The Book of Jem

Carole Hailey

To Helen
With much love

Carole
x

Watermark Press

Published in UK by Watermark Press 2020

A CIP catalogue record for this book is available from the British Library

ISBN: 978-1-8380043-1-6

Typeset in Book Antigua

Cover design by nb-design.com

Printed by Imprint Digital

Watermark Press
Unit 77 Penn Street, Duo Tower, London, England, N1 5FF
www.watermarkpress.co.uk

For my family

WHITEOUT

1

Eileen

Only I know the truth about what happened and because I wrote the Book of Jem, my truth is the one that will be remembered.

Jem told me that she had a migraine that first morning. I was with her many times when she had one and what she did was drink tea and eat two pieces of bread with honey, unless there was no honey in which case she had jam, anything really, so long as it was sweet.

When I decided to write Jem's story and make a permanent record, I asked her questions such as *was it definitely honey you had on your toast that first morning?* But she just shrugged. She didn't care about the details. However to do this properly I need to include as much information as possible, so I'll fill in the blanks as best I can.

It's pretty safe to assume she woke in agony because I've heard her describe the migraines as shafts of fire inside her brain. She will have swung her legs over the side of the bed, levering herself into a sitting position, holding her clothes at arm's length, squinting at them through half-closed eyes, keeping her head as level as possible. When she walked, she would have slid her feet along the floor in a slow glide – even her own footsteps could make the pain worse.

Bathroom first, fumbling for a patch to stick to the inside of her right wrist, then the kitchen and a large mug of tea. In between gulps of her drink, I assume she ate bread slathered with honey.

At some point she made the surprising decision to go for a walk. She put on a black jacket and wound a bright red scarf around her neck – I know this for certain, because it's what she was wearing when she arrived here. Tying the laces on her boots must have been impossible without moving her head and probably made her feel sick all over again, but eventually she was ready to leave. She took a small green rucksack to carry a bottle of water and her migraine patches. If she brought anything else with her, I've never seen it.

Jem never told us anything about where she used to live or what she used to do. She always said that since it was all going to be gone soon, there was no point thinking about it. *Never look back* was one of first things she said to me.

But, if I'm going to tell her story properly, I do need to look back a little, to try and imagine her life before she came here. She must have worked in the factories because she's never mentioned working the Files and so what else would she do? She probably lived in one of those micro-homes – I've seen pictures of them – the ones with an all-in-one living, kitchen and sleeping area plus a miniscule bathroom where she kept her toothbrush and a hairbrush, snagged with strands of her short, dark hair. No cosmetics. She wasn't wearing any when she arrived and although I offered to order some for her, she refused. I'm not surprised: Jem didn't need any help to look beautiful.

I think she must have lived by herself because she never talked about anyone, and no-one from her past has ever come looking for her. In any case, I like the idea of her being alone before she came here. It feels appropriate somehow, like she was saving herself for us.

When Jem walked away from her life that morning, the pain in her head will have pulsed in time with her stride. She will have gritted her teeth – well, perhaps not actually gritted them because

2

that would have made it worse, but there must have been a mental gritting of teeth as she focused on the business of walking – hoping that the exercise would speed the drug through her blood.

At some point, Jem turned off the road and headed up the hills between wherever she came from and Underhill, pausing at some point to apply another patch to her arm, relieved to feel the slight scratch on her skin as the drug was released into her blood. She walked as fast as she could while breathing through her nose, so that more oxygen would be forced into her lungs, cycling the drugs around her body until, eventually, the migraine began to unclip itself from her brain.

At some point before the top of the hill, Jem told us that she stopped walking and sat on a tree stump. She drank from the bottle of water and looked around, surprised by how high she had climbed. In the early hours of a migraine, Jem focused almost entirely on her body: no unnecessary head movements, drink tea, eat something sweet, put one foot in front of the other, breathe through the nose. It was almost impossible for her to receive anything but the most basic of inputs and so it was only when she finally stopped that she realised just how far she had walked.

From her vantage point on the remains of the old tree, she saw that she was alone on the hillside. A recent storm had dumped the rest of the leaves on the ground and above her was a crosshatch of naked branches. Every few seconds, the wind stirred clumps of leaves into small vortices, before releasing them to patter back to the earth. It was cold and getting colder – it was the start of Whiteout after all – so she decided that she had better head back down.

It was at that point that she heard a voice telling her to carry on up the hill. Even Jem admits that it was a disappointingly mundane first communication. She looked around the deserted hillside and called out things like *hello* and *who's there?*.

She said there was a slight pause before the voice replied, but when it did, it again urged her to keep going up the hill. The voice was husky, with a faint trace of an accent that Jem couldn't place. Once, I heard her use the word seductive to describe it although usually she just called it low-pitched. Apparently, when she heard it that first morning, she felt the migraine patch tightening on her arm as her skin gathered into goose-bumps.

'Who are you?' Jem called, getting to her feet and peering through the trees into the darkness beyond. Her head immediately felt worse and she forced herself to take some deep breaths. It was then that the voice said that if Jem wanted to call It something, she could call It God.

At that point, it didn't cross even her mind that it was *actually* God who was speaking to her. I suppose she assumed someone was playing a joke on her although I have no idea who she thought might have been doing that, perhaps an ex-boyfriend (or girlfriend, because I don't know what Jem's tastes were in this regard, although believe me, it's something I've thought about a lot) and she was trying to decide if she was more scared or angry when the voice once more urged her to go up the hill, saying she should climb to the top, down the other side and keep on walking until she found the people who were waiting for her.

I can see Jem as clearly as if I had been there on the hill with her. She wore emotions like clothes: they were always visible and for me, who knew her better than anyone, they were easy to read. For example, when she was angry she puffed up her little frame like a bird and wrapped her hand around the back of her neck, rubbing hard at the place where her hair feathered into the pale skin of her neck. I'm sure this is what she did on the hillside, before shrugging and saying, 'You don't exist.'

There was a long pause, presumably as God decided how best to reply and Jem said that when God did eventually speak, It sounded remarkably relaxed about her denial of Its very existence.

A lot more passed between Jem and God on the hill that first morning and although she kept most of it to herself, that hasn't stopped me wondering what I would have done if it had been me that God spoke to and honestly, I think I would have died of fright because, as far as we know, Jem was the very first person to hear from God since It was banned.

2

Kat

So many times I wish I'd taken my family and run screaming into the hills. If I'd had even the slightest idea of the devastation that girl would cause, I would have done just that. But I couldn't possibly imagine – how could I? – the catastrophic chain of events that began the day she came wandering into our village.

The first day, the day she arrived, all I knew for certain was that the air was heavy, weighed down by something I couldn't place. Excitement? Danger? Fear? I wasn't sure, but things didn't feel quite right as I swallowed the last of my tea and emptied the dregs on the ground around the slender trunk of my elder tree.

'There you are. Tea leaves. Good for your roots.'

My fingers were freezing as I fumbled to get the top back on the flask. I had been staring at the hills for days, waiting for the leading edge of the snow clouds to appear. I hated Whiteout, hated the way the daylight dimmed to a dank grey, how the air made my throat burn and my joints ache. I kept telling myself the sooner it started, the sooner it would be over, trying to trick myself into feeling better. It wasn't working.

I rubbed my palm against the rough bark of the tree.

'You'll need to lend me your strength for what's coming,' I said, my voice booming around the graveyard. I wrapped my hand tightly around one of her branches and hoped the Elder Mother was listening. I wasn't sure if I was talking about Whiteout, or something else. Whatever, I'd need her help to face it.

I'd already spent too much time there and turned away reluctantly, pushing my way past the brambles. I stopped briefly by the smallest of the broken headstones, tucked behind the crumbling stone wall. It was cracked horizontally into two pieces and I bent down, putting a hand on each half. With my left forefinger, I traced the name. *Holly Jane Jenkins*. Baby Holly was the youngest person in the graveyard – four weeks and two days old when she died – and the last to have been buried there.

I ran my hand over the words on the other half of the stone, although I knew them by heart: *Beloved daughter, granddaughter and sister, Earth has one gentle soul less, Heaven one special angel more*. How unfortunate for Holly's parents that they had chosen those words to commemorate the brief life of their daughter. If only they had avoided the mention of Heaven and angel, the tiny headstone might have been left unbroken.

Leaving the dead behind me, I slipped through the gap in the wall. The hills flanking the village cast long shadows, during Whiteout it took hours for the sun to rise high enough to give any warmth and I walked fast, eager to get home. The track through the village was rutted by years of storms and I had to concentrate to avoid the potholes lurking below thin skins of ice.

When I first saw Underhill it had looked unfinished, with its jumble of cottages huddled together along one side of the street without a matching row opposite. The first people to settle at the foot of the hill, all those years ago, had only managed to find a narrow seam of rock brittle enough to cut and even then the sharp slope meant that there were five or six rough steps to get from the street down to the front doors.

Our house was almost exactly in the middle of the village. Ed, his parents, his grandparents and probably their parents before them, had all lived there, although their home had now been my home for nearly twenty years. When I reached the bottom of the steps, Lily waved at me from next door, and stopped arranging the pots of herbs on her kitchen windowsill long enough to hold up a mug. It was tempting, but once she got started, Lils did like to talk and I had a busy day ahead of me, so I shook my head and mouthed an exaggerated *sorry*. She flapped her hand at me, we'd see each other later.

I closed the front door and leaned against it for a moment, letting the silence settle around me. In recent months the cottage had begun to feel crowded when Ed and the twins were at home. I felt guilty for even thinking such a thing, but teenage arms and legs seemed to take up so much space. I made myself a tea then sat down at the kitchen table. I loved the table, which Ed had made from an oak tree downed by a lightning strike. He'd made most of our furniture although he didn't hesitate to give things away if there was an opportunity to swap them for something we might find useful. Just after the kids had been born, someone mentioned that they liked our dining chairs, so he swapped two of them for half a dozen chickens. It was years before he'd got around to making any more. But I drew the line at the table: that was staying right where it was.

As so often happened, the sight of baby Holly's headstone had reminded me of my parents and even after all these years, as I sipped my tea, I could hear their voices as if they were right there at the table with me, going over and over the same old arguments.

'Gravestones are just lumps of granite put there by grieving families,' my mother would say, banging her knife on the table. 'What's the harm leaving them where they are?'

'They're a symbol,' my father would retort through mouthfuls of food, his appetite always fuelled by an argument. 'How can we truly be free of religion with millions of stone markers as a reminder?'

My father had been very tall and very thin, despite his love of eating, with a cloud of wispy white hair all around his head. I called him Dandy, because when I was little I thought he looked like a dandelion bobbing in the breeze. He moved constantly, as if he was always trying to be somewhere else, and even as we ate, the food would wobble on our plates as his knee jiggled up and down, rocking the table.

'God lost his usefulness as soon as we crept out of the Dark Ages. Belief in religion has no more credibility than what, Kitten?' he'd ask, waving his fork in my direction.

'No more credibility than the belief that the sun orbited the Earth, Dandy,' I'd reply, blushing as he smiled his approval between mouthfuls.

I looked up from my tea, surprised for a moment to find the chairs empty, but my parents were long dead; they had never even been to Underhill. I drained the rest of my tea and stood up, I had things to do, I couldn't waste time sitting around thinking about the old days.

*

Snow arrived before the girl.

When she eventually came wandering along the lane later that day, I was at the kitchen sink watching the white flakes floating to the ground, twisting a cloth around my hand so tightly my fingers had gone numb. I shook out the pins and needles and stared through the window. She was a tiny slip of a girl, barely older than a child, and at first glance there was absolutely nothing about her to indicate how much damage she would inflict on us all.

She walked slowly, hands buried deep in her pockets, face turned to the clouds, letting the snow drift onto it. The tip of her tongue poked through her teeth – the only point of colour on her pale face. As she passed our house, she paused, glancing down and I turned away, embarrassed to be caught staring.

Already a crowd was gathering, which wasn't surprising. Strangers hardly ever came to Underhill, but the mood was still tense after a group of Uplanders had come down several weeks earlier, setting fire to one of the cottages on the outskirts of the village, and taking advantage of our panic to break into a house at the other end of the track, snatching as much as they could carry. We'd put the fire out before it could really take hold, and they hadn't taken much; but still, it was a worrying development.

I was tempted to stay inside but ignoring the girl wouldn't make her go away. Face your enemies head on, Dandy used to say, that way they can't stab you in the back. The twins had already rushed outside, completely ignoring me when I'd shouted, 'Willow, Ash, put your scarves on.'

I popped my head around the living room door and found Ed exactly where I knew he'd be – slumped in his chair, staring blankly out of the window.

'There's a stranger in the lane,' I said.

'Ash told me.'

'Are you coming out?'

He didn't answer, so I went to stand in front of him, giving him no choice but to look at me.

'Lots of people are out there already, shall I wait while you put your boots on?'

'I've been outside all day,' he said. 'I've no need to spend my evening out there as well.'

Sometimes, when I listened to other people complaining about their partner's annoying habits, I found myself wishing that Ed would shake himself out of his lethargy long enough to develop a habit, one that involved something other than staring out of the window. Thankfully, he always found the energy to go up to the turbines since we all relied on him to keep the lights on in

Underhill. But recently Ed had no interest in doing anything else. I couldn't remember the last time he'd done any of his carpentry. When he wasn't up at the turbines, or asleep, he was slumped in his chair. There was no doubt that Whiteout made his job harder, and I'd been trying to convince myself that his lethargy was because of the time of year. If I said it often enough, I could almost ignore the part of me that knew Ed was suffering from something far more serious than a case of the Whiteout blues.

'Sure you don't want to come outside with me?'

He reached up and squeezed my fingers. 'I'm sure, love. Just make sure Willow doesn't decide to bring the stranger home, won't you? You know what she's like.'

By the time I got into the street half the village was gathered around the girl. Snow was falling heavily, the lane was already white, and people were stamping their feet and blowing on their hands while they waited for Molly to arrive and decide what to do. I have to admit, the girl didn't strike me as particularly dangerous that first day. She was older than the twins, but not by much, perhaps late teens, maybe early twenties, it was difficult to tell because her skin was so blanched from the cold. When she coughed, even the inside of her mouth was white. She was wearing a black jacket, a red scarf, and a defiant stare.

I squeezed through the crowd and made my way over to where Lily was standing.

'What do you make of this, Lils?'

'She must be crazy. Why would anyone choose to walk over the hills at the beginning of Whiteout?'

'I know, you'd have to be mad to even try.'

I looked around, caught Laurel's eye and smiled at her. She smiled back gratefully, then fussed with Mila's blanket, wrapping it more tightly around her daughter. Several people were openly staring at the baby, not bothering to disguise their hostility even

11

though Rob was glaring at anyone who so much as looked in their direction.

Molly had finally puffed her way down the street and the crowd parted to let her through. When she touched the girl's arm, she flinched.

'I'm Molly,' she said. 'I do the community admin.'

The girl frowned, as if she had no idea what Molly was talking about.

'You know,' Molly said. 'I do the applications for new arrivals, leavers, that sort of thing.'

The girl still didn't react, and I began to wonder if there was something wrong with her.

'You must be freezing,' Molly said. 'What's your name, love?'

Lily nudged me and nodded towards where Willow was elbowing her way through the crowd. Recently, my daughter had become supremely reliable in her ability to do the exact opposite of what I wanted her to do, which in this case meant putting herself right in the middle of things. Her hood was pushed back, the snow settling on her thick, blonde plait. I called to her, but of course she ignored me, squeezed past a couple more people and came to a halt in front of the girl.

'Do you understand us?' Willow asked.

The girl nodded.

'What's your name?'

The stranger looked my daughter up and down, then finally she spoke.

'Jem.'

Her lips barely moved, and people turned to each other, trying to work out what she'd said.

'Be quiet,' called Molly. 'Let the girl speak.'

'Hello, Jem,' Willow said. 'I'm Willow. Where have you come from?'

Jem waved her hand towards the hills.

'Over there.'

Each word was carried from her mouth on a little puff of breath that hung in the air.

'Why are you here?' my daughter asked, and all around me people started pushing forward to hear the answer.

'I was told to come.'

Several people called out, 'Who told you to come?'

Later that night, I lay in bed wondering whether I'd somehow known what the girl was going to say before she said it, because while my neighbours were jostling and crowding closer, eager to hear her reply, I was already drawing back, trying to put some distance between us.

'God,' the girl said, her voice barely a whisper. But then she lifted her head and said loudly enough for everyone to hear, 'God told me to come.'

3

Eileen

I should probably explain why I made the decision to call god *God*, and why, for the purposes of the Book of Jem, God is an It, rather than a He or a She or a They.

At school, they made us sit through hours and hours of what they called Compliancy Class. Everyone hated Compliancy Class, which was basically just endless talk about how important the Laws were, why we had to obey them at all times, and how it was the worst thing ever for someone to flout them. At the end of each class, we'd be given multiple choice tests that only a total idiot could possibly fail, such as: do the Laws allow membership of non-authority approved organisations? *A) Yes, B) No, C) In certain circumstances.* And of course, there was always someone who answered something other than No, so then we had to listen to the teacher going on all over again about whatever particular Law it was.

The lessons about religion focused mainly on how some people who had believed God was real convinced themselves to kill other people who believed God was real. I guess they wanted us to understand the traps so we could avoid them ourselves. But there was a lot they didn't tell us. For example, I often wondered if some religions were better than others, were there ones that made you wealthier, or healthier? We weren't told things like this because they didn't want to make religion sound interesting, so mainly we learned about how all religions were a lie, made up by rich and powerful people to trick other people into fighting against each other so that the rich and powerful people could become even more rich and powerful.

In one of the earliest classes, when I was quite little, we had to memorise some of the names for the supernatural beings of different religions. Where I'm from, *God* was the name that most people had used, but I can still remember some of the others: *El, Yahweh, Elohim, Jehovah, Allah, Parvardigar, Krishna.* I made up rhymes to remember them. But, Jem calls god *god* so I'm sticking with that. And it always used to be spelt with a capital letter, like an actual name, so *God* it is.

And as for why God is neither a he nor a she nor a they? Well, that's simple. Jem has said that sometimes the voice sounds like a man, sometimes like a woman, and once or twice apparently it even sounds like a child. It seems that God doesn't want to let on what gender it is, and so I've decided that God can be an It.

That first afternoon when Jem appeared, I only really got a glimpse of her face poking out above that red scarf. Even though she was so cold and so white, she still looked beautiful, like a cloud floating along the lane.

There was quite a bit of pushing and shoving after Jem said that God had told her to come to Underhill. Everyone wanted to get a good look at her, but she planted her legs in the snow and shoved her hands in her pockets – even then it was obvious that she was so much stronger than she looked.

'Give the girl some room,' Molly shouted, after Jem had spoken. Everyone obligingly shuffled back a little, and I took the opportunity to push myself forwards, so I could get a better look at her. It took everyone else much longer to realise, of course, but from the moment I saw her, there was never, not for one single second, any doubt in my mind about how important she was. I tried to memorise everything about my first proper sight of her, from the sturdy boots, thick with mud from her climb over the hills, to how perfectly her clothes emphasised her tiny frame – I even remember thinking that she could do with a bit of fattening up. And then there was her beautiful, serene face, rising from her red scarf and topped by her short black hair, blanketed in a layer of snow. I pushed back my hood, so the snow could collect on my head too.

'Now then, my dear,' Molly said, dropping her voice to a more manageable volume. 'You've obviously come a long way, and I know it must all be very confusing. I'm sure you don't know what you're saying, do you?'

Mentioning God by any of Its names was technically against several Laws, and I knew only too well how some people would take any opportunity to pretend to be outraged, so I kept a close eye on the back of the group where people like Kat and her cronies stood huddled together, making sure they weren't about to run off and notify Jem.

For once in her life, Molly actually made a sensible decision, because she decided to ignore what Jem had said and focus instead on what we were going to do with her. It was nearly dark and wherever Jem had come from must have been hours and hours away, so she couldn't be expected to turn around and go straight back. The question was, where was she going to spend the night?

If only I had been a bit braver from the beginning, pushed myself forwards, said she could stay with me, how differently it might all have turned out. Instead I was so distracted watching Jem that I didn't listen to what was going on. But then, she wasn't paying attention to the conversation either, she was staring down the road. I turned a couple of times to try and see what she was looking at, but there were just the cottages and beyond them, the silhouette of the wind turbines up on Front Hill.

At some point, I realised that the decision had been made that she would stay with Lily and Cooper. Lily was already saying, 'She can have the room at the top, the bed's all made up, as long as she doesn't mind the sound of mum snoring in the next room.'

At the time, I was annoyed that I hadn't spoken up, but it's only with the benefit of hindsight that I saw how each of these early decisions led us all along a path that would eventually affect every single person in Underhill.

*

Back at home, I couldn't stop thinking about her. I replayed over and over in my mind the moment that she had mentioned God, and each time a shiver went down my back which made me squirm. I imagined reaching out my hands, touching her pale cold face, running my fingertips over her lips. Why hadn't I said she could stay with me? I'd have been happy to sleep on the sofa if she'd been here. Actually, I'd have been happy to sleep on the floor.

I tried to imagine what she would be doing, stuck in that house with Lily, Cooper and Lily's repulsive old mother, Ruby. I got to my feet and started pacing around the room. Eventually I couldn't bear it any longer and I threw on my coat, shoved my feet in my boots, and went out.

When it's dark in Underhill, it's properly dark. Apparently, in the past, before the Wars, there used to be so much electricity that everything was lit up all the time and, in some places, you couldn't even see the stars. Nowadays though, after the sun goes down, the only light outside is from the moon.

With all the snow clouds, the night was black, but I have wandered around the village so often when everyone is sleeping that I could have found my way to every single house with my eyes closed. To get to Lily and Cooper's, I went down to the back of my garden, skirted around the pond, making sure not to slip on the ice, pushed the loose fence panel to the side, squeezed through, replaced the panel and set off along the narrow path, arms outstretched, trying to avoid walking into any trees.

I counted off the houses as I passed them. At the bottom of Laurel and Rob's garden, I stopped for a moment and listened. The sound of baby Mila crying always made me feel confused and a bit unhappy, so I hurried on. The tenth garden was Lily and Cooper's. They didn't have a fence and I squeezed through the bushes. Fortunately for me, most people couldn't imagine why anyone would want to approach a house through the back garden when they could just go to the front door.

There was a light on in the living room. I walked towards it slowly – I hadn't been to watch Lily and Cooper for a while and I couldn't quite remember what was in the garden. I wasn't sure if they had any of those ridiculous old statues that some people have. Ever since I broke my toe on an over-sized concrete owl, I've learned to be more careful. I hunched below the windowsill, then slowly raised my head. I knew it was going to be almost impossible for anyone to see me outside in the dark, but even so, I'm always really careful when I'm doing my watching.

The sight of Jem literally took my breath away. She was sitting in front of the fire looking so young and vulnerable. She had taken off her coat, which was on the back of a chair with that red scarf of hers folded neatly over it, and she was wearing jeans and a blue jumper. In front of her was a plate of food, but she wasn't eating. Lily was sitting opposite her, but there was no sign of either Cooper or Lily's mother.

I felt a sudden rush of anger that it wasn't me in there with her. Of course, no-one would have thought of me or suggested that Jem stay with me. I had been left out of things again, just like always. I forced myself to calm down, pushing the anger back inside, storing it up to use when I really needed it. At least by looking through the window, I could stare at her without being seen.

Lily was talking, jabbering away as she always did, and Jem was just sitting there, not saying anything. I wasn't surprised. She was so far from home, she was exhausted and now she was being forced to listen to Lily droning on and on. The talking finally finished and Lily got to her feet, loosening her grey hair before scooping it up again into a ponytail. She put a hand on Jem's shoulder for a moment and I imagined it was my hand on her shoulder, tickling my way along the sharp line of her collar bone. Lily left the room and a moment later a light came on upstairs.

Left by herself, Jem still didn't move and I marvelled again at how perfectly her short dark hair framed her face, and how huge her eyes were. I just knew that if she looked at me, her eyes would see me properly, she would see the me that no-one else saw. Despite the freezing night air and all the snow falling on my head, I felt really hot.

Suddenly, Jem got to her feet and came over to the window, pushing her face up close to the glass. I didn't think she would know I was there – there was a light behind her and I was standing in complete darkness – so at first, I didn't do anything. I *couldn't* do anything. Our faces were so close that I could see little cracks in the skin at the corners of her mouth. They looked sore. I could feel the blood pulsing in my fingertips and it was all I could do not to reach out and press my hand on the glass, but then she started fiddling with the window catch and I turned and fled. I don't know if Jem knew that I was outside the window that night. She never said and I never asked.

*

I was still rushing when I got back to my garden and I forgot to take care and slipped on the ice at the edge of the pond, falling onto my knees. It really hurt and I had to concentrate hard not to cry out. I lay there for a minute, feeling the snow settling on my face, but when I began to get too cold, I got up, hobbled into my house, shut the door and sat on the floor. I cried for a while. My trousers were torn at both knees and as I mopped up the blood, I cursed myself for not being more careful: new trousers would cost money I didn't have. I pressed my hands over my scraped knees and watched the blood oozing between my fingers. I tried to distract myself by thinking how exciting it had been watching Jem through the window and I think I must have been sitting on the floor for quite a while because by the time I took my hands away, my palms had stuck to my knees so they started bleeding all over again.

Eventually, I got to my feet and made a cup of tea. Then I sat at the table and tried to think sensibly about Jem and what she had said when she arrived in Underhill. What would make someone walk over a mountain to come to us? Why would she say that God had spoken to her? I couldn't make any sense of it, which was surprising since I already knew for certain that she was going to change my life.

It wasn't then that I decided to write the Book of Jem, but it was then that it first crossed my mind that someone needed to do it. Sitting there with my bloody knees, upset and excited at the same time, I thought back to all the classes that we'd had on religion and once the blood had finally stopped running down my legs, I went to fetch my notebooks.

I know it's old fashioned, but I've always loved writing on paper although I have to use tiny writing, because even the smallest notebook costs a ridiculous amount. When I was at school, if I found a class interesting, I'd go home and transcribe the notes that I made from my Tab into a notebook, which no-one else bothered to do. My grandmother got me into writing. She had beautiful handwriting and when I was little, I'd pestered and pestered her to teach me how to write like she did. I am very proud of my writing. Each page is beautiful and there's always been something about being able to touch words that I've written myself that makes them seem more real.

Of course, once my affliction started, writing was the only way I could express myself properly. When I write, I'm in control of the words, whereas when I speak, the words are in control of me.

History was my favourite subject at school and I flicked through pages and pages of notes that I'd made for essays such as: Discuss The Rise of Extremism; Examine The Use Of Religion To Justify Terrorism; An Analysis Of The Development And Availability Of Chemical Weapons; Why Did Four Billion People Die In the Wars? Discuss.

I'd got top marks for that last essay.

Seeing my notes again reminded me how whenever she was teaching the History of Religion my teacher would get herself all worked up, slamming her fist into her palm for emphasis over and over again while she'd said things like, 'Think of religion as a recipe. You take a group of people, usually poor people or miserable people. We'll call them the *victims*. Add to the victims a *supernatural being*. Then invent stories designed to make the victims believe that their unhappy lives will improve if they worship the supernatural being. Stir it well, bring to boiling point and there you have it: a religion.'

My notes summed it up as: *Recipe for religion = miserable people + supernatural being + invented stories*, but in the margin, I'd added some questions such as: Why was it necessary for the people to be miserable? If religion was a lie, why did so many people believe it? Why were there so many different religions? If religion made people happy, then why did they end up fighting each other? I never did believe it was as simple as my teacher said.

I turned over the page, and there it was, just as I had remembered it. According to my History of Religion notes, each religion had individuals who claimed to speak on behalf of their particular god. These people were called prophets. Every religion had prophets. And every prophet had a book which described what they did and what messages they received from their gods.

I'd never seen one of these old prophet books, but I'm sure that's where my idea came from because it wasn't long after that first night that I realised that if there was any chance that what Jem was saying was true, if God really was talking to her, then that made Jem a prophet. And if she was a prophet then her story had to be told.

Someone needed to write the Book of Jem.

4

Kat

I stood at the top of the stairs watching Ed lace up his boots. He moved stiffly, as if it was the end of his day rather than the beginning.

'How did you sleep?' I asked, although I already knew the answer. He carefully tucked the ends of his laces inside his boots then glanced up at me. The circles below his eyes had deepened overnight and his face looked bruised.

'I didn't.'

Obviously, we were none of us getting any younger, but in the last few months, Ed's scalp had begun to shine through his previously bushy hair and his body was noticeably softening, apart from his fingernails which were brittle and always snapping. I used to hate how he bit his nails whenever he was thinking about something, but they no longer grew long enough for him to do that. I reached out and put my arms around him, trying to remember the last time I'd seen him laugh. At first, he resisted but then he leaned into me and hugged me back.

'Oh love,' I said, my voice muffled by his shoulder. 'You've got a long day ahead of you.'

'I'd better get going,' he said, pulling away from me so abruptly that my arms were left hanging in mid-air. 'George stayed up there again last night.'

Ed had recently begun to teach the young man how to repurpose the piles of long discarded machinery to keep the turbines turning – Underhill would need people with the skills to replace Ed and his brother when the time came. George lived in one of the smallest cottages in the village, with his parents, an aunt and his grandparents, so he often chose to stay up on the hill and sleep in their work hut. It was pretty basic: mattresses, table and chairs, and piles and piles of tools, but I was envious of the solitude that George had up there. I would have enjoyed lying in the darkness, matching my breathing to the sound of the turbine arms slicing through the air: eighteen rotations a minute, eighteen breaths a minute.

'Before you go,' I said to Ed, lowering my voice so it wouldn't carry to the kitchen where the twins were having breakfast.

He frowned, obviously wanting to get on. 'What is it?'

'I'm worried.'

'Why?' he asked. 'What is it now? Has Willow been sneaking out again?'

'No, nothing like that,' I said, holding both his hands, making sure I had his attention. 'I'm worried about the girl that came yesterday.'

Ed sighed. 'Is that all? I'm sure she's ok, staying with Lily and Cooper.'

'I don't mean I'm worried *for* her.' I tried to find the right words to make him understand. 'I'm worried *about* her. I think she's going to cause trouble.'

Ed zipped up his coat. 'Right, I see. So this is another one of your feelings, is it?'

'Don't say it like that, Ed. It sounds as if you think I'm mad.'

'Well, you know, sometimes I wonder if you are,' he said, shaking his head. 'You're the only person I know that talks to a tree.'

'I'm not hurting anyone.' My voice was rising – this was not how I'd wanted the conversation to go.

'That's easy for you to say. If I've said it once, Kat, I've said it a million times: if anyone realises what you're doing in that graveyard, you could find yourself notified. And then what would happen?' He shook his head. 'It's selfish.'

'You're a fine one to talk,' I shot back. 'You don't do anything but sit in that bloody chair nowadays. I'm surprised it doesn't stick to your arse when you stand up.'

And there it was. The frustration. The anger. Always waiting, just below the surface. Sometimes, it made me itch so badly it was all I could do not to rake my nails down the length of my body, tear myself open in my desperation to let it out. I looked down and realised that I was already scratching the inside of my left arm. I tried to rub away the red lines, then forced my arms down by my sides.

'I'm leaving now, Kat,' Ed said, his voice small and hard. 'I'm leaving to walk for nearly an hour, shovelling snow from the path, so that I can get up to the turbines. Then I'm going to spend the day making sure that there's enough electricity to keep our lights on. Then I shall walk back down the hill, probably when it's dark and certainly when it's freezing cold, no doubt having to shovel yet more snow out of the way. So, yes, I probably will want to sit down and relax this evening, if that's acceptable to you?'

The quiet click of the door behind him was much worse than if he'd slammed it and I stood in the hallway wondering how I had managed to let the conversation get so out of hand. Ed was a good man. He loved our kids. I loved him, and I was pretty sure he still loved me, although possibly not right at that moment. Love was not always enough though. I missed the old Ed, the one that rarely made an appearance nowadays, even when he was sitting right opposite me.

I went into the kitchen and Willow said, 'Were you and Dad fighting again?'

She was doing her best to sound bored, but the kids hated it when we argued. Ash avoided looking at me, concentrating on scraping up the last of his breakfast.

'Well?' demanded Willow, glaring at me. '*Were* you fighting with Dad?'

'It was just a disagreement, nothing for you to worry about.'

'It was about Jem, wasn't it?' asked Willow, pushing her bowl away and standing up. 'Can I go round to Lily's and see her?'

'No, you can't. There isn't enough time before class.'

'But Mum, it was *me* she talked to yesterday, so I should go and see if she wants to speak to me again. Maybe she wants to tell us something else about God.'

I slammed my hand on the table and both children jumped. 'How dare you say that word in this house?'

'It's only a word, Mum, there's no need to get so annoyed,' Willow said, rolling her eyes in the way that she knew infuriated me.

'You know it's more than that. Anyway, since when have you had the slightest interest in religion?'

I loved my daughter, but Freedom knows she knew how to wind me up. Whatever I said, she would say the opposite. Whenever I asked her to do something, she would do something different. Ed assured me it was a phase and I knew he was right, but that hadn't stopped my relationship with Willow beginning to feel like a relentless, unwinnable battle.

I took a deep breath, one argument that morning was enough, I didn't have the energy for another. I picked their bowls up.

'You two need to get a move on or you'll be late for class.'

'It too cold to go out,' said Willow. She nudged her twin. 'Isn't it, Ash?' He nodded.

'Here's an idea then, why don't you put on an extra jumper?'

'You always say that.'

'Oh for Freedom's sake, if you stopped using the same reasons to try and get out of doing what you're supposed to do, then I wouldn't have to repeat myself.'

'But Mum...'

I slammed the bowls down. 'I don't want to hear another word or else I'll pull you out of classes for good and you can spend your whole lives working the Files.'

It was an empty threat and they knew it, but I didn't care, I just wished we could get through a single morning without Willow winding me up.

I'd never expected to have a child. Why would I? Nobody did, and the best way to deal with it was to simply assume that it would never happen. When we found out that not only was I pregnant but that I was having twins, we didn't believe it: the chances were so astronomically small that we told ourselves that there must have been a mistake, that there could only be one heartbeat inside my growing belly. We remained convinced that it was a mistake, right up to the point that Ash was born seven minutes after his sister.

In those first few months, we were overwhelmed by people wanting to know how we had managed it. Was it what we ate? Or, what we didn't eat, perhaps? Did we only drink water piped from the tanks? Perhaps we avoided drinking the tank water, was that it? Did we have access to a secret supply of food from uncontaminated land? And then there were all the other questions. I lost count of how many times I was asked where, when and how we had sex. The questions were personal, intrusive and desperate. But we had no advice to give. We'd simply been very, very lucky.

Of all the things that changed in my life after the kids were born, what I was most unprepared for was just how often I didn't feel lucky. I knew how I was supposed to feel – I only had to look at the infertility rates, which continued climbing long after I'd had the twins – but a bunch of numbers didn't help me cope with the tedious, repetitive work that went into raising children. I was supposed to feel like the most fortunate person in the world, but all too often my primary emotion was guilt, a constant, unrelenting undercurrent of guilt because I didn't feel as lucky as I knew I should. I loved the kids more than anything, of course I did, but I didn't always love how they made me feel about myself.

The pair of them were already late by the time they left and I watched from the door to make sure they were hurrying along the road towards the house that doubled as their school, before I went back to the kitchen to make myself a cup of tea. I really wanted to go to the graveyard and see the Elder Mother, but it would have to wait. Perhaps I could go later in the day, although looking through the lengthy list of ordering to be done, it seemed unlikely.

Laurel would want to order for Mila, which would take a while, but several others hopefully wouldn't take too long since they were all people who relied on working the Files to make money, which meant that they could never afford to order much. Lily and Cooper were also on my list and I decided to go there first; hopefully Lily's chatter would cheer me up and, although I was reluctant to admit it to myself, I was curious to see how the girl was getting on. I left my tea half-finished, checked I had everything I needed in my bag and pulled on my boots and coat.

*

The front door opened so quickly that I wondered if Lily had been standing behind it, waiting for me to arrive. She came out onto the doorstep.

'That girl's a strange one,' Lily said, jerking her thumb over her shoulder.

'Oh yes?'

'Barely said a word to us since last night. I think there's something wrong with her. Maybe she's unstable.' Lily shivered. 'It's freezing out here, let's go inside. Perhaps you'll get more out of her than I've been able to.'

I followed her through to the living room at the back of their house.

'Jem, this is Kat,' Lily said. 'She's come to do our order.'

The girl didn't look up. She was pale, despite the heat coming from the fire, and there were faint red marks along her cheeks – acne scars or traces of old scratches perhaps. Her dark eyebrows sat fiercely above her small features and her shoulders were hunched, she looked like she was poised to flee at any moment. With one hand, she was twisting the fingers of the other into painful-looking plaits.

'Hello, Jem. How are you feeling today?' I asked, trying to sound kind.

When she didn't reply, I said, 'It was my daughter, Willow, that spoke to you yesterday in the street. Do you remember?'

Jem lifted her eyes and for a moment she looked familiar, like someone I'd known long ago, although that was ridiculous – she was barely older than the twins and I couldn't possibly have met her before.

'Of course I remember,' Jem said. 'Why wouldn't I?' She returned to contorting her fingers.

I looked at Lily and shrugged. 'Shall we get on with the ordering, Lils? I've got a lot to get through today.'

Lily led me back into the kitchen. 'See?' she hissed. 'She's so strange. Do you think she's got *stability issues*?' She mouthed the last two words.

'I don't know. Possibly,' I said. 'Have there been any more mentions of you know what?'

Lily shook her head. 'Thankfully not. I mean, I don't mind

putting her up for a few nights, but Mum's already threatening to notify her if she mentions the G word again, although I'm sure she won't actually do it.'

I didn't have the time for one of our endless conversations about the authority, so I just pulled the Tab out of my bag without replying. I had been responsible for Underhill's ordering for several years, and usually tried to make sure I was finished by early afternoon so I could take my time placing the orders, scheduling deliveries and organising swaps of any unwanted items – the prohibitive cost of returning them meant they almost always found a home somewhere in Underhill.

Lily was fussing over the Tab – she always behaved as if she might find exciting new things to order, although she never did – when Jem appeared in the doorway. I glanced at her. She was chewing her lower lip, raking her teeth over the cracked skin and there was a smudge of blood on her chin.

'What are you doing?' Jem asked.

'Ordering,' I said. 'I organise the deliveries.'

'Why doesn't everyone buy their own stuff?'

'There's only one drone delivery a week, so we have to co-ordinate the orders. Doesn't it work like that where you're from?'

Jem shrugged. Lily was wrong, the girl didn't have stability issues, she was just plain rude.

Lily looked up. 'Is there anything you'd like us to order for you, Jem?'

I tried to catch her eye, she shouldn't be wasting her money on the girl, but Jem was already shaking her head.

'No,' she said. 'It won't matter anyway.'

'What won't matter?' I asked.

'Nothing will matter. Now God has returned, everything is going to change.'

'Jem,' said Lily, fiddling with a little wicker basket in the middle of the table. 'You know you mustn't talk about the G word, don't you? I don't know what it's like where you're from, but here we take the Laws very seriously. You do know what they say about religion, don't you? I mean, there's Law One for a start: *There is no god.*' She winced as she said the word.

'I know that's what you tell yourselves,' said Jem. 'But you're wrong. God went away for a while, but now It's back and It sent me here.'

'Why?' I asked. Lily shook her head. She was unwinding strands from the basket, clearly very uncomfortable with the conversation, but I was curious to understand what the girl was trying to achieve by spouting such nonsense.

'Why here? Why were you sent *here*?' I asked.

'I don't know yet. But this is where I must be.'

Lily got up abruptly and went over to the windowsill where she started moving pots of herbs around. My kids had always found Lily's obsessive ordering and re-ordering of her plants highly amusing; they had even gone through a phase of trying to guess the order they'd be in when they came home from school, keeping an elaborate scoring system for months. What they didn't know, because I hadn't told them, was that it was one of my friend's many coping mechanisms. When she was unhappy, or felt out of control, or when her mother was being particularly difficult, Lils shoved the chipped pots of mint and rosemary and parsley around, convinced that if she could just get them in *exactly* the right places, things would get better. Of course it was silly, but like almost everyone else in Underhill, she found ways of pretending that the difficulties and frustrations of her life were just temporary, she had become an expert at tricking herself into believing that one day she would find the key that would unlock the better, happier, easier life that was waiting for her. We all did it in our own ways. We never really talked about it, but almost all of us believed it. If we just did *this*, then surely, finally, *that* would happen.

I watched as Jem looked slowly around the kitchen until her gaze finally came to rest on me. She stared at my arms, and I realised she was looking at the mess of tiny scars all over them. She smirked and I felt a sudden burst of anger. Who was she to judge me? I pulled my sleeves down and stared back at the girl. Her lips parted as if she was going to say something, but in the end, she just got to her feet and left the room. A moment later, a chair scraped against the floor next door.

Lily turned towards me, her face pale. 'You see?' she hissed. 'She's clearly unstable. Mum's terribly upset about the whole thing. She won't come out of her room – she said this morning she heard Jem talking to herself for hours last night on the other side of the wall. She's threatening to leave if we don't kick the girl out, although I've no idea where Mum thinks she'll take herself to.'

I grinned; Ruby was cantankerous at the best of times and it was difficult to feel too sorry for her.

Lily returned my smile but then shook her head. 'It's not funny, though. To be honest, I wish we'd never offered to have her here. I've already said to Cooper that if she's going to go on about the G word, then she'll have to leave. Someone else will have to take her in.'

*

It was the last house on my list and I knocked hard, in case Laurel was upstairs with the baby. I'd left my gloves somewhere and my hands were freezing. I rubbed them together, looking up at the banks of heavy cloud – the next wave of snow was on its way. The orders had taken longer to get through than I'd hoped mainly because of some unexpected items: new medicine for Molly, trousers for Eileen – she'd somehow managed to rip holes in her other pair – and other bits and pieces that would take a while to source. I definitely wouldn't have time to go to the graveyard.

The door finally opened and Laurel peered out. When she saw who it was, she managed a small smile and opened the door properly.

'Come in, come in, I know how much you hate Whiteout.'

As soon as I was inside, Laurel bolted the door behind us.

'Still having trouble?' I asked.

Her smile had already disappeared.

'Rob thinks I'm being too sensitive, but I can't bear seeing how everyone looks at her.'

'Come on, it's not everyone,' I said. 'Most of us are really happy there's a baby in the village.'

Laurel shrugged and turned away, but not before I saw her tears.

'There'll always be jealous people,' I said, following her into the kitchen. 'They want what they can't have, particularly when it comes to fertility. You've got to try and put it out of your mind. Mila is a beautiful, healthy baby. Focus on that.'

'Was it like this when you had the twins?' asked Laurel. 'Was everyone really awful to you?'

'Back then the chance of getting pregnant wasn't quite as bad as now, you know?'

Laurel nodded.

'There was still a lot of jealousy, though,' I said. 'And there were a lot of horrible comments. Some people actually asked me why I thought we should be allowed to keep both our children when most people couldn't have one. We were even offered money, ridiculous amounts actually, to give one of them away.'

Laurel nodded again, but I could tell she wasn't really listening, so I pulled the Tab out of my bag.

'Right, let's get this done. Have you decided what you want to order? There's still a bit of space left on this week's drone, so you could use up some of Mila's baby allowance.'

She ordered quickly and as soon as she had finished, I put my coat on, keen to get home.

'Try and ignore the jealousy,' I said. 'I know it's hard but focus on how amazing it is that you and Rob are in the one percent. Too many people can't accept that they won't have children and letting them upset you won't change anything.'

Laurel nodded. 'Rob says the same.'

Upstairs, Mila was awake and it sounded like she might be about to wind herself up into a full-blown tantrum.

'I'd better go up to her,' Laurel said, getting to her feet. 'Thanks, Kat.'

Outside, I stood for a moment and looked along the road. The turbines rose from the top of Front Hill, their arms slicing through the underbelly of the clouds. It was easy to miss them during Whiteout, camouflaged in their slender, grey casings, but like everyone else, I always looked towards them whenever I was outside, checking they were still turning. My anger with Ed had disappeared and I was just left with the guilt. Ed was doing his best – he didn't deserve the criticism that I found it so easy to fling at him – I would make it up to him that evening. I nodded an apology towards the turbines, hoping he knew how sorry I was.

I didn't see anyone else as I crunched along the frozen ground. The snow was already banked on either side of the track, the start of walls that would rise higher and higher over the next few weeks, forming a roofless tunnel, enclosing us within in our little community. Keeping the snow levels on the main track manageable, and the paths to the purification tanks and up to the turbines clear was a back-breaking job which paid hardly any money, but there was never any shortage of volunteers. Many people were happy to do almost anything rather than work the Files and who could blame them? Puzzling over Files of long dead victims of the Wars, trying to attach names to images of decomposing bodies was horrible, traumatic even. But for those that didn't have animals to farm, or who weren't skilled at making things, there were so few ways to earn money.

Now the ordering was done, my thoughts returned to Jem. I didn't agree with Lily that Jem was unstable. It wasn't instability that I had seen as the girl stared around the kitchen. No. Behind that sullen gaze was something far worse.

5

Eileen

I found out that they were going to discuss Jem at the monthly meeting. Although it was at Molly's house and she was on my List of Enemies, I decided to make an exception and go along.

My new trousers hadn't yet arrived, and I didn't have any others, so I'd patched the rips with bits of material that I cut from the back of the sofa. Every time I bent my legs, the rough fabric rubbed against the scabs on my knees.

Before they banned religion, people went to places called churches to talk to God. The manager of each church, who was called a priest because he collected the money, lived in a big house next door to the church. Molly lived in the old church manager's house which was the largest house in Underhill.

Molly's gross abuse of the community administration job was the reason that she was on my List, which I kept in one of my grandmother's old notebooks. Even though I used the tiniest writing, the notebook was nearly full, because each time someone moved up or down a place I had to write the List out again. I kept it locked away in case the notebook fell into the wrong hands, although most of my neighbours would have been too ignorant to understand what they were looking at.

At the time of the meeting, Molly had been occupying the number one spot on the List for over a year, ever since my failed application to move away. I wanted to go somewhere else, not to the factories of course, but somewhere where people would hopefully be a bit more like me. I spent weeks working on my application, putting in lots of helpful information about my interests, but I didn't receive a single response. Not one. I'm sure that that bitch Molly didn't even put my name forward for relocation, let alone share my application with communities looking for new residents, so I was stuck in Underhill for the time being. Which meant that Molly was stuck at number one on my List.

It was only when Jem arrived that I realised how fortunate it was that my application hadn't been successful. I mean, imagine if I hadn't been in Underhill? I would never have met her. How terrible would that have been? And also nobody else would have thought to write the Book of Jem, so if I hadn't been forced to stay here against my will then she would never have had a prophet book. Anyway, on the night of the meeting at Molly's house, that was all still ahead of me.

When I got there, everyone was in their usual groups. Someone asked me why I was limping, but I just ignored them and sat down, unsticking my trousers from the scabs on my knees. I didn't speak to anyone because unnecessary talking was always something I avoided.

I did like watching other people though, that was one of my interests, so I made sure to sit where I had a good view of the room. Apart from Molly, there were quite a few other people who I'd Listed. Kat was there too, of course and Ed was with her – poor man, being partnered with her, he would have been so much happier with someone different, someone more like me.

I had always quite liked their daughter Willow, ever since she had given me a present some years ago. Ed had made it for her when she was really young. It was a series of interlinking boxes carved out of a single piece of wood, which he'd polished and polished until it shone. There was a gold-coloured ball which you dropped in at the top and then you had to move and tilt the boxes to get the ball through different tunnels and holes, so it would drop out of the bottom. I'd often seen Willow carrying it around with her – she obviously loved it – but it wasn't until she left it on the wall outside their house for me that I realised how beautiful it really was.

I kept it in my Treasure Cupboard so no-one could see it, particularly not Kat when she came to take my orders, darting her horrid eyes all over the place, staring at all my belongings. I would have much preferred to get things delivered by private drone, but I didn't have enough money. It wasn't that I didn't like working the Files, I'd never understood why people made such a fuss about it. I mean it's true that when there was advanced decomposition it could sometimes be impossible to make a positive identification, but usually if I stared at a picture long enough, turning it around and looking at it from different directions, then I'd eventually work out what it was – half an arm, say, or a bit of buttock – which always gave me a bit of a thrill. Obviously if there was an identifying mark then I'd hit the jackpot, but even if I worked the Files all day every day, I still wouldn't make enough money to get my orders delivered privately.

Jem wasn't there when I arrived so each time the door opened, I sat up and smiled, waiting for her to come through it. Then Lily and Cooper came in, with Lily's desiccated hag of a mother, Ruby, and I realised that Jem must have stayed behind and wasn't going to come at all, which was very disappointing because I'd only gone to the meeting so that I could see her.

Molly started off by reading the monthly communication from the authority. She droned on about a community that I'd never heard of which had been forcibly relocated to the factories in a city somewhere because of consistent flouting of the Laws. That was another reason why I never went to the meetings. I mean, I had better things to do than to listen to that sort of stuff. Frankly I don't care about most of the people I know, let alone those I don't.

Eventually Molly started reading out the latest amendments to the Laws, which were called *clarifications*. There were always clarifications about what was and wasn't included in the ban on religion and it was impossible to keep up. For example, there was that time when there had been a lot of talk about how, at certain points during the year, particular constellations aligned with the turbines. For a while, some people in Underhill genuinely believed that if they stared at the night sky long enough through the blades of a turbine, then some great revelation would happen. Something like that anyway. People are so gullible and it's not just in Underhill, because apparently there had been talk of similar nonsense all over the place, until one month the clarifications said that religion included astrological predictions and just like that the star-gazing stopped and everyone moved on to snowflake counting or predicting cloud formations or some other such rubbish.

Anyway, I must have stopped listening because by the time I tuned in again, Molly had finally moved on to talking about Jem. I waited for an opportunity to mention a few ideas I'd had about how we could help her settle in, but it quickly became apparent that most people hadn't a clue what a wonderful thing her arrival was for Underhill. All they wanted to go on about was what they should do if she kept talking about God.

'She keeps mentioning that word and she's adamant that she's been sent here for a purpose,' Lily said, in that annoying whiny voice of hers that made me want to slap her until she shut up. I mean, why had Lily bothered to ask Jem to stay with her if she was just going to moan about it? And, as far as her having a purpose in coming to Underhill, well, of course she had a purpose. I could have told them that. It was obvious from the moment I saw her. In the end though, I decided to keep my opinions to myself – it was their loss if they were too stupid to understand.

I was getting really bored, but then I had an idea. I stood up and started edging towards the door, trying not to draw attention to myself, although Kat was staring at me, as usual. It always felt as though she was trying to read my thoughts, not that there was any chance of that, there's far more going on in my head than she would ever know. Anyway, I finally got to the door and opened it, slipping outside. As soon as I closed it, I realised I'd left my coat behind, but I could hear everyone laughing, and I couldn't face going back inside.

It was snowing heavily by then, so I tried to run along the street to keep warm, but the combination of the snow and my scabby knees meant it took me a few minutes to get to Lily's house, and I was freezing by the time I knocked on the door. I stood back, arranged my face into my best smile, putting my hands palm-up in a friendly gesture.

To my surprise, Willow opened the door. She stood there, staring at me and I stared back at her, until eventually I managed to say, 'I c...c...came to see Jem.'

The cold often made my affliction worse.

Willow frowned, and it was only then that I remembered that she had never seemed to like me as much as I liked her.

'You'd better come in, then,' she said.

I'd never been into Lily's house and I wasn't sure where to go so I just followed Willow, who led me down the hallway. I stopped in the doorway of the room that I'd been staring into from the garden on the first night. Then Jem lifted her head and looked at me and I wanted to run over and give her a big hug, but I knew what some people thought about uninvited displays of affection, so I restrained myself.

It was stiflingly hot. Someone had forced as much wood as

possible into the stove and shut the air vents, so the heat was radiating directly into the room. Willow's face was bright red although Jem's was as pale as when she'd been outside in the snow.

I could feel myself starting to sweat and I held my arms close against my sides hoping that I wouldn't get damp patches on my shirt.

Willow laughed. 'You can go into the room, you know. She won't bite.'

She was trying to make me look stupid, but I made sure to keep the smile on my face as I walked across to where Jem was sitting.

At first, I couldn't really believe that I was so close to her. After I'd got myself comfortable on one of the chairs, unsticking my trousers from my knees, I started to introduce myself to Jem. I stumbled over my words which made Willow laugh again and I suddenly realised how wrong I'd been to ever think that I liked her. In fact, at that moment, I wanted nothing more than to shove her head into the fire. I was so busy imagining holding her down while her face melted and wondering if she would smell like pork chops that I didn't hear what she was saying, so I ignored her, turned to Jem and shoved my hands firmly under my thighs.

'I want to know about why you've c...c....c...' I paused and took a deep breath. 'Why you're here.'

Jem smiled, and I knew that she'd been expecting me.

Next to her, Willow was nodding.

'That's what I asked too,' she said, and I felt embarrassed for her. She really needed to try and act more mature while she was in Jem's presence.

'Look,' Willow continued. 'I'll have to get back soon, Mum will be really annoyed if she finds out that I was here, so what can you tell us or is it all a big secret?'

Jem looked at Willow and then at me and I stared into her eyes. I've often tried to think of ways to describe them because *blue* doesn't come close to doing them justice. There were tiny darts of gold around her pupils and her irises were the same colour as the sky just after the rain stops. Her lashes were curled in a uniform row, not like the scraggly ones I've got. See? Even trying my absolute best, I still can't describe how beautiful they were. But what I can say is that the first time I properly looked into Jem's eyes, I shivered. I hoped she hadn't seen me do it, but then the corners of her mouth twitched and I knew that she understood that we were going to be special friends. For a moment, it was like nothing else existed except me and Jem, until Willow broke the silence, 'Well? Is it a secret?' she demanded. So rude, just like her mother.

Jem shifted her gaze to Willow and I felt hollow. I wanted more than anything for her to keep looking at me.

'God sent me here,' said Jem.

'But God doesn't exist,' said Willow, lowering her voice when she said the word *God*. 'It's Law One: *There Is No God.*' She held up her left hand with her fingers splayed, as if she was a toddler. 'First: *There Is No God.*' She folded down her left thumb. 'Second: *Religion Is A Lie*'. Down went her left forefinger. 'Third: *Personal Responsibility Is Everything.*' Middle finger folded. Compliancy Class obviously hadn't changed since I'd sat there folding down my own fingers.

'That's what I believed until a few days ago,' said Jem, thankfully interrupting Willow before she could recite any more of the Laws.

'So, what happened to change your mind?' asked Willow. She was really beginning to irritate me, jumping in, showing off, asking all the questions that I wanted to ask. I could only imagine how annoying Jem must be finding her and I accidently-on-purpose straightened my leg and kicked Willow hard with my boot.

'Ow,' she said, glaring at me.

'Sorry,' I mumbled. 'I didn't know your f…f…foot was there.'

I wiped my face on my shirt sleeve. The room was so hot that even my ears were sweating and I tried to dry them with my fingers.

Jem sat back in her chair and her sweater rose up her arms. Her hands were tiny and above them the knobbly bumps of her wrists looked like molehills.

'What changed my mind,' she said, and I leaned in close. 'What changed my mind, was that God spoke to me and told me things.'

'What sort of things?' asked Willow.

Jem frowned. 'Private things,' she said and she sat back in her chair, so I sat back in mine.

'Is that it?' asked Willow, sounding disappointed. 'God told you some private things and so you came here? But why? Why here? Why not go somewhere else? I mean, you could have picked somewhere where something actually *happens*. Somewhere people do something other than just work the Files and don't have to rely on a drone if they want something. I mean of all places, why would you come to Underhill?'

Jem looked at Willow, but I wanted her to look at me instead, so I said, 'Are you only allowed to talk about it with certain people?'

I glanced at Willow, proud that my words had come out so easily, but she didn't seem to have noticed. She was so self-absorbed.

'God has sent me to save Underhill,' Jem said.

'S…s…save it from what?' I asked.

'I don't know yet,' Jem said. 'God will reveal everything when the time is right.'

I looked around the room, but apart from the beast of the fire, there was nothing to see; there was certainly no revealing happening. Jem pulled her chair closer to the table, we all leaned forward and for the first time I smelt her lovely clove smell.

'Can I trust you both?' she asked.

I sniffed and wiped my nose with the back of my hand, hoping some of her scent would be caught on my skin, so I could smell it later, when I was at home, in the privacy of my own bedroom. Willow and I both nodded. What I really wanted to say was that she should just trust me and didn't need Willow, but I couldn't concentrate because Jem had reached across the table and taken hold of our hands. Her palms were cool and I hoped she didn't mind that even my knuckles seemed to be sweating. A log cracked in the fire and I jumped. Jem smiled at me.

'I'm going to need help,' she said and I nodded. I was ready. I was so ready.

'I need to know who I can trust when it begins.'

'What's going to happen?' asked Willow.

Jem ignored her and linked her fingers more closely with mine. I squeezed her hand tight.

'It's not going to be easy, but when the time is right, will you help me?'

'Yes,' I said, immediately.

'Why not?' Willow said, then laughed. 'Mum'll hate it.'

She stood up. 'I'd better go. Don't tell Mum I was here,' she said, looking at me. I stared back at her. I had no intention of telling Kat what her daughter was up to.

'I'll see you again soon, Jem,' she said. 'I'm only next door.'

I imagined her putting a glass to the wall, listening to Jem in Lily's spare room. It wasn't fair that I could only stand outside the house in the garden, hoping to catch a glimpse of her through the window. Willow did up her coat and tied a scarf around her neck.

'I wish I had a red one like yours,' she said, stroking Jem's scarf where it was folded over the back of the chair. 'It's a lovely colour. Well, see you soon,' she said to Jem. She looked at me. 'Bye, then.'

When she left I stared at Jem, not really able to believe that I was alone with her, but then she got up and said, 'I need to go out.'

'It's s...s...snowing.'

'I have to go.'

'Where? Where are you going to go? Do you want to come over to my house? It's only a few minutes away. I can make you a cup of tea. Or something to eat. You could come and stay,' I said, plucking up the courage to say what I had wished I'd said when she arrived. Or at least that's what I thought I said, but I'm not sure if my words came out properly because all she said was, 'I've got to go somewhere I can hear.'

'Hear what?' I said, but then I realised. 'Oh, you mean s...s... somewhere you can hear God? Are you getting a message? Is It t...t...talking to you now?'

Jem didn't reply, she just laced up her boots, put her jacket on and wound the red scarf around her neck.

'Can I c...c...come?'

I wouldn't get very far in the snow without my coat, but I could always run back to Molly's and collect it.

She shook her head. 'No, I'm going alone. I need to listen.'

'I won't s...s...speak,' I babbled, desperate to go with her.

Jem shook her head and left the room and before I knew what was happening, I heard the front door open, then close.

By the time I got out of the house, up the steps and onto the road, she was gone.

6

Kat

The fire was blazing and too many people were crammed into the room. Poor Molly had sweat pooling in the creases of her neck: her new medicine didn't seem to be making much of a difference, and she looked exhausted by the time we finally got around to discussing what we were referring to as the *Jem issue*.

Nobody actually believed we should notify the girl, but that didn't stop a few troublemakers winding everyone else up by pretending that they did. It was always the same. And of course when it came to any discussion about religion, it was always those same few annoying people who somehow convinced themselves that *their* specific peculiarities – the way they celebrated every full moon, or obsessively counted the days it rained, or noted the formations of birds flying overhead – didn't flout the Laws. They told themselves that those things didn't count, whereas when someone mentioned how meaningful it was that the snow had drifted in a different pattern along the side of the road, they would frown, purse their lips and shake their heads at the crossing of the line between harmless superstition and religion.

The power of self-deception in the post-religion age: I could almost hear Dandy saying the words. If he were still alive, he would have had a field day with the people right there in that room, not to mention a career's worth of research material.

The endless shifting between what was considered religion and what wasn't also happened to be the reason why I had never told anyone about the Elder Mother.

Of course, it wasn't just religion that caused problems. The authority seemed to have nothing better to do than to send clarifications about all the Laws so it was almost impossible to stay up to date. For example, there was the ever-changing list of banned weapons. Guns had always been classed as weapons of course, and we all agreed with that. But sometimes we got notices about this or that tool being newly classified as a weapon. I'd lost count of how many times Ed had had to request an exemption for the tools he needed for the turbines. Why on earth couldn't they just make lists for the Laws and stick to them? I'd come to the conclusion long ago that the people at the authority genuinely enjoyed spending all of their time thinking up new clarifications, new ways to make the lives of ordinary people like us just that little bit more difficult.

But of course, in the end, despite one or two people muttering about notifying Jem, the one thing that everyone agreed on was that no-one wanted to give the authority a reason to turn its attention to Underhill. Molly said that the girl couldn't be expected to go anywhere during Whiteout, but as soon as snowmelt arrived she would persuade the girl to leave and that was good enough for us.

The meeting was coming to an end when there was a loud thud against Molly's front door. Whatever was outside started wailing, quietly at first but becoming steadily louder until the noise reached a crescendo somewhere between a howl and a shriek. Several people flanked Molly as she crossed the room, grasped the door handle and yanked it open.

For a moment, I didn't recognise Eileen. I'd seen her leave the meeting earlier, sidling out, as shifty as ever, but now she was in the doorway, shivering violently, eyes closed, mouth open, making a horrible keening noise that set my teeth on edge. Her hair was plastered to her cheeks and she was covered in snow. Molly reached for her, put an arm around her and pulled her inside, bustling her towards the fire.

'Sit down, Eileen,' she said, but the girl stayed on her feet, rocking slightly from side to side. I went over and took hold of her arm, Lily took the other, and we lowered her into a chair. Abruptly, she stopped wailing, and instead buried her head in her hands, smudging tears and snot around her face.

A blast of cold air hit my neck – I looked up and saw several people hurrying out.

'Is it the Uplanders?' Lily whispered.

I shook my head. 'Can't be. They'll be in the hills until snowmelt.' I sounded more confident than I felt, and Lily looked unconvinced as more people left, calling a hurried goodnight over their shoulders.

Eileen's teeth had finally stopped chattering and the snow was melting into her clothes. I tried to get her to take her jumper off, but she just crossed her arms over her chest and stared stubbornly at the floor.

'What's happened?' Molly asked, and when Eileen didn't reply she said more urgently, 'Is it the Uplanders?'

Eileen shook her head, to the relief of everyone still in the room.

Molly lowered herself to the floor, squatting in front of the chair. She put her hands on Eileen's knees, but the young woman flinched and pushed them away.

'Look, Eileen,' Molly said. 'I know you're upset.'

Eileen nodded.

'We want to help you. But unless you tell us what the matter is, we can't, can we?'

Eileen shook her head, then took a deep breath.

'Sh…sh…sh…' She swallowed, took another deep breath and tried again. 'Jem's gone.' A long wail carried the words from her mouth.

I rolled my eyes at Lily, who squeezed the tip of her nose and raised her eyebrows – each time Eileen moved, a pungent smell rolled up towards us, vaguely reminding me of a decomposing animal.

'But why are you so upset?' Molly asked. I admired her patience, I could already feel the anger prickling my skin and I clenched my fists to stop myself raking my fingernails down the inside of my arm.

Eileen's eyes were so swollen, she had difficulty focusing on anything. She wiped her nose on her sleeve, then took a few more shuddering breaths.

'W…w…we…'

She paused, looking up at me, and I forced myself to nod encouragingly. She rubbed her palms along her thighs several times and when she finally spoke, the words tumbled out as if they were racing to escape.

'I was with her. W…w…we were having such a lovely time; b… b…but then she said she needed to go and talk to God.'

There were some unnecessarily dramatic gasps around the room and a few people actually backed away, as if she was contagious. Lily's mother Ruby, who had been preparing to leave and already had one arm in her coat, lifted her hand and pointed a trembling finger at Eileen.

'Shame on you. Shame. On. You.'

Eileen gave no sign that she'd heard Ruby, she just carried on plucking the patches on her trousers.

'Notify her,' said Ruby, loudly.

Molly shook her head. 'We agreed a plan and we'll stick to it.' She raised her voice. 'There will be no notifying.'

Ruby went over to Eileen and pushed her face close until the younger woman had no choice but to look at her.

'Flouter,' Ruby hissed. Specks of her saliva glistened on Eileen's cheeks, but Eileen just tugged down the sleeve of her jumper and wiped her face on it.

Lily held Ruby's coat so her mother could put her other arm into it.

'Don't get yourself worked up, Mum.'

The old woman spun to face her daughter. 'Don't patronise me. I lived through the Wars. I saw what was done in all the many names of God,' she said, spitting out the final word, her mouth twisting with hatred. 'You're all making a terrible mistake. We should notify this evening.'

After the door banged shut behind her, there was silence in the room. A flush of red spread down poor Lily's neck, I caught her eye and gave her a sympathetic smile.

Molly held my arm and heaved herself to her feet, grunting softly – she looked so tired that I reached out to squeeze her hand. She smiled at me, then looked down at Eileen.

'Did Jem say where she was going?'

Eileen shook her head and her eyes filled with tears. She pointed across the room to where her coat was slung across the back of a chair.

'She w…w…wouldn't wait.' The sobbing started again.

Annoyed by the melodramatics, I was about to suggest to Ed that we go home, when he spoke for the first time all evening.

'I think we should try to find the girl.'

'Why would we do that?' I said. 'No-one forced her to leave.'

Ed frowned. 'She's only a few years older than our kids. She'll die up there if we don't find her.'

Eileen's wails grew louder. I was scratching my arm again and I forced my hand to my side.

'If you find her, what then?' I asked.

Ed looked at me blankly.

'You find her. What will you do then?' I said, my voice

betraying my irritation.

'I don't know. Maybe we should notify her.' He shrugged.

'What is the point of finding her if we're just going to do that?' I asked.

'You think she's better off dead?' he said, sounding appalled.

'You know I didn't say that,' I shot back.

'You didn't have to,' he said. 'It's obviously what you think.'

'Why do you always have to make every conversation so bloody difficult?' My voice was shrill. There was a pressure on my arm and looking down I realised Lily had wrapped her hand around it. The room had fallen silent, everyone was listening to us, including Eileen, who was wearing a spiteful little smile.

I took a deep breath.

'That girl is not our responsibility. She arrived here from who knows where, spouting nonsense about the G word. Now she's decided to leave. Well, good. It's one less thing for us to worry about.'

Lily nodded. 'I agree. She's not a child, if she wants to go, then so be it.'

I smiled at her gratefully, but Ed turned to his brother. 'What do you think?' he asked.

Leroy shrugged. 'I don't mind going up the turbine path, see if we can find her.'

'Well there's a surprise,' I said. 'Agreeing with your brother, like always.'

Leroy ignored me and started cleaning his nails, using the middle finger on his right hand to excavate the nails on the other.

I turned back to Ed. 'For Freedom's sake, why couldn't you just keep your mouth shut? We should leave the bloody girl–'

'I think Ed's right, Kat,' said Molly, interrupting me. 'I know Jem's not one of ours, but we offered her shelter and if we don't find her she'll be dead before sunrise.'

I couldn't believe it. No-one really wanted the girl in Underhill, apparently except for Eileen, and since when did her views count for anything? I'd known the girl would be trouble before she even arrived, and frankly it was a relief to hear that she'd left. That is, until Ed decided to organise a rescue party.

Eileen stood up. 'I'm c…c…c…'

Ed interrupted her, 'You're not coming.'

'I'm her friend.' This time, Eileen's words came easily, and her face was set in a mulish expression that I knew all too well.

Ed shook his head. 'It's too dangerous, you don't know the paths well enough in the dark.'

Eileen ignored him, fumbling with the buttons on her coat.

I looked from one to the other: they were both as mad as each other as far as I was concerned.

'We don't want to lose you as well now, do we, Eileen?' said Molly, mildly.

Eileen threw herself back into the chair, looking sulky.

In all, half a dozen people familiar with the hill paths offered to go. Molly handed out torches which were all pre-Wars, held together by little more than bits of string and grubby tape, but Molly always made sure the batteries were kept charged and when Ed turned his torch on to check it, cupping his hand over the light, his palm glowed orange. He bent to give me a kiss, but I stepped back so his lips just skimmed my ear.

'I'll be home soon,' he said and hesitated for a moment, hoping for a reply, but I looked away.

*

Lily persuaded me to walk Eileen home with her. I agreed, thinking that it might help me calm down, but as we picked our way along the street, trying to avoid stepping in puddles, I wished I hadn't bothered. There was an occasional flash of light from the search parties making their way up the paths, but other than that, the dark was absolute and although I couldn't see the falling snow, I hated the way that it tickled my face.

It wasn't until I'd been in Underhill for a few years that I began to understand how the community assumed the traits of each season. During Whiteout, the mood was heavy and brooding, with little laughter, the people colder, less caring. If anyone had been harbouring thoughts about leaving to work in the factories, they would always make their application during snowfall.

For homework once, the twins' teacher asked them to find a picture that they believed best represented each season. I forget what they found for the others, but I have never forgotten the image that they decided to use for Whiteout. It must have been taken in a year when the snow came too early and fell too long. At first glance, the picture looked like an ordinary snow-covered field, a sheet of white with tree branches poking through it. But when you looked closer, you realised that they weren't trees, but legs. Dozens of animals, marooned among the drifts of snow piled up around them, had suffered some mass contagion of panic and all thrown themselves sideways and upside-down in their frenzied efforts to get away. Smothered where they lay, their frozen legs rising stiffly from the snowy field. Every season brings its own issues for us to deal with, but it's only Whiteout that I fear.

Listening to Eileen's phlegmy breath catching in her throat as we walked, my anger drained away and I almost felt sorry for her, which was a rare feeling in the ten years or so since her parents had died. It had been so awful, the way people started to mention that they hadn't been seen for a few days, but not bothering to check up on them until Ed – always the rescuer – took it upon himself to break down their front door. In the same room as the bodies of her parents, he found sixteen-year-old Eileen lying under a table, knees drawn up to her chest, tears streaming down her face. He had bundled her out of the door and straight to our cottage. After that, every night for weeks I'd wake to the sound of crying, and still half-asleep I'd go to the girl.

'Why are they dead? Why didn't I die too?' she would sob, but I had no answers for her. It was just so horribly *unfair*. They had been a tight-knit threesome who kept themselves to themselves, as much as anyone could in Underhill. Eileen's parents were both scientists who had devoted their lives to the desperate race to develop a replacement for failing antibiotics. The pair of them died only weeks before the new drugs were available and every time I remembered the terror that had accompanied every cough and sneeze back then, I thought of Eileen's parents.

I caught my foot in a divot and stumbled slightly, my arm brushing against hers and she pulled away as if she'd been stabbed. It hadn't always been that way – back then, after she'd first come to us, she wouldn't let me out of her sight. She followed me around like a duckling, to the point where she would even hover outside the bathroom, knocking every few minutes to make sure that I hadn't escaped through the window. Then there was the time I woke up and found Eileen stretched out on the floor of our bedroom, head propped on an arm, watching us sleep.

Eventually, we also became aware of some of her other less endearing habits. With hindsight, it was obvious the stealing had been going on for a while, perhaps since the first days that she had come to us, but we hadn't wanted to blame a girl so broken with grief – it was simpler to assume it was one of our kids, and it wasn't until I went to Eileen's house to pick up some clothes that I found my mother's necklace, some of my father's books and a couple of Ed's carpentry tools stashed in the back of a wardrobe. Ed wanted to forgive the girl – he always was too soft – but that was the beginning of the end of her time with us and after we'd been on the receiving end of one too many of Eileen's lies, I told her that it was time to return to her own home. She had never forgiven me.

'Why did you go and see Jem?' asked Lily suddenly. 'I don't mind that you went to my house, but why did you go?'

Eileen didn't reply and it was impossible to see her expression in the dark.

'Why are you so upset about the girl?' Lily said, determined to press her for an answer.

Eileen sniffed and I could hear her weird hiccupy-breathing.

'Only I know w…w…what's really going on.'

'What is going on?' asked Lily.

Eileen just laughed, so we walked the rest of the way in silence. The frigid air had found its way inside my clothes and I was shivering by the time we reached Eileen's cottage. We waited for her to fiddle with all the various locks that she insisted on having and I started to say that she should let me know if there was anything she needed, but before I could get the words out, Eileen slammed the door in our faces. As I followed Lily up the steps, the sound of bolts being drawn across the door bounced around the street.

*

Later, with the twins finally in bed, I stoked up the fire and sat down to wait for Ed. I was embarrassed that people had seen us arguing – I was far too old to be behaving like that. My temper was always quicker to rise if I hadn't had a chance to visit the Elder Mother, but that wasn't Ed's fault. Nothing he had done was out of character and he hadn't deserved my outburst, but I never seemed to learn.

Right from the beginning Dandy had had concerns about my compatibility with Ed. He worried that I wouldn't have the patience to deal with Ed's emotional frailty, that it would bring out the worst in me. I believed I was strong enough for us both, that I could carry Ed when he needed me to. And many times I had. But sometimes, my father was right: I was impatient, I didn't give Ed the sympathy he needed, or deserved.

'Speaking professionally and not as your father,' Dandy had said, not long before I made the move to Underhill, 'Ed's issues mean he'll always be a *seeker*. He'll always be looking for answers that don't exist. And that will make it hard for you both, Kitten.'

I got to my feet, trying to distract myself by looking at the photographs that hung on our walls. They were all pictures of Ed's mother's ancestors, and whenever I looked at them I had pangs of nostalgia for a life I'd never had. As far as I knew, the people in the photographs were doing things that had been considered perfectly normal in their day, although I couldn't imagine doing them myself.

In one photograph, two girls, not much older than the twins, were grinning at each other outside a grubby yellow building with the words *Aeropuerto de Palma de Mallorca* picked out in huge metal letters. Below that was another picture of the same girls, flat on their backs on towels laid on sand, eyes closed, their skin burned a painful red, white strings hanging from their ears. Every time I looked at it, I was surprised all over again by how startlingly oblivious the girls seemed to be to the number of young children on the beach with them.

In a larger photograph on the other side of the fireplace, one of the same girls was older, sitting with a man in a vehicle without a roof. She was smiling at the person taking the picture and there was something about the shape of her chin, topped by the neat rows of teeth, that reminded me of Ed. A man's arm was draped over her shoulders while his other hand rested on the pregnant mound of her stomach, his face obscured by her thick blonde hair. Ed knew nothing about where these people were from, or what they had done with their lives and he'd have happily consigned the pictures to a cupboard, but I liked their company.

The photograph that I looked at more than any of the others, the one that I recreated in my mind when I couldn't sleep, was taken in something that I knew had been called a super market. The two girls were much younger in this photograph, the eldest was perhaps no more than ten years old and she was holding large tomatoes up to her eyes, while the other had squashed her nose flat with an oversized cucumber. Both girls were laughing, their mouths wide, tongues like red petals.

Beside them, a woman was pushing a metal basket on wheels, forehead wrinkled in a frown of disapproval. What fascinated me wasn't the girls, but the rows of fruits and vegetables stretching into the distance on either side of them. I recognised apples and pears and there were piles of potatoes, but a lot of the other food I could only identify by colour. Fat balls of orange were piled alongside slim, yellow fruit that had been called bananas. The quantity and variety of food was staggering, and just thinking about it was enough to make my mouth water. Before I had seen the photograph, when I had tried to picture what a super market might be, I had always imagined a set of oversized tables, loaded with meat, potatoes, bread, the usual staples; I had never thought in my wildest dreams that it was a place where countless different foods stretched to infinity under the glare of overhead lights.

I knew the past was a time of disgusting waste and decadence, I knew how electricity had been consumed as if there was a limitless supply, how more food was thrown away or left to rot than was ever eaten, and how absolutely everything required the use of the plastic that ended up choking the earth. Worst of all, energy and food had been used as weapons. Those who had them used them to get more, while those who didn't have enough energy or food were desperate for them. We'd learnt all about those people – the ones who had nothing – and how they had used religion to justify taking what they wanted.

Yet despite everything that I knew about life before the Wars, when I looked at the photographs of Ed's ancestors, it didn't stop me wishing I could visit them, just for a moment, to see whether the past really had been a place that was as colourful and plentiful as it looked.

I was still lost in the pictures when Ed finally came home. He shivered in front of the fire, stripping off his coat and unlacing his boots before dropping into his chair. I handed him a blanket which he pulled tightly around his shoulders, reminding me of Ash, who always tucked his bedclothes around himself like a cocoon, even on the hottest nights.

I waited for him to speak, but he just sighed, his breath escaping in a long hiss, so I went over to the small wooden cupboard on the other side of the room and carefully lifted out two crystal glasses. They had belonged my grandmother Rose but, unlike Rose herself, they had survived the Wars.

I put the glasses on the table beside Ed's chair and poured mead into them, then pushed one into his hand.

He opened his eyes and looked down at the glass as if he'd never seen it before. He glanced at the bottle and then up at me.

'Why are we drinking this?'

'Whatever happened out there tonight, you look like you need it. I know I do,' I said, knocking the contents of the glass back in a single gulp. I poured myself some more, then looked at him and said, 'I'm sorry. You know? For earlier?'

He lifted the glass to his lips, then hesitated and said, 'It's been a strange night.'

'You did your best, Ed. It's not your fault you couldn't find her. Poor girl, she won't survive the night in these conditions.'

It was easy to feel concern for the girl, now she had gone.

He took a sip. 'It's always surprising how good this stuff is, considering what it's made from,' he said, grinning.

For as long as I'd known him, Ed's brother had nurtured yeast cultures as if they were babies, turning swathes of heather into a potent mead. Each year he would present us with a bottle. The bottle itself had been used many times and had *Leroy's Luck* etched roughly into the glass, the elaborately curling tail of the first L underlining the rest of the letters. I tilted it towards Ed and he nodded, so I poured him some more then picked up my glass and went to sit on the other side of the fire. I sipped slowly, enjoying the burn of the alcohol as it traced a path to my stomach.

'We found her,' said Ed.

I sat forward, nearly spilling my drink. 'What do you mean, you found her? Where?'

'Assuming she's still where I left her, then she's about half-way up Front Hill, just off the main path.'

'How did you know where she was?'

'Leroy spotted a break in the snow.'

'So why didn't you bring her back with you? What have you been doing all this time?' My hand shook as I took a large gulp of mead.

Ed got to his feet, letting the blanket fall in a heap on the floor, and went to stand by the fire. I couldn't tell what he was thinking. Had something awful happened to her and he didn't want to tell me?

'Oh, love. Was she dead?'

He shook his head and turned to look at the photographs on the left-hand side of the fire. Then he moved across and looked at the ones on the other side, then started pacing up and down in front of me.

'So, what happened?' His silence was annoying, and I tried to ignore the urge to drag my nails down the soft underside of my arm.

He stopped close to my chair, looking down at me.

'You're going to think this is crazy. Promise me you won't get annoyed? I don't want another argument.'

'Neither do I, but we're going to have one if you don't tell me what happened.'

He started pacing again, glancing over at me every few seconds as he spoke.

'She'd managed to push through the drifts, although I don't know how she did it without tools. She was at the end of a track that she'd made, burrowed into a bank of snow, curled into a ball. She was so still that at first we thought she was dead, that she'd taken herself up there to die like a wounded animal, you know?'

I just nodded, not wanting to interrupt him.

'Leroy went to let the others know we'd found her, and I stayed to make sure she was okay. I cleared the snow away from her head, brushing it off her face and that red scarf of hers.'

He suddenly stopped and stared at the ceiling; I followed his gaze, but all I could see were the beams, cracked with age. When I looked back at him, he was grinning broadly and I smiled, hesitantly. He resumed his laps of the room – he hadn't been so full of energy for ages.

'She was talking,' he said.

'Really? What was she saying?'

He laughed, holding his arms above his head, stretching the kinks out of his back.

'Perhaps I'll go and finish that chair.'

'What?' He was making no sense.

'You know, that chair I'm making?' he said. 'To replace the broken one.'

'It's the middle of the night, it's Whiteout and you want to go to the barn and make a chair?'

He looked crestfallen. 'I suppose you're right. It can wait until tomorrow.'

He made his hands into fists and bumped them together several times. 'I need to do something though. Tire myself out before bed.' He gave me a look that I hadn't seen for a while. 'Or, how about we just go to bed?' He winked, but tempting though it was, I wasn't going anywhere until I knew what had happened.

'Finish telling me first, would you?'

He picked up his glass and knocked back the rest of his drink, then went over to the photographs again, first one side of the fire, then the other, then back, all the while humming something I didn't recognise.

'It's funny,' he said, 'when I look at these people, I don't feel anything, no connection, no blood ties, nothing.' He laughed, bitterly. 'If only I felt the same way about my father's family, eh love?'

I ignored him – it certainly wasn't the time for *that* conversation.

'You said the girl was talking…?' I tried again.

'What's that?'

'The girl. You found her. She was talking.'

'Oh yes, well obviously I couldn't understand what she was saying.'

'Why's that? Was she speaking in a different language?'

He looked at me, frowning, suddenly serious.

'You won't like this.'

I couldn't bear it any longer. 'For Freedom's sake, just spit it out.'

'OK, but don't say I didn't warn you,' he said. He turned to face the fire, so I couldn't see his expression. 'She said she was talking with God.'

Leroy's Luck washed around my stomach and I thought I might be sick.

'Ed, love, you're exhausted,' I said, trying very hard to keep my voice level. 'You've had no sleep and you've been working so hard. Let's go to bed, see how you're feeling in the morning.'

'I'm fine,' he said. He grabbed my hands, pulling me to my feet and putting his arms around me. For the life of me, I couldn't understand what he was so happy about. 'I feel great, Kat, better than I have in a long time.'

'You're not making any sense,' I said, leaning back to look at him. 'You follow a strange girl onto the hill in the middle of a snowstorm, find her half-buried and speaking nonsense; now you reckon you're feeling great.'

'She wasn't speaking nonsense.'

I sighed, it was hardly the point, but I decided to humour him. 'You said you didn't understand what she was saying.'

'Look, I know it's ridiculous, but if she really was speaking to God, why would you expect me to understand what she was saying?'

'I don't,' I said, helplessly. 'But you've got to realise why I'm finding this impossible to understand. Earlier this evening you said you wanted to notify the girl.'

'Come on, you know I didn't mean it,' he said. 'I'd never notify anyone. All I'm doing is telling you what happened. We went up the hill, we found the girl, she told me she was speaking to God.'

I wanted to scream and struggled to keep my voice calm when I said, 'Let's go to bed and…'

'Now there's an offer I can't refuse,' he said, pulling me close.

'…and tomorrow I'll book some time for you to Wave Dr. Lawrence.'

'I don't need to speak to Dr. Lawrence.'

'I think it would be a good idea, love,' I said, carefully. 'You're not quite yourself. Don't you see that?'

He shook his head. 'You're always worrying. Come on, let's go to bed.'

He took my hand, but I had one final question.

'Where's the girl now? Why didn't she come back with you?'

'I wanted her to. But don't worry about her, she'll come back to us soon.'

Later, after Ed had fallen asleep, his arm heavy across my stomach, the last thing on my mind was worrying about Jem. Instead, my thoughts were full of how we would manage if Ed really was about to have a full relapse: weeks or even months of persuading him to attend his therapy sessions with Dr. Lawrence on the Wave; the cost of chemi-patches we couldn't afford; the continual, exhausting, tiptoeing around him that the twins and I would have to do. Not to mention the effect that it had had on Ash last time: nine years old, sobbing, desperately worried about his father and overwhelmed with concern that the same thing would happen to him.

I had no idea where I would find the strength to go through it all again. The worst part was that this time, I'd known. I'd known that his old problem was coming back, and I'd known that the girl was trouble. I just hadn't known that the two things were connected.

7

Eileen

They stopped me from joining the search for Jem. That bitch, Kat, and her moronic friend Lily practically tied me to the chair so I couldn't go – I'm not sure how they knew, but they must have realised, even then, how important I was. I found bruises on my shoulders later, but I didn't care because by then everything had already changed forever.

After the search party left, the two of them hustled me down the street and practically threw me through my own front door. They pretended to be concerned about me but I knew they just wanted to come in and have a nose around, so I politely wished them goodnight, waved them up the steps to the street, and shut the door.

It was only then that everything that had happened that evening really hit me, and I slid down the wall until I was sitting on the floor in my hallway. Jem had held my hand. I couldn't remember anyone ever holding my hand, apart from my parents. And she had looked at me as though she was seeing me, *really* seeing me, not like how everyone else's gaze slides over me as if I'm not even there. Jem wanted to be my friend. She had asked me to be ready to help her and she told me that she needed me. I had been ready to do whatever she wanted, but then she left. Why? Why did she leave me? Maybe she hadn't believed me. How could I prove myself to her?

After lying on the floor for a while, I started shivering, so I went upstairs to the room at the front of my house, the one with the best view of the street. I unlocked my Treasure Cupboard, pushing aside the stack of my parent's syringes and the little glass bottles of drugs which they had used for their experiments, to get to the binoculars which had belonged to my great-grandfather, Nikon. Apparently, he had used them to look at birds – I suppose there must have been more around back then.

Even though I used them almost every day, I was always surprised by how heavy the binoculars were. I rubbed my finger over the little silver-coloured plaque with my great-grandfather's name on it, pulled a chair up to the window and made myself comfortable, prepared to wait for as long as it took. During Whiteout, the hills around Underhill are usually invisible at night, so when I held the binoculars up to my eyes it was strange to see the flashes of light from the torches bobbing along. I kept thinking about Jem up there all alone, but I had to stop myself crying because then I couldn't see through the binoculars.

I don't know how long it was before the light from the torches swung back towards the village, but I stared at each pinprick of light as it came closer, trying to work out if Jem was with whoever it was, but there was no sign of her. Leroy came past my house and then, later, Ed. I wasn't at all surprised that he was the last to come back – of course he would spend longer than anyone else trying to find her, that was just the sort of man he was.

As he walked towards me, I waited for him to look up. It was our secret sign: every day when he went to and from the turbines, he would look up at the window and I would look back at him. This time however, he didn't even glance in my direction; he was obviously being discreet.

It was only after he reached the steps that led down to his own house that I realised what it meant. The search parties had all returned but Jem had not come back. I put my hand against a crack in the window pane and pressed my thumb along it until a line of blood ran from the pad. I watched it gather into a heavy scarlet ball, then drip onto the floor where I scuffed it into the carpet with my foot.

*

My thumb had stopped bleeding, my eyelids were almost too heavy to keep open, my knees itched and my shoulders hurt from where I'd been forcibly manhandled by Kat and Lily but finally, a line crept across the sky above the hills and the night began to lift. As the black turned to grey, I was certain that the light would return Jem to me.

The first thing I saw was her scarf, bright red against the snow. I stared through the binoculars making sure it was really her, half-convinced that I was imagining it, but it was definitely Jem walking down the turbine path. I jumped up from my seat, then collapsed on the floor where I lay for several minutes, waiting for the pins and needles to go. As soon as the feeling came back in my legs, I raced downstairs and out onto the street.

Jem was weaving about all over the place and I thought she was going to fall over, but then Ed rushed past me and gathered her into his arms. I can't honestly say which one of them I was more jealous of at that moment, but I managed to put my feelings to one side and went to offer my services.

'Not now, Eileen. We need to get her inside.'

There was no excuse for such rudeness, but I followed Ed down the street anyway.

'Is sh…sh…she ok?' I said, but he ignored me until he reached the steps that led down to his cottage.

'I can't carry her down these,' he said, lowering Jem onto the ground and putting one of her arms around his neck. 'Can you take her other arm?'

Together we helped her down the steps, although Jem wasn't really being very co-operative, so it was more a case of dragging her to the front door, then Ed picked her up again and took her inside. I followed, shutting the door behind me.

It was years since I'd been in his house and the old yellow carpet in the hallway was still there, even dirtier than before and worn through in patches. I was amazed all over again to see the old photographs on the walls and I was trying to find my favourite one – a little red cottage, with a mountain in the background – which I used to spend ages looking at when I was staying there, when I realised that Ed and Jem had disappeared and I hurried to find them.

He had taken her into the living room. The furniture had been moved since I'd last been in it, but I was familiar with the layout from all the evenings I'd spent in their garden. I knew which was Ed's favourite chair – a couple of years ago he had repositioned it to face the window so I could see him properly – and I was surprised, and yes, I must admit, a little bit jealous when he lowered Jem into his chair. She slumped into it, curling up like a plant when the sun goes down. I went over and patted her head a few times, but she didn't seem to like me doing that very much. Then I realised that she was trying to tell me something so I bent down, sniffing hard to smell her lovely clove scent. She seemed to be having difficulty speaking.

'My,' she said.

'Yes?' I said.

'My…'

'Your w…what?'

'Migraine.' The word came out fast and loud, like an explosion. 'Migraine,' she said again. 'Need patches. In my bag.'

I looked at Ed and said, 'Her bag's at L…L…L…'

I took a deep breath, and he stared at me, so I stared back, wondering why he was being so slow, but eventually he clapped his hands together and said, 'Her bag's at Lily's. Right. I'll go and get it.'

As soon as he had left, I knelt down next to Jem's chair and rubbed her arm.

'I'm here. I'm ready.'

She didn't reply, so I tried again. 'I'm ready, like you asked. Tell me what to do.'

'What's going on?' said a voice behind me. Kat was watching us from the doorway.

'Why are you here?' she said, tapping her fingers on the doorframe. 'And why is she here, for that matter?'

Kat's face was all puffy, and her hair was sticking out all over the place. I assume she'd only just woken up but, honestly, she could have made an effort before coming downstairs – personal grooming clearly wasn't a priority for her. Poor Ed. I was imagining how I would do my hair if I was with him, when she interrupted my thoughts.

'Where's Ed?'

'N…n…next door,' I said, but she looked at me as though I was speaking a foreign language.

'Next door. At Lily's.' I spoke slowly, making sure I enunciated all the syllables properly – if she wanted to behave like an imbecile, then I had no problem treating her like one.

'Why?' Honestly, the woman simply had no manners at all.

'To get Jem's bag. She's g…g…got a migraine.'

Kat looked at Jem and frowned. Then she shrugged, walked over to the fire, and pointlessly stirred the embers with a poker. When she stopped, she turned to look at me.

'Frankly, I'm surprised the girl's even alive after being outside all night. How did she get here?'

'I was waiting for her. So was Ed,' I said, not bothering to keep the pleasure from my voice when I informed her that Ed and I had been spending time together. It was thrilling to see her look of annoyance.

'Well, Eileen, you can go home now. I'll keep an eye on her.'

'I d...d... don't think so,' I said. 'I'm s...s...staying right here.'

I knew what Kat thought of Jem. She was probably wishing she'd died up on the hill, and I crossed my arms to show her that I meant what I said.

There were footsteps on the staircase and Willow rushed into the room, closely followed by Ash. They paused, gaping at the sight of Jem. Willow tried to catch my eye, but I just looked at the floor.

'Jem,' Willow said. 'Why are you here?' She went over to her and put her arms around the girl, behaving like a foolish teenager. Out of the corner of my eye, I saw Kat shaking her head.

Ed came into the room with Jem's backpack and held it out to her, but she didn't take it, so I grabbed it for her. Inside it there were several packs of migraine patches and I ripped one open, shoved Jem's sleeve up and slapped it on her arm.

'Do you need anything else, Jem?' asked Kat, finally remembering her manners.

'Do you have bread and honey?' Jem said.

Kat shook her head.

'Jam, then?'

'Willow, go and get her some bread and jam,' said Kat.

'And tea,' added Jem.

Willow looked distinctly unimpressed but left the room.

'Ash, go with her,' Kat said. 'You both need to eat breakfast, or else you'll be late for class again.'

Kat pushed Ed out into the hallway, and I went to stand behind the door so I could hear them.

'Why did you bring her here?' Kat was obviously trying to talk quietly but I could still tell she was annoyed.

'Where else was I supposed to take her? Lily doesn't want her there.'

'Well I don't want her here. And why is Eileen here, draping herself all over the girl? This is ridiculous, Ed. I thought we talked about this last night. You're ill.'

I filed away that interesting piece of information to consider later, in the privacy of my own home. Meanwhile, on the other side of the door, Kat was really getting worked up.

'You need help,' she was saying. 'What you don't need is to be bringing troublemakers into this house.'

I know Ed would have defended me if he'd had a chance, but she just carried on talking right over him.

'I'm going to book an emergency Wave session for you with Dr. Lawrence, like we talked about.'

'You talked about it, Kat, but obviously you didn't listen to what I was saying. I've brought Jem here because I want to understand what happened last night.'

'This is crazy,' said Kat, and it sounded like she was stamping her foot, so I put my eye against the gap in the door frame to try and see what they were doing. Behind me, Jem chuckled quietly.

'I'm going to go and get Molly,' Kat said. 'We need to sort this out. And keep an eye on Eileen. You of all people should know that we can't trust her.'

I didn't hear what they said after that because I was concentrating really hard to stop myself from picking up the poker, running out into the hallway and ramming it into her back. I was still doing my special breathing when Willow came into the room carrying a plate of thickly cut bread slathered in jam. She seemed surprised to see me behind the door and I thought she was going to say something, but then she thought better of it and went over to Jem, shoving the plate into her hand. Ash trailed in after her with a mug of tea.

Kat slammed the front door as she left, and shortly after that, Ed practically pushed Willow and Ash out of the house to go to their classes. He came back into the living room and sat next to me, where I was watching Jem eat. Each time her teeth parted, tiny dimples appeared in the mounds of her cheeks. I have to admit, although the dimples were mesmerising, she was looking pretty terrible otherwise: her lips were cracked and blistered and looked as though they had been vigorously scoured; her hair had dried into clumps which gave her a mildly deranged look; she was shivering, despite the fire and the mug of tea which she took great slurps of in between mouthfuls of bread. The whole time she ate, she kept looking round the room, side to side, up and down, craning her neck to stare behind her. I kept trying to see what she was looking at but whenever I turned back towards her, she would be staring somewhere else.

When she had finally finished all the bread and tilted the mug to drain the last dregs of tea, she put the plate on the table next to her and settled herself more comfortably in Ed's chair. Next to me, he shuffled forward until he was sitting right on the edge of the sofa. He reminded me of a baby bird preparing to launch itself into the air for the first time. I lifted my hand from my lap and casually put it down near his leg, but he pretended not to see it.

'Do you feel well enough to talk about last night?' he asked Jem.

I wanted to know about last night as well, but Jem just licked a spot of red jam off one of her fingers. The glimpse of her tongue made me shiver. She closed her eyes and let her head fall back against the chair.

'When you're feeling better, then,' Ed said, looking disappointed and shuffling back to safety on the sofa.

*

It took hours for Jem's migraine to ease and in all that time she didn't move from Ed's chair and I didn't move from the sofa. Ed didn't go up to the turbines all day, which led to another heated debate between him and Kat. I don't know the rules of a happy partnership, but it seems unlikely that whispered arguments in the hallway are a recommended part of the arrangement.

Lily kept popping in and out and having secret conversations with Kat in the kitchen, while they banged pots and pans around unnecessarily loudly. Molly waddled in, but when Jem didn't seem inclined to answer her questions, she manoeuvred herself around and left, asking that someone let her know when Jem was well enough to talk.

At some point, Kat went out again. She was gone for nearly two hours, which was a relief because we could finally relax without her miserable face appearing in the doorway every few minutes. While she was gone, Ed tried to get Jem to talk to him again. He squatted by her chair and started speaking in a really low voice, so I couldn't hear him. I didn't like that at all, so I got up and stood near them, pretending to look at some old photographs on the walls. Ed was speaking so quietly that all I could hear was the odd word like *snowfall*, *night* and *understand*, and I actually heard him say the G word, not just once but several times.

After their classes were finished, Willow and Ash came home and sprawled in front of the fire, playing a game. I offered to play it with them but they said only two people could play, so I just sat and waited.

By the time Jem was finally well enough to talk to us, quite a group had gathered in the room, including several from my List of Enemies. Obviously I was pleased that my neighbours were finally beginning to realise what a special person my best friend was, but I would have preferred it if they all just went away and left me alone with her.

In the end when she spoke, I was there, of course, and Ed, Willow and Ash. Kat and Lily were huddled together against the far wall, whispering like they had been for most of the day. Molly had come back, and as well as all of us, there were another six other people present in the room that day to hear Jem's Vision.

Laurel was there with baby Mila. She said she'd come to check with Kat if the drone had been, but that was just an excuse because everyone knew it wasn't coming until the next day. She'd brought Lia and Fred with her for some reason, although they just sat side-by-side holding hands without speaking, being their usual ignorable selves.

Those dreadful women Petra and Tish had also turned up and of course they'd not even been there for a minute when their bickering started. That's all they do. Bicker, bicker, bicker, all day long. I really don't know why they stay together. Petra said Tish had pushed ahead of her through the doorway, then Tish accused Petra of hogging the chair they had squashed themselves into. Petra said Tish had knocked her elbow when she was trying to drink her tea and Tish said Petra had taken the bigger slice of cake that Ash was passing round. On and on and on. Jem was frowning at them, which wasn't surprising because I myself had fantasised several times about creative ways to silence their bickering once and for all.

Clearly Jem had had enough of their arguing because she actually got out of her chair at one point and went to kneel in front of them.

'You're really sliding about, aren't you?' she said. 'Sliding and slipping around each other. What you need is something to hold onto. Something to lift you free of yourselves and bind you together.'

Well. Who knows what *that* meant but it certainly did the trick, because they both looked startled, stopped talking and didn't say another word.

When I thought about it afterwards, I realised that I shouldn't have been surprised, not when you consider that she was bringing a message from God, but even I was shocked when Jem got up from her chair and fell onto her knees, spreading her arms out wide, palms up. She stared at the ceiling the whole time that she spoke and although her neck looked as fragile as a twig, her eyes were blazing like suns.

It was the smell though, that was most unexpected. In the beginning, the smell of burning was so strong that everyone kept looking to see if something had fallen from the fire, but after a bit it faded to the charred smell you get from a piece of wood that has somehow survived when everything around it has burned to ashes.

Nobody said a word while Jem was speaking. Nobody moved or coughed or scratched themselves. Everyone in the room was still and silent, even baby Mila, whose eyes were wide as she stared at Jem, her thumb plugging her mouth.

I know exactly what Jem said because afterwards I went straight home and wrote it all down. Her words that day are near the beginning of the Book of Jem and I've read them so often I can recite them by heart, and indeed I often do.

Arrivals 2:3-15

God called me to the hill and told me to prepare for a visitor.

I knelt on the ground and although the snow was all around me, I was not cold.

A woman appeared before me, stepping out of a golden light. Knots puckered her flesh, and when she reached a hand towards me, she had long, long fingers, with knuckles of stone and blackened, cracked nails. Tufts of white hair rustled around her head and deep within her scorched-

leather face, her green eyes stared at me unblinkingly as she told me her story.

This is what she said.

I am the earth and the earth is me. I am one of the infinite strands of God.

For the longest time, I lived among the plants and the animals and I was happy. But even as the plants and the animals thrived they did not need me, and I wanted to share myself with something that needed me.

I asked the wind to help me find a purpose, and it blew me towards a stream. I asked the stream for help, and the waters bore me to a stone, which directed me to a forest. There, deep inside the forest, I found people and I knew that they were what I was looking for.

For many, many of their lifetimes, the people and I were happy. They made great fires to keep me warm and they offered me gifts. In return I gave them food to fill their bellies, I blew away the storms that threatened their crops and I turned aside the pestilence that threatened their bodies. They needed me and I loved them and I was full of joy.

But one day, the people asked for my help to leave the forest and find new homes. The wind and the stream, the plants and the animals were afraid of the people and did not want them to leave the forest. But the people pleaded with me and because I loved them, I promised to help them.

Before I gave my promise, I asked the people for a vow which they gave gladly. They vowed that as they spread across the earth, they would nurture it, they would respect the plants and the animals, they would keep the streams running fast and the wind blowing clean. Finally, they vowed to always remember to share the earth with everything that lived upon it.

For a time, they honoured their vow.
For a time, they remembered.
For a time, they shared.
For a time, all was good.
But, slowly, they began to forget.
And then they forgot to remember.

Instead of nurturing the earth, they poisoned it. They saturated it with chemicals and toxins until the land and the streams and the winds were too weak to give life to the plants and the animals, which sickened and died. And as the people watched the crops fail, and the beasts falter and their own babies slip too early from their mother's bellies, they searched for something to blame.

They searched and they searched, and finally they said it was me that had done this, and they named me wicked and banished me.

But I ask you, the visitor on the hill said to me, the heat of her tears melting the snow, who is the wicked one? She who fulfilled the promise she had made? Or they who betrayed their vows?

8

Kat

I talked, she listened. If only I could say the same for everyone else in my life. I often wondered what it said about me that my longest relationship was with someone who had never said a word. That was the thing about talking to the Elder Mother though: she gave me space to speak and listened without judgement and most days that was all I needed.

I knew talking to a tree was on the limits of acceptable behaviour, in fact if I was being really honest with myself, I knew it was the wrong side of the line and there was no doubt, as Ed never tired of saying, that it could cause me a whole heap of trouble if anyone ever found out. But I'd been doing it since I was younger than the twins were now, when the arguments back home were a whole lot worse than the occasional disagreement that Ed and I had.

I'd been hanging around outside our house, trying to pretend that the sound of my parents' shouting wasn't really carrying halfway down the street, when one of our neighbours asked if I wanted to come in for a cup of tea and a piece of cake. I don't know if it was Sally or Rhea who asked me that first time – they'd lived together so long and resembled each other so closely that most people thought of them as a single person. If they minded that no-one bothered to remember which one of them was which, they never said.

They had no children or grandchildren and looking back on it,

I think they were happy to have a youngster around. They'd ply me with cake and let me spend hours at a time leaning against piles of precariously balanced books. I'd never seen so many books in one place and I don't suppose I ever will again. The two old ladies encouraged me to read everything and anything: *No knowledge is bad knowledge*, one or other of them was fond of saying, *provided you know what to do with it*, and often I'd find myself picking up the next book while I was still turning the final pages of the previous one.

Whenever the arguments at home became so bad that my parents' voices came through the wall, the deliveries of cake became more frequent, accompanied by quiet murmurs and pats of sympathy, and after they left the room, I'd reach for the unpromisingly named *Spirits in the Trees: Pagan Beliefs*.

It had taken a while before I'd even bothered to look at the book. One of the old ladies had pointed it out when I'd first started going round there, saying something like, 'If only everything was like it was back then,' but I wasn't interested in history, generally I preferred more modern books. What people got up to before the Wars bore so little resemblance to my world that the problems they faced just seemed stupid.

What finally made me pick the book up was the picture on the cover. The photograph was of a tree, taken when it was heavy with new leaves, the colour of gold. The tree stood alone on the slope of a hill, and some trick of the light meant that the sunlit fields behind it were the same rich, golden colour. It was a beautiful tree, but that wasn't what made me pull the book onto my lap and open it; it was the fact that when I looked really closely, I realised that someone was standing in front of the tree. I hadn't noticed them at first, maybe because of how far away the photographer must have been, but also because of the way the shadows fell, so the person blended into the tree trunk. Although I spent ages squinting at the picture, I couldn't tell whether it was a man or a woman, or even a child. The only detail that stood out clearly was their bright red scarf.

I often wondered if the photographer knew that the person was there. Perhaps it was some relative? A daughter? A partner? Or perhaps the photographer didn't know, perhaps the person in the scarf just happened to be standing there by accident, at the exact time the picture was taken. Did they even know they were on the cover of a book? I pointed the hidden person out to one of the old ladies and she looked at it closely.

'You've got a decent pair of eyes on you. I've lost count of the number of times I've looked at this book, but I've never noticed that.'

She put a piece of cake down beside me and left me to my reading. As I turned the pages, I tried to find other people hiding among the trees, but no matter how hard I looked, I couldn't find any others.

When I eventually settled down to read the book properly, I found that each of the twenty chapters was about a different tree. Long ago, the book explained, people believed that trees had spirits, and they used to talk to the trees, and ask them for help with their lives. Although I didn't realise it until later on, it must have been because I was so unhappy with everything going on at home that I decided to copy those long dead people and pick myself a spirit tree to help me with my life.

The beautiful tree on the cover was an ash and had there been any ash trees left, then it would have been an easy decision, but when I asked Dandy where I could find an ash tree, he said, 'There's none left, Kitten. They've all gone.' After that, I very nearly opted for the rowan tree. It was The Lady of the Mountain and I loved the name, not to mention that it had gorgeous red leaves that were almost as beautiful as the ash, but in the end, I chose the elder tree, which was an unlikely choice. It was the ugly cousin of the ash and rowan, but I didn't choose my spirit tree for how it looked on the outside, I was fascinated by what the book told me lived on the inside.

The spirit who lived inside the elder tree had many names, some of them were beautiful – White Goddess, for example – others were less flattering, Old Crone was particularly unpleasant, all hairy warts and hooked nose. However, to me, the spirit in the elder tree was always the Elder Mother, who I thought of as being like an honorary great-aunt, modelled on two kind, cake-delivering old ladies.

According to my book, the Elder Mother was the *mother of daughters, defender of homesteads and healer of fevers.* She and her daughters lived in the trees and as long as the people living nearby respected the elder trees, she would look after them. If someone wanted to cut down an elder tree, they had to make an offering and give the Elder Mother time to leave before they started chopping.

Once I had settled on her, I began to talk to the Elder Mother as I had never talked to anyone before and all my thoughts, good, bad, happy and sad, began to spill out. It took practice to talk without receiving a reply. The book hadn't told me how I was supposed to address my spirit tree, and over the years, I had developed my own way of speaking to the Elder Mother, but at first, standing in front of the elder tree at the back of my parents' garden, I regularly stopped mid-sentence, feeling stupid.

One time, Dandy came outside while I was muttering away.

'What's that you're doing, Kitten?'

He looked so weary. My parents' relationship had reached its most exhausting point, a few months more and it would finally come to an end. He was staring at me curiously, waiting for my reply and I was about to tell him about the Elder Mother and how she was my tree spirit, but at the last second, I stopped myself. He would be angry if he knew what I was really doing. Angry but also disappointed, which would be far worse. My father, the academic – back in the days when it was still possible to make a living from being clever and thoughtful – had spent his whole career studying what he referred to as our *innate propensity for religion* and he was convinced that it was the single most catastrophic creation of all time. I knew how the conversation would go.

'*What is religion, Kitten?*'

I had no doubt what he'd want to hear, he'd told me often enough.

'*Religion is a lie. It's a belief in non-existent supernatural forces.*'

'*And yet, little Kitten, you somehow don't think that that includes tree spirits?*'

I wasn't sure if talking to the invisible Elder Mother did actually count as religion, but I knew there would be no doubt in Dandy's mind.

'I'm just practising something for school tomorrow, Dandy,' I said eventually, hating the lie.

When I came to be with Ed, I felt an immediate connection with the elder tree at the back of the abandoned graveyard. I took comfort from choosing to believe that the Elder Mother that had listened to my teenage confessions was the same Elder Mother that I talked to about my new life in Underhill.

When I was completely honest with myself, I had to admit that I was never entirely convinced that trees really did have spirits. I loved the idea of it, but when I tried to imagine how the Elder Mother could possibly inhabit the tree, the whole idea was ridiculous. It seemed unlikely that she writhed along the branches, stretching herself into the gnarled tips. However, all these years later I still went to the graveyard to see my tree as often as possible. I had tried stopping a few times – usually after Ed wound me up about the risk of being notified – but after a couple of days of not talking to her, I'd have vivid red lines tracking along my arms, from where I'd scratched myself raw. One time it was so bad that I couldn't fight the urge to take my clothes off in the middle of the day and scratch and scratch until I made the skin on my stomach bleed. I went back to the graveyard that same afternoon.

'Why is she here?' I asked the Elder Mother, the day after Jem had told us about her supposed vision. I was squeezing my hand so hard around the trunk that the knots dug painfully into my palm.

The Elder Mother remained silent and I sighed. I pressed my forehead against the tree. The bark was scarred with gashes and the leafless branches pointed skyward, stretching away from the tangle of ivy at the foot of the tree. During Whiteout, the trees sucked their vitality back into their roots, pushing deep underground, retrenching to survive and I wished I could do the same, wished I could ignore everything else until the sun returned, rising high enough above the hills to bring us some warmth.

I felt a familiar thickening in the air that meant the drone must be approaching. I'd stayed too long and had to hurry out without saying hello to baby Holly. A break in the snow meant the clouds were high enough for me to watch as the drone followed the route towards the touch-down site, slightly above and to the right of the hill ridge, giving the turbines a wide berth. As it swung in towards Underhill, the dark shape gradually resolved into the sleek lines of the drone.

I turned off the track and into the close-cropped meadow, trying to catch my breath. As the drone hung motionless above me, running through its landing procedures, I found myself thinking, yet again, about how in the years before the Wars, there was supposed to have been more than a million people flying through the air at any given moment. I couldn't imagine a million people anywhere, let alone the idea of so many bodies sealed up together inside metal boxes and it was unbelievable to think that people did it for pleasure – as far as I'm concerned flying is only for birds and drones.

The drone engaged its landing pads, locking them into position below the curve of its belly, then dropped smoothly onto the patch of cleared ground, rocking lightly before it powered down, shuddering as it switched itself off. On clear days, the sunlight glinting off the panels was blinding, but when the clouds were piled overhead, it was a uniform grey-black – apart from the purple logo, of course. I walked over to the recessed access pad and reached my hand up to Wave authorisation. There was a brief pause, a series of barely audible clicks, a short high-pitched whine, then the belly slid open.

A full container, indistinguishable from all the others, was lowered to the ground. As the empty container on the far side of the site was lifted into the drone, I confirmed that everything was in the new one, checking each item off one by one. It wasn't often that mistakes were made, the orders were picked automatically when I placed them, but occasionally there were errors and it was so much simpler not to accept an item, than to try and return it later. I checked off the final thing – Eileen's new trousers – and Waved receipt. The drone gave another shiver as it switched itself back on, then rose smoothly into the air, before accelerating away from Underhill.

Accepting the order was easy; the difficult part began when I had to unload all the items from the container into the cart. Fortunately, the empty container was very light and so it was easy for me to push into position ready for collection next time but once the cart was full, it was ridiculously heavy. The irony wasn't lost on me: it was so simple to get the orders to us – they were picked, packed, and transported through the sky with minimal effort; and yet, I thought, as the wheel of the cart rolled backwards and almost ran over my foot, moving everything the final few metres to the barn was so bloody difficult.

No doubt some communities had more sophisticated methods of transportation, just as we had a relatively reliable supply of electricity when many didn't. We did the best with what we had. In the years since I'd moved to Underhill, the opportunity to share resources externally had pretty much dried up and we were almost entirely reliant on the food we produced ourselves. Sometimes the animals were fed better than us, to give them the best chance of reproducing and continuing to provide us with meat. Ed and I were extremely fortunate, of course. He worked with the turbines, I did the ordering, but for most of my neighbours there was very little opportunity for anyone to make any money other than by farming or working the Files. That, or move to a city.

I heaved the cart over a final bump and as it rolled into the barn, the sweat tickled uncomfortably as it ran down my back – once it started to dry, I'd be freezing. I sorted the packages, tallying them with the individual orders and put Molly's medicine in my bag to drop off later. While I waited for everyone to come and collect their orders, I poured myself some tea and wandered over to Ed's work bench. It was in the corner of the barn, with his carpentry tools locked away in a chest underneath. The half-finished chair was still there. Despite wanting to rush out and work on it two nights ago, he hadn't been to the barn since.

I wasn't at all happy that Jem was still in our house, but Ed was insistent and I couldn't bear another fight. What with her and the kids, it had been impossible to find an opportunity to talk to him properly. He'd refused to Wave Dr. Lawrence, and I hadn't pushed it. He was full of energy, but it wouldn't last, and I was becoming increasingly concerned that if we carried on ignoring things, it would be so much worse in the end.

I tried to put my worries out of my mind and concentrate on handing out the orders. Eileen was the last to arrive, coming into the barn so quietly that I jumped when she thrust her hand out for her new trousers. I reached for the parcel, then hesitated and turned back towards her.

'Has Jem told you why she came to Underhill?'

She looked startled for a moment and her forehead drew itself together into a brief frown, before her face settled back into its usual slab-like expression. She didn't say anything, just jiggled her arm impatiently in front of my face.

'Well? Has she?'

'N...n...n...' Eileen shook her head, then opened her mouth wide, gulping air like a fish.

'No.' When the word finally shot from her mouth, she pressed her lips firmly together, clearly she had no intention of saying anything else.

I sighed and pushed the trousers towards her.

'If you do know anything about why she's here...' I said, but I was talking to myself, she'd already grabbed her parcel and fled.

*

By the time I'd taken Molly her medicine, I was exhausted, but when I saw Jem's coat and scarf hanging in my hallway, I seriously considered turning around and going back out. Perhaps I could go and have a cup of tea with Lily? But then I thought, no, it's my house, I'm not going to let that girl make me feel like a stranger in my own home.

I hesitated in the kitchen doorway watching her shovelling food into her mouth, flicking through a pile of books. Some of them were Dandy's textbooks – ones he'd actually written – and I treasured them, they lived on a bookshelf in our bedroom and no-one was allowed to touch them without my permission. The nerve of the girl, going through my stuff.

She was oblivious to the fact I was watching her. I scratched my arm. Clearly, she'd had a shower at some point during the day, which meant there wouldn't be enough water for Ed when he came home. It had washed away the after-effects of her night on the hill – her black hair was gleaming and her skin glowed. She looked newly made, like she'd been birthed fully formed from the snow. Despite her evidently large appetite, she was tiny and had folded herself into the chair in a way that took up hardly any space at all.

A drop of milk fell from the spoon onto the page she was looking at, but she ignored it, casually turning the page over, not caring that it would be stained for ever. I strode across and pulled the books away from her, piling them up on the end of the table.

'Don't touch these,' I said. 'Some of them are very old.'

'Why have you got so many books about God?' she asked.

'They're not about God. They're about the sociopsychology of religion. That's different. They were my father's.'

'Books don't help you understand God.'

'My father didn't want to understand God,' I replied. 'He wanted to understand people who believed in God.'

I got up and poured some hot water over the last of my tea – I'd need to mix up some more.

'We'll be having dinner soon,' I said.

Jem shrugged and put the dirty spoon on the table.

I sat down opposite her, and wrapped my hands around my mug, ignoring the urge to reach across and slap her. I took a deep breath and watched her pick at a bit of skin next to the nail on her left forefinger, picking and picking until she worried an edge free and peeled a tiny strip of skin back. A bead of blood appeared and she sucked her finger.

'Why are you here?' I asked, determined to get her to talk to me. Years of dealing with Willow had taught me how to out-stubborn anyone.

She finally looked at me and the corners of her mouth turned up into something approximating a smile, then she pulled the bowl back towards her, picked up the spoon and had another mouthful, chewing loudly. I pulled the bowl out of her hands and put it in the sink. Yes, it was petty, but it made me feel better and I leaned back against the counter-top with my arms folded.

'Your little performance, all that *I had a vision* and *God was talking to me* rubbish, might convince some people,' I said, deliberately keeping my tone light, as if I was talking about the weather. 'But you and I both know there is no such thing as God and you did not have a vision, so I'll ask you again, why're you here?'

Jem delicately touched the tip of her tongue to the corners of her mouth.

'I know where you were this morning,' she said.

'Sorting the orders. I do it every week.'

'Before then. I know where you go.'

'I don't know what you're talking about.' I stared at her, but she just stared back, so I picked up a cup and started cleaning it, rubbing the inside so hard that it squeaked.

'This isn't about me,' I said.

'Isn't it?' she asked. 'You may not like it, but you're just the same as everyone else, Kat. All of you trying to find something that will fill the great gaping hole inside yourselves, even if most people don't realise that's what they're doing. Anyway, there's no point denying it. I told you, I know where you go.'

I slammed down the cup, spinning round to face her.

'Don't you dare threaten me. Tell me why you're here.'

'God told me to come here.'

'Enough. Seriously. Just stop lying.' She'd wound me up so much that I was yelling and I hated that I couldn't control myself. I dragged my fingernails down the inside of arm so hard that I broke the skin. The sight of my blood calmed me and I took a couple of deep breaths before I spoke again.

'What do you want from us, Jem?'

'I don't want anything. I know you don't want to believe me, but God *did* tell me to come here and God *did* tell me to go up the hill and soon I will understand what it means.'

'What it *means*? It doesn't *mean* anything, you stupid girl.'

She was staring at the smear of blood on my arm, and I yanked my sleeves down.

'You leave Ed alone, do you understand?' I said, jabbing my finger at her. 'He's vulnerable. He needs stability, not some, some....'

'Have you asked him how he feels? Maybe he's curious. Maybe he wants to know more.'

'Why are you shouting, Mum? Also, when's dinner?'

Ash was standing in the doorway with Willow hovering behind him. There was a mark around her throat.

'What's happened? Are you okay, Willow?'

'Yeah.'

'Have you cut yourself?' I gestured towards her neck. 'There. Are you hurt?'

Willow shrugged. 'It's nothing.'

I went over to her and realised that she'd tied a piece of red string around her neck. I ran my finger over it – it was so tight that it was cutting into the ridges of cartilage in her throat.

'Why have you got string around your neck?' I asked, wearily, already knowing I wouldn't get a proper answer.

'I felt like it.' Willow brushed away my hand. 'When's dinner?'

As I turned away, I saw Jem smile approvingly at Willow.

*

During the night, I woke from a bad dream. My legs were tangled in the covers and I kicked them free, then reached across to Ed's side of the bed, trying to reassure myself that the terrors hadn't followed me into the bedroom.

He wasn't there. I sat up and felt for my jumper, pulling it over my head, then I got out of bed and crossed the room, stubbing my toe on the corner of the bed. I stood on one leg, rubbing my foot, and opened the bedroom door. Voices drifted up from the kitchen and I crept down the staircase. I sat on the bottom stair, leaning my head against the banister and scratching my arm.

'…all the Laws, all the rules, they're just ways for the authority to control us,' Jem was saying and her voice had lost its sneering tone – she sounded sympathetic, almost kind. 'They want us docile, obedient. The way they see it, the authority is the *only* authority. Of course they don't want us to seek out God. They don't want us asking questions and they certainly don't want us looking for answers, other than the ones they decide to give us. But there is another way. We can choose freedom. We can choose God.'

I got to my feet, intending to go and ask Ed to come back to bed – the last thing he needed was to listen to that girl spouting more rubbish, winding him up, making him believe there was a quick fix to all his problems – but then he started speaking and I sank back down onto the stairs, unable to believe what I was hearing.

Not long after I first met Ed – when it became obvious to us both that our relationship was becoming serious – he had said that there was something that I needed to know about him. I'd no idea what to expect, so when he told me about his grandfather it was a complete shock. Actually, *shock* is the wrong word. At first, I couldn't take it in. His grandfather was Abe Pask. The man I'd learned about at school. The one they called 'The Designer of Death'. That was Ed's grandfather? I just sat there for a very, very long time until eventually when he couldn't bear my silence any longer, Ed said that he understood if I wanted to leave, if I never wanted to see him again. But I already loved him by then, so I held his hand and said that I was glad he had told me, glad it was out in the open, and that it didn't make a difference to me – I wanted to be with him – and in any case, Ed wasn't his grandfather.

That was the thing about the Wars – so much had been done that could never be forgiven, that there was no choice except to try and forget. Our duty was to look to the future and by then I was certain that my future was with Ed.

As far as I was aware, he had never told anyone else – except Dr. Lawrence – who his grandfather was. The burden of Abe Pask, the memory of him, the genetic link to him was a burden Ed carried so heavily that sometimes I was convinced it was going to crush him completely, but I don't even think that he and Leroy talked about it, and certainly Leroy had never had Ed's problems. I told Dandy and he had had quite a bit to say about it all of course, but I'd already made my choice, time had moved on and our focus, the focus of everyone, was to make the best of what was left. So, the idea that Ed would tell his story, make his confession, to the devious, *dangerous* young woman in our kitchen appalled me.

In the kitchen, Ed's voice had a catch in it and I knew he was on the verge of tears – which made two of us. I couldn't bear to hear any more of his misery and that girl's false sympathy, so I ran back up the stairs and into our bed where I pulled the duvet over my head, wrapping myself up into a tight ball. Tears came, but I only let myself cry for a minute before I pulled myself together. I had to be strong if we were going to get through this.

First thing in the morning, I would contact Dr. Lawrence and arrange an emergency session for Ed.

After that, I would do whatever I needed to do to make sure Jem left our home and never came back.

9

Eileen

Talking is overrated.

When I was little, I used to talk all the time. My Dad had a nickname for me: Little Miss Chatterbox. She was a character in an old book that his mother used to read to him. Each night, when he put me to bed, Dad would make up stories about Little Miss Chatterbox. One night, she might be a farmer, singing to the cows as she milked them; the next night, Little Miss Chatterbox lived long ago and flew planes to places that aren't there anymore. Mostly, though, she was a scientist, inventing medicines like my parents did.

In reality, I think Dad just liked the name and when I interrupted him and Mum while they were working he used to always do a really exaggerated sigh and say, *Here's Little Miss Chatterbox*, starting slow and low, and getting high and loud, so that he always said box in a really high-pitched showy voice. Mum and I would roll our eyes at each other, but secretly I loved it.

Most of the games I played with my parents involved storytelling. Every mealtime, we would take it in turns to say sentences and each one had to follow on from the one before, Mum, Dad and me, one after another, until we'd told a complete story. As I got older, and I started using my grandmother's notebooks, I began writing stories down. When they were as good as I could make them, I used to read them aloud to Mum and Dad and they would both sit at the kitchen table with their eyes closed so I knew that they were completely focused on listening to me.

When I read aloud, I used to love the way the words felt in my mouth. The way some words sounded hard, like *bad* or *hate* – when I said them my tongue and lips would be all stiff. But for other words, softer words like *Mum* and *love* my tongue would go all floppy. But after my parents died, I didn't talk much – if they couldn't hear me then there didn't seem to be much point.

After a while, I found it difficult to speak at all. I tried only using words that I hadn't used with my parents, but that was impossible. Talking just reminded me of all the things that I would never be able to say to them. Then my affliction started and words became my enemy. I couldn't seem to push them out, they invaded my mouth, got trapped under my tongue, lodged behind my teeth, stuck in my cheeks. That's why I only speak when I really absolutely have to.

It's okay though, because the words come easily when I write things down and it doesn't matter that I can't say them out loud. Everyone else is too busy talking, words spilling out of their flapping mouths any which way, without any respect for what they mean. I consider each word that I write, I cherish it and that is why, even after everything, I really was the only person who could have written the Book of Jem.

There was quite a lot of disagreement in the room immediately after Jem told us about her Vision. One or two people just said she was making the whole thing up, whilst everyone else was trying to work out what it meant. Obviously, I just kept my opinions to myself and went home and wrote it down in the Book of Jem.

The next major thing that happened was a couple of days later when I decided to give my new trousers a trial outing. I wasn't going to go very far, I just intended to check in with a few of my regulars. I slid my legs into the trousers. My knees were still scabbed and the material felt rough, like they were made from old carpets or something, but I hadn't had the money for anything better.

I did some stretching, both for the benefit of the trousers and myself, and then I went out of my back door. The temperature had dropped again and it was too cold to snow which presented some challenges: I wouldn't be able to stop moving for too long, or else I might freeze to death, and unless it snowed at some point during the night, my footprints would be on display in all the gardens that I went into. There wasn't much I could do about that though, so I hurried down to the path at the back of the houses, trying to warm myself up.

Before anything else, I wanted to check up on Jem. I'd been round to Ed's house a few times, but Kat had refused to let me in, even after I had banged on their door thirty-seven times. Eventually, I found out that there had been an *altercation*, as it was being called, and Jem wasn't staying there any longer but was now with Laurel and Rob. It was the third place she'd been since she'd come to Underhill, but she still hadn't come to stay with me.

Since Mila was born I hadn't been to watch Laurel and Rob very often, but I knew their garden was easy to navigate because there were no pointless statues or unnecessary ponds, and I crept along the grass border towards the house. I also knew that they had a vastly over-sized fireplace in their living room and so they almost always kept a window open, even during the depths of Whiteout, which was fortunate since I might otherwise have ended up just watching everyone that evening without hearing very much of anything. At the sound of voices from inside, I abandoned all caution, took three quick steps to get right up close to the window and peered into the room. I couldn't believe my eyes.

Given how the rest of the evening went, I suppose I should explain who was there: Jem, of course, sitting in the chair nearest the fire with her red scarf wound tightly round her neck, looking as beautiful as ever. I've explained before how good I am at interpreting Jem's emotions and I could tell straightaway that she was already frustrated by the questions about her Vision and God. If only everyone understood her as easily as I did.

Laurel and Rob were there as well, which was fair enough, after all it was their house. Laurel was holding baby Mila. Watching her, I felt a tingling in my arms like they needed something solid and warm to stop them from flying up. Rob had one hand on Laurel's leg. Affection make my palms itch. It's like people are doing it to each other on purpose to make me feel bad, and as I watched, he squeezed her leg, just above her knee. It's so pathetic, the need some people have to touch someone else.

Anyway, that paled into insignificance compared with how I felt when I saw Tish and Petra, lounging on the floor by the fire. I've cross-checked the date and can confirm that as of that evening, they were fourth and fifteenth on my List of Enemies. Petra had her hand stuffed full of tissues. She had a chronic allergy to life as far as I could tell – forever sniffing, coughing, kneading her forehead with her fingers in a way that was designed to make us feel sorry for her, although of course I saw right through it. Petra was only really on my List because she was Tish's partner. Tish was far, far worse. She was on my List because she was a bitch who I did not like one little bit. Suffice to say, I was not happy to see them lolling about on the floor, in front of Jem, bickering away between themselves, just like always.

I was less annoyed about Lia and Fred being there because they were so ignorable although there had been a time when I'd thought that perhaps Fred and I could have been friends. I'd even written him a note, asking him if he'd like to get together for a conversation or maybe more. I agonised over whether to give it to him, but in the end, I plucked up the courage to slip it under their front door. I never received a reply.

They were older than me, maybe about forty, but the additional years hadn't given Lia any substance: she was a completely *in*substantial person, both physically, in that she looked like a twig, and personality-wise, in that she didn't really have one. That's probably why she had never been on my List – she didn't have enough personality to have done anything that would have warranted giving her a place on it.

At the time, I did wonder how Jem knew that none of these people were really what an Underhill person was *supposed* to be. I mean, there's always the same inner circle who arrange the parties, make the food, shout the loudest, laugh the longest, tell each other how wonderful they are, how lucky they are to have each other. Even if they had got down on their knees and begged me, I would never have consented to become part of that group, with their cloying, nauseating *niceness*. Others avoided it too. When I thought back on it, it occurred to me that maybe it was precisely because they had never been part of the Underhill clique that the people gathered around Jem understood her from the beginning.

In any case, none of that meant that I was happy to see them, especially when I realised that the only other person in the room was Ed. I couldn't believe it. Ed and Jem. Jem and Ed. Together, without me. No matter what I did, no matter how hard I tried, I was always left out of things. I forced myself to do my special breathing and at the same time I rubbed my new trousers over my knee scabs until they started bleeding. Blood always soothes me. It helps me to know how easily life could end. I just have to make the blood flow and keep it flowing, and that would be it. All over.

Once the blood was trickling down my legs, I could concentrate on what they were talking about and the first thing I noticed was how they were all saying the G word and no-one was being weird about it.

'Let's just say, for the sake of argument, that God was talking to you,' Ed was saying.

'God was talking to me.' Just the sound of Jem's voice made me want to climb through the window to get to her, but I forced myself to stay still.

'Ok, ok, but why you? And why Underhill?' That was Tish, of course. Always so aggressive and bitchy and argumentative.

'I don't know why Underhill, and I don't know why me, but what I do know is that I was sent here to help you find what you're all searching for.' It made my heart hurt to hear Jem's calm certainty in the face of such doubt.

'And what's that?' asked Tish.

'The part of yourselves that was ripped out when God left. You're all looking for something that will mend the damage inside yourselves. But whatever you try, whatever new things you believe in, it's never enough, is it?'

There was silence inside the room and I noticed that everyone was looking at the floor, or at their hands, no-one was looking at anyone else.

'And I think you know why it's never enough, don't you?' Jem continued. 'It's because that big, dark, painful wound inside you is God-shaped and the only way, *the only way*, to sew yourselves back together is to use God as the thread.'

I was beginning to get horribly cold. I poked myself in the cheek, but I couldn't feel my fingers and my face was completely numb. Beside me was an old set of garden furniture. I shuffled round and sat down on one of the chairs. There were a couple of slats missing and the chair rocked a bit under my weight but then stayed still and I got myself comfortable, pleased that the new trousers were so thick – they gave me some padding. I wrapped my arms around my body and jiggled my feet up and down, trying to warm up a bit.

Tish was speaking again.

'My father died protesting the ban on religion.'

I have to say, I hadn't known that, although it explained why she was such a troublemaker: clearly it was in her genes. 'He didn't even believe in God, but he thought everyone should be free to choose what to believe.'

'It's the authority that stops us from having the choice,' said Fred, which was surprising because he spoke so rarely. 'They tell us that by putting religion behind us we're free, but we're not are we? Because we're not free to make a choice. We're not free to choose God and we're not free to choose religion. All those endless clarifications they send us. All those rules about what we can and can't do. It hasn't exactly made our lives better has it?'

Everyone was shaking their heads, and I realised that I was doing the same. Fred hadn't finished though.

'Do they really think that if they tell us over and over that God doesn't exist then eventually we'll all just say *oh, ok then*? Really? Are we all that gullible?' He took a deep breath and let it out slowly. Then he said, 'I'm not going to let myself be told what to believe any longer. If I want to believe in God, then that's exactly what I'm going to do.'

'I think the fact that they banned God might actually be proof that It exists,' said Tish. 'I mean think about what else they banned. Guns, for example. They existed, didn't they? Or… chemical weapons, say. They existed. And all the other things that the Laws have banned. They all existed. Think about it for a minute. Why ban so many things that existed but just one thing that didn't? As far as I'm concerned, that's proof right there that God exists.'

She sat back in her chair and folded her arms, looking so smug that I had to do some immediate special breathing to stop myself hurling a chair through the window at her. Petra was grinning and I thought she might be laughing at Tish, but when she said, 'I think I might understand why God might have picked Underhill,' I realised that her smile signified a temporary truce between them.

'Why?' asked Ed and Petra turned to him.

'If anyone needs a break,' she said, 'it's us. We all do our best. Like you, Ed. You're up at the turbines, day in, day out, trying to keep them turning, making electricity for us all. Nobody helps. Nobody cares. Same with the farmers. Slogging away, trying to nurture enough animals and grow enough plants to feed everyone, despite the contaminated soil. Nobody helps with the food, do they? They don't care about us. The authority's quick enough to send a census drone each year, but they never give us any assistance do they? Of course they bloody don't. If I were God, I think I might look at a bunch of people struggling to make the best out of their shitty little lives and think, *them*, I'll help them.'

There was silence in the room for a moment, presumably while they all considered their shitty little lives, then Lia spoke, and her tiny, insubstantial voice was so quiet that I had to hold my breath to hear what she said. 'How do we know that God wants to help us? What if it's another trap, like the authority?'

Was there no end to their doubts? Poor Jem.

Before she had a chance to reply, Laurel said, 'I think... I'm sure God's going to help us. I think It's already been helping us for a while,' she said and bent over Mila, sniffing her neck, muffling her voice so I had to strain to hear what she said next.

'Mila was a miracle baby – you all know that. Natural conception. No drugs or lab involvement. Don't you think perhaps it's a sign that God was already here with us?'

'I think that might be going a bit far,' said Ed. 'I mean, spontaneous conceptions do still happen.'

'Yeah, but what're the chances nowadays?' said Rob, then he

reached over to squeeze Laurel's thigh, so I looked away, back at Jem. 'One in two or three million? Seems to me there's more chance of God existing and sending us Mila as proof, than there is of a spontaneous conception.'

'Maybe there's been other signs,' said Tish. 'Other things that we've not seen.'

'Like what?' Petra asked.

Tish glared at her, obviously their brief truce was over. 'I don't know, I'm just saying.'

Ed cleared his throat. 'There's another angle to this. If God *did* send Jem to Underhill then what is Its reaction going to be if we don't believe what she's saying?'

'Well, I don't need any more proof,' said Laurel, holding Mila up, like she was offering her as evidence. 'The question is, what are we supposed to do next?'

Everyone looked at Jem and she gave them the tiniest smile and said, 'I need to understand the Vision. God will reveal the meaning to me and when I know that, I will know what we must do.'

The leg of my chair gave way with a loud crack, tipping me forwards into the rest of the garden set, which fell in a pile on top of me. When I looked up, the window had been pushed wide open and several pairs of eyes were staring at me.

'Eileen. Obviously,' said Tish.

'I thought Molly had spoken to you again about creeping round outside?' said Petra, then her head disappeared inside the room and I could hear her blowing her nose.

Molly had spoken to me about my nocturnal activities, but while she was talking to me I was thinking about how enjoyable it would be to tie her up and paper cut her to death, although I do realise what a waste of paper that would have been. The upshot was that I hadn't paid any attention to what she was saying.

I must admit, I did feel a bit embarrassed to be found lying on the ground below the window, but these people had driven me to it. If only everyone would learn to include me, then things would be so much simpler for us all.

Jem said, 'Eileen should join us, she has an important job to do,' and as one, everyone turned to look at her for a moment, then turned back towards me. I smiled up at them, suddenly feeling a whole lot better. Perhaps it had all been a big misunderstanding, Jem must have wanted me to be there with her but hadn't known where to find me. I stood up, disentangling myself from the legs of a small table and tried to brush the snow and mud off my new trousers, although I was sure they would already be stained.

Leaving the furniture in a heap, I made my way around the side of the house, feeling with my hands along the wall because it was too dark to see anything. Fortunately, the house was only attached to its neighbour on one side and there was a narrow passageway to the left, which I shuffled down, sliding my feet along carefully, trying to avoid any trip hazards. I emerged at the front of the house, where Laurel was waiting by the door holding Mila.

I pretended to have a stiff neck – it was a bit sore anyway from falling off the chair – so that I could keep my head turned away from the baby. I couldn't avoid her smell though, and it made me feel weird inside, as if I was hungry or something, and I pushed past Laurel as quickly as possible.

I had been in this house once before, with my parents, when I was little. When Laurel's grandmother had been really sick, she had volunteered for one of my parents' experiments. I had been given a big piece of cake and told to stay in the kitchen, but I stashed the cake in my bag for later and crept upstairs where I saw Dad injecting the old woman. She died soon afterwards.

Laurel led the way down the hall and into their living room, which was small and square, but with their gigantic fire, which was a relief because I was in urgent need of some warmth. Jem smiled at me when I entered the room and everyone else stared.

'What's this job of Eileen's then?' asked Tish, clearly unable to believe that I actually had anything to contribute.

Until that moment, it hadn't occurred to me to wonder how Jem knew that I was writing the Book of Jem. I mean, I had clearly heard her say to the others that I had *an important job* to do, but at that point, all I'd done was write down her Vision and I hadn't even told her that I had done that, let alone that I had decided to write a prophet book. I must have been frowning because she looked really sad for a moment, then she turned to the others.

'It's up to Eileen to tell you what her job is,' she said.

Everyone looked at me and straight away words started to jam in my throat. I could feel them piling up, one on top of each other, cramming into the narrow gap between my tongue and the roof of my mouth. I shook my head to try and dislodge them, hoping to loosen them a little so that I could force some of them out, tell people what I was doing. Instead the words swelled even larger and I had to concentrate very hard on my breathing, on squeezing air through the tiny crevices between the words and down into my lungs.

Jem came over to me and stood close. Really close, so I could see myself reflected in her pupils, twin Eileens staring back at me. There was a strong smell which reminded me of the pinecones that my Mum used to burn each Freedom Day, which is ironic now I come to think of it – the smell when Jem talked about God is the same smell that was used to celebrate the day that God was banned.

The room darkened and I wondered if the fire had gone out, but when I looked it was still burning brightly, although it was very far away, like it was at the end of a long tunnel. I looked back at Jem. An old woman was standing in her place, smiling at me through an impossibly wrinkled face.

'Wh…Wh…Wh…' I tried, but there was no chance of words dislodging themselves. I shook my head and puffed my way through a few breaths before attempting something different, eventually managing to force out 'Jem?'

The old woman smiled, her wrinkles dissolved, her face smoothed and once again Jem was standing in front of me.

She leaned forward until her lips were almost touching mine. I shivered and closed my eyes and she kissed me. She kept her lips pressed against mine for a long time, but eventually I felt her pull away and opened my eyes. A tiny thread of saliva hung between us.

Then she whispered, 'I'm listening.'

I breathed her in, drawing her deep inside me. I felt strange, like my stomach was being tickled and for a moment, I didn't recognise what it was. Then it came to me. I was happy.

Suddenly, I realised that my words had unblocked themselves. They were bumping against my lips, wanting to be free, eager to rush out, to tell people my thoughts, but before I could speak, Tish the bitch got in first.

'It's always the same with you, Eileen. It's always just secrets and lies.'

Petra nodded in agreement, with an extra-hard sniff for emphasis. They weren't bickering now, were they? Of course they weren't. Not when there was a chance to gang up on me.

I looked around the room – it was clear that no-one was interested in anything I might have to say, so I decided not to waste my newly liberated words on them. My work on the Book of Jem would stay a secret. These people didn't deserve to know what I was doing, they were too ignorant to appreciate it. But when I looked at Jem, the happiness in my stomach grew – it was enough to know that I could have spoken had I wished to.

Later, when I was in bed, writing the next entry in the Book of

Jem, and trying to remember exactly what had happened that evening, how Jem's lips had felt on my mouth – soft, moist, plump – and how I had sucked her breath deep into my lungs, I started wondering again how she had known I was writing the Book. Had God told her? Had God talked to her about me, about Eileen?

It wasn't until much, much later – months later, in fact – that I realised that she might not have been talking about the Book at all that evening. Maybe she had already known the *other* job I would have, the *other* part I had to play in everything.

That night though, I decided not to spend any more time thinking about it and turned my attention back to the last few words that I had written.

Stories 1:3

And the wise Prophet looked at the lonely young orphan whose words were stuck in her mouth and saw that they were choking her. The Prophet kissed the orphan and breathed a wise and powerful breath. The orphan opened her mouth, taking the breath deep inside her and at once she felt her words slipping and loosening until they fell easily from her lips.

MUDBOUND

10

Kat

There was a problem with the turbines, so we had to delay our snowmelt party. I barely saw Ed while he, Leroy and George worked around the clock, squeezing into the hut together each night to try and get a few hours sleep. Until the turbines turned properly again, electricity was strictly rationed. Fortunately, I was well-practised at cooking over an open fire, although the shortage of properly seasoned wood gave everything a faintly acrid taste.

The transition from Whiteout to Mudbound is difficult at the best of times. It's almost as if the drifts of snow leave us stranded far apart, so when it eventually melts we have to work hard to come back together. The last few weeks of Whiteout had been particularly bad weather-wise, and everyone was really looking forward to the party, so when it was postponed you could almost see the misery seeping out of the cottages.

The turbine problems brought many of our issues into sharp relief. No-one was going to come and help us sort them out, no-one but us even cared whether they got fixed or not. Our community paid its taxes to the authority, but we received hardly anything in return – educational resources for the kids and the right to consult a doctor on the Wave, although usually we relied on Petra who'd been a nurse in one of the factories before she came to Underhill. There was precious little else from the authority, so when the census drone appeared in the sky at the end of each Whiteout, cataloguing us, our land and water, and our precious animals and crops, it became the focus of much of the pent-up anger and frustration.

Every year, people would try to evade the drone and confuse the census, while others claimed to have an infallible way to attack the thing, but none of it ever worked. The drone hovered above us, out of reach, seeing everything. Just like the authority. I've never understood the purpose of the census anyway – I mean nothing ever changes, we're never offered any additional help. They scrutinise us, itemise us, and categorise us, then everything goes on exactly as it was before.

That's why the snowmelt party is always such a welcome distraction. We usually have it when the air is filled with the sound of cracking ice and trickling water. For a day or two, we're suspended in that wonderful moment when everything is clean and new, and we're carried along like the melting snow, rushing towards brighter, warmer days. But this year, by the time the turbines were fixed and the party was re-arranged, we were well and truly Mudbound.

It only takes a week, sometimes less, before everything is coated in mud – Underhill turns brown, the stream slows, weighed down by sludge, and walking along the street becomes a viscous, gluey effort. It's horrible. And my neighbours, especially the ones that have always lived in the village, suddenly want to stick together, as if the forced isolation of Whiteout has left them desperate for company. It takes me twice as long to do the ordering because of how everyone is in and out of each other's houses, sharing gossip, drinking tea, and moaning about the mud. It gets everywhere. Great long streaks of it along floors and walls. Handprints on the doors. It even turns up in the bedclothes.

So, by the evening of the party, I was ready to enjoy myself and as my family assembled by the front door, I hugged each of them in turn. Willow hesitated for a moment when I held out my arms, but then shuffled a half-step towards me. We'd had yet another argument a couple of days before. She was getting behind on her schoolwork because she kept disappearing for hours on end. I knew she was spending some of her time with Jem and the group of misfits she had collected around her, but she refused to talk to me about it until, in the end, I exploded.

'I'm not stupid, Willow. You've never shown the slightest interest in religion. I know full well you're only doing it to antagonise me, and it has to stop. Do you understand? It has to stop *now*.'

She shrugged, and I had a brief moment of hope. Surely it wouldn't be long before my feisty, temperamental daughter's tendency to flit from thing to thing would push her away from Jem and onto something new. She'd been like it ever since she was little. Each obsession was profound, all-consuming, until just as suddenly as it had begun, it ended. When she was younger, there had been that time – weeks it went on for – when she wouldn't leave the house without a toy that Ed had made her. It was a sort of puzzle, a little ball that rolled around intricate boxes, carved by him out of a single piece of wood. She loved it so much that she had even insisted on sleeping with it – the corner of the wood pushed against her soft cheek. Then one day it just disappeared. She tried to tell us that it had been stolen, but obviously that wasn't the case. I mean, who would steal a toy from a child?

I just had to keep reminding myself that the thing was, with Willow, if you pushed her, she shoved back twice as hard. I needed to be patient, keep my mouth shut – no matter how difficult that was – and hope that soon enough she would move on from Jem to something new. Our argument before the party hadn't ended well, though. Before she'd flounced off, she'd yelled at me, 'You're just trying to turn me into you. What have you actually *done* with your life, Mum? You take the orders, wait for the drones, follow the rules, obey the Laws, all the time spouting "yes authority, no authority, whatever you say authority". Well, I get to choose what I do with my life and I want something different from you and you know what? I'm going to start by leaving school.'

But then the next day she'd got up as if nothing had happened and gone to school, oblivious to the fact that I had to change the outfit that I'd planned to wear for the party, swapping it for something with long sleeves to hide the livid marks where I'd torn into my skin after her little outburst.

Nevertheless, the party was finally here, and I wasn't going to let anything get in the way of our enjoyment of it. Besides, when it came down to it, we weren't doing so badly, Ed and me. Even the grubby bit of string that Willow was insisting on wearing around her neck and all her hot-tempered outbursts didn't detract from how quickly she was growing up, and although our boy was still more boy than man, I was proud of both our children.

'I love you all,' I said, spontaneously. Willow rolled her eyes, Ash blushed, but Ed reached for my hand as we left the house. We picked our way through the mud towards the barn and everyone except Ash managed to avoid the worst of it – inevitably he put his boot in a big slick which splashed up his trousers.

The barn had been tidied for the party and everything was shoved to one side, leaving a large open space. Antique bunting was strung around the walls, the colours faded so much that the little triangles were practically see-through. No-one could remember where the bunting came from originally, but it had been used at every party for as long as I had been in Underhill and presumably for years before that. After each party, we took it down, carefully folding it to keep it safe until the next time.

In one corner, tables were loaded with food that had been brought over during the day. There wasn't much variety so soon after Whiteout and the dishes were mainly egg-based, but the kids were delighted to see a decent selection of cakes and the smell of the sheep that Camman was roasting made my mouth water. The old bath which we always used for punch had been scrubbed clean that morning and was already full by the time we arrived. No-one bothered with a recipe, and it was well understood that no matter what the ratio of alcohol to juice, one cup would get you into the party mood, two cups would find you talking to people that you might otherwise choose to avoid, and three would guarantee a splitting headache in the morning. If you were foolish enough to drink any more than that, no-one would expect to see you for days. Still, we never judged anyone, there were few enough opportunities to enjoy ourselves.

'Don't drink the punch,' was all I managed to say, before the twins slipped away. I linked my fingers with Ed's, and for the first time the tension that I'd been carrying ever since the beginning of Whiteout eased a little. We dipped our cups in the bath, the contents tasted strongly of blackberries and I sipped it cautiously, tapping my foot in time with the music. The Underhillbillys had been practising for weeks, and they'd promised to play some new songs.

The barn was filling up and there was a lot of laughter as everyone tried their best to forget their latest grievance with authority, or the recent depressing soil toxicity results, or all the million and one other daily problems we faced just to get by. A different song started, people were singing, and I let myself be caught up in the atmosphere, happy to be there with Ed, another Whiteout behind us.

Then Jem arrived.

She paused in the doorway surrounded by a gaggle of sycophants, waiting to be noticed. Framed by her black hair and that red scarf that she always draped around her neck, her face was so drained of colour that it was almost translucent. It had been weeks and weeks since her arrival, surely she must be bored with Underhill by now? I had really hoped that with the end of Whiteout, the girl would melt away with the snow and go back to wherever she had come from, but we were two weeks into Mudbound and there was no sign that she was going anywhere.

I stared at the group gathered around the girl, trying to work out what they could possibly see in her. I just did not understand the appeal. She didn't have any great physical presence: she was short, plain and had clearly made no effort for the party. Every time I saw her she wore an unpleasant expression that hovered somewhere between judgemental and disdainful, and yet the little group of supporters gazed at her raptly, hanging on to her every word.

Eventually, they moved away from the doorway, and as they passed us, Ed let go of my hand. After I'd kicked her out of our house, I had tried to put the girl out of my mind. There was enough to worry about, what with making sure Ed kept his appointments with Dr. Lawrence and trying to stop Willow sneaking out of the house. Then, a few weeks before the end of Whiteout, both twins had gone down with a nasty dose of snowflu. Half the village had had it, but thankfully Petra always kept a decent stock of anti-viral patches. Thank Freedom we'd all made it through Whiteout without any deaths this year, and the only significant injury was when Ruby slipped on ice and broke her ankle, although her biggest complaint was that it meant she had to stay home and miss the party.

Although I'd been too busy to spend much time worrying about Jem, I still felt sick whenever I remembered the night I'd overheard Ed talking to her about his grandfather. I'd made her leave the next day, she moved in with Laurel and Rob, and stayed out of my way ever since. Once, when I went over to take Laurel's order, I asked her what Jem did all day.

Her face lit up. 'We talk. She helps with Mila. And she goes for walks.'

I knew about the walks. Apparently, she only ever went up the turbine path. I also knew, although I'd heard it from someone else, that Ed had regularly cleared the snow for her which I wasn't happy about, but because we argued every time we talked about her, I'd decided that the best thing for both of us was if I kept my views to myself, at least for the time being.

'And what does she do when she's up there on Front Hill?' I asked Laurel, but she had just looked away and concentrated on her order. With the extra allowance they got for Mila, Laurel and Rob had been able to absorb the cost of feeding Jem. In any case, they had more food than most because Rob helped Camman with the animals in return for meat.

Lily was pushing through the crowd towards us, concentrating on holding two drinks steady.

'Sorry Ed, I couldn't manage three,' she said when she reached us, winking as she thrust the larger cup towards me. 'Cooper was looking for you, he's over by the food.'

'Food sounds like a good idea,' Ed said and wandered off in the direction of the tables.

'You're playing catch up.' Lily said. 'I've had two already – both of them *after* Leroy added his mead.'

Looking at her flushed face, I sipped the punch cautiously.

'It's even more revolting than usual,' I said.

'Yup, although after a few swigs you can't taste it anyway.'

She smiled, proving her point by taking another large gulp, before nodding towards the group around Jem.

'So much for Molly persuading her to go at snowmelt.'

'She tried, but the girl's in no hurry to leave. Laurel and Rob are happy for her to stay with them, and she's not using the G word any longer, at least not in public and of course Molly's adamant we shouldn't involve the authority.'

'That's what we all think, isn't it? Or have you changed your mind?' asked Lily.

'Of course not, I just wish I knew what the girl was up to.'

'Well, she's not going to be here indefinitely. Presumably she'll have been picked up in the census, so someone's going to start asking questions.'

I had another sip of my drink. It really was disgusting. 'Molly says it's impossible to get a straight answer from the girl about her plans.'

'Have you noticed…' Lily started, then hesitated.

'Noticed what?' I said. When she didn't say anything, I said, 'Come on, spit it out, noticed what?'

Lily finished her drink in one gulp, burped, then giggled.

'I'd better not have any more.'

'What were you going to say?' I wasn't going to let her off the hook that easily.

She waved her empty cup towards the group huddled around Jem. 'They've all got red thread tied around their necks. At first it was just Willow, but now they're all doing it – like it's some sort of club.'

I looked over and as I watched, Jem reached out to Tish, who bowed her head as the girl ran her finger back and forth along the barely visible thread.

'Now, *that's* weird.' said Lily.

I looked around for Willow, relieved she wasn't part of the huddle around Jem but anxious that I couldn't see her, until I realised that none of the youngsters were in the barn. No doubt they'd sneaked some of the punch outside. We'd all done it, but I hoped they wouldn't drink so much that they were ill or get so muddy that I had to spend the whole of the next day washing clothes.

The Underhillbillys started another tune, one with a fast beat, and there was a rush to dance. It was hot and I was thirsty, but I didn't want any more alcohol, so I was trying to find some water when Ash appeared at the door of the barn. He was shouting and I could tell he was upset but no-one paid him any attention and I was pushing my way towards him when the rest of the youngsters poured through the door. The music stopped abruptly, but because they were all yelling over each other, it took a few seconds for their shouting to resolve into a single word. *Fire.*

*

The Uplanders use fire like I use the Wave: as a way to connect to the world. They spend most of their lives disconnected from us, yet when they set the flames licking up the corner of a building, they create a moment of connection. We rely on fire to heat our homes, but our greatest fear is uncontrolled flames.

Thankfully, for most of the year there's no shortage of water – we have the stream, the stock ponds and, of course, the purification tanks. But when there's a burning, getting water to wherever it needs to be can be difficult and the street is always lined with barrels filled with water, ready to be rolled to wherever they are needed.

The Uplanders must have been spying on us. Either that or it was just our bad luck that they had chosen snowmelt party night to come down from the hills. Their usual tactic was to set fire to a building at one place in the village, then loot somewhere else. Distract us over *here*, take what they can over *there*. But, thanks to Molly's insistence on weekly drills, everyone knew what to do.

It wasn't my job to help to put out the fire. Instead, I was in one of the groups tasked with trying to prevent looting so, shouting at the kids to stay where they were, I ran out into the street. To my left, flames were shooting up the side of one of the storage barns, but I turned my back on it and hurried along the road as fast as I could through the mud. Several people ran to their houses, to find whatever they could use as weapons: pokers, knives and one or two antique guns – which were illegal but useful, particularly if the Uplanders didn't realise that no-one had any ammunition.

As I jogged along the road to the cottages that we were responsible for checking, I hoped the kids had done what they were told for once and stayed in the barn. Ed would be helping to put out the fire, but all thoughts of him disappeared when I saw that the door to Lily's house had been kicked in. I rushed down the steps with the others and into the hallway.

'We've got guns.'

'Come out now.'

'Uplander bastards.'

Alcohol made us sound braver than we felt.

Two of my group went upstairs, one checked the kitchen, and I went into the living room, so I was the first to see Ruby lying on the floor. I rushed to her side, relieved that her eyes were open and she was blinking.

'In here,' I yelled, and Fred appeared in the doorway, an old bread knife held out front of him, his hand noticeably shaking. When he saw Ruby, his eyes widened.

'Is she…?'

'She's conscious,' I said. 'Go and get Lily. Bring Petra as well.'

'There's no-one upstairs,' he said. 'You okay staying here while we check the rest of the cottages?'

'Yes, but get Lily first. She'll be further along the road.'

Ruby groaned, and I leaned close.

'Did they hurt you?'

To my relief, she shook her head. 'Bastards scared the shit out of me.'

I struggled not to smile – Ruby was a cantankerous old woman and if she was able to be angry, I was pretty sure she'd be okay.

'Can you sit up?'

She grunted, struggling to lift herself onto her elbows. I put my arms under hers, braced myself to take her weight and pulled her into a sitting position.

It was then that I heard a muffled whimper coming from behind the sofa, so quiet that I thought perhaps I'd imagined it, until I glanced at Ruby and saw my fear reflected in her eyes. I squeezed her hand, put my finger to my lips and reached for the poker by the side of the fire. I crossed the room, then hesitated. My heart was banging painfully in my chest, but the longer I waited the more scared I was becoming, so taking a deep breath, I held the poker straight out in front of me and rushed around the side of the sofa.

I couldn't believe my eyes.

Jammed into the corner, half sitting, half lying, was a young woman. At first glance, she looked like every other Uplander: she was covered in mud, her matted hair caught up in a dirty cloth and judging by the smell, it had been weeks since she'd had a wash. A blanket was wrapped around her waist several times to make a rudimentary skirt which fell just below her knees and here and there, patches of a vivid orange pattern were visible, oddly bright against the mud. Another filthy blanket was draped over her shoulders, enveloping her arms and the top half of her body. Her boots were surprisingly well made – they must have been stolen. Despite the heat from the fire, she was shivering violently.

I watched as her gaze flicked between me and the end of the poker, only centimetres from her face. I had somehow expected that the Uplanders' semi-feral living, their choice to cut themselves off, would harden them, make them vicious, so what I did not expect was the vulnerability which radiated from the young woman cowering on the floor in front of me.

I lowered the poker slowly, without loosening my grip on it.

'I'm not going to hurt you,' I said. 'Can you stand?'

She shook her head and her eyes filled with tears. I wondered how she had managed to survive Whiteout. As far as I knew, during the long weeks of snow the Uplanders sheltered in long-abandoned houses, systematically ripping them apart to burn for heat. I'd heard that they often went days without eating – surviving at the very limit of existence. For years, there had been a standing amnesty for them to turn themselves in, go to the cities, where they would be housed and given a job. But they chose to stay living between worlds, not prepared to accept the drudgery of factory work, but unable to find another place prepared to take them in – without personal records, they couldn't apply to join a community, and without a place in a community, they had no personal records.

'What's going on over there?' Ruby's voice made us both jump.

Keeping my gaze fixed on the woman, I said, as calmly as I could, 'There's someone here.'

Ruby gave a little shriek.

'She's not going to hurt you,' I said. 'I think, perhaps... she's not well.'

The woman pulled the blanket more tightly around herself and the bulk of her body strained against the material.

'Why are you fussing over her? *I'm* the one that was attacked.' Ruby's voice was sharp, and I took a step back and glanced over at her, relieved to see that the colour had returned to the old woman's cheeks. She scowled at me, which had to be a good sign.

'Lily will be here any second, Ruby.' I turned back to look at the woman on the floor. 'I think something's wrong with her.'

'Nothing that turning her in wouldn't cure.'

Ignoring Ruby, I put the poker down behind me and crouched by her side. The terror in woman's eyes was real.

'It's ok,' I said, softly. 'I want to help you.'

She was the second young woman to arrive unannounced in Underhill since the beginning of Whiteout. This time however, I hadn't sensed that anyone was coming and it was only when I thought about it later that I realised how different it felt compared to when Jem had turned up because, despite everything I thought I knew about the Uplanders, even despite them burning the barn, all I wanted to do was to help this woman slumped on the floor in front of me.

There was another whimper and the woman looked around frantically, obviously trying to find a way to escape.

'It's okay,' I said, again.

'It's far from okay,' said Ruby. She was angry and scared, and I was about to go back to her when the woman pushed herself up a little and the blanket slipped from her shoulders, falling to her waist. When I saw what she had been hiding under the folds of the filthy, threadbare blanket, I suddenly understood. Cradled in her arms, so new to the world that it was still streaked with his mother's blood, lay a tiny baby.

11

Eileen

Truths 6:1-17

The Prophet Jem often walked on the hills to hear the voice of God. One day, she told the believers to come with her, so they followed her and when she turned from the main path, forging a narrow track through the snow, they followed her there, too.

As they watched, she knelt on the ground, unconcerned by the snow or the wind or the cold. When she spoke, they were overcome by the sweetness of her voice, and the beauty of her face, delicate and pale above her red scarf.

Holding out her hands, she said,

'Come close. Come close and I will tell you the words of God.'

The faithful drew close and as she spoke her breath warmed the freezing air and they no longer felt cold.

This is what she told them.

'I have come to prepare you. God has a plan for the people of Underhill.'

One among them called out, 'Where is God? I cannot see It.'

And the Prophet replied, 'God is everywhere.'

When she said this, some of the people looked about fearfully, while the doubts of others were clear on their faces, but when the Prophet saw their fears and their doubts, she laughed.

'You do not need to see God to know where It is. God rustles with the leaves, It tumbles along the rivers, drifts with the snowflakes. God is in every flower, every animal, every breeze that caresses your face.

'God is a rope bound from countless threads. Each of you is a thread of God. Everything that was, everything that is, and everything that will be, is part of the rope of God.

'For the longest time, people on earth knew what they were, they understood that they were threads of God and they kept the binding strong. But, gradually, centuries passed, and the people began to forget, until finally the knowledge of what they were had left them. Then, they tried to separate God's threads, pulling them apart, picking and tugging at them until the rope frayed and split into many pieces.'

Tears spilled from the Prophet's eyes, burning holes in the snow.

'But I am here to tell you that God has re-bound Itself. It is once more an unbreakable rope, able to bend and twist, yet capable of lifting the heaviest burden.'

A voice called, 'What is God's plan for us?'

'God has not forgotten the promise that was broken by people when they left the forest and spread across the earth. God will have Its revenge.'

'What promise did we forget?' asked one.

'I didn't make any promise,' said another.

The Prophet summoned her patience and reminded those who still doubted.

'Long ago, we promised to nurture the world and everything in it, but we failed to keep our promise.'

There was silence as they considered her words.

'You said God has a plan for us. What is the plan?' asked

the most faithful follower of all, showing the others by her words how to accept what the Prophet said, without doubt or hesitation.

'God will reveal Its plan when It knows that you are ready to hear it. But first, you must begin the preparations.'

'Why would God choose to reveal these truths to you?' called out a faithless one.

'I was of no consequence until I was chosen by God to hear Its words,' said the Prophet. 'I am but a thread like you. We are all God's threads.'

'But why did God send you to Underhill?'

And the people continued to ask questions, and the Prophet continued to answer them.

The reason I finished my entry in the Book of Jem at that point was because I couldn't bring myself to write down all the ridiculous questions everyone was asking. I failed to see why it wasn't enough for some people to know that Jem was revealing God's words, without having to interrogate her about the details of who, what, where and why.

I mean, just think about it for a moment: God's words were being revealed to us. To us. To a handful of people, most of whom, let's be fair, weren't exactly worthy recipients of such a gift.

I said from the outset that I was going to write a prophet book to record God's messages to Jem and it's also important for me to include details to explain what happened to make it end like it did, but that doesn't mean that I'm going to waste space in my precious notebook writing down the inane drivel of ignorant people. If I had asked Jem at the time, I'm sure she would have agreed that it was far more important that I captured the essence of what happened – the truth-behind-the-truth, if you will – rather than confining myself to faithfully transcribing a series of often rather dull events as they occurred.

The reality was that there was a lot of standing around up there on Front Hill that first time, practically freezing to death while we listened to the *God has a plan* message. After that, we met in Laurel's house until snowmelt.

Although Jem said that it was important to try and get other people interested, that we needed to bind together as many Threads as possible to fulfil God's plan, we had to be careful who we talked to because we didn't want to risk being notified. Being one of God's Threads was the first time in my life that I'd voluntarily been part of a group and it felt good, but I don't mind admitting that I was concerned that the more people who joined us, the less time Jem would have to spend with me. As it was, I was having to arrive for the meetings earlier and earlier to make sure I could sit or stand next to her.

I'd started tying a piece of red thread around my neck and although at first I had difficulty swallowing, when I looked at myself in the mirror, it reminded me of Jem's scarf, so I left it on. After a while, when I had got used to it, I realised that as soon as words started jamming up in my mouth, all I had to do was to run my finger back and forth along the thread, think about the time when she had kissed me, and the words would loosen themselves.

I wanted to know what the plan was, but Jem said that it was important for us to receive the details slowly, because God had to be sure that we were ready. We got into a bit of a routine at the meetings, which always started with some hand-holding, which I found profoundly disturbing. After one particular occasion when I was forced to stand between Tish, her damp fingers linked with mine and baby Mila, who, no matter how hard I squeezed her tiny fat fingers, tried to squeeze back even harder, I asked Jem if maybe I could just hold her hand each time, but she smiled, said 'No,' and explained how holding hands with each other was symbolic of God's Threads being bound together like a rope.

There were many mentions of threads and rope in those early days, which became quite tedious. I considered mentioning to Jem that perhaps it was time to move things along, but of course she was the prophet, I was just the one writing her story. I kept reminding myself that not everyone was as quick on the uptake as me and it did seem to be the case that the more frequently people heard her say something, the more they seemed to be convinced by it. I suppose that's what a lack of intelligence does for you.

Those first weeks, there were generally the same handful of us at every gathering. Occasionally Ed would come – one time he brought his brother although Leroy left as soon as Jem had finished speaking and didn't come back again for ages, not until a lot more people had become Threads. Willow sometimes came as well, although she was always late, arriving just as we were finishing the hand-holding and I was trying to extricate my fingers from whichever sweaty palm they'd been linked with. Early on, Willow had copied my idea of wearing a piece of red thread – once she even tried to claim that she had thought of it first, but I set her straight and she never said it again. By snowmelt, almost all of the Threads had string tied around their necks, except Ed and baby Mila, but that was only because Laurel was worried she might choke.

After the hand-holding, we would all sit down – most of us on the floor – and look up at Jem who always remained standing. She would point at each of us in turn and say, 'You are one of God's Threads. You have a purpose.' Our purpose was still a mystery. Sometimes, it seemed like she was just about to reveal it to us, but then she would shake her head and frown and mutter as though she was having a conversation with herself, and say, 'It's not time.' I'm sure she would have been happy to tell me, after all I had been there from the start, but it was almost impossible to get her alone without some of God's other Threads being around.

Finally, just after snowmelt, Jem announced that it was time for us all to gather on Front Hill again, she said we were ready for her to reveal the next part of God's message. So, it was really very irritating when that was delayed because of what happened on the night of the party.

*

Before Jem came to Underhill, I hadn't enjoyed the parties. There was a lot of inappropriate affection on display and also, depending how long my List of Enemies was, it could be quite tricky to find anyone that I was prepared to speak to.

There was one horrible Freedom Day party, when there had been a shortage of juice to dilute the alcohol and everyone had drunk far too much. I was always very sensible – as soon as the room began to spin, I would take myself outside and stick my fingers down my throat, which always made me feel better. On that particular night, I had stayed where I was, kneeling on the ground, trying to decide whether to go back in for another drink to take away the taste of vomit, or go home.

I was still weighing up my options, when two people came stumbling out of the barn and right in front of my eyes, started doing sex. It's not easy to find the words to convey quite how absurd they looked. First of all, he started frantically fumbling beneath her top, trying to push it up and over her chest. In the end she had to help him out – she has the sort of breasts that arrive in a room well before the rest of her – and she did a great deal of wriggling before they were finally uncovered. Then, their fumbling switched to his trouser area, which also went on for a long time because they both seemed to be completely flummoxed by the fastening. In the end, he had to back away and concentrate properly on undoing it.

I'd never seen people doing sex so close-up before, although of course I had seen it through windows. There were a few things about the mechanics of it that I didn't understand, but I didn't really feel I could ask anyone about. For example, I had seen the different possible variations, men together, women together, men and women together. The last one, frankly, always tended to look like the man was sawing away at a piece of wood. In all variations though, one of the things I didn't understand was how and when they decided to change positions. Was there a signal that I couldn't see? Or a special word? And why did people sometimes not change position? It was important to understand this, so that when I eventually did sex, I knew the rules.

Despite how repulsive it was watching them, not to mention the disgusting sucking noise that was coming from their general vicinity, I realised that I should probably make the most of the opportunity to learn, so I crawled towards them, unfortunately forgetting about the little pool of sick in front of me, which I put my palm into. I was so close that I could have reached out and wiped my hand on the back of his leg.

They had finally finished dealing with their clothing issues, she was leaning against a tree and sure enough, he had started doing the sawing movement. She was giggling which, when I thought about it afterwards, was a surprising response, particularly given how seriously he appeared to be taking it. But then suddenly, she stopped laughing. She was staring over his shoulder and when he eventually realised that she wasn't paying attention to his efforts, he stopped sawing and looked round to see what she was staring at.

It was me.

She was staring at me.

'Really, Eileen? This is what you're reduced to doing now?

Sneaking around watching people having sex?' she said.

'Fucking freak,' he added, unnecessarily.

I didn't dignify their comments with a response. Instead, I got to my feet, which took a couple of attempts because I was still feeling the effects of the alcohol. As I walked away, they shouted some really hurtful things after me, so, remembering what my mother used to say about such people, I mumbled *promiscuous pieces of filth* under my breath in time with my footsteps. In the morning, I would update my List and move them up several places.

Although I was blameless in the whole sorry episode, the experience had left me feeling wary about going to another party, but this snowmelt party would be different. I was part of a group. I was one of God's Threads.

Before we went, Jem called us together at Laurel's.

'Remember,' she said, clasping her hands tightly together in that way she did when she was saying something important. 'A bound rope makes all threads equally strong. Don't let others pull you apart.'

I practised smiling as I looked around at the other Threads, almost feeling happy to be bound together with them. It was probably time to consider removing most of them from my List.

The party started well. It was the first time I had ever actually arrived at a social function with anyone since my parents had died, and although people still stared at me, I knew this time it was because they were jealous that I was with Jem. Ed kept glancing over in our direction and I was sorry to see him looking so sad. Jem had explained that he had some knots to unpick and until he could do that, he wasn't ready to be bound with the rest of us. I knew what his biggest knot was – she was standing right next to him.

We stuck together, just as Jem had told us to, until the young people came running in. After that, things fell apart a bit. I didn't have anything to do during an attack by the Uplanders, I hadn't bothered to go to the meetings that Molly had arranged, instead I'd taken my own precautions, ordering more locks for my front door and hiding things in my Treasure Cupboard. I thought maybe us Threads could just stay at the party and carry on enjoying ourselves, but most people seemed more interested in throwing water at the fire and trying to find the Uplanders, so in the end I just went home and went to bed, which meant that it wasn't until the next day that I found out about the woman and her baby.

*

Because Laurel and Rob had baby equipment in their house, the Uplander woman, Lorne, and her baby went to stay with them. It must have been a bit of a tight squeeze, what with Jem being there as well. The baby was a boy and, I kid you not, she had called him Stone. Stone? There is no way to make that name sound other than it is – thick, dense and heavy – but apparently that's the name she'd decided on. Clearly, creativity was in short supply among the people from the hills.

Lorne didn't speak much when she first came, and when she did her accent made it sound as if she had a mouth full of mud, so I really had to concentrate to understand her. Because the woman had only given birth to Stone a few hours before she came to Underhill, Molly had waddled over to Laurel's house to announce that she would be given time to recover before any decisions were made about what to do with her.

Lorne told Laurel that none of the other Uplanders doing the raid had been aware that she was planning to stay behind and even she herself hadn't been certain whether she would stay. It was the first time anyone in her group had ever had a baby. They had been preparing to leave the shelter where they had spent Whiteout – soon the farmers would be heading back up onto the slopes, and so it was time for them to travel deeper into the hills. But the nights were still very cold, she had no clothes for Stone, and she was worried whether she'd be strong enough to make the journey.

They'd picked Lily's house at random, thinking we were all at the party, not realising that Ruby had stayed behind. It was a shame they didn't do something other than just scare the old cow, which would have done us all a big favour, but the Uplanders weren't interested in hurting people, they just wanted to steal things, so unfortunately all they did was give Ruby a fright. It didn't stop her demanding sympathy for days afterwards, although I successfully managed to resist giving her any.

After Lorne had been at Laurel's for a couple of days, Jem again said we should go back up the path and she would finally tell us more about God's plan for us. We all trooped up the hill and found Ed already there – Jem had asked him to bring along some lengths of rope and stakes which he had used to mark out an area for us Threads to stand in while Jem did her propheting. Given how significant that place would become, it's strange to remember how uncomfortable I felt that first time, penned in by the ropes.

All the Threads at that time were there and Lorne had come as well, with Stone – there was a piece of cloth tightly wrapped around the pair of them, keeping him strapped to her front. She'd obviously had a wash at some point and seeing her dressed in clothes that Laurel must have lent her, I was surprised how similar she looked to the rest of us. I guessed she was probably about the same age as me although it was difficult to tell because she hadn't taken very good care of herself: her remaining teeth were in a shocking state – one good shake and they would probably fall out. She was so thin that her head was concave at her temples, and her hair was the same colour as the mud that we'd trudged through to get up the hill. Her skin was the oddest thing though: it had a strange translucence that seemed to take on the colour of the sky, so when it was cloudy, her face and hands were brown, but when the sun came out, she looked almost yellow. It was as if, by spending so long living among the hills, the topmost layer of herself had been absorbed into them.

Lorne displayed no curiosity about why we'd all walked up the path and were standing around inside some ropes. All in all, she wasn't much of an advertisement for Uplander intellect. She stood next to Laurel and they leaned in close, whispering to each other but it seemed I wasn't the only one finding it difficult to have another baby around because I saw Mila stretch her fat little hand towards Stone, poking her fingers into his side. I surmised from his flood of tears that his tiny body wasn't quite as hard as his name suggested.

I was relieved when Jem finally started speaking.

Looking around to make sure we were all focused on her, she said, 'We have witnessed a miracle.'

I had always understood that a miracle was a sort of lie which was designed to convince people to believe in God and included impossible events like people running over the sea and women having spontaneous sperm-free pregnancies. Not all religions had miracles: some prophets managed to say what they wanted to say without wrapping their messages in unbelievable stories. That's what I was doing in the Book of Jem – telling it like it was, or more accurately, like it should have been. So, I was really surprised when Jem said there had been a miracle and I wracked my brain trying to work out what it was.

Seeing our confusion, she said, 'Stone is the miracle.'

We all looked at Stone, who was trying to stuff his fist into his mouth. He had managed to get the whole thing halfway down his throat and his cheeks had turned bright red before Lorne realised what he was doing and pulled his fingers out of his mouth. As he gasped for air, I looked at his hand, gleaming with his own saliva, and wondered if the point Jem was making was that it was some sort of miracle that he had even managed to survive his first few days.

Jem usually wanted us to work things out for ourselves. Although she would regularly give speeches, usually about threads, rope and broken promises, most of the time when we got together she would make cryptic comments about what God had said and let us try and figure out what she was talking about. I was better at this than the others and when I understood what she was saying, she would smile at me as though no-one else existed, which more than made up for the other times when she clamped her jaw tightly together and refused to look at me. I couldn't bear it when I disappointed her.

'Stone has been sent to us as a sign,' she said again, giving us a final chance to understand.

This was more familiar territory. People in Underhill were used to seeing signs, or at least, thinking they did. In my opinion, far too much time was spent looking for signs – in the clouds, in the stars, in the direction the wind blew, which foot someone used to step into or out of a house or the patterns of leaves on the street. You name it, someone would see a sign in it. And of course, this compulsion to see signs everywhere wasn't religion, was it? No, of course it wasn't. Religion was bad, religion was forbidden, but the signs? Well, the signs were just, well, *signs*. Ridiculous. However, regardless of all that, I was almost certain that this was the first time anyone had seen a sign in a baby.

Everyone shuffled their feet as best they could in the mud, looking confused, and it was quite obvious that no-one knew what Jem was talking about, so I arranged my expression into the one that indicated that of course *I* understood, but that I would give the slower Threads time to work it out for themselves. Jem looked round at us all, then sighed, impatiently.

I didn't bother to record the whole of what followed in the Book of Jem, there were far too many questions, answers, doubts, ifs, buts and maybes. Instead, I wrapped everything up into a concise summary, so I'll let the entry speak for itself.

Stories 6:21-30

The air grew dark and lightening flashed across the sky. At the first clap of thunder the Prophet lifted her hands to cover her face; at the third clap she lowered them, and she looked as ancient as the oldest hills. When she spoke, the earth trembled, and the Threads dropped to their knees.

'We humans made an agreement with God,' the Prophet said. 'In return for the freedom of the world, we gave a promise to nurture the plants, the birds, the animals and each other. But we forgot our promise. We became destroyers. We fought and fought and when we were still not sated by death, we fought some more. When the old weapons no longer satisfied us, we made chemicals to burn ourselves from the inside out: skin peeled from our bones, blood leaked from our organs and breath rushed from our lungs. We took the world to the brink of an abyss, then kicked it over the edge. In our frenzy to massacre each other, we strangled the plants, we razed the forests, we tortured the beasts, starved the birds and choked the seas.

'And after we did this, after we made the world a temple to extermination, what did we do? We blamed God. We told ourselves that it was God who had caused the murder of four billion people, that it was God who had brought about the extinction of so many species. We said God was to blame for

the poison in our water, it was God who put the toxins in our food and God who caused our childlessness. We said religion is evil so there will be no more religion, we said God did all this, so there will be no more God.

'God's message is this: God rejects our false accusations. God renounces what has been done in Its name. God will take revenge and Its revenge will be terrible beyond imagining, for the coldest ice will freeze our blood until it no longer pumps through the veins of humanity.

'God has chosen Its weapon for revenge and that weapon is Underhill and the baby Stone is a sign, for after God has wrought Its revenge, Underhill shall be the cradle of every person who walks on the earth.'

12

Kat

I shook the tea leaves around the trunk of the elder tree, she'd be glad of the nourishment, and touched my fingertip to one of the buds dotting the branches, overlapping purple scales topped by tiny, ragged crowns of shoots. For as long as life returned to my Elder Mother each year, I had a reason to feel hopeful.

Shrugging off my coat, I laid it on the ground and settled myself onto it. Everything was already so muddy that a little more wouldn't make any difference and at least the mud cushioned the ground underneath me. I had a free day ahead: despite Willow's protestations, the twins were at their classes, I'd finished the latest ordering, and other than dropping in to see Lily, I had no plans. There was time to sit for a while with the Elder Mother. Besides, I had something on my mind that I wanted to talk to her about.

'She still hasn't left,' I said.

I always spoke aloud because I had realised long ago that if I only talked to her in my thoughts, they would drift onto other things and I'd end up thinking about what to make for dinner, or whether the kids had done their chores, or how Ed was doing. Speaking aloud was the best way of keeping focused on my connection with the Elder Mother.

After the attack by the Uplanders and all the fuss about Lorne and her baby, when things had calmed down a little, my thoughts returned to Jem. The fascination that some of my neighbours had for her hadn't waned, in fact it seemed to be growing and a steady stream of people visited her at Laurel and Rob's house. Apparently, a group of them regularly met halfway up Front Hill and I'd heard rumours that Jem was actually preaching there, invoking God in her little speeches.

Although we all knew that what she was doing was against the Laws, no-one was stupid enough to notify her and invite the authority to scrutinise our lives. She wasn't causing any actual harm and as Molly had put it, at least it was keeping some of the more irritating people in Underhill occupied. She had looked horribly embarrassed as soon as she said that – obviously she'd remembered that Ed and Willow were among them – but I knew what she meant. Whenever I thought about the girl, I had the urge to scratch myself, tear my skin, and consequently, I was covered in red welts. Surely Jem must be getting bored of whatever game she was playing?

Out of the corner of my eye, I saw a flash of colour on the far side of the graveyard near a large pile of smashed headstones. A few seconds later, I saw it again, there was definitely something there. I picked up my jacket, shook the worst of the mud from it and went to peer through the tangle of gorse.

Lying on the mud was the Uplander, Lorne, curled into a tight ball, reminding me of the first time I'd seen her, squeezed behind Lily's sofa. One of her hands was resting on a fragment of headstone. Her eyes were closed and her cheeks were wet.

I thought about creeping away, leaving her to her tears, but she looked so miserable that in the end I said softly, 'Lorne?'

Her eyes snapped open and she sat up, rubbing her face, leaving dark streaks of mud down her cheeks.

'What are you doing here?' I looked around. 'Where's Stone?'

'Laurel's looking after him.' She'd been working hard to soften her accent and it was already easier to understand her.

'What are you doing here?' I asked again, but she didn't answer.

She was gripping a piece of broken granite and I crouched down to look at the words carved in the stone.

'And God shall wipe away all tears from their eyes,' I read aloud.

The next bit was missing, then there were some letters and numbers that I didn't recognise: *v l tion 21:4*, and underneath that there was part of a name, *Olivia Har...*

'Who was Olivia?' I asked.

She traced the letters with her hand and looked up at me. 'My great-grandmother.'

'She lived in Underhill?'

Lorne nodded.

It had never occurred to me to wonder if she'd had relatives in our village. As far as I knew, Uplanders weren't territorial – they didn't claim a connection with any particular place. Other than during the worst of Whiteout, they were constantly on the move in the high lands, travelling huge distances in their search for food, going wherever their feet took them.

'Is that why you brought Stone here? Because of Olivia?'

Lorne nodded again and sat up straighter, hugging her knees to her chest.

'I want him to have a home,' she said. 'My father left Underhill as soon as he was old enough. He never came back, but every night when I was a kid he would tell me stories about his home under the hill and when we walked we used to sing the doors.'

'What do you mean?'

Lorne took a deep breath and then to my surprise, she started singing.

'Red, then blue, then green and green. Three more red, then second blue. Green and red and red then blue...'

Her voice faltered, and she blushed.

'It's the colours of the front doors. I can sing the whole street.

Of course, when I got older I realised that Dad only made me sing to try and stop me moaning about how much my feet hurt. The colours aren't the same now, they must have changed since he lived here.'

She looked so sad, and I felt sad for her, for a little girl who had once blocked out the pain in her feet by singing the colours of the front doors of a place she had never been to.

'And Olivia?' I asked.

She traced the letters of Olivia's name on the headstone.

'Dad's grandmother. He told me about this place,' she said, gesturing around her.

'About the graveyard?'

She shrugged. 'I didn't know the name for it. Just that there was a place, from before, where you could visit the dead. I like that. On the hills we never get to visit our dead. When Dad died, he was dug into the ground, then we moved on and never went back.'

'And when you found out you were pregnant?'

'I didn't want my baby to have the same life I did. We were always walking. Walking, walking, walking, but never arriving anywhere. I told some of the others about the village under the hill – said I thought it was a good place to try stealing. That's why *they* came down of course, but I came because I wanted to bring Stone home to Olivia.'

She started crying again and without thinking, I held out my arms and she shuffled towards me and pressed into my embrace, wrapping her arms around me. I rocked her back and forth, smoothing her hair as if she was one of my children.

'Poor girl,' I said. 'You're home now. You've come home.'

I let her cry herself out. Above us, the rooks chattered noisily, passing on messages of utmost importance. A few years ago, the Underhill rooks had suffered a near catastrophic decline, but with the arrival of Mudbound this year they were back in force and I was glad of the cacophony over my head.

Eventually, Lorne unwound her arms and moved away from me a little, smudging more mud around her face as she rubbed her tears away.

'You're a kind person,' she said. 'Not like what some of them say…' her voice trailed off and she glanced at me, embarrassed.

'Don't worry,' I said. 'Holding grudges is a full-time job for some people in Underhill.'

Lorne smiled uncertainly, then she scrambled to her feet. 'I've got to get back.'

'Stone will be missing you,' I said.

'Yes. But it's nearly time to go up as well.'

'Go up where?' I asked.

Lorne flushed. 'I mustn't say. You've been so kind, but I mustn't say.' She reached over and touched the back of my hand.

'Thank you,' she said, and hurried out of the graveyard.

*

I popped round to see Lily and ended up staying much longer than I intended. It took her a while to stop obsessively pushing her little herb pots around the kitchen window sill, and when she finally did she threw herself into a chair and started crying. She hated being Mudbound – every year she spent most of the season threatening to move away – and some of the Files she'd worked on recently had been particularly traumatic, which had left her completely wrung out. On top of that, Ruby was being even more trying than usual – she hadn't forgiven Lily for being at the party when the house was broken into and she was making her daughter's life very difficult. Lily wouldn't let me leave until I promised to drop in again later and I left her scrubbing away at some plates so hard I thought she might actually scrub right through them. Still, I supposed it was better than pointlessly rearranging pots of herbs.

I wanted to clear my head, so I decided to go up to the turbines and surprise Ed with a picnic. I brewed some of the lavender tea that he loved and decanted it into a flask, packed some food in a bag and set off to walk up Front Hill.

One of the things about being Mudbound is the effort it takes to get anywhere. For the first few days, my legs ache, I'm out of breath, and I have to work really hard just to walk down the road. But then my muscles start to toughen, my breathing settles into the rhythm of the new season and everything becomes much easier. We all lose weight during Mudbound – it may be filthy, but it's certainly good for us.

As I passed Laurel and Rob's cottage I glanced through the kitchen window, but there was no sign of anyone and I was determined not to let thoughts of Jem accompany me on my walk. I tried to focus instead on the pleasure of being outside without having to rush from house to house to get the ordering done, or struggle to unload the drone, or nag the kids to study, or all the other things that generally filled my time.

It was a beautiful day, the sort of day that showed Underhill off to its best. The sky was a patchwork of blue and white and although the ground under my feet was uniformly brown, above a certain height the hills were green – the mud tended to slide down towards the village. Looking at the hills reminded me of Lorne. Even though she'd led the Uplanders to us, I couldn't help but admire her strength, everything she'd been through: struggling to survive up there, going through childbirth in terrible conditions, making the decision to return to Underhill. I hoped she would stay, I'd speak to Molly, see if she could speed up the application, if Lorne's family was from here, it should be relatively straightforward.

The path started to rise, and I concentrated on matching my breathing to my footsteps, welcoming the thumping of my heart as it pumped my sluggish post-Whiteout blood around. It made me think of something Dandy had told me, about how before the Wars people let themselves get so large that lots of them had to use a wheeled chair to get from place to place. When he first told me, I thought it was a joke, after all we've only got one life, one body, why wouldn't you cherish it, give it the best chance to carry you wherever you want to go? However, Dandy was adamant that it was true.

'There was so much that had gone wrong back then, Kitten. Maybe we needed the Wars to wash away all the bad stuff.'

I had been horrified. 'You can't say that, Dandy. Billions of people died. You can't really think that was a good thing.'

'I didn't say it was a *good* thing. I said perhaps the Wars were needed to rid us of all the bad things. You know how in some places fires burn for days, leaving the land all dead and black, but when the plants grow back they're always greener and stronger than before? Perhaps humanity had got itself into such a state before the Wars, that the same thing had to happen. I mean, physically we were fucked from preventable diseases we inflicted on ourselves. And emotionally and mentally, we were equally as fucked, doing unimaginably awful things in the name of God, or Allah, or Yahweh or whatever other fucking name people wanted to use.'

His use of the word fuck always increased exponentially with how strongly he felt about what he was saying. No-one else said it with such venom and when Dandy felt really strongly about something, he would add emphasis by putting an extra syllable on the end, so it sounded like he was saying *fuckeduh* or *fuckinguh*.

He ran his fingers through his hair, which was waving wildly around his head and I suspected he had forgotten that it was his twelve-year-old daughter he was talking to. Perhaps he thought I was one of his students.

'My point is,' he was saying, 'that as terrible as the Wars were, perhaps it was the only way to get everyone to do something about the fucked*uh* way that they were living their lives.'

He must have seen something in my face because he said in a milder voice, 'Sorry, Kitten. Am I upsetting you?' But then he continued without waiting for an answer. 'The point is that we no longer have the luxury of ignorance. Religion gave everyone a safety net because it gave them permission to think it's okay to abuse your body, because it'll be restored to perfection in heaven. It's okay to behave badly, because God will forgive you. It's even okay to kill others, as long as you're doing it in the name of God. You do understand why it was so evil, don't you, Kitten?'

The thing was, I'd understood then and I still understood, because there was absolutely no question that religion had damaged the world, terribly and forever. But, all those people had died before I was born and although I understood a monstrous thing had happened, I couldn't grieve for people I had never known. What I did grieve for were the ash trees that I'd never had a chance to see, and all the other plants and animals that were gone forever thanks to the poison spread over the world by people in the name of their gods. When religion was finally banned, there was no doubt in my mind that it was for the best. The most important thing was personal responsibility. For ourselves. For each other. For our planet.

Annoyed that I couldn't even enjoy a walk without my thoughts taking me to places I'd rather not go, I thought about Ed and how nice it would be to have lunch with him – the turbines had needed a lot of attention recently and he'd been spending more time than usual up on the hill. I wasn't that far away, I could see the top of Lucy's blades slicing through the sky and if I hadn't stepped in a thick slick of mud, which made me stumble and look down, I might have missed the mess of boot prints leading along a narrow track that split from the main path and headed off to the right. If I hadn't seen those boot prints, then I wouldn't have stopped, and it was only because I had stopped that my breathing eased enough for me to hear her voice, carried towards me on the breeze.

Jem's voice was unmistakeable, with its curious lack of modulation so that everything she said was delivered at a single pitch. Almost without thinking about it, I turned and followed the trail of boot prints. As I got closer, I made out snatches of phrases: binding together, cleansing the world, and several mentions of the G word. I rounded a corner and there she was, standing with about a dozen others inside an area that had been cordoned off with lengths of rope. They were all standing in a circle with their eyes shut, holding hands.

'God renounces what has been done in its name,' Jem was saying. The rest of them nodded in time to the words as her voice droned on. Then I saw Ed. He had his back to me, on one side he was holding hands with Eileen and on the other, although I didn't want to believe it, Willow. I ducked underneath the nearest length of rope.

'What the fuck are you doing?'

At the sound of my voice, Jem abruptly stopped talking and the entire group turned towards me. Ignoring them all, I stared at Ed.

'Well? Do you want to tell me what's going on?'

I turned to Willow. 'And you, young lady, why aren't you at school?'

Ed extricated himself from Eileen's grasp and held both hands out towards me, but I stepped back, I couldn't bear for him to touch me. He looked unconcerned that I'd found him there and even managed a smile, before he said, 'I was going to tell you about God's Threads.'

I raked my nails down my arm and clenched my jaw together so hard that it was a wonder that my teeth didn't shatter, but when he gave me another dopey half-smile, I couldn't keep it in any longer.

'You stupid idiot. There was I, thinking it was the turbines that were keeping you busy. But all the time, you've been listening to this poisonous bitch spout all this... this... nonsense about God. Not to mention encouraging our daughter. What are you thinking?'

I glared around the circle. 'It's not just him, you know. I've got news for you all. There is no God. It might be against the Laws, but nobody should need a Law to tell them that God doesn't exist. It's just an evil made-up story to justify all the sick, twisted things that people did to each other.' I looked at Ed. 'You know that better than anyone, don't you?'

He flinched, but I didn't care. I was furious with them all, standing around on the side of the hill, lapping up her rubbish. I mean, I knew that Eileen had had some sort of weird fetish about Jem from the moment she arrived, but I had hoped that the likes of Fred and Lia would have come to their senses by now. Lorne was there too, with Stone bound to her chest, doing her best to avoid catching my eye. They all just stood there impassively, some of them still holding hands.

'Don't you lot get it? It's evil. You're all deluded.'

I held my bag up to show Ed. 'I was coming to see you, wanted to surprise you. Thought we could have some lunch together.' I laughed bitterly. 'Guess that makes me as stupid as you.'

Ed took a step towards me and in a voice that was so calm that it sounded like he was discussing the weather or something, he said, 'Let's go up to the turbines and talk.'

'You're joking, right? You want me to sit and pretend everything is fine, when you've been sneaking around behind my back, encouraging Willow to do the same?'

He reached for me and this time I let him take hold of my arms, which he pressed hard against my sides, like he was trying to push my anger back inside, then he turned to Willow, 'I think you should go home. Your mum and I need to talk.'

She frowned, and I waited for the inevitable argument, but then Jem said to her, 'Go on,' and my daughter just nodded and walked away. What on earth? I stared after her, unable to believe what I was seeing. Willow never listened to me like that.

'Kat,' said Ed. 'Come up to the turbines and we'll talk.'

One by one, everyone turned away from us, linking hands and reforming their circle. Lorne gave me an embarrassed little smile and Eileen shuffled round to close the gap left by Ed. She was the last to reach out and take hold of the hands either side of her, and even when she had completed the circle, she continued to look over her shoulder at us.

I looked at Ed. I took a deep breath. And another.

'Okay,' I said. 'Let's go and talk.'

*

The main path was wide enough for us to walk side-by-side, but I went on ahead, trying to force myself to calm down, balling my hands into fists to stop myself tearing at my skin. Arguing never got us anywhere, we had never resolved anything that way, and if I was being honest, it hadn't been a complete surprise to find him there. Had I actually hoped to catch him with Jem? Was that what my idea of a surprise picnic had really been about? I stamped up the path, focusing on Lucy's arms sweeping round.

As I gained height, the rest of the turbine column came slowly into view. I had always loved how, because of the way that the hill rose in several stages, Lucy emerged teasingly from the earth until finally, where the path levelled out, her full height was revealed. Behind me, Ed was muttering to himself and now I was closer, I saw that her arms weren't going around as fast as they should have been in the stiff breeze – the pitch of her blades was wrong.

I looked over my shoulder.

'Do you want to go and sort Lucy out?'

Judging by his look of surprise, he'd obviously been expecting me to shout at him. He shook his head.

'I've been trying to fix her for weeks,' he said. 'I don't know what else to do.'

I squinted at Faraday and Hinton, relieved to see that at least they seemed to be working normally.

I looked back up at Lucy. She was the faithful one, the one that kept on turning no matter what, even when Faraday and Hinton were playing silly buggers. She used to have a different name, but when Ed's mother died, his father had re-named her Lucy, said that it made him feel close to his wife when he was up on the hills, the sentimental old fool.

'What's wrong with her?'

Ed shrugged. 'I'll just go and tell Leroy and George that we're over here.' He nodded at Lucy. 'Why don't you go and sit? I'll be back in a minute.'

I climbed the five metal steps bolted to the base of the turbine and settled myself on the platform, leaning against the door that opened into Lucy's inner workings. I tried to pretend everything was okay, unpacking the bag, shaking out a little cloth, pouring a cup of the lavender tea, then setting out bread, cheese, boiled eggs and some of the preserved pears that Ed loved.

'I'm glad you're here.'

He was standing at the bottom of the steps, looking up at me.

'I'm still furious,' I said. 'You have to start talking to me. I need to know what's going on with you. And why you're making Willow think it's okay to be part of it.'

He sat down beside me on the platform and took a pear, eating it slowly, savouring the sweetness, then he tore off a hunk of bread and reached for the cheese.

'What was all that about?' I asked. 'All of you standing around, holding hands. And what are the *threads*?'

Ed pointed up at Lucy's arms, slowly sweeping around above our heads.

'She's dying,' he said.

'She can't be. Your father always said she'd see us out, us and the kids. Lucy's got decades of life left in her.'

Ed shook his head.

'Well he was wrong. And it's not just Lucy.' He nodded towards Faraday and Hinton. 'They're all dying.'

'Oh Ed, you'll fix them, you and Leroy between you, you always do…'

'No,' he said, and the despair in his voice stopped me in my tracks. 'I'm doing everything I can, I've tried everything that Dad taught me, everything I've learned myself. I've spent hours, days, on the Wave, trying to find a way to fix them.'

'You've got to keep looking. Or… or…' I desperately tried to think of a suggestion. 'What if we ask someone from the authority to come and help you?'

'You know that won't happen, Kat. No-one cares about our turbines. If the authority finds out that they're dying they'll just see it as an excuse to break up our community. I mean, you've said it yourself enough times, give them the flimsiest excuse to relocate people and they'll do it.'

'There must be something we can do.'

He slumped against Lucy's door, looking completely exhausted. 'I Waved someone Dad trained with and he put me in touch with an engineer who works on one of the big factory arrays. Leroy and I spoke to him last week, told him what's been going on and he agrees with me.'

I pointed at the five dormant turbines beyond the sub-station, none of which had turned for years.

'Can't you get them working again?'

He shook his head. 'Where do you think we get the spare parts for Lucy and the others? They're just shells, there's hardly anything left inside them. Anyway, we pulled up the cables that connect them to the sub-station years ago.'

'What's any of this got to do with Jem?' I asked, changing the subject, not ready to let myself even begin to think about what the consequences would be, what the death of the turbines would mean for every single person in Underhill.

'I don't think her arrival is a coincidence,' Ed said, glancing down at my hands which I'd balled into fists. He reached over and smoothed my fingers out, then lifted my palms and kissed the grooves of half-moons left by my nails.

'Of course it's a coincidence,' I said. 'She's got nothing to do with the turbines, unless you think she's up here sabotaging them?'

He snorted and said, 'You're funny,' but he wasn't smiling. 'She's not the reason the turbines are failing.' He reached for another piece of bread, but he didn't eat it, just sat there, crumbling it between his fingers. 'But the more I think about it, the more I think Jem has the answer to how we'll survive when they do.'

'What are you talking about?'

'Will you just listen to what I have to say without jumping down my throat, Kat? Will you do that?'

I nodded my head, although he really needed to start making some sense soon.

'Jem has told us that God is going to renew the world…'

'*Renew* the world?' What? Had he lost his mind? I mean, seriously, had he actually gone mad?

'For Freedom's sake, just listen.' His voice was urgent. He squeezed my hands and I pressed my lips together.

'When you think about it and believe me I've been thinking about it a lot over the last few weeks, it does make sense. Just suppose that God does exist, that God always existed. And what if people, humanity, whatever you want to call us, what if we were supposed to nurture the world, to look after it? What if we promised to do that? And then we, people like my monster of a grandfather, and so many other people, we broke our promise to God. We brought the world and everything in it to the brink of destruction, I mean, think about all the contaminated land, all the toxins in the food chain, all the extinct species. I think Jem is here to tell us that God has had enough.'

'You don't need to lecture me about how humanity fucked up the world, Ed. But it's quite some leap to get from the horror of the Wars to believing in some mythical god figure. And even if, just for the sake of argument, we say it's true, why on earth would this God choose someone like Jem, of all people, to tell us all this?'

'Why not, love? I mean, really, why not? Who should It choose?'

'Not her.'

'I think it's the message that you're struggling to accept, Kat. Not Jem herself.'

'No. It's Jem. She's devious and manipulative and I don't trust her.'

My voice caught, I was on the edge of tears. It was ridiculous, I mean, who would believe this rubbish?

But I knew.

I knew exactly who would believe it because I could hear Dandy's voice so clearly he might as well have been sitting there with us.

'Ed will always be a seeker, Kitten. Not like you. You'll confront the challenges that this changing world will throw at you. But Ed's different, he's vulnerable. There's always the danger that when things get tough, people like Ed will seek comfort in irrational beliefs. The paths to God can never be completely destroyed. They can only ever be obscured.'

My father said a lot more. He had approached it like he did his lectures: assembled the facts, backed them up with examples, and made the same points over and over again as he tried his very best to persuade me to rethink my relationship with Ed, to find someone less emotionally fragile to build a life with. In the end though, it didn't work. I loved Ed, I thought I could be strong enough for us both, and that was that.

So, thanks to Dandy, I understood it. I understood why, by listening to Jem, Ed thought he might find some hope, some relief from the burdens he carried. But just because I understood, did not mean that I could, or would, accept that it was the right thing for him to do.

Ed very obviously thought otherwise and he was still talking, hoping to persuade me to take him seriously. 'God is going to renew the world, to start all over again, and when that happens, everyone will be cleansed. Everyone but us.'

'What do you mean, *everyone but us*?'

'That's what Jem is telling us, Kat. Humanity is going to be wiped from the face of the earth. Everyone will die except us. But we are going to be saved.'

'Why us? Why are we going to be saved?'

'Because God has chosen Underhill as the place where humanity will start again.'

He smiled then, and I realised with horror that he had no idea how crazy he sounded. I stared across the hill, letting my eyes follow the motion of Hinton's blades, tracing their path through the air, two, three, four times before I turned to him.

'Why do you believe her?'

He reached over, cupping his warm hands around my face. He gave me a kiss and said, so quietly I could barely hear him, 'I can't *not* believe her, love. The turbines are dying and when that happens, I think…no…that's not right…I'm *certain*…only God can save us.'

13

Eileen

You should have seen Kat's face when she found me and Ed holding hands in the Binding Area. It was hilarious. He'd started to come to the meetings more regularly – Jem said that he'd unpicked some of his knots and was ready to be bound. He didn't say much, but Jem had explained that it was okay for Threads to take their time, that some people would need longer to fully understand how to accept God's Messages into their lives.

Take Lia, for example. She had always been a bit pointless, making her way through life without leaving an impression on anything. Fred obviously saw something in her, but I had no idea what it might be. After Lia became one of God's Threads, though, once she was bound to the rest of us, it was clear that the reason she had been so unencumbered by anything resembling a personality, was so that God could fill her with Itself. Lia seemed to expand in front of our eyes, as the Messages poured into her and forced their way into all that empty space that she'd been carrying around inside her. I must say, I was finding it very satisfying to be one of the strong Threads helping to lift the weaker and less popular ones, although when I said that to Lia I'm not sure she really understood, she just stared at me for a moment, then laughed. She probably found it all very overwhelming, poor woman.

The point was, Ed was still very reticent about doing much more than turning up to the meetings and holding my hand, but at least he was there and that was progress. He obviously hadn't told Kat though, because that day she just appeared from nowhere, yelling and screaming. She untied a piece of rope from the stakes and started whipping it around her head. Eventually she got tired of that, so she dropped it on the ground and ran towards Jem, shouting the most awful things. At one point she tried to hit her, but I stepped in front of Jem to stop Kat reaching her. I would have rather died than see her hurt Jem.

After Jem sent Willow home and Ed finally dragged Kat away, we all went back to what we had been doing before she arrived, which was listening to Jem talk about the Messages. I'm sure you can imagine the endless discussions we had about what it all meant, particularly the bit about *Underhill shall become the cradle of every person who walks on the earth.*

Sometimes I found it quite hard not to be irritated that God felt it necessary to deliver Its Messages to Jem in such a roundabout way. First of all, there was all the stuff about people living in the forest and a frankly unbelievable story about the wind and streams saying that they didn't want anyone to leave, which was followed with a rambling tale about broken promises, cleansing, renewals and cradles. I mean, wouldn't it have been clearer if the message had been: Everyone's going to die, apart from you lot?

I did ask Jem why everything was so vague, but she just said that it was not for us to question the intentions of God, and that It used stories to make it easier for us to understand the Messages. I guess I just had to accept that everything moved at the pace of the slowest Thread, and it made sense that some people were too stupid to understand what Jem was telling us unless it was delivered in this way.

An unfortunate result of the endless discussions about the *soon Underhill will be the cradle* part of the Message was that Laurel and Lorne began to behave like they were special, just because they had managed to produce babies. At our meetings in the Binding Area, they both made a point of standing next to Jem, so that when the rest of us listened to her speak, we were forced to look at those two as well. It wasn't always easy to maintain good thoughts about the other Threads.

When I wasn't at the Binding Area, or working the Files, I was doing the other thing that I enjoy doing when we're Mudbound. I know some people don't like the mud, but I really appreciate how it slows everyone down when they're walking along the street and I get a permanent groove in the fleshy bits of my palms from holding great-grandfather Nikon's binoculars up to my face for so long.

There is always something interesting to look at, which I wouldn't necessarily see if it was raining or snowing. For example, in the space of only a couple of days, I saw the following things. I saw Willow and Ash arguing at the top of the steps leading down to their house. I saw Lily coming out of her house in tears. I saw Ed's apprentice, George, come down the turbine path and head to the barn that was burned by the Uplanders and then, a few minutes later, I saw Willow going there too. I saw Kat going in and out of everyone's houses, supposedly to do the ordering, although I'm sure she was taking every opportunity to spread poison about Jem. I saw Tish and Petra having an argument in the street, but there was nothing new about that. I saw how often Ed was up at the turbines and how little he was at home. I watched Molly waddling along the street and right outside my house, I saw a particularly thick slick of mud catch her boot and trip her up. She seemed to be in quite a lot of pain and she stayed crumpled on the ground for ages. At one point she looked straight at my window and I wondered if the sun was glinting off the glass of the binoculars, so I put them down and went to get a drink. When I came back, she was still lying on the ground and it wasn't until

Fred came along and helped her up that she was able to limp home.

One afternoon, I watched Laurel and Lorne holding their babies in front of themselves like trophies as they came down the street towards my house, talking and laughing. It made me so angry all over again, how they considered themselves more important than the rest of us. More important than me. Me. The first and truest follower of Jem. The first to understand how special she was. The first of God's Threads. The one who was writing the Book of Jem. Lorne had been in Underhill hardly any time at all, but already she was more important than me, or at least, her stupid baby was. Why wasn't I as important?

Then it hit me. *Of course* I was important. The end of the Message which went on about cradles must be meant for *me*. How had it taken me so long to realise? Jem was speaking about me. She had probably known all along – she always tried to make us work out the meanings of things for ourselves. It had taken me long enough, but suddenly everything was clear.

I needed to have a baby.

I flew out of my seat by the window, almost dropping great-grandfather Nikon's binoculars, but once I had put them safely down, I rushed over to my Treasure Cupboard. I stabbed myself on one of dad's syringes, but I didn't care, I reached right to the back and pulled out the notebook with my List of Enemies in it. By turning it upside down and back-to-front, it was almost like having a brand-new notebook. On the back page, which was now the front page, I wrote, *Plans for a baby*. Then I tapped the pencil on my teeth and considered what to write. Obviously, there was one item that I couldn't do without, and I wrote down 1) *Sperm*.

I needed to think very carefully about who I might be prepared to accept it from. Ed was a no-brainer, of course, and I wrote his name down. He had demonstrated his ability, since Kat had had two for the price of one from him. He was kind to me. He was one of God's Threads. We held hands in the Binding Area. There were all sorts of reasons why Ed would be a very good candidate to provide me with sperm. However, there was an obvious downside – our child would be the half-sibling of Willow and Ash, which would mean a permanent connection to Kat, which was obviously not something I relished.

Underneath Ed's name, I wrote Rob's. He had also proved capable, and I didn't really mind the thought of our baby being related to Mila, just as long as the thing didn't cry as much as she did. The list seemed a little short though, and I knew I should have some other options, to maximise my chances.

Another thought occurred to me – what about Ash? Given Ed's productivity, there was a good chance that Ash's sperm would be pretty capable as well. I wrote his name down, but then after a moment, I added a question mark. After all, that would make my baby Kat's grandchild, and I really wasn't sure I could cope with that.

I wondered how quickly I would get pregnant. Since the meaning of the Message was now clear, presumably none of the usual fertility issues would affect me. I was a bit vague on how this could be, since I had no choice but to eat food and drink water from the same sources as everyone else, but that was God's problem to sort out, not mine.

I decided to go and ask Jem whose sperm she would recommend. Also, perhaps she could ask God whether I should actually do sex, or just get the man to hand some over and I'd sort the rest out myself.

Jem was in Laurel's sitting room with Lorne, who was feeding Stone. The sight of Lorne's veiny breast was repulsive and when she said, 'The Threads are bound,' I just mumbled a reply under my breath.

'I need to talk to you about something of the utmost importance,' I said, looking at Jem. I loved the way my words always slipped so easily from my mouth now whenever I talked to her.

'The Threads are bound,' she said, and immediately I was ashamed that I hadn't greeted her properly.

'The Threads are bound,' I said.

'It's good to see you, Eileen.'

Out of the corner of my eye, I saw Lorne's nipple pop out of Stone's mouth.

'I need to talk to you,' I said, again.

Jem waved me towards one of the cushions on the floor but I put my mouth close to her ear and allowed myself two long, deep sniffs, before I hissed, '*In private.*'

Jem smiled at Lorne and said, 'We'll continue later,' and I badly wanted to know what they had been talking about, but then Jem said, 'Come up to my room,' and all other thoughts left my head.

She got to her feet, her head barely reached my chin, which always made me feel protective of her. I was so excited – in all the weeks she had been in Underhill I had never been in her room before, despite the hours I'd stood in the garden looking up at the window, wishing I could be there with her.

Following her up the stairs, my nose was level with her calves and it was difficult not to reach out and touch the fine black hairs on her legs. At the top, she turned left and walked along the small corridor to the end. Laurel and Rob's room was on the right, and so the first room on the left must be where Lorne was staying although the door was shut, so I couldn't see in.

All of a sudden, I felt shy. I had imagined this moment so often – mainly when I was in bed and couldn't sleep – but now it had finally arrived, I was really worried that I might do the wrong thing. Then Jem said, somewhat impatiently I thought, 'Well, come on then,' and I went into her room.

She shut the door behind me and gestured to a small cushion on the floor.

'Sit yourself down.'

I tried to fold myself onto the cushion and as she settled herself into a chair opposite, I wondered if any of the others had been up here. I liked the thought of being the first person to be alone with her in her room.

'I've had a thought,' I began, eager to tell her my news, but at the same time she said, 'Let's begin with a moment of reflection about our purpose as God's Threads.'

She shut her eyes and as her breathing slowed, I took the opportunity to look around the room. There was a small wooden bed which didn't look nearly as comfortable as my parents' bed where I slept. It had lots of woollen blankets piled on top of it and there was a thin pillow scrunched into a ball. Above the bed the window was framed by heavy blue curtains. When I was in the garden, those curtains were closed far too often for my liking. Jem's little rucksack rested against one of the legs of the bed and next to it there was a selection of clothes that the Threads had provided for her. They were all neatly folded and piled according to their colour with her red scarf draped over the top of them. I ran my finger along the thread tied around my throat.

There was nothing else in the room and in some obscure way I felt disappointed, I'm not sure exactly what I had expected, although I had hoped that there would be something significant to indicate that God's Prophet slept there. At some point while I had been looking around the room, Jem had finished reflecting on our purpose and was watching me.

'Faithful Eileen,' she said. 'Ever-present Eileen. What can I do for you?'

I was a bit taken aback when I heard my new titles, but I didn't let myself be distracted from what I had come to say.

'I'm excited.'

'How so?'

'I've realised what God's plan is for me.'

Jem didn't look as thrilled by the news as I'd expected.

'It's not given to everyone to know the intentions of God, Eileen.'

'I know that, I know God only speaks to you,' I said. 'But you know how we've been talking about interpretations of the Messages?'

Jem nodded, so I carried on, 'Well, I've worked one out.'

'And what is it?'

'I'm going to have a baby.'

Jem didn't say anything straight away and she couldn't seem to decide whether to look pleased or shocked, although she eventually settled on pleased. She got out of her chair, took my hands, helped me to my feet and then put her arms around me. I hoped we might stay like that for a while, but she pushed me gently away from her, holding me at arm's length.

'This is wonderful news, Eileen. A pregnancy so soon confirms the prophecy. Remember? *Underhill will be the cradle*. God is beginning to lift the burden of infertility from Underhill, so that humanity may be born again.'

I felt myself blushing with pride.

'I expected more pregnancies. God told me they would be a sign that we were moving along the path towards the Cleansing,' she said, and then smiled at me. 'Forgive me, Eileen, but it hadn't occurred to me that you would be one of them.'

I ignored this rather strange comment and said, 'I'm part of God's plan, aren't I?'

She laughed and pulled me back into a hug. 'Yes,' she said and rocked me from side to side. 'Yes, you are. I'm so happy.'

She pulled me over to the bed and we sat down on it, together.

157

I was so thrilled to be next to her, on her bed, that I almost missed what she said next.

'So, how far along are you? When are you due?'

'Oh, I'm not pregnant,' I said, rubbing one of the blankets between my fingers, it was lovely and thick, and I wondered if she might let me have it.

When I looked up, I was surprised to see she was frowning.

'You said you were going to have a baby, Eileen.'

'That's right.' I took the notebook out of my pocket, thumbed through it to the page headed *Plans for a baby*, and held it towards her.

She barely glanced at it, so I explained, 'I wanted to talk to you about my list of possible sperm-providers.'

She pushed her fingers into her temples and said, 'I'm getting a migraine.'

I couldn't believe it, we hadn't had a chance to talk about my plans at all, and I had no idea if she thought I should use Ed, Ash, Rob, or perhaps someone else entirely.

She reached for her rucksack and felt around inside for one of the patches. I watched her peel it back, push her sleeve up and stick it onto her arm.

'Please, Eileen,' she said, shuffling back on the bed, then lying down, pulling the blankets around her like a nest. 'On your way out, can you ask Lorne to bring me some bread and honey.'

I waved my notebook at her. 'What about God's plan? Shouldn't we discuss the details?'

'Another time.' She was slurring her words, which meant the migraine was going to be a bad one, so I leaned over, kissing her first on the forehead and then either cheek, just like my mother used to do to me when I felt poorly, and left the room.

*

For a few days after that, whenever I tried to talk to Jem alone, there were always other Threads hanging around, and I still hadn't managed to speak to her when it was time to get together again in the Binding Area. I went early, hoping to catch Jem before anyone else arrived, but to my annoyance, there were already people up there, including a few newcomers – obviously some of the other Threads had been spreading the word around the village – looking at the arrangement of ropes and stakes that marked out the Binding Area. I said, 'The Threads are bound,' but no-one replied.

Ed arrived with Leroy, who had started coming to the meetings again. Unlike Ed, who looked worn out, Leroy was full of energy, jiggling around from foot to foot, occasionally leaning over to say something to Ed, who barely seemed awake enough to reply. Leroy was younger than Ed by a few years and as I watched the muscles in his arms tensing and relaxing each time he moved, and how he kept running his fingers through his thick hair, like he was checking it was still there, I realised I might have just found my answer.

The meeting started slowly because the new people had to be instructed on how to hold hands and say, 'The Threads are Bound.' While we were getting through that I tried to imagine what the baby would look like. Leroy was one of my favourite colours – a shade of wet mud – and I was sure that combined with what my dad used to call my *honeyed complexion* there was no doubt that we would produce a well-toned offspring. Names would be an interesting decision, I mean, if my child was destined to renew humanity, then it had to be called something rather better than Stone. It would have to be a name that represented everything: Proton or Seed, or perhaps Beginning. Something inspiring.

Finally, Jem moved things on to the next phase of the gathering, when we discussed the interpretation of the Messages and I filed away my proposed names for consideration later on. Perhaps I would suggest them to Leroy and let him pick his favourite.

'Today we will consider the timing of God's revenge,' said Jem. 'The Threads will remember these words from the Message, *God will take revenge and Its revenge will be terrible beyond imagining for the coldest ice will freeze our blood until it no longer pumps through the veins of humanity*, and I want to begin our discussion by considering when the revenge will come to pass.'

'Soon,' called out Lia, and I looked at her approvingly, happy that she was continuing to benefit from being bound to us stronger Threads.

'And why will it happen soon?' asked Jem.

Lia blushed and reached for Fred's hand. 'Stone is not the only sign,' she said. 'There's something…'

'We'll talk of signs later,' interrupted Jem. 'First, consider the question of God's revenge. What indications do we have in the Message itself about when it will happen?'

Those of us that had been Threads since the beginning watched smugly while the newcomers looked at each other in confusion – we knew the answer, because we had already discussed it several times before. In the end Tish put them out of their misery.

'*The coldest ice will freeze our blood*,' she intoned, in that overly dramatic voice she always used when quoting the Messages. No-one could get a word in edgeways when Tish got started, although it didn't really matter because everyone was still looking blank.

'When is there a lot of ice?' Tish asked impatiently, as if she was talking to children. It was unacceptable, the way that she was getting above herself. Behind her, Jem was frowning.

Finally, someone called out, 'Whiteout? There's a lot of ice then.'

Before Tish could reply, Jem stepped in front of her.

'Thank you, Tish. And yes, that's right. God shall take Its

revenge at the next Whiteout when It shall Cleanse everyone on earth.' She paused a beat, as she always did at this point. 'Everyone, that is, except us.'

A voice called, 'What exactly do you mean by *Cleanse*?'

Jem opened her arms wide and fell to her knees, which she often did when she wanted to make sure the gravity of her message would be understood.

'God will have Its revenge, and no-one will be spared...' here there was another pause, '...apart from us.'

Apparently, not all the new Threads were completely ready to hear the Message because there was some concerned muttering and one or two of them actually looked scared.

'What about people in Underhill who *don't* believe?' someone asked. 'What about them? Are they going to be Cleansed as well?'

'God has chosen Underhill as the place where humanity will be Renewed. Everyone in Underhill will be saved for this purpose, but those who are most closely bound to God shall be raised up higher than the rest.'

'What about–' someone started to ask, but Jem interrupted before they could finish.

'Anyone in search of the truth can come and see me later and we will talk about the Messages. Now. Let's move on to signs. Has anyone got any new signs to tell us about?'

Across the circle, Ed and Leroy appeared to be arguing about something and I watched them anxiously. I had some affection for Ed, however my loyalty now had to be to Leroy. But Ed would be the baby's uncle, so it was important that they maintained cordial relations and I was about to go and offer to mediate, when Lia spoke up once again.

'I'm going to have a baby.'

Jem glanced at me, clearly irritated on my behalf that someone had stolen my idea.

'Are you actually pregnant, Lia?' she asked.

'Nearly eight weeks. It's got to be a sign, hasn't it?'

'Of course it's a sign,' said Fred. He put his hand protectively across Lia's stomach, looking so smug that it was all I could do not to pick up one of the stakes at the edge of the Binding Area and smash his face in.

'We had all the tests years ago,' he said, 'and the chance of natural conception for us was even worse than most couples, it was something like one in ten million, so it must be a sign.'

I tuned out for a while. Other people talking about themselves gets very boring very quickly and I wish that more people realised how a little bit of self-awareness goes a long way. Because I wasn't completely concentrating on what was happening, I'm not sure whether what I later wrote in the Book of Jem was *entirely* accurate, but I managed to get most of it down.

Preparations 1:1-5

The Threads held hands and bound themselves to the miracle that was growing within the belly of the one called Lia, then the Prophet stepped forwards and spoke these words.

'God is cleansing the toxins from our earth and our plants. God is preparing the people of Underhill for Renewal. It has sent this new life as a sign that what has been told will soon come to pass.'

But then the voice of the Prophet became louder and to those gathered around her, her words were like thunder and they cried out in fear, for they were deafened and they did not understand what they must do.

'I ask you now, Threads of God, what should we do to prepare ourselves? What burdens must we assume? What sacrifices must we make to ready ourselves for the Cleansing of the earth and the Renewal that will follow? Each of you

must ask of yourself, what must I do? What is God asking from me? What preparations must I make to be sure of my place in the cradle of the earth?'

And the words crushed us, and as we fell to our knees in the mud and knelt there in fear, a great fire came down from the sky and wrapped itself around the Prophet until she shone as brightly as the sun and in that way we knew that she truly spoke the words of God.

That's the gist of what happened anyway. The next few weeks might have involved nothing more than handholding, binding and Lia going on and on about her pregnancy, but fortunately it was all completely overshadowed by what happened next.

14

Kat

I asked Leroy to come for dinner, so I could talk to him and Ed together, and try again to convince them to tell everyone about the turbines. Even if it didn't work, I had to try.

If I'm honest, I wasn't in the best of moods when Leroy turned up. Earlier in the day Willow had disappeared again. I was sick and tired of her coming and going when she chose, with absolutely no thought for the rest of us. Ash claimed not to know where she was, but he was clearly upset.

'Have you two had a fight?'

'No.'

'You'd tell me if there was a problem between you?'

He shrugged – whatever the matter was, he obviously wasn't going to tell me.

Willow's attitude was getting worse. I understood that she wanted to push the boundaries, of course I did. I'd done it myself: she was growing up fast, it was natural for her to feel that our house, our family, was too unexciting, too small, too ordinary, whatever it was that she was feeling. I just wanted her to finish school before making any decisions, but she was missing classes again and spending far too much time hanging around Jem. This particular obsession was lasting far longer than most, but I hadn't given up hope that she would get bored of the girl and her stupid messages. Of course, while ever Ed was part of the group, it basically made it impossible for me to tell Willow that she shouldn't be. If her father was doing it, she'd yelled at me, more than once, then so could she.

I tried again with Ash.

'Ash? You'd tell me if there was something wrong with Willow?'

'For Freedom's sake, Mum. Stop going on.'

He stomped out of the kitchen and thundered up the stairs into his room. When he slammed his door, it shook the house. I was envious. I wished I could just run away from everything and slam a door on the world. I couldn't remember the last time I hadn't been worried about something.

It wasn't only me. The mood in the village was fragile at the best of times, but since Jem's arrival, we seemed to have split into two groups. There were those of us who were increasingly worried about everything, all of the time, and then there were the others who, thanks to the rubbish that girl was spouting, were doing a very good job of convincing themselves that they need never worry about anything ever again. The firm grip with which we held our community together was slipping. What would happen, I found myself wondering, if we let go altogether?

And, of course, Ed still hadn't told anyone else that the turbines were dying. I couldn't even begin to imagine what was going to happen when the news got out, but nevertheless, I hated keeping it a secret.

'Let me just tell Molly,' I'd pleaded. 'She needs to know. We need to make plans.'

'No, Kat, wait until I know how much longer they're going to keep turning.'

'But it might be too late by then…'

'Look, they're not going to stop overnight. They'll carry on for a while – just not for the decades Dad thought they would.'

'People need to know what's going on. They have a right to

know.'

'Yes, they do, but I don't have the answers that they'll want. Not yet. I'll tell them as soon as I have. You've got to trust me, Kat. Please? Promise me you won't tell anyone.'

I hated secrets, and I only agreed because of how worried I was about him. It was the slightly better of two bad choices. Lily had definitely guessed something was wrong, and several times I'd found myself avoiding her questions, blaming my mood on my irritation with Jem, or Willow, or anything else I could think of.

That's why I wanted to talk to Leroy and Ed together, to try again to convince them that they had to start telling people about the turbines. Once the meal was finished, I shooed Ash upstairs, and made the three of us some lavender tea.

'It's really hot, wait until it's cooled down a bit,' I said, handing them both a mug, then bringing my own drink over, I sat at the end of the table with Ed on my left, Leroy slouched opposite him.

'You need to tell everyone about the turbines,' I said, getting straight to the point.

'Not yet,' Ed said, glancing at Leroy, obviously they had anticipated this.

'People have a right to know,' I said. 'We need to make plans. We might only have a few weeks.'

'It'll be longer than that,' Ed said.

'Whatever. A few months, a year, two years. But in the end the turbines are going to stop working and Underhill will have no more electricity. That *is* right, isn't it?'

They both lifted their mugs and gulped their tea, their Adam's apples bobbing up and down at the same time.

'Is that right?' I asked again, struggling to force down the anger tickling the back of my throat. I couldn't afford to lose my temper – this was too serious. We had to start making plans, and we could only do that if we stayed calm, but Freedom knows, it wasn't easy.

I was finding it almost impossible to stop myself raking my fingernails down the inside of my arm and I wrapped both hands around my mug, clinging on to it tightly.

Ed nodded. 'Yes, and as soon as we can estimate how much longer the turbines are going to work, *then* we'll tell everyone. But until we know that, all we'll be doing is creating unnecessary panic.'

I turned to Leroy, who was running a finger round and round the top of the mug, making a squeaking noise that set my teeth on edge.

'You agree with him?' I asked.

He grunted something that might have been a yes or a no, I couldn't tell.

'Leroy, *please* stop making that awful noise.' He frowned, but at least he stopped.

'Do you agree with Ed?' Seriously, it was worse than getting the kids to talk.

'I guess. Jem said we should wait...'

'*Jem* said? You've told *her* about the turbines?'

Leroy flushed and looked across the table at Ed, who said, 'I told her. I thought it might be a sign.'

'A sign of what?' I couldn't believe it. They wouldn't tell the people who actually lived in Underhill, but they'd told her.

'A sign of *what*?' I asked again.

'A sign that we are on the path.'

'*What*? What are you going on about?'

I felt as if my head might explode with the effort it was taking not to shout. Or throw something. Or run out into the street, screaming.

Then Ed said, 'There are signs,' and I shivered, even though I wasn't cold. 'Signs that we are on the path to Renewal. The babies. Another pregnancy...'

He was talking about Lia's pregnancy. I was thrilled for her. The one-in-ten-million baby never actually happened to someone you knew. Except in this case, it had, and I knew how desperate she and Fred had been for a child. Years ago, she had asked me hundreds of questions about how I'd managed to get pregnant. She was so desperate that she had overcome her shyness long enough to present me with a list of things she wanted to know, her face flushed and her voice wobbly as she asked me about frequency, position, duration, whether I put my legs up afterwards, and for how long. Even after all this time, I was still embarrassed when I remembered our conversation. None of it had helped though and I always suspected that she thought I had kept something from her, but I hadn't. Other than not talking about my Elder Mother, I didn't keep secrets from anyone. Until now.

'You can't really believe that Lia's pregnancy proves anything that Jem's saying is true? It's just one pregnancy, Ed.'

'But Mila was only born a few months ago. Then Lorne turned up with Stone. And now Lia. No community as small as ours has three babies at the same time. It means something.'

'Why? Why must it *mean* anything? It's a coincidence. Coincidences do happen. Once Lia's had her baby, chances are there won't be another birth here in our lifetime.'

Ed smiled one of those annoying half-smiles that made me want to slap him.

'In any case,' I continued, 'I still don't understand why you decided to tell a complete stranger, someone who is flouting the Laws, that our village will run out of electricity decades earlier than we expected, yet you don't think it's news worth sharing with anyone else.'

I banged my hand on the table so hard that my fingers buzzed with pain.

'Surely you've got to see how wrong that is?'

Ed reached across the table and put his hand over mine, but I couldn't bear him to touch me and I pulled my arm away.

'It won't matter, Kat,' he said, and I couldn't believe how relaxed he sounded. 'That's the thing about God's Messages.'

'How can you say that? Of course it matters. It matters more than anything. Without electricity, we'll be no better than the Uplanders, except we don't know how to look after ourselves like they do.'

'Jem says that everyone in Underhill is already bound to God, even those who have yet to accept it. When the time comes, we will renew our promise to God and God will look after us.'

'And that's it?' I asked, incredulous. 'You think this God of Jem's is going to wipe everyone out except us, and then after our miraculous survival we'll no longer need electricity. Why is that? Is her God going to come and operate the turbines for us?'

I wished one of them would shout back so at least we could have a proper argument, but they both sat there with patient looks on their stupid faces which made me feel like a toddler having a tantrum while they waited for me to wear myself out.

'Leroy,' I said, and waited for him to look at me. 'Tell me what you really think about this.'

He shrugged, but I wasn't going to let him off the hook. 'Listen, it's one thing to suddenly decide to believe in God. I don't like it one bit, but I suppose I just have to accept that that's what you've decided to do. However,' I paused, and took a deep breath, trying to order my thoughts, 'it's altogether another thing to somehow believe that this God of yours is going to help us when the turbines fail. *Surely* you can see how ridiculous that is?'

He took another sip of his drink, then another, but eventually he spoke.

'The turbines are failing. Hinton's been struggling for weeks, although he's always broken down a lot. Dad used to call him the lazy one. He said any excuse for a break and Hinton would take it.'

'Leroy, the history of the turbines is not the point right now.'

'It is the point,' he mumbled.

'Why? Why is it?'

He looked at Ed, then tilted his mug towards him, examining it intently as if he might find the answer inside.

'The point is that we're used to Hinton's ways,' said Ed. 'But recently, since the beginning of Whiteout, as soon as we fix one problem with him, immediately there's another one. We've had issue after issue with the hydraulics, the motors, the coolers – Leroy's spending more time up at the top of Hinton than he is in his own bed. It didn't used to be like that. We don't know why it's happening now, but we do know that it started at almost exactly the same time that Jem received the first Message.'

'Oh come on, that proves nothing. It's a coincidence, hardly even that. Remember when Faraday was offline for a month a few years ago, right in the middle of Whiteout?'

'Of course I remember, love. One of his gear shafts sheared off and we had to wait ages for a replacement.'

'So? Get more replacements now.'

'This is different. They're dying.' Ed rubbed his eyes, looking so worn out that I felt a sudden pang of guilt. 'Don't you think if there was a way to fix them I'd have tried?'

I honestly wasn't sure any more. Were the turbines really as bad as he was saying? Perhaps he was exaggerating their problems to try and ingratiate himself with Jem and her stupid Threads. Surely Ed couldn't be causing the problems himself, in order to be able to claim that they were some sort of *sign*? No, no matter what issues Ed had, I couldn't believe he would do that. He wouldn't sabotage the turbines. He wouldn't, would he? I pushed the thought away.

'Let me get this straight,' I said. 'You told Jem about the problems with the turbines because you think they're a sign that the end of the world is coming?'

'I think, all things considered, that it's likely that the fact the turbines are dying is a sign that we are on the path to Cleansing and Renewal, yes,' he said.

His deliberate choice of words that presumably Jem herself had used was chilling. I sipped my tea, but it tasted bitter, so I pushed my cup away and turned to Leroy. I didn't really have much hope of getting through to him – it was always been the same, where Ed went, Leroy followed – but I had to try.

'I suppose you know Ed's been speaking to Dr. Lawrence again?'

He nodded, and I continued, 'I can see why Ed might be feeling vulnerable at the moment, susceptible to what this girl's saying.' Ed tried to interrupt, but I was determined to have my say. 'You've always been okay, Leroy. What your grandfather did has never affected you, so I just can't understand why you would listen to all this nonsense.'

'Has it ever occurred to you that what you call *nonsense* might actually be true?' Leroy asked.

'No, I can't say it has.'

He thought for a long time about what to say next and then he leaned across the table towards me.

'Maybe you should consider that Jem might be speaking the truth. Think about it. The turbines were fine until she started receiving the Messages, but now Lucy and the others are dying decades earlier than they should be. Why is that? The easy thing to do is to dismiss what she's saying, but rather than do that, why don't you try listening instead? What if our problems have nothing to do with the turbines themselves? What if Jem is telling us the truth? What if she is telling us over and over again, until we all hear and understand? Ask yourself Kat, what if what she is saying is true?'

*

The next day, I went to see Lily. She was in a terrible state and I think Cooper hoped that I might be able to calm her down. To be honest, it was a relief to think about something other than the dying turbines, and Ed somehow convincing himself that it was connected with Jem's arrival and the Threads. *The Threads*. What sort of stupid name was that anyway?

Lily looked as unhappy as I felt. She was slumped on a chair at the kitchen table, holding on to a cushion as if it was the only thing stopping her from slithering onto the floor. Ruby was in the chair opposite, sitting bolt upright with her silvery hair wound high on her head, hands folded in her lap, lips firmly pressed together. She glanced at me as I walked in, then returned to staring at her daughter, almost like she was expecting something to happen.

I sat down and put my arm around Lily. Her eyes were swollen, there were clusters of little white spots around her mouth and flaky patches of skin along her hairline. She always struggled with being Mudbound – years ago she'd told me that being stuck in the mud always reminded her just how stagnant her life was – but I'd never seen her this unhappy.

'If I have to work another File, I'm going to go mad.'

Ruby sniffed loudly. Why didn't she just go upstairs, or make a drink or do anything rather than just sit there, radiating disapproval? I patted Lily's knee.

'I'm sorry, Lils.' It was a useless thing to say, but there was nothing that I hadn't already said to her many, many times before.

'It's torture, making people spend their days looking at bits of dead bodies. What's the point?'

She knew the point. We all did. What was left of society had a responsibility to try and identify those who died during the Wars, to try and put a name to the pictures and, wherever possible, match unclaimed assets to descendants. Back in the day, panic about the risk of contamination meant that bodies were burned almost immediately. They'd been photographed, but there was no DNA testing, nothing like that. Flesh which had reached a certain state of decomposition was sometimes impossible to identify, but if the person working a File puzzled away at the pictures long enough, it was often possible to find enough to make an identification and match the body to the database. Another victim named. Another File closed.

Working the Files was a horrible job, one that I had done for a while before I took over Underhill's ordering, and even now, years later, my dreams were haunted by images of chemically disfigured faces, and swollen, blackened limbs. But so often there was no choice for people but to work the Files. The thing was, if you didn't work in one of the factories the opportunities to earn money were limited, but for people who couldn't otherwise find work, there were always the Files. How else were people like us supposed to make money? A few months ago, it had been announced that the billionth File had been closed. So many years of working the Files, and still only a quarter of the dead identified.

Lily grabbed my hand, squeezing hard as her tears started falling.

'Pull yourself together,' said Ruby, looking faintly disgusted by the sight of her daughter's crumpled face. She really was a deeply unpleasant woman – I didn't know anyone else who got so much pleasure out of being so thoroughly horrible. However, the sound of her mother's voice at least had the effect of making Lily sit up and wipe her face, her despair hardening into anger.

'Okay, mother. I'll spend my whole life cataloguing the dead shall I, until finally I'll just be dead too. What is the point of that?

Maybe I should just skip the life part and go straight to the death part. What would you do then, mother? Without me here to look after you? What would you do?'

Ruby stared back impassively, only a slight curl of her lip betraying her thoughts.

A shadow passed in front of the window – it was Molly, making her way down the steps, still limping from a nasty fall in the street a few days earlier. Lily took a deep breath and managed a smile in my direction before going to open the door. Molly limped into the room and lowered herself onto a chair.

'Ash told me you were here,' she said, looking at me. She glanced at Ruby and Lily but didn't say anything else and there was an awkward silence until I asked, 'Do you want to go next door, to my house?'

Molly cleared her throat, looking uncomfortable. 'I suppose everyone's going to find out soon enough. Someone's notified Jem.'

Outside, water was dripping from the roof and pinging off something metal and I counted the drops while I tried to take in what she'd said. Lily looked horrified and a thin smile played along Ruby's lips.

Lily was the first to break the silence. 'Who notified her?'

'I don't know,' Molly said. 'The authority Waved me, as a *courtesy* they said. They're sending an investigator because they've been notified about potential religious activity in Underhill. I suppose there was a chance that they might not have done anything about it, but we'd already been flagged because of the undeclared people that showed up on the census.'

'Are you going to get into trouble?' Lily's voice wobbled, on the verge of tears again.

'For not registering the girl when she arrived? Probably.'

'There's Lorne and Stone as well,' I said.

'Yes,' said Molly. 'I'll get their application in later today. I'll probably just get a slap on the wrist for that, though – it's obviously the notification about religion that they're really concerned about.'

I couldn't believe it. Despite everything I thought about Jem and the nonsense that she was spreading, I was adamant that we shouldn't notify her and I'd been completely certain that we all felt the same. Far better to have one stupid young woman running around saying things that shouldn't be said, than risk turning the authority's attention towards Underhill. I mean, only the other day there had been news of the forceable relocation of yet another community. It was somewhere up north and apparently, it wasn't even the Laws on religion that they'd flouted, it was something much less serious.

According to the rumours we'd heard, they had discovered a stash of guns and a load of ammunition, but rather than handing everything in, they decided to teach themselves to use them. Someone had notified them and the authority sent an observation drone which saw people firing guns in a field. I have to say, it was pretty stupid to have done it in the first place, it wasn't exactly a difficult Law to stick to. But nevertheless, one misstep, their community was disbanded and everyone shipped off to a city to work in the factories.

Maybe there was more to the story, I couldn't be sure, but it could so easily be us. I mean, I had more reason than most to want the girl gone, but there was no way I would have notified her. Now that it had actually happened, what would it mean for Underhill? What about the so-called Threads? What would happen to them? Fuck, what about Willow? What about Ed?

'What did you say when they told you?' I asked.

'I was surprised, obviously,' Molly said, 'since I had no idea that anyone had notified her. Look, we've got no choice. What's done is done and we'll just have to deal with it.'

I nodded – it was like everything else, when the authority made decisions, nothing we said or did made any difference. I thought about my visits to the graveyard. What if I hadn't kept them as secret as I'd hoped? Surely whoever came would have better things to do than worry about my conversations with the Elder Mother.

I realised Molly was talking to me. 'I need your help, Kat,' she was saying.

'Of course, anything...'

'I need to get the records up to date. You know how far behind I got during Whiteout.'

I nodded, but before I could say anything, Lily said, 'Why would anyone do this? Why would someone deliberately involve the authority and risk everything we have?'

'Maybe someone thought it was time the Laws were enforced. Maybe someone thought the girl needed to be silenced.'

They were the only words Ruby had spoken since Molly had arrived and little flecks of saliva flew from her mouth, landing on the table and glistening in the sunlight. Before I realised what was happening, Lily was already out of her chair and standing over her mother.

'It was you, wasn't it?'

Molly turned to Ruby, shock written across her face. The old woman reached up and patted the top of her hair, pushing a stray strand back into place. She pulled up the corners of her lips, although the effect was more of a snarl than a smile.

'So what if it was me? Someone should have done it weeks ago.'

'What have you done?' Lily wailed.

Every time I remembered what happened next, it was like it had happened in slow motion. Lily clenched her hands so hard that it looked like her knuckles might burst through her skin, then, just for a moment, she relaxed them, so they hung loosely by her sides, before her fingers straightened. Even when she pulled back her arm, her elbow forming a perfect right-angle, finger-tips twitching, Ruby remained cloaked in self-righteousness, refusing to acknowledge what was about to happen. Lily put all her strength behind the slap and her hand connected low on her mother's cheek. The impact was jarring, the sound deadened by the contact with Ruby's jawbone.

Lily sat back down and touched her fingers to her own cheek, stroking the place where her mother's face was already turning red. Ruby hadn't moved but, as the outline of Lily's hand on her face deepened in colour, the old lady tilted her head just a fraction.

'You've always been a wicked child,' she said, spittle clogging the corners of her mouth.

Molly reached across to touch Ruby's arm, but Ruby shrugged her off. I looked at Lily. We'd been friends since the day I'd arrived in Underhill, and of the two of us it was *me* that had the temper, *me* that acted without thinking, then regretted it later. Lily had always been the one that I could rely on to calm me down, to point out when I was being unreasonable. I could count on the fingers of one hand the number of times that I'd seen Lily lose her temper and certainly never as spectacularly as this.

I was used to her complaints about Ruby, of course, about how selfish her mother was, how she constantly criticised Lily, even as she relied on her and Cooper for everything, as she had for years. As far as Ruby was concerned, nothing Lily did was ever good enough. But now my friend was wearing an expression that I had never seen before – she looked empty, drained, finished, as if she had put everything of herself into the slap.

'Lils…' I said, but I didn't know what I wanted to say.

Ignoring the other two, she looked at me and said, 'I'm done with this. Starting now, there's going to be some changes around here. I'm going to start putting myself first. I'm going to do whatever I need to do to never work any more Files. And, I am not going to let that woman...' she nodded towards her mother, '...bully me ever again.'

15

Eileen

Truths 8:1-4

…and so it was that jealousy of the Prophet, of the strength of her binding to God, and of her wisdom and beauty took hold among the faithless, and their jealousy grew like a weed, until one of them, a wizened and evil old woman, scarlet by name and sinful by nature, betrayed the Prophet to those that would hunt her down and punish her for the Messages which she had brought to the people of Underhill.

When God's Threads learned what had been done, they were fearful that the Prophet would be taken from them and they would not know how to continue to bind themselves to God without her.

However, the Prophet herself was fearless.

'We are on the path to Cleansing and Renewal. The signs are clear, and the binding cannot be unpicked. I am but one of the Threads, God's rope will remain strong without me.'

But the people did not want to be without their Prophet and so they begged her to take action to remain safe. When she did nothing, they pleaded with her to speak to God and seek Its guidance. When the Prophet saw how fearful the Threads were, she went alone to the Binding Area and lay herself down on the mud, and for all of one day and all of one night she waited for God to tell her what she must do. When dawn came on the second day, the Prophet was tired and thirsty, and a great pain began inside her head and she lifted her eyes to the horizon, and it was then that she saw a great presence on the hill top, its arms stretched wide to embrace the people of Underhill and in that moment the Prophet understood what God wished her to do.

It's tempting to claim that it was me that suggested that Jem go and hide inside a wind turbine, but I am nothing if not truthful, so it wouldn't be right to say that it was my idea. It was God that told Jem what to do.

Hiding in a turbine was a big secret and most of the Threads didn't know where Jem was going, but before she left, she called us all together at Laurel's house. It wasn't the most relaxing of meetings; Jem was pacing around the room, but because most of us were sitting on the floor, we kept getting in her way. Petra made a ridiculous fuss when Jem stepped on her hand, and after that she stopped wandering around. Jem was obviously on edge, which I guess is hardly surprising given that she knew that she was about to be shut away inside a metal tube, but her mood infected everyone else and even the babies seemed to be competing to see who could cry the loudest. Laurel said that Mila was teething, but that's no excuse. I mean, we all have teeth.

In light of the latest Message, everyone talked a bit about the preparations they were making for Cleansing and Renewal. Judging by the suggestions, there was a long way to go before some of the Threads would be able to be sure of their place in the *cradle of the earth.*

In between all her usual coughing and spluttering, plus whining on about her sore hand, Petra kept going on about stockpiling supplies, which was obviously stupid, because after Cleansing, God will lift up the Threads and provide everything we need. No-one had to tell Petra how ridiculous she was being though, because when she was talking, Tish started tutting really loudly and rolling her eyes so they practically disappeared inside her head. Petra got the message pretty quickly and spent the rest of the meeting sitting in silence, apart from the constant sniffing. Her sullen look made my palms itch.

Willow had come along to the meeting as well, but I don't know why she bothered, because she didn't say a word. To be honest, she looked terrible, and I wondered if she'd been sneaking out at night to meet George again. I had done my best to keep an eye on her, doing my duty as a considerate neighbour; I had even gone over to the old barn a few times, to see what they were up to, although I suspected Willow was trying to avoid me, because I never saw them there.

Fred started talking about the delivery drone. He had his arm wrapped around Lia's back with his hand resting on her stomach and every time he wanted to emphasis his point, he patted it. It must have been annoying, but Lia just stared into space, smiling to herself, as if she was listening to something the rest of us couldn't hear. Anyway, in between all the stomach tapping, Fred worked himself up into quite a state about the drone – he thought we should stop using it right away, because it was part of everything that would be swept away by God at the Cleansing. He said we should start getting used to life without orders but I didn't agree – I mean, it's one thing to know that God is going to provide for us, but it's completely another to voluntarily stop ordering things before It starts doing that.

'We need to prepare ourselves,' Fred kept saying, even though it was clear that no-one was remotely interested in anything he had to say. 'After Cleansing and Renewal, there will be no deliveries.'

'That's because there won't be anyone out there to order from,' said Leroy, without looking up from the thread he was unpicking from the sleeve of his jumper. I smiled at him; it was such a relief to know that the baby would have two intelligent parents.

'It feels a bit...strange.' Lia's voice was quiet. 'I mean, I know we don't often see outsiders, but at least we know they're there. What'll it be like when there's no-one else out there? When it's just us? No authority or anything. What if something goes wrong?'

'Nothing will go wrong,' said Fred, drumming away on her stomach. 'God will lift up the Threads, keep us strong. Just like It sent us our miracle.' I was pretty certain that if their miracle had developed ears, it would be desperate for Fred to stop banging on Lia's stomach and give it some peace and quiet.

'Still, it will be a very big world for not many people,' Lia said, and I saw her shiver.

Jem straightened up in her chair – she'd clearly heard enough.

'More babies will come,' she said, in that tone of voice that ended all discussion. 'Underhill is the cradle. The Threads are the carpenters.'

There was silence while everyone absorbed this new piece of wisdom, then Lorne said, 'Should we be trying to get more people to come to Underhill before Cleansing?'

It was always such an effort to understand her, what with her Uplander accent and all, deliberately garbling her words in an effort to sound exotic. 'I thought about going to find my people, see if anyone else wants to come here.'

I looked at Jem to find out how to react to this suggestion. She thought about it for a bit, then said, 'More people in Underhill at Cleansing means more genetic diversity after Renewal, which is good. But they have to be the *right* people. They have to be ready to bind with the Threads, to be bound to God. *Are* your people the right people, Lorne?'

Lorne looked uncertain. 'Maybe.'

'The most important thing is to keep our binding tight. At

Cleansing, all the loose, frayed, split, broken and snapped threads of humanity will be swept up and thrown away and all that will remain will be the one, true, strong, bound rope of Threads.'

That was our cue.

'The Threads are Bound. The Threads are Bound,' we chanted over and over, our voices steadily growing louder. 'The Threads are Bound. The Threads are Bound.' I ran my finger back and forth along the red thread around my neck. 'The Threads are Bound. The Threads are Bound.' The words filled me up until there was nothing else except the feeling of God pulling steadily on the rope, lifting me up. The roots of my hair stretched and tugged, and I started rising up onto the balls of my feet. All around me, the Threads were standing as if something was about to happen, but then Willow suddenly rushed out of the room. Ed followed her and after that no-one seemed to be in the mood to hear more about the preparations that we were supposed to be making.

So, it was only by accident that I found out about the plan to hide Jem in one of the turbines. I'd gone over to Leroy's. Baby planning was going well. I'd done several lists, one with the names I'd thought of, another with some of the positions that we might assume during the conception, things like that. I'd already worked out the genetically probable hair, skin and eye colour of the baby, but I wasn't sure I knew enough about Leroy to make assumptions about the child's temperament and it had occurred to me that it might be helpful to find out a bit more about Leroy's habits, his likes and dislikes, which my mother had always said were important when you were getting to know someone. One final visit, and I would have all the necessary information to make the relevant projections, after which I would be ready to share them with Leroy.

His window was open, which was fortunate because it meant that from my position between two bushes I could hear everything that he and Ed were saying about hiding Jem and how Hinton would be the best turbine because he wasn't working. That was news to me. From the village, we could see the very top of Lucy's blades as they turned, and I always assumed that over the brow of the hill Hinton and Faraday were also turning, just like she was. One of my earliest memories was going up Front Hill with my parents for the turbine festival. From my position on Dad's shoulders, I felt like the tallest person in the world and he let me stay there the whole time, even while we made the offerings to Faraday, Hinton and Lucy. He only lifted me down when it was time to sit on the grass and eat the food.

They were talking about how they would shut Jem inside Hinton in the morning, and I knew she would want me to be there, so as soon as there was enough light, I set out along the path up Front Hill. It was hard work wading through all the mud and then the others didn't arrive for hours, so I was really sleepy by the time I finally saw them coming. I got to my feet and waved at them, but nobody waved back.

When they reached Hinton, Leroy said, 'What are you doing here?'

It occurred to me that perhaps he was hoping I'd gone up there to see him, so keeping my voice gentle I said, 'I came to make sure Jem was okay.' Leroy looked disappointed and I smiled at him kindly – maybe we would have time to talk after Jem had been locked in.

Ed's boots clicked on the metal steps when he went up to unlock the door with a big bunch of keys. The rest of us waited at the bottom while he selected the key for Hinton's door and fitted it into the lock. I have always appreciated a sturdy lock and I wondered if there might be a spare one lying around that I could have. I would ask Leroy later on, after the chat about our baby.

Ed turned the handle, and the door swung open revealing a

black space. He looked down at us. 'You coming up?'

For a moment, Jem's foot hovered over the lowest step, and I wondered if she was trying to delay the moment when she would be locked inside. But then she rushed up and stood beside Ed on the platform. I looked at Leroy and he nodded at me to go next. Not only a gentleman, but a person of few words, just like me.

I walked up the steps, focusing on swinging my hips from side to side, which I had heard was appealing, sexually speaking. I was concentrating so hard on doing that that I nearly tripped on the top step, but when I was safely on the platform, I turned back to see what effect my efforts had had on Leroy. Unfortunately, he had his back to me and was looking across the hill towards Lucy.

'Her pitch is wrong again. I'll go and take a look,' he called to Ed and marched off without waiting for a reply. I considered going after him – perhaps he had made up a problem, so we could have some time together – but then Ed said to Jem, 'I hope you don't mind the dark,' and I remembered that my place was with her. I reached for her hand and squashed her fingers together, comfortingly.

'I've put some blankets in there for you, but it'll be very dark,' Ed said.

'God lights the way,' Jem murmured, peering through the doorway. I looked in as well. Inside was a metal platform and on the opposite side from the door Ed had laid out the blankets. It looked quite cosy, all things considering.

Leroy shouted something across from the bottom of Lucy. I couldn't make out what he was saying but Ed must have understood because he said, 'I'd better go and help him. I'll come back in a bit, check there's nothing else you need.'

He went down the steps and jogged across to Leroy, where they stood together, pointing up at Lucy's blades.

'You don't need to stay.' The sound of Jem's voice bouncing off the inside of Hinton's curved walls made me jump.

'It's okay. I'll settle you in,' I said, stepping through the doorway. The long column stretched far above my head. It was a sort of off-white colour, like dirty snow, and there was a narrow metal staircase reaching to the top. Thick black cables hung down the walls and there were metal struts at regular intervals all the way up. Other than that, it was empty. I went over to the blankets that Ed had laid out, picked them up and shook them, then put them back down. There was a big container of water, which I moved to the side a little, and a smaller one with some food inside, which I lifted over to the other side of the water. A bit further away was a bucket, but I didn't touch that.

'All sorted,' I said, brightly. 'Is there anything else that you'd like me to do?'

Jem sat on the blankets, crossing her legs and leaning against the wall.

'Shut the door, will you? Let's see what it's like,' she said.

The door was so heavy that I had to use both hands to close it, and once it was shut, the darkness was immediate and absolute. I've always hated the dark, unless I'm outside of course, and I had to force myself to breath normally. I put both my hands flat against Hinton's wall and slid down slowly until I was sitting on the platform. Thankfully, there was a tiny whistling noise after each of Jem's breaths, and I calmed myself by counting them. Nothing could hurt me while I was with her and I counted thirty-one breaths before she spoke.

'If someone had told me a year ago that God would send me to a place where I'd be shut inside a wind turbine, on a hill, in the middle of nowhere...' Her laughter bounced around the walls. 'Well, I'd have said they were mad.'

'Where did you live before you came here?' She had no idea just how often I'd wondered about this. I shifted along the floor a little bit, towards where she was sitting.

'Where we come from isn't important, Eileen. God is leading us away from what is behind us.'

I stifled a sigh, or at least I hoped I did, and screwed up my eyes, but the blackness inside the turbine was total, I couldn't even see the edges of the door. I ignored the urge to feel for it, push it open, let the daylight in. Perhaps this was what death was like – a black space, filled with silence.

'Will you tell me something about your life from before?' I asked, trying to keep my voice calm.

'Why is it important to you?'

I almost told her then about the Book of Jem. I almost told her about how I was writing a prophet book, just like they did in the past. I almost told her how all the things that she said, and all the things that she did, were written down in one of my grand-mother's notebooks, the special one that was dark green with big white dots and a thin pink ribbon that you could use to mark the page you were on, and how there were different sections with names like Arrivals and Stories and Truths. I almost told her how completely happy I had been, since she had arrived in Underhill and I had started to write the Book of Jem.

Looking back, perhaps if I had told her that it was the first time that I was doing something that really mattered to me, then everything might have ended differently. So many times, I have asked myself how things might have changed if I had taken that opportunity to tell her that when I went to bed each night, I no longer hoped I wouldn't wake up. Perhaps I should have tried harder to find a way to tell her that I was finally happy that there would be a next day, and a day after that, and a day after that. I loved being one of God's Threads, it gave me an itchy, tickly feeling deep inside every time I remembered that I was one of the people who had been chosen to start everything over again. My life had a purpose. I had a purpose. And it was all because of her. I so nearly said all of that to her right there, in the darkness inside Hinton.

But I didn't.

I wish now that I had.

But in the end when she asked me why I wanted to know about her life before she came to us, all I said was, 'I just want to know.'

She didn't say anything, and I opened my eyes as wide as I could, trying to look through the darkness. For a moment, I was sure I could see a woman lying on her side on the blankets, a hand stretched out towards me. Through her smile, her mouth was forming my name, but she didn't talk and although I tried so hard, I couldn't get the one word that I wanted to say out of my mouth. It was too big a word, too important, and it swelled behind my teeth and wrapped itself around my tongue. *Mum*. In the end I said nothing and when I blinked there was just blackness again. I carried on slowly edging around the wall towards Jem.

Suddenly, she spoke. 'I'm no-one special. If it wasn't for God, I'd be working in a factory.'

'You worked in a factory?' I said, but she didn't reply.

I thought of something else to ask. 'Won't your parents be missing you?'

'They're dead.'

I waited for more, but she was silent. That didn't matter, though. After all, I wasn't writing the Book of Parents of Jem.

I said, 'Like me, then? Dead parents.'

She coughed, and I realised that I wasn't very far away from her now – I had come most of the way around the wall.

'No, Eileen, not like you. When your parents died, you had people to look after you, to make sure you were ok.'

I wanted to explain, to tell Jem how it was only Kat that had looked after me and that she hardly counted because everyone knew what sort of woman she was. She had even tried to turn her own husband against me, although of course he had been too clever to fall for her conniving ways. But I didn't get a chance because Jem was saying, 'There was no-one there for me. I was on my own. I was on my own for a long time, until now.'

I was so happy to be here for her and my smile was huge, then she added, 'Until God found me,' and I realised she wasn't talking about me after all.

I carried on around the final stretch of the wall towards her, trying to think of something else to ask.

'Why do you think God chose you?'

There was another silence, and I counted her whistling breaths. She really was very noisy when she breathed. She didn't say anything for so long that I wondered if she had fallen asleep, but finally she said, 'It's something I ask myself every day. Why me? All I can think is that perhaps it's *because* I was no-one. Perhaps God found someone empty to fill with its Messages. Perhaps what made me special was simply that I was not special.'

That was going too far. I mean, she was the most beautiful, the most kind, the cleverest person I'd ever met, and, even more than that, she had unstuck my words, but before I had a chance to say anything, she was off again. Having finally managed to get her talking, I began to wonder if she would ever stop.

'Perhaps the real question is why I was so accepting of what God wanted to say to me. But even when I was a young child, even as I was learning all the bad things about religion, I always wondered about the other side of the story. Why weren't we taught about that? I mean, nothing is all bad is it? There's always another point of view. What was God's point of view? I always wanted to know that. Maybe I was an open door, and all God had to do was to walk through.'

I finally felt her breath rolling towards me and at the same time my hand touched the edge of the blanket that she was sitting on. I felt around until the tips of my fingers touched her hand. I ran my tongue over my lips and leaned close.

The light flooded down on us, so sudden and bright that I had to screw my eyes shut. This was it. God was binding me together with Jem and I was so ready for it.

Then Ed's voice boomed into the turbine.

'Time to leave, Eileen.'

The daylight pouring through the door was blinding and I had to make tiny cracks in my eyes to look at Jem.

'Shall I stay? Keep you company?' I asked, but in the doorway Ed shook his head and said, 'No-one should be missing from Underhill. We need to keep everything as normal as possible. You know the story we've agreed. A stranger passed through, she's left, it's just a wasted trip for whoever's coming from the authority.'

I stepped out onto the platform and Ed poked his head back inside.

'You're going to be ok in the dark?' he asked Jem. 'Molly has all the torches but we can't ask her for one, else she might guess where you are.'

Jem smiled at us. 'You have provided the shelter. God will provide the light.' She looked so beautiful – at that moment her binding with God must have been very strong.

'I'll come and check on you when I can,' he said.

Jem settled herself on the blankets.

'The Threads are bound,' she said.

'The Threads are bound,' I replied.

Ed swung the door over. 'The Threads are bound,' he said, then pushed it shut and locked it. Black rubber sealed the door tightly against the frame. Because I was turning away, I almost didn't see the light that suddenly flared around the edge of the door. I turned back, and the light was so brilliant that it looked like we had locked the sun inside with Jem. I knew then beyond any doubt that God was with her.

'D...d...did you see that?' I said, but Ed was busy watching Leroy who was dangling on a rope halfway down Lucy. When I looked again the light had gone, leaving only a locked door between Jem and whoever was coming to find her.

16

Kat

The man came from the north, his vehicle bumping down the hill, skirting round the worst of the mud patches. I'd arrived in something similar myself, and I could still remember how sick I'd felt as it bounced over the rutted ground. The journey seemed to go on for ever. Dandy had once told me that before the Wars, when there were roads joining every community to every other community, everyone had their own vehicle. I couldn't imagine where they all needed to travel to.

Only after I'd watched it roll past the purification tanks did I go down the steps and into my house. Molly had spent days cautioning us all against showing our anger, or frustration, or whatever other emotion we might want to express to the investigator.

'It's just a box-ticking exercise,' she'd said, sitting at our table a few nights earlier. 'Face-to-face interviews are just a formality after a notification. It doesn't mean the authority will actually do anything.'

I could tell how much effort she was putting into trying to sound unconcerned, and I understood why: the calmer we all appeared, the less suspicious we would seem. That's what we were hoping, anyway.

Willow, who had actually been at home for once, leaned over and whispered something to Ash, but when I frowned at her she straightened up in her chair, her face falling into the sullen look that was fast becoming her usual expression. Had teenagers always been so difficult, or was it something peculiar to the world we lived in nowadays? There were far fewer kids for them to mix with than back in the old days of course, and often I wondered if that might have something to do with it.

With a glare at Willow, I turned my attention back to Molly.

'There's no sign of Jem,' she was saying. 'If anyone knows where she's gone, they're not telling me.'

I glanced at Ed, sure he knew more than he was letting on, but he was fiddling with a sliver of wood, staring at it intently.

'So, I'll be telling them the truth,' Molly said. 'Which is that Jem came to Underhill, we let her stay during Whiteout, and now she's gone.'

'And what about the Messages?' Willow asked.

My heart sunk. Of course she would choose now to be in one of her difficult moods.

'What do you mean?' Molly said.

'What about everything Jem's said? About Cleansing…'

'Enough, Willow,' I said. 'Jem has gone.' My voice was shrill – since when had winding me up become my daughter's primary objective in life?

'But Mum, you don't understand. The Messages…'

'Willow. *Stop*. Please, just *stop*. Jem's gone, so will you just stop going on about it.'

Willow looked at Ed, presumably hoping for support, but he continued scrutinising the wood, paring it into smaller and smaller pieces with his thumbnail. Willow pushed back her chair and stormed out of the room.

'I'll talk to her later,' I said to Molly. 'She knows we don't want to give the authority anything to be concerned about.'

In the end, Ed said he'd speak to her. They spent a long time in the kitchen with the door shut and I resisted the temptation to stand outside and listen. As soon as they had finished, Willow rushed out of the house.

'She'll be ok,' was all Ed would say, and I had to content myself with that.

Molly had suggested that everyone stay inside when the investigator arrived – the fewer people he saw, the less chance someone would say something they shouldn't. We knew he'd interview Ruby, of course, but other than her we didn't know who else he might want to speak to. It would probably depend on how much he believed of what Ruby said, which in turn would depend on how well Lily delivered the story that we'd agreed on. I'd been helping her practice. *My mother's not in a good way*, she said, over and over, while trying to look suitably sad. *Sometimes she gets confused* – she'd accompanied that one with a little shake of the head, until I told her it looked too staged. My personal favourite was, *if you're lucky, she might have a lucid few minutes*. Maybe it was wrong of us to pretend that the old woman's faculties were failing, that she was incapable of rational thought, but I didn't feel guilty, not when I thought about how she'd treated Lily, not to mention that it was Ruby's fault the authority had turned its attention towards Underhill in the first place.

We all knew what to say if we were asked about Jem, or Ruby, but once the investigator actually arrived and the morning wore on, I started feeling more and more anxious. Had Lily managed to put enough doubt in his mind about Ruby? Who else was he talking to? I'd scratched at my skin until both my arms were bleeding and in the end, I tried to distract myself by going through the admin records on the Wave again, even though I knew they were completely up to date. It was all there in meticulous detail: the animals we relied on; the food we produced; calculations of levies and taxes, and dates of payment; death records; the recent application for Lorne and Stone to become residents. Was that really all our community amounted to? How could it be that our lives, the lives of everyone in Underhill, could be condensed into just a few pages?

Even though I'd been half-expecting it, when there was a knock at the door, my heart lurched. The man on the doorstep was tall, one of the tallest people I'd ever seen, and he was holding a Tab out towards me although I barely glanced at it because the large red trisected circle on his jacket – the authority logo – left no room for doubt as to who he was.

'You'll have been expecting me.'

It wasn't a question, so I didn't give him an answer. Instead, I said, 'Come in,' and led him along the hallway. 'I hope your trip to Underhill isn't a waste of time.' I ushered him into the kitchen. 'It seems a bit over the top just because we provided a young woman with shelter during Whiteout.'

'It's never a waste of time to investigate a possible flouting of the Laws.'

'I suppose not,' I said, waving him towards a chair. I watched him fold his legs awkwardly underneath my table and realised that I didn't know his name – I should have looked at his identification when I had the chance. I smiled but he didn't smile back, just dropped his gaze to the Tab on the table in front of him. Was it really necessary to be so rude? What was wrong with a bit of common courtesy? I sat on my hands to stop myself scratching.

He raised his head. 'Why didn't you notify this Jem person? You do know that everyone has a duty to notify flouters?'

'She was never going to be here for very long and a few mentions of the G word hardly seemed worth troubling the authority about.'

'It's not your place to make that decision, unless you believe yourself to be above the Laws.' He paused. 'Do you?'

'Do I what?'

'Believe yourself to be above the Laws.'

'No, of course not.'

'Did you have any conversations with her?'

'Yes, she stayed in our house for a few nights.'

'And did she talk to you about religion?'

'No.'

'What did you talk to her about?'

'I spent most of my time encouraging her to leave Underhill. We certainly didn't have cosy little chats together.'

I couldn't help my flippant tone. If he really thought that I'd welcomed the girl into our home, then he was an idiot. He made a note on his Tab.

'What's your opinion of religion?'

I thought of the elder tree, patiently waiting for me in the graveyard.

'Religion is evil,' I said. 'I do not and have never believed that religion is anything other than lies made up to control people and persuade them to do terrible things.'

He held my gaze for so long that I began to feel uncomfortable, but I refused to look away. I *believed* what I said. My relationship with the Elder Mother had nothing to do with it. He made another note. I wondered what he could possibly be finding so interesting.

'I understand your partner maintains the community wind turbines?'

'Yes.'

'And he was one of those that encouraged all this talk about God?'

He practically spat the word out.

'Ed is vulnerable,' I said. 'Have a look at his medical records. He's been in treatment on and off for most of his life. Sometimes he looks for answers to things that are unanswerable.'

He bent over the Tab, searching for Ed's records. I had no doubt what his reaction would be, and sure enough, after a minute or so, his eyes widened and his eyebrows practically disappeared into his hairline. Eventually he lifted his head, and said, 'Your partner is Abe Pask's grandson? *The* Abe Pask? The Designer of Death?' To be fair to him, he didn't sound as horrified as I thought he would. Not as horrified as I had been.

'Yes,' I said. 'But Ed is nothing like his grandfather. He works very hard to keep the lights on in Underhill, he's a wonderful father and a great partner, but he carries his problems close to the surface. The girl saw a little of that, I think, and she tried to take advantage of it. As I said, Ed is vulnerable.'

I couldn't stop myself remembering how appalled I'd been, sitting on our staircase listening to him open up to Jem about his grandfather.

'Look, she was a manipulative young woman,' I said, trying to make him understand. 'She said a few things that she shouldn't have and perhaps some people listened for a little longer than they should have. But that's all there was to it.'

'I'll need to speak to Ed.'

'He's up on the hill with the turbines.'

'I'm authorised to interview anyone that may have relevant information. Look, I'll show you.' He picked up the Tab, but before he could find whatever he was looking for, I said, 'Okay, fine.' Frankly, I didn't want to spend another minute with him, but if he was going to go and talk to Ed then I wanted to be there, so I just said, 'I'll take you.'

*

The sky was pale blue, washed with the sort of sharp sunlight that we only see during Mudbound. I stopped to let the man catch his breath and deliberately avoided looking along the track leading to where I'd first seen the Threads standing together like stunned animals. Perhaps that's where Jem was hiding, although it seemed unlikely – it was too exposed.

Well before we reached the turbines, I could see George at the bottom of Hinton shouting up to Leroy who was hanging from ropes near the top. Hinton's blades weren't turning, and neither were Faraday's, which meant that yet again Lucy was the only one working, but I couldn't worry about that now. One thing at a time. Ed was outside the sub-station and as we came over the brow of the hill, he turned and shaded his eyes with his hands, watching us walk towards him. I reached him first and gave him a kiss.

'Ed, this is the investigator. He wants to talk to you.'

Ed smiled, and they shook hands. Then he pointed to their little hut beside the sub-station.

'Let's go in there.'

I started to follow them, but the man said, 'Not you. I'll interview him alone.'

'Why don't you go and sit at the top of Lucy's steps, love?' Ed squeezed my hand. 'They're in the sun at the moment, so it'll be nice and warm.'

I watched them go inside, then I walked over to Hinton. George grunted something that might have been hello, before rushing off, obviously not wanting to hang around and talk to me.

'How's it going?' I shouted up and Leroy lowered himself slowly down on the ropes, until his feet were dangling just above my head.

'I'm just trying a new fix. Best if you stay clear.'

Leaving him to pull himself back up, I walked across to Lucy, feeling like I'd just been dismissed. At the top of the steps I sat down and leaned against the door. Ed was right, it was lovely and warm. The ground around Lucy was rock hard. The mud always dried out on top of the hills first, a thick crust forming before spreading down the hill and by the time it reached the village, the sticky, dirty mud was gone for another year. Judging by how quickly the ground by the turbines was hardening, Dust would be here before we knew it. My eyelids were heavy, and I let them fall shut for a moment, enjoying the feeling of the sun on my face, and slowing my breathing to match the regular swoop of Lucy's arms rotating above my head.

I must have fallen asleep, because the next thing I knew, Ed was shaking my shoulder, and when I opened my eyes, I realised that I must have been there for quite a while, because the sun was behind Lucy and the air had turned chilly. The investigator was standing at the bottom of the steps staring up at me and I scrambled to my feet, embarrassed.

'I've just given Ronan a tour,' Ed said, looking surprisingly relaxed.

Ronan, was it? I certainly hadn't expected them to be on first name terms.

'I've always wondered about these turbine arrays,' the man – Ronan – said. 'It's remarkable how they're still working in such isolated places.'

Ed nodded. 'And I showed him the storage batteries as well and told him about that inter-community electricity project that was proposed a while ago. I mean it was obvious that it was never going to work, wasn't it, love? It's a constant battle just to coax enough power for Underhill, let alone have any spare. The blackout flickers had already started by then, hadn't they?'

He grinned, clearly waiting for me to agree. I nodded, confused. Why on earth was he so happy?

'There's hardly enough electricity for all of us down in the village, let alone any excess to share,' Ed said.

'I have to say though, it's so impressive what you manage to achieve in such a remote place.' Ronan sounded positively friendly. I was always surprised by just how much some people were completely fascinated by anything to do with pre-Wars technology, able to go on and on for hours about nacelles and hydraulics and transformers and who knew what else. And of course, no-one loved it more than Ed although, by the look of it, he seemed to have found a match for his enthusiasm. It sounded like they had spent more time discussing the turbine array than Jem, which was no bad thing.

'I even gave him a look inside a turbine, although I imagine it was a bit of an anti-climax,' said Ed, chuckling. He never chuckled.

'Well,' Ronan said. 'I'm not sure what I expected to see other than cables. But still, it was good to see inside… which one was it? Hinton?'

'Faraday,' Ed said. 'It was Faraday. Hinton's the one that my brother's working on, you wouldn't want to go inside him, his cables are live at the moment.'

He was lying, I was certain he was lying. I knew for a fact that the cables inside the turbines were never live – they weren't even dangerous – they were far too well insulated for that. I squinted up at Leroy, hanging near the top of Hinton. Ronan followed my gaze, frowning and for a moment, he looked like he might be about to say something, but then he turned back to Ed and held out his hand.

'Thanks so much for the tour. Really, it was great.'

*

The scream pulled me out of my sleep so abruptly that for a moment I was too scared to move. Although it was dark in our bedroom, I could hear Ed slamming his hand into the wall over and over. I sat up and reached across to him, but his arm jerked towards me and smacked the side of my head. I gasped, then moved away and said, firmly, 'Ed. Ed. Wake up. Wake up, love.' He fell silent and I waited. It always took him a while to wrestle the demons back into his subconscious.

Eventually, I whispered, 'Was it a bad one?'

He groped for my hand, holding it tightly.

'Blood. So much...' He gasped, and I knew he was seeing it all over again. 'All that pain.'

'You didn't hurt anyone Ed. You've never hurt anyone.'

That wasn't quite true – I rubbed my cheek which was stinging, but he would be even more upset if I told him he'd hit me.

'But *he* hurt people.'

He was talking about his grandfather, of course. Always his grandfather. After Ed first told me about him, I had spent hours reading everything I could find about Abe Pask until I felt stained by the horror of it all. In the pictures he was a thin man, with slicked-back hair and shirt sleeves too short for his arms. Somehow, it made it worse that he looked more like an overgrown schoolboy than a scientific genius, let alone a genocidal maniac.

Try as I might, and occasionally I had tried, I could not imagine being so sick and twisted that I would use my position and talent to design weapons with the sole purpose of killing as many people as possible. And then the hubris, the sheer arrogance of the man, to give such terrible things away to anyone who was fighting in the name of *his* God. Surely he knew? He *must* have known what would happen once the chemicals were out there, once others got their hands on them. He must have. He was too clever not to understand what the consequences would be. But he claimed that he'd done nothing wrong. His God had told him to develop the weapons, and his God had told him who to give them to. Not his fault. Just God's will.

That's why it was the right thing to do when they banned religion. No-one needed to look any further to justify the decision than the monster who, in the name of his God, had infected the entire planet and been one of the principle culprits responsible for four billion deaths.

And then there was his grandson. Ed was completely blameless, but in the darkness of our room, he was sobbing.

'He did what he did in the name of a God,' he said. 'In his mind, his religion justified his actions.'

'You aren't your grandfather, Ed, and you're not responsible for what he did.'

'Maybe I have a chance to try and do something to make up for it, though. I know I can't make up for the past, but maybe I have a chance to do some good in the name of God.'

I'd never wished anyone dead before, but if Jem had been in front of me at that moment, I would have cheerfully put my hands around her neck and suffocated the life out of her, I wanted to make her suffer, like she was making Ed suffer. It had taken so many years of therapy before he had even begun to believe that his grandfather's evil was not his evil. But just a few short weeks of listening to her lies was threatening to undo all the progress that he'd made.

If only Ed could be more like Leroy about it. His brother was sickened by what Abe Pask had done of course, but he accepted, and always had, that he himself carried no blame. Neither of them did. So why couldn't Ed see that the very worst thing that he could do either for himself or for anyone else, was to suddenly start believing that there really was a God and do anything, *anything*, in the name of religion? The evils of the past could not and would not ever be erased by believing the lies that had caused them in the first place.

I propped myself up on a pillow and stroked Ed's damp hair. I had no idea what to do for the best. If only I could talk to my father. Maybe he would have known how to convince Ed that none of this was real. I knew from what I'd read in my father's books that Ed's new-found belief was an illusion he was creating to try and shift the weight of his burdens away from himself, onto Jem and God. I understood that he didn't know he was doing it, that it was subconscious, but the more I tried to explain it to him, to make him understand how he was kidding himself, the more stubbornly determined he was to listen to what Jem was saying. How could rational logic possibly compete with glittering promise of a guilt-free world?

It was too much to hope that the girl had actually left. All the so-called Threads were taking her departure far too calmly for it to be true. I was almost certain that she would reappear and when she did, we'd be right back where we started.

Ed's breathing changed; he was asleep and with luck, the rest of his night would be dreamless. I pulled the covers up to my chin and thought about the investigator. He had only spoken to a couple of others after Ed, so hopefully Molly was right and the whole thing had just been a pointless box-ticking exercise. In any case, he'd refused to tell us what his recommendations would be, just that he would make his report and we'd be told what measures would be taken. Measures. That could mean anything. It could mean everything, if we were all forcibly re-located. Stupid Ruby. Reckless, deluded Threads. And most of all, evil, dangerous Jem.

Molly and I had stood outside her house, trying not to show our relief as we watched Ronan fold his long legs inside the vehicle like an insect retreating into its lair. It was already getting dark, and as it rolled back past the purification tanks, lights had flicked on at the front of the vehicle, two yellow beams picking out the way ahead.

I was still wide awake when a window squeaked open downstairs and then, a few seconds later, after my daughter had squeezed her way through it, there was another squeak as she closed it. I counted the creaks on the stairs, then her bedroom door opened and closed. It had to stop, all this creeping around, going missing for hours at a time. It really wasn't good enough. And that was before I even got started about her pretending to hang onto Jem's every word. Willow wasn't her father, she didn't have Ed's excuse. She was just a teenager looking to cause trouble. A *clever* teenager who knew her mother well enough to seize the perfect opportunity to wind her up.

But teenager or no teenager, enough was enough. She was part of this family, and she had to start behaving like it.

Careful not to disturb Ed, I pulled on some clothes and crept out of our room. I hesitated outside Willow's door, not really sure what I was going to say. I wanted to try to find a way to get through to her, to convince her that she should stick with school, and stop disappearing for hours at a time, make her admit that the whole Jem thing was just a temporary distraction. When it came down to it, I missed my daughter and I think all I was really hoping to achieve as I grasped her door handle was to remind her how much I loved her.

I pushed the door open. She was only wearing a pair of knickers and I must have startled her, because she didn't cover herself up before she spun round to face me. I was completely unprepared for what I saw.

Below swollen breasts, latticed with blue veins, my fifteen-year-old daughter's stomach was swollen with a small but unmistakeable bump.

DUST

17

Eileen

My throat felt naked without the thread, but every time I heaved into the bowl, it cut so deep into my neck that I thought it was going to slice my head off. From where I was slumped on the floor, I could see the red string hanging over the edge of table, the end of it trembling in time with my pulse, as though it was still attached to me.

I studied the contents of my stomach. Most of the food hadn't been properly digested before it came back up and everything solid had come out some time ago, so now I was just vomiting yellow slime, which smelt horrible and tasted even worse. I'd heard Laurel talking to Willow about the beginning of her pregnancy and how sick she had been, but Laurel always exaggerated and besides, she couldn't possibly have felt as ill as I was feeling.

Judging by how much I was sweating, it had to be past eight o'clock, which would mean I'd been sitting there, puking into the bowl, for at least an hour. I hate Dust. Not only is it unbearably hot, but the short nights make it tricky for me to do my watching. Even when there are a few hours of proper darkness, most people have their windows and doors open all night long so the risk of being seen is high. I've perfected the technique of examining the ground as if I've lost something, but they still don't like me being in their gardens. Consequently, I always feel out of the loop.

I took a few deep breaths, gauging the likelihood of doing more vomiting, and was pleasantly surprised to find that the sickness seemed to have passed, at least for the time being. I put the bowl on the floor, manoeuvred myself onto my knees, then stood up slowly, holding onto the back of a chair. At first, I was a bit wobbly and had to swallow hard a couple of times, but I felt better once I'd re-tied the thread nice and tight around my throat.

I tipped the contents of the bowl into the sink and turned on the tap. Nothing. I turned it off, then on again. Still nothing. Nobody had told me there was going to be a water shut-down. There had been a meeting a few days ago to discuss what they called *scheduled drought measures*, but I had been far too busy to go, and in any case, who cares about a little water shortage when we're so close to Cleansing and Renewal?

I did my best to push the vomit down the plughole with the end of a spoon, but the bigger lumps were surprisingly firm, and I couldn't squash them through the little holes. The smell was so bad that for a moment I thought I might be sick again, but I managed to control myself long enough to get out of the kitchen. I couldn't sit around all day: I had places to be, people to see.

*

The heat in the street was awful, and my backpack stuck to my shirt immediately. I hated the way the air danced and shimmered just ahead of me, never letting me catch up with it. It was teasing me, and I hated being teased. I dragged myself along the street, seriously considering adding "Dust" and "Heat" to my List of Enemies, but I forgot all about that when I passed Kat's house and saw her dipping a cup into a large pan of water, tilting her head back as she drank. *She'd* obviously known about the water shut-down. Had they kept it a secret from the Threads? I'd have to talk to Jem about how to deal with such blatant discrimination.

I was sure the path up Front Hill had become steeper since the last time I'd been on it, and I wished I had eaten something before I left, but I hadn't seen Jem for nearly two days and I needed to be with her. I'd feel better when I got there, and perhaps by then I'd feel well enough to eat some of the food I was taking for her.

I stopped for a moment and shifted my backpack from two shoulders to one, trying to cool down a bit. High overhead, there was a glint from one of the Raptors. Following the investigator's visit, Underhill had been put under what Molly said were *observational measures*, although she had sounded no more concerned than as if she was asking for a cup of tea. *Monitor drones. Keeping an eye on us. Confirming our compliance.* She looked delighted to be trotting out the official phrases, which made me wonder if she'd actually asked the authority to send the Raptors, just to try and make things more difficult for us Threads. Another example of discrimination.

I was the only one clever enough to think of calling the observation drones *Raptors*. No-one else would have known what raptors were. Among great-grandfather Nikon's collection of books – the contents of which I could recite by heart, although so far there hadn't been a suitable occasion to do so – was a whole book devoted to them. In the introduction, it said: *Raptors are bird species with exceptional vision allowing them to detect prey during flight. The name raptor derives from the Latin rapere meaning to seize or take by force.*

Come to think of it, I'm probably also the only one who knows what Latin is. Great-grandfather Nikon might have spoken Latin, I suppose, I'm not sure but I think everyone who spoke it died during the Wars. I did try to explain to Jem about Latin and raptors and why it was so clever of me to call the observation drones Raptors, but I think she was bit distracted at the time because when I tried to give her a little test afterwards, she didn't remember what I had said. Not everyone is as able to retain information as easily as me.

Initially, I wasn't certain whether I should mention the Raptors in the Book of Jem. On the one hand, they aren't part of the Threads or the Messages, but on the other, they were only observing Underhill because of Jem. And it seems to me that anything to do with her should be in the Book.

In any case, who am I to decide what is important and what isn't? All I can really do is set down everything that Jem says and everything that happens, and those that come later – my readers – will make up their own minds. I decided that I would mention them but that I wouldn't over-emphasise their importance, so I simply included the following.

Stories 19:1
One day, several Raptors appeared in the skies. They searched for the Prophet ceaselessly: they were all-seeing, they never tired and needed no food. They hovered high above the land, biding their time, waiting to snatch up their prey and steal her from the Threads. But the Raptors' cold, silver eyes could not see inside the sanctuary of Hinton.

Of course, I could have just called them observation drones rather than Raptors, but I was trying to show what it was really like being watched by them. As I've explained before, sometimes telling the truth behind the truth means making sure that the people who read the Book of Jem in the future are able to understand what was really going on. In any case, it would have been a shame not to use such an inspired metaphor.

In reality, the Raptors were only observing Underhill, and didn't seem to be concerned with anything happening on the hills, although it *is* true that they couldn't see inside the turbines – something about the metal, or the electricity – I couldn't quite hear

Leroy and Ed's conversation clearly enough to make it out. For most of the time, we didn't even know the drones were there – they were too high and too quiet – but on really clear days, when the air wasn't filled with dust, you'd sometimes see a brief flash in the sky. That was a Raptor.

I adjusted my backpack and started trudging up the path again. I really was feeling weak after all the vomiting that morning, but I guess that's what food-poisoning does for you. The left-over scrag-end must have gone bad in the heat; it had tasted pretty disgusting when I had eaten it the previous night, although not nearly as bad as when it was coming back up. Just thinking about it made me want to start vomiting again and I began to imagine that I could smell meat cooking, which was clearly impossible since I was halfway up Front Hill. To try and distract myself, I thought about how pleased Jem would be to see me.

After Underhill was placed under observational measures, Jem decided to carry on living in Hinton. Not only was she hidden from the Raptors there, but there was less chance of another notification if she wasn't wandering around Underhill. Because it was important for Jem to spend time with all the Threads, to strengthen their binding, a rota was put in place to help her with various tasks. I was not at all happy about the allocation of certain jobs. For example, although I would have been fine about taking food to her every day, it was not appropriate for such a senior Thread as myself to have to carry her bucket out of Hinton to empty into the hole that Ed had dug some way away. When I raised it with her, all Jem would say is that it was important for all Threads to experience humility as part of their preparations. I could only assume that Jem must have already experienced sufficient humility because she never emptied the bucket herself.

Most of the time, she didn't let anyone stay in Hinton with her, not even me, although Willow slept there the first few nights after she ran away from home. I suppose it was inevitable that people were jealous of my relationship with Jem, given how close we were and how much she relied on me, and I guess I shouldn't have been surprised when Willow tried to come between us. It was pathetic really, the way she used her pregnancy, bleating on about how *mum won't listen to me* and *I can't stand living at home* to try and get sympathy. It didn't work though, Jem saw right through her and after a few days Willow moved into the hut next to the substation with George and that was that.

Jem spent a lot of time shut inside Hinton, alone with God, preparing our path to Cleansing and Renewal, but after she'd been living there for a while, she asked us all to gather together near the turbines because she wanted to tell us something.

Obviously, I wrote about what she said in The Book of Jem.

Stories 4:7-12
A long time before the Prophet first heard the voice of God, three giants came to live on the hills above the village. They were called Lucy and Hinton and Faraday, and they towered above the people of Underhill. They were immensely strong and tickled the clouds with their long thin arms.

They loved the wind more than anything and whenever it blew, they turned their arms, whirling them faster and faster, trying to catch the breezes and the gusts, the squalls and the storms. Through the snow and the rain and the mud and the dust, whenever the wind blew, their arms would whirl, and their happiness could be heard across the hilltop. Only when the wind went away did their arms grow still.

Certain people from the village possessed great wisdom which they used to make warmth and heat from the spinning of the giants' arms. Lucy and her brothers loved the people who tended to them so attentively and even when their arms

*became stiff and weary and it hurt to move them, they still
forced them to turn to make the people happy.*

*One day, after they had been standing on the hills for too
many years to remember, the Prophet came among the
giants, fleeing from those who would harm her. She was
embraced by Hinton who vowed to shelter her and protect
her from anyone that might wish to hurt her.*

*To show her gratitude, the Prophet gathered the Threads
together.*

*'God led me from peril and brought me here to a place of
safety,' she said. 'Hinton protects me from those who would
harm me. The Threads must never forget what he has done.'*

*And ever after, the Threads did remember that Hinton
and Lucy and Faraday were bound together with them, and
that they too were lifted by God, as a reward for the kindness
that they had shown to the Prophet Jem.*

I was covered in dust by the time I finally reached the top of the
path and as I came over the brow of the hill, I saw Willow sitting
outside Hinton. Of course she would be there, hanging around,
hoping to get yet more praise for being pregnant. When I got a
little closer I realised George was there too, pulling weeds out of
the ground at the bottom of the steps. I gritted my teeth in
anticipation of another barrage of self-congratulatory drivel about
how fantastic the pair of them were, just because they had
managed to do sex and conceive a child.

Ever since we had found out that Willow was going to have a
baby, all the Threads except me had been behaving like she was
really important, and George had been strutting around like he
was the king of the turbines or something. Of course, he couldn't
really strut because he was so short, and he looked more like a
chicken: breast out, head bobbing.

When I reached Hinton, I got down on my knees to kiss the bottom step which was one of the recent rules that Jem had announced was *necessary to prevent the rope fraying*, then called up to where she was sitting in the doorway.

'The Threads are Bound.'

George was the first to reply, although I hadn't actually been talking to him.

'The Threads are Bound.'

Just the sound of his voice was enough to make me look around for some sort of implement to silence him. It was only a matter of extreme good luck for him that there hadn't yet been one within my reach whenever I heard his lispy, obsequious voice. He'd become a Thread the day he found out that he was going to be a father, and unfortunately for the rest of us, he seemed determined to be the *most* committed, the *most* dedicated, the *most* nauseatingly perfect Thread. He didn't even have the brain capacity to realise that it wasn't about what you *did*, or at least, it wasn't only that, it was about what you *were*. And what he was was a weak little man-baby, with nothing to say for himself, whose only talent in life appeared to be his ability to produce a single fertile sperm. It seemed highly likely that this would remain his only achievement until the day he died.

In the absence of anything that I could shove in his face to shut him up, I pushed past him and climbed the steps. At the top, I waited for Willow to move so I could sit down next to Jem and when she didn't, I nudged her leg with my boot until she shifted over and made room for me to squeeze myself between her and the doorway.

'Here you are,' I said, handing my bag of food to Jem. When she reached for it, her hand was shaking.

'Another migraine?' I asked.

She nodded, wincing.

'Oh well,' I said. 'It could be worse.' I wasn't exactly sure how, but it was better than saying nothing and at least she hadn't eaten putrid scrag-end.

'It was bad during the night,' she said. 'But Willow brought me some bread and jam earlier.'

Willow smiled, smugly. She was sitting very close to the edge of the steps and I tried to calculate how easy it would be to accidentally push her down them. I did a fake yawn and stretched out my left arm, the one closest to her.

'Ow!' she said in a whiny little-girl voice, holding her cheek, although I'd barely touched her. It really wouldn't take much effort to apply sufficient force to roll her down the steps, so that I could be alone with Jem. I opened my mouth to do another yawn.

'Eileen?' Jem said, stopping me mid-yawn.

I looked at her.

'I need you to go to the Binding Area, to get things ready for the meeting later.'

'But I've only just got here.'

'The ropes need to be checked before everyone arrives.'

'Why can't Willow go?'

'Willow and I have things to talk about. Plus, she shouldn't be walking about too much in this heat. It's not good for her to tire herself out.'

Why didn't anyone care about whether I was tiring myself out? No-one ever bothered to ask how I was feeling.

But then Jem gave me one of those special smiles that she reserves just for me and, leaning close, she said, 'You're the only one I can trust to prepare the Binding Area properly. You're the only one who knows how I like it.'

I bent my head closer, so the edge of her scarf tickled my cheek, and sniffed deeply, letting the smell of her fill me up.

She was right, of course.

*

There was quite a crowd at the Binding Area. The middle of the day was a bad time to hold the meeting: the sun filled the sky, we were all covered in dust, and sweat was pouring off everyone. The light washed the colours away, leaving everything the same shade of bluey-white, hurting my eyes and making me squint. All the Threads had come, and I congratulated myself on having made the Binding Area a little larger.

Lia and Willow stood together in one corner with Fred and George either side of them, and in another corner Laurel and Lorne stood with their babies, who were in some sort of heat-induced stupor. Even among the Threads, people didn't seem to be able to resist making little cliques, so I went and stood next to Leroy – I could make my own clique, thank you very much.

It was one of the meetings where Jem had instructed us Threads to invite non-believers to come and listen. Apparently, it was important to reach out to those who were still unbound, because God had told Jem that an important preparation for Cleansing and Renewal was for us to try and mend the people in Underhill who were frayed or split or otherwise not yet part of God's rope. Since Underhill had been put under observational measures, there had been an increase in the number of people who wanted to listen to what Jem had to say, even if they weren't yet ready to become Threads. It was ironic, really, how the authority had sent someone to threaten us, but all it really did was bind the Threads more tightly and make non-Threads want to know more about us.

Having said that, if it had been up to me, I wouldn't have bothered inviting the unbound. I mean, they were all going to be around after Cleansing and Renewal, everyone in Underhill was, and the fewer Threads there were, the fewer of us would be in charge, telling the others what God wanted them to do. When I tried to explain that to Jem though, she told me that one of my preparations for Cleansing should be to replace pride with compassion. I had no idea what she was talking about.

Despite my doubts about inviting the unbound, I can't deny that some people always stayed afterwards to find out more about God and the Messages. They would queue up to speak to Jem, and sometimes I would help them pass the time by telling them about how I was the first Thread.

Once we'd got through the hand-holding, which was almost bearable because I was standing next to Leroy, Jem climbed onto the wooden platform that Ed had made for her. It was positioned at one end of the Binding Area, so she could look down on every-one, the Threads and the unbound.

'The Threads are Bound,' she called, and when we replied, a few voices from outside the ropes murmured it with us.

'The time for Cleansing is near.' Jem always began in the same way. 'But first let us acknowledge how God gave us a sign of Its commitment to Its Threads.' She tilted her head back, so we all dutifully copied her, squinting up at the sky. I was always surprised by how often the sky wasn't actually blue: in Whiteout it was grey and dim, whereas during Dust it was so bright and pale that it was a sort of yellowy-white that made my eyes sting if I looked at it for too long. We all stared up at the Raptor-free sky while Jem went on and on about how the arrival of the drones signalled both how close we were to Cleansing but also how God was on our side – because they were only watching Underhill and weren't in the skies above Front Hill. I must admit to having the occasional thought that perhaps it was more to do with budgetary constraints at the authority, but since Jem was getting her information directly from God, I had to assume that she had access to the truth.

'We must strengthen our preparations,' she was saying, when I finally looked away from the sky. 'We must show God that we are ready for what is to come. That we are worthy of undergoing Renewal. That we trust God to lift us. We must demonstrate that our binding is so tight that not even a needle can pierce God's rope. Who among the Threads will testify?'

Willow's arm was the first to shoot up and I rolled my eyes, but Jem smiled and beckoned her onto the stage where she gave her a big hug. It was only after Willow had pulled herself away from Jem that I realised I'd bitten the inside of my cheek so hard that I could taste blood. Willow cleared her throat, as if she was going to make some big new announcement.

'George and me are preparing for Cleansing and Renewal by having one of God's babies.'

Right on cue, all the Threads started shouting about how special Willow was, how loved she was, how tightly bound to God she was, how she was one of the *Mothers of the Renewed World*. This had been going on for weeks, and each time was as nauseating as the first. I was doing my best to brace myself for another round of endless, unbearable Willow-worship, when Kat bellowed, from outside the Binding Area, 'It's not *God's* baby, Willow, it's *your* baby.'

Kat wasn't there because she was interested in being bound, she was always just hanging around wherever Willow was.

Willow turned slightly so she didn't have to look at her mother, then continued. 'I am proud to be a Mother of the Renewed world. There can be no greater honour than to have one of God's children. There is no tighter binding to God than to bear the babies that will build the Renewed world.' She sounded so smug that it was all I could do to stop myself grabbing one of the stakes that held up the ropes and ramming it into her stupid, fat belly.

Lia rubbed her own pregnant stomach and gave a little cheer, even though Willow was just repeating word-for-word what Jem had said many times before. I was fully expecting her to whine on with the rest of what Jem always said, about how it was an affirmation of the Messages, that the pregnancies were proof that God was going to save Underhill, blah, blah, blah, but surprisingly Willow didn't say anything else. She was looking at Kat, who was crying, probably wishing she was one of the pregnant ones, although she was far too old for that. It was Ed that I felt sorry for. He had gone to stand near Kat and as I watched, he reached across the rope and tried to take her hand, but she pulled away from him, so for a moment his arm just hung there outside the Binding Area, like it didn't know where it was supposed to be.

I couldn't waste my time thinking about them, though. No. I was excited. Soon it would be me up there on the platform, announcing my pregnancy, although obviously I would be far more restrained about it. Now I was over my food-poisoning, it was time to speak to Leroy. In fact, as soon as we'd finished in the Binding Area, I'd ask him to come for a walk with me. I'd tried to talk to him several times already, but he was always too busy – which wasn't surprising since he kept the turbines going practically single-handedly – but today was the day. I felt in my pocket for my notebook. He was going to be so impressed when he saw all the lists and projections that I'd done. I'd show him the plans and then, after he'd seen everything, we would get down to it. It occurred to me that after all the scrag-end-induced vomiting, I should probably have brushed my teeth, in case he wanted to do some preliminary kissing, but it wasn't my fault that the water had been turned off.

I'd stopped paying attention to what was going on in the Binding Area, and by the time I looked back at the platform, Willow had been replaced by Fred who was rehashing his usual topic about ordering, and how we shouldn't be doing it any more. Everyone was getting restless and Jem had lifted her hand to stop him, but he added, 'I've also stopped working the Files because there's no point since everyone but us will be dead after Renewal.'

This was a new preparation, and Jem nodded her approval, before ushering him off the platform.

'My Threads,' she said, raising her voice to make sure she could be heard. 'My Threads. We must do more. God needs us to do more. We must prove ourselves worthy of what is to come. Who has it within themselves to be bound most tightly to God?'

Apart from Jem, I was the one that was obviously most tightly bound to God, and I was trying hard to remember any preparations that I'd done, when there was a commotion outside the Binding Area. Camman, Amber and their lumbering sons, Dull and Stupid – which weren't their real names, but I could never be bothered to remember them – were trying to climb over the ropes. A while ago they claimed that they didn't have time to become Threads, what with all the livestock that they had to look after, but I happened to know that on more than one occasion recently they had gone up to Hinton to see Jem, so it wasn't a complete surprise to see them at the meeting.

Having pushed their way through the crowd, Camman had actually managed to get one of his legs over the rope. He was astride it but then Leroy gave him a shove and Camman just managed to grab hold of the rope before he swung round so he was upside down. While he rocked gently from side to side, his hair brushing the ground, Amber called across to Jem, 'Our family has heard you. We are ready to become Threads. We have made preparations.'

Jem stepped off the platform and crossed the Binding Area. She held a hand out to Camman, who removed his right hand from the rope and promptly collapsed on to the ground. He rolled over and Jem helped him to his feet. Then she turned and held the rope down so that Amber could step over it, followed by Dull and

Stupid. Jem took Camman and Amber by the hand and led them back to the platform.

They had always been an unpleasantly pale family, and standing next to Jem, it was apparent that they were also unnecessarily tall. The heat clearly didn't suit them because they were all very pink and damp. Farming was an odd choice of profession for people so ill-suited to being outdoors.

Amber cleared her throat and I had a horrible thought that there might be about to be another baby announcement. There had better not be, it was definitely my turn next.

'We are ready to be bound,' Amber said, and Camman and the boys nodded their huge heads, sweat flicking from their bright yellow hair in all directions. 'In preparation for Cleansing and Renewal, we have killed all our animals. God will provide.'

'We cut their throats,' Camman added, 'so they would have a thread of red around their necks and God would bind them to Itself. Then we burned them.'

No wonder I'd thought I could smell meat cooking.

No-one else appeared to be thinking about that, though. All the unbound on the other side of the ropes began shouting and screaming about how we were going to starve to death, but I didn't pay any attention to them because I was watching Jem. She lifted Camman and Amber's hands – huge, dirty farmer's hands bursting with knuckles – to her lips and kissed them, running her mouth back and forth between them like their fingers were made of silk. I shivered.

Then she raised her head.

'Our binding is strengthened by your actions,' she called, ignoring the racket coming from outside the ropes. 'God sees your faith and will reward you. After Renewal you will be among the Threads that bind all other Threads. God will see your faith and It will raise you up.'

This was our cue, and we started chanting: 'The Threads are Bound. The Threads are Bound. The Threads are Bound.'

We called faster and faster, clapping in time with the words. Willow and Lia wrapped their arms over their stomachs, swaying from side to side. Laurel and Lorne jiggled Mila and Stone up and down. Camman, Amber, Dull and Stupid had dropped to their knees on the platform, so Jem could Thread them. Once the red string was tied around their necks, they kissed the ends of Jem's scarf, then stretched their pale arms up towards the sky, sobbing. Someone started stamping their feet and we all joined in. With each stamp we kicked up dust and it swirled around our legs, so we looked like we were floating above the earth.

'The Threads are Bound. The Threads are Bound. The Threads are Bound.'

The clapping got faster, our feet shook the ground, the smell of burning meat drifted across the hillside, and still we chanted on and on, our voices so loud that we drowned out the terrified cries of the people outside the Binding Area.

18

Kat

The smell of burning flesh was everywhere. The heat made it worse and the wind carried flakes of charred meat down from the hills, blowing them in through open windows and depositing them all over the house, like tiny offerings.

I'd never had much to do with Camman and Amber. We relied on them for meat and milk – they had more animals than anyone else – but their house was half-way up Back Hill and they had always kept themselves to themselves. Whenever I went to take their orders they had always given every impression of being devoted to their livestock.

So, how could they have killed their animals? And then burned them. What had they been thinking? Here was the madness of religion at its worst: the belief that the greater their sacrifice, the faster they would be propelled along the path to wherever it was they thought they were headed. Some days it felt like I was the only sane person left in Underhill. It wasn't just Camman and Amber, there was an increasing number of people who were calling themselves Threads. I mean, we'd been extremely fortunate that the authority had only imposed observational measures on Underhill, but even though we'd got off lightly compared to so many other places, the appearance of the drones overhead had still had the effect of driving yet more people into Jem's arms and everywhere I went, there were conversations about the Threads.

I knew what was happening. It was how it had always been. Religion was a disease passed from person to person, each transmission making it a little stronger, a little more immune to reality. While each new convert reinforced the commitment of those who already believed, each new believer became another voice calling for the rest of us to join them. But despite all the different reasons my neighbours had for talking themselves into becoming Threads – and Freedom knows the hours and hours that I'd spent reading Dandy's books had shown me just how many and various those reasons might be – nothing would persuade me to think of them as anything other than gullible, deluded fools.

Ridiculous theories kept circulating, like how their God had intervened to make sure that the drones only observed Underhill and not the hills around it. I mean, obviously God had nothing to do with it – it had far more to do with Ed charming the investigator with all his talk of the turbines and old technology. The anger towards the authority was understandable, but far too many people seemed to be convincing themselves that the drones were somehow evidence of the *start of the end* that Jem was apparently always going on about.

Ash was fascinated by the observation drones. He was the first to call them Raptors – because of their similarity to the birds – and the name caught on quickly. However, whatever we called them, they were still hovering high above our homes, watching us, feeding our discontent, which in turn was pushing people towards Jem.

The drones were causing other issues. I was increasingly concerned for Molly who said she could hear them all the time. She claimed that there was a constant high-pitched whining noise and it was driving her mad. I couldn't hear it and I don't think anyone else could either. The whole point of the observation drones was that they watched us, unseen for the most part, and unheard. But that didn't help Molly.

And as if that wasn't enough, there was Ed's continuing refusal to talk to anyone about what was going on with the turbines, which was going to cause a whole new crisis when the news did eventually get out. Even Lily appeared to be in a world of her own: when she wasn't finding new ways to punish her mother, who barely left the house any more, she seemed to be actively avoiding me. That hurt, but nothing, *nothing*, came close to how upset I was about Willow.

My little girl was having a baby. My baby was going to be a mother. At first, I was appalled. I wanted to kill George, to scratch out his eyes for even daring to look at her. She was fifteen and pregnant. The night I'd found out, I had dragged Ed out of bed, pulled him along to Willow's room, and pushed him through the door. Willow had put on some clothes, hiding the evidence.

'Tell him.'

She clamped her jaw together and I could see myself in the set of her face.

'Tell him.'

'Tell me what?' Ed asked, looking from me to her.

'Tell your father.'

She looked scared then. She was only fifteen, it was too young. Ed was staring at her, but still she said nothing.

'She's pregnant,' I said, and with the words my tears came, hot and desperate. That night I cried for my daughter, and I cried for my damaged husband, and for my son, who came into Willow's room, still half-asleep, looking bewildered as he sat holding his twin's hand, but most of all, I cried for myself. I squeezed my girl close and sobbed, but eventually, I sat up and wiped away the tears. Someone had to be strong.

At first, I tried to convince myself that everything would be okay. George was a good lad, and I wasn't so naïve that I didn't know that people got together younger and quicker than they had in my day. And, in some ways, there was much to celebrate. After all, my daughter was having a baby and not in my wildest dreams had I let myself hope that that might happen for either of our kids. For a few days, I almost believed that I was happy.

But, as Dust arrived and the ground beneath us began to crack open, our family cracked open too. The most difficult thing to deal with was how Willow had convinced herself that her pregnancy was one of the *signs* that the Threads were always going on about.

'Why don't you get it, Mum? Underhill is going to be the cradle of the Renewed world and me and George are having one of God's babies.'

'Listen to yourself, Willow. You're not making any sense.'

'No, *you're* not making any sense.'

It was impossible. On the one hand, being pregnant meant Willow was having to learn a whole new level of responsibility impossibly quickly; but on the other hand, she was still so young, answering back, refusing to talk sensibly about any of it. She was still determined to see me as the enemy and I'd lost count of the number of ways I had tried to get through to her, to make her see how she was being used.

'People like Jem will latch onto anything they can to promote their agenda.'

'It's not an *agenda*. Jem says the Messages are *real*.'

'Sweetheart, of course that's what she says, but you know better than to believe there's about to be some sort of mass cleansing of the world. You've got to stop listening to all this nonsense and start focusing on the baby.'

'I'm a Mother of the Renewed world. God will take care of me *and* the baby.'

It was terrifying to watch Willow playing along with a story that some non-existent being was looking after her, somehow guaranteeing that her and her baby would be okay. I took no comfort at all from knowing that, unlike Ed, Willow almost certainly didn't believe in Jem's God. The problem was that she loved all the attention that she was getting. I mean, what teenager wouldn't want to be told how wonderful they are, how special they are, how they're carrying the future of the whole of humanity? What teenager wouldn't keep doing whatever they needed to do to remain the centre of such adulation? Particularly, it seemed, when she knew how just much it upset me.

When I was really honest with myself, I knew that the whole situation could have been avoided. If I hadn't been so strict with Willow, always moaning at her, telling her off, then perhaps she wouldn't have been so keen to find ways to annoy me. She had only latched onto Jem because she knew how much I would hate it, and now that she was getting all this attention, why on earth would she want it to stop?

On top of that, all she had to do was to trot out the but *Dad's a Thread* line and I'd have nowhere to go. I felt like I was fighting an unwinnable battle, I couldn't give up. I had to keep trying to get through to her, to convince her to do the right thing for herself and her baby, to make sure that the pregnancy went as smoothly as possible and stop her obsessing over Jem and her stupid, deluded, lies.

But then everything got so much worse.

Willow left.

She'd already been spending a lot of her time – far too much time – up at the turbines. It was an open secret that Jem was living inside Hinton, where she was ideally placed to keeping on filling Ed's head with rubbish, making him believe that he was somehow on a path to redemption. Willow had been up there a lot as well, seeing George, and of course I couldn't stop her, but it had never crossed my mind that she would move up there permanently.

One afternoon, a few weeks after we'd found out that Willow was pregnant, I'd come home from sorting the orders. I walked down the steps, automatically glancing through the kitchen window next door, hoping to see Lily waiting for me, mug in hand, ready for a tea and a chat. She wasn't there, and her little herb pots were in the same arrangement that they'd been in for days, for some reason she'd stopped pushing them round the windowsill. She must have found some new superstition to try – no doubt I'd hear about it soon enough.

When I let myself into the house, all was quiet. How often I wished I could go back to before last Whiteout, when the cottage seemed too full of my family. I'd take the noise, the mess and the lack of space any day over the silent, tidy home it was now. I pottered around for a few minutes before I heard Ash, but as soon as I realised he was there I went straight upstairs and stood outside his door. There was no doubt about it, he was crying.

'Ash, sweetheart, what's the matter?'

There was no reply, so I opened the door and looked in. My boy was lying curled up on his bed, covered by the duvet. I crossed the room and pulled it back. He looked terrible, like he'd been under there for ages, sobbing.

'What is it? What's upset you?'

At first, all he would say was, 'she's gone,' and it took me a while to realise why he was so distraught, after all Willow was always banging her way out of the house, disappearing for hours. Eventually though, I understood that this time was different. This time, Willow had no intention of coming home. She had told Ash that she had a responsibility as a Mother of the Renewed World to bind herself as tightly as possible to the Threads. Apparently to do that, she needed to go and be nearer to Jem. She tried to persuade Ash to leave with her and, thank Freedom, he didn't go but that afternoon Willow broke something inside Ash, something that I knew would take a long time to heal.

From that day on, Willow had refused to speak to me. When I went up to the turbines to see her, she would shut herself inside Hinton, or barricade herself in the hut where she and George were sleeping. I took baskets of food and bundles of my clothes because hers would no longer fit over her growing stomach. I'd plead with her, banging on the door until my fists ached.

'Sweetheart, please talk to me. I love you. Please.'

Sometimes she'd look at me through one of the windows in the hut, but she wouldn't speak to me. Ed kept trying to reassure me that she was fine, that everything would be okay, but it wasn't enough. Whenever I knew they were going to be gathering in their meeting place, I'd go there too, desperate to see her, but as soon as she caught sight of me, she'd turn her back on me. My wilful, stubborn daughter had cast me in the role of the enemy and it seemed there was nothing I could do about it.

In my desperation I tried asking some of the Threads to help me persuade Willow to come home. She was just a child, I said, over and over, a child that was pregnant. She needed to be at home with me. She needed to have access to the Wave, to medical advice, to proper food, to a warm bed. I had hoped that Laurel might help, after all, she was a mother, surely she would understand how I was feeling?

'You've got to try and persuade Willow to speak to me,' I said, forcing my hands by my sides, so I didn't tear into my skin with my nails. 'I just want a chance to explain why she needs to be at home.'

Laurel shook her head. 'Willow is where she needs to be,' she said, and I knew then that she wasn't going to help. 'She needs to be with Jem. She is preparing for her role after Cleansing and Renewal. She is carrying God's baby, just like Mila is one of God's babies. God will not let any harm come to Willow, she is a Thread and her binding is tight.'

They all spouted the same rubbish. Why could none of them see how dangerous it was for Willow to be pregnant and stuck up on a hill, rather than at home with me, where I could look after her? The longer it went on, the riskier it would become for her, but the only thing I could do was to keep going on up to the turbines and to their stupid meeting area and try to convince Willow to change her mind.

It was pointless asking Ed to help. I'd gone on about the danger to our daughter, to our grandchild, until I was blue in the face, but he just said the same as everyone else. In any case, he was spending practically every waking hour up at the turbines, trying to work out how much longer we had before they stopped for ever. At least, that's what he said he was doing. He had told me that he hadn't known about the pregnancy, that he was just as shocked as me, and I chose to believe him. At first, I was pleased to see how excited he was about becoming a grandfather, but then it became obvious that he was most thrilled by the fact that Willow's baby was another bloody *sign*. First the turbines, now our grandchild. Even with everything I thought I knew about how religion worked, it was still almost unbelievable to see how successfully Jem persuaded people to believe her lies.

I mean, I could understand her appeal to people like Eileen. She had always had a slippery grip on real life, and most of the time it was difficult to believe that there was very much happening at all behind her blank expression. If anyone paid Eileen even the slightest bit of attention, she'd swing her cow-like gaze onto them, and keep it fixed there, ignoring all other distractions until she got bored, or found something more interesting to focus on.

But most people weren't like Eileen. In fact, many of the so-called Threads were individuals I had always considered intelligent, and as each week passed people who had previously found the whole idea of religion just as repugnant as I did were rushing to tie grubby bits of red string around their necks. And, once they'd crossed that line, it was like they had to constantly prove to themselves that they'd made the right decision, by trying to be the *most* fervent, the *most* committed Thread among the Threads. Had their lives before Jem's arrival really been *so* bad, that these people – most of whom I had known for years – were just waiting for someone, anyone, to come and seduce them with make-believe promises of an impossible future?

When I thought about it afterwards, I suppose it wasn't a surprise that Lily would start to show an interest, although she tried to hide it from me. I'd gone along to one of their meetings because Willow would be there and if nothing else, I could at least see for myself if she was looking well. The Threads had started inviting those of us that they called the *unbound* to the meetings, to *unpick their knots and prepare for binding* as they liked to say, while listening to whatever rubbish the girl was spouting. So, although I had expected to see a few other people standing around on that particular day, I honestly hadn't expected to see Lily.

Inside their meeting area, the Threads were milling about waiting for things to begin. I ducked under the nearest rope and went over to Willow, but as soon as she saw me that stubborn look that I knew so well shuttered her face. I had had to get used to it, the way that she almost seemed to slide away from me, to absent herself whenever I tried to talk to her. I knew from bitter experience that there was nothing to be gained by making a fuss or staying inside the ropes – I'd already been bundled out one too many times, so I ducked back under the barrier, which is when I spotted Lily and went over to her.

'I didn't expect to see you here,' I said and then, when she didn't reply, I looked at her properly and saw she was blushing.

'Lily?'

She shook her head. 'I've just come to listen. That's all.'

'Lils, not you as well?' I wasn't sure I could bear it.

'I'm just listening. There *has* to be something more, Kat. I just want to hear what she thinks it might be.'

No. Not Lily. Not my best friend. Soon there would be nobody left on my side, except the Elder Mother.

'There has to be something more than *what*?' I asked, but then everyone inside the ropes reached for each other's hands and started chanting that stupid chant of theirs. It got louder and louder, their voices invading me, forcing their way inside, until my heart was beating in time with their words. Each time I went to one of their meetings my claustrophobia got worse, but I couldn't not go because I had to see Willow. Their chanting squeezed the breath out of my lungs, and even though I was on an open hillside, I felt trapped, crushed by the weight of their stupid, ignorant belief.

Afterwards, I looked for Lily, hoping to walk back down with her, but she was with a small group of people hovering around Jem, waiting to speak to her. After that Lily avoided me, which took some doing given she lives next door.

*

With the smell of burning meat in my nostrils, I walked down the street to the graveyard. I almost didn't care any more about people finding out about the Elder Mother. After all, with a full-blown religion in full swing on Front Hill, who would care that I went to visit an elder tree?

It was another scorching day. Willow's baby was due at the beginning of Whiteout, but for the moment we were in the middle of Dust, and I was warm and dry, which was a relief because if I'd had to cope with all this stress during Whiteout, I might have just given up altogether and dug myself into the snow. I walked through the graveyard towards the elder tree and it wasn't until I was pushing through the huge stands of nettles – nettles were one of the few things that loved Dust even more than I did – that I saw Lorne. She had trampled down some weeds, and was sitting with her legs crossed, leaning against an unbroken headstone, feeding her son. When she saw me, she smiled and held Stone up to me.

'Can you hold him for a second? My legs have gone numb.'

She straightened her legs, then reached for her son. He was whimpering, and she guided him to her nipple.

'He's not finished yet,' she said, and as if agreeing, Stone started sucking greedily. His eyelids fell shut and he lifted his tiny hand, letting it drop onto the curve of Lorne's breast.

I smiled at her, 'He's growing fast.'

'It's not surprising, given the amount of milk he gets through.' She ran her hand over his head, but his newly grown tufts of hair refused to lie down.

'I haven't seen you here for a while,' I said.

'I often come to see my great-granny.' She nodded at the pieces of Olivia's headstone on the ground next to her. 'But I don't like to come in when you're here. I don't want to disturb you.'

Surprised by her thoughtfulness, I watched Stone feeding, imagining the day when I would be watching my daughter feeding her baby.

'Willow's doing well,' Lorne said, guessing my thoughts.

'Is she?'

'Of course. I mean, she's healthy, isn't she? George seems nice. And she's got you.'

'It's not me she wants. It's Jem.' I spat the name out of my mouth with such venom that I almost expected to see it land on the ground between us.

Lorne pulled a little green hat over Stone's eyes, then she wiped the back of her hand along her forehead. There were sweat patches under her arms.

'Willow is where she needs to be...' she began, but I put my hand up and thankfully she stopped.

'Please,' I said. 'Don't. It doesn't matter how many of you say it, or how often, it won't make it true. What my daughter needs is to be at home with me where I can look after her and make sure she's healthy and happy.'

'It's natural that you'd be concerned about Willow,' Lorne said, frowning, 'and of course I understand that. But what I really can't understand is why you're so angry about the choices that other people make.' She was still frowning, looking at me like I was a puzzle she was trying to solve. I scraped my nails along my arm, digging into myself so hard, I could feel my tendons flex.

'Wouldn't you be angry?' I asked 'I mean my daughter's been kidnapped and...'

'Willow hasn't been kidnapped,' Lorne interrupted before I could wind myself up into a full-blown rant. 'She's *chosen* to be where she is. Nobody is forcing her to do anything.'

'Maybe not physically. But there are other ways of making people do things. If you all want to delude yourselves that a non-existent God is somehow going to make your lives better and solve the world's problems then that's fine. What is *not* fine is when my pregnant daughter gets caught up in it as well.'

'Can't you just be pleased that people are enjoying being part of something bigger than themselves? That goes for Willow too.' She sounded so matter of fact, as if it was my point of view that was the strange one. 'And even if you can't,' she continued, 'I still don't understand why it makes you so angry.'

I took a deep breath. 'Religion is illegal, religion makes vulnerable people do bad things.'

'I know what the Laws say,' she said, then hesitated for a moment. When she spoke, she sounded almost shy. 'I knew other people like you, you know. Up there, where I lived. People with a special connection to trees. I know why you come to the grave-yard.' Whatever reaction she saw in my expression made her smile. 'It's not really all that different, is it?'

I stared at her. She knew about the Elder Mother? Really? And she hadn't told anyone? After a few moments, she looked down at Stone and as I watched her settling him on her lap, I suddenly blurted out, 'I've lost control of things.' I shocked myself with the words even as I said them.

Lorne said nothing, focusing on Stone, putting a thin square of cloth over his face, carefully overlapping it with his hat to keep the sun off him.

'Ed, Willow, they're part of something I don't belong to. I feel like they're becoming strangers.'

'You could try and understand.' Lorne smiled. 'Any one of us would be happy to explain our beliefs to you.'

'It's not that. I mean, I do understand. Some of it anyway. My father was a professor. A Professor of Why, he liked to call himself. He used to tell people he specialised in the *why* of religion. It was actually Religious Social Psychology, but the point is that he talked to me about it all the time, so I understand what's happening a lot better than most. But just because I understand it doesn't mean I have to accept it. My father said that even before the Wars they'd begun to realise that religion was a weapon used to take away people's ability to think for themselves. That's what Jem's doing. She's an infection, she gets inside here.' I tapped the side of my head. 'You've all convinced yourselves that Jem is offering you something real, but she's not.'

I was grateful for the silence that settled between us. There was a streak of blood on my arm and I licked my thumb and rubbed my skin until it disappeared. Eventually I said, 'Why you, Lorne? That is something I don't understand. I mean, you'd been here, what was it, a week when you were *threaded*?' I felt the sneer on my face as I said the word.

She didn't answer straight away. I liked that about Lorne, the way she took time to think before speaking. It was a quality I could have done with myself.

'Before I answer that,' she said at last. 'Can I ask *you* something?' I shrugged, and she said, 'What is religion?'

I rolled my eyes. 'Oh come on. You know that as well as I do.'

She didn't look away, she was obviously expecting an answer, so I allowed myself a roll of the eyes and a loud tut before reciting the first definition I could think of.

'The belief that supernatural beings direct the actions of believers.'

'Exactly,' she said and chuckled, although I didn't see what was funny. 'You know you're quoting straight from the Laws, don't you? And you know that the Laws were made by people that you and I never met who decided that they had the right to tell us what religion was? So, why is that you're prepared to accept their opinion as correct? Do you see what I'm saying, Kat? Why have you decided that the opinion of some people at the authority about religion is more valid than anyone else's opinion?'

'It's not that simple. All those deaths that happened in the Wars were because of what people believed their God was telling them to do.'

'That's not the fault of God, Kat. That's the fault of the people who used God for their own purposes.'

I shook my head, it wasn't that straightforward. There was absolutely no doubt in my mind that banning religion had been the right thing to do.

'Look,' Lorne said. 'I don't let anyone, not even Jem, decide who my God is. Only I have the right to decide that. I don't even know if my God is the same as Jem's God, but what I do know is that everything that was done in the Wars was done without a moment's thought for the planet and the plants and animals that lived on it. When I heard the Messages, they made sense to me. There *should* be a reckoning, not just for what humans did to each other, but for what we did to everything that we once shared the world with. I want the Messages to be true, and I want God to be real and I want my son to be one of those who starts over again and gets it right this time. I'm not being *told* to believe, Kat, I *choose* to believe.'

We sat in silence again, for a long time. A thumping noise drifted across from the purification tanks – whenever the water levels dropped too low, the mechanism inside the tanks became audible. I thought about Willow, but that was hardly surprising because I was always thinking about Willow. The pain of my daughter living up on the hill, away from me, was constant and unrelenting – an open wound to be both protected and picked at. I was exhausted, and so, so worried, desperate to find a way to persuade her to come home, where she would be safe.

The sun had moved round in the time we'd been sitting there, and I shuffled back a little, trying to find some shade, although Lorne seemed unconcerned, tipping her face up to the sky. She made it all sound so simple. She saw God in the goodness of plants and animals, and the evil of humans in the chemicals that clotted the streams and poisoned the earth. But it wasn't that simple. It wasn't.

Eventually Stone began to stir, his little fists punching the cloth over his head.

'I need to get back,' said Lorne. 'But before I go, there's something I'd like to show you.'

I held Stone while she got to her feet, then I followed her to a corner of the graveyard opposite my elder tree. There was a patch in the undergrowth, where someone had ripped out the weeds and cleared away the broken headstones.

'I've been bringing water, but I didn't want to tell anyone until I was sure it was going to survive.' She shifted Stone to her other hip and reached for my hand, linking her fingers with mine. I took a step forward, holding my breath. In the warm soil of the graveyard, barely taller than my knees, was a sapling, and although I couldn't be completely sure, not until I'd compared it with the pictures in my book, I was almost certain that I was looking at an ash tree.

*

My excitement was short-lived. Ash was only vaguely interested that I'd seen a tree which was supposed to have been extinct for decades – one that was so important to me that we had named him after it – and although Ed listened when I told him about the sapling, he said he was too tired to come to the graveyard to see it. In any case, I had work to do that evening. There had been a big drop in orders recently, there was always less ordering during Dust, but there was a significant reduction on previous years. Nevertheless, there were always my regulars and Molly's medicine had nearly run out, so I needed to make sure there would be more on the next drone. I'd just finished when there was a flicker and the Wave broke, but there was enough light from the moon for me to see my way upstairs, where I slid into bed beside Ed.

I wasn't entirely without blame for what happened next. After all, he was pretending to be asleep, but I knew he was awake, he never slept well at the height of Dust, it was too hot. I suppose I was feeling just a little happier than I had for a long time. Willow was looking as well as could be expected and I was still trying my best to believe that she might tire of living up on the hill and come home of her own accord. And, of course, I'd seen the ash tree and as my *Spirits in the Trees* book said: *Ash heals the loneliness of the human spirit*, and there was no doubt that I was sick and tired of feeling lonely.

I rolled across the bed. Ed was on his side facing away from me and I reached over and put my arm round him, feeling the familiar contours of his chest. I hated how distant we'd become and if we couldn't talk ourselves closer, then I would just have to try and find another way back to him. I trailed my fingertips lower, forcing myself to go slowly, teasing him, just as he liked it. Below his stomach, I moved my hand in little circles, barely making any contact, waiting to hear the catch in his breath, waiting for him to turn to me. He shifted slightly, angling his hips further away from me, not yet ready to give up the pretence that he was asleep.

Two could play at that game and I slid my fingers back up his stomach, onto his chest, as if I wasn't even aware of where my hand had been a moment before. I knew he wouldn't be able to wait much longer and I pressed myself against him. Then he shifted once again and because I was thinking about how much I wanted him to turn to me, I wasn't focusing on where my hand was, so when he moved, my arm slipped off his shoulder and my fingers briefly touched the thread around his throat. He jerked away from me so violently that he nearly fell out of the bed.

'Don't touch that.'

He swung his legs onto the floor and sat on the side of the bed for a moment. I reached for him but when he felt my hand on his back, he got up and started pulling on his clothes.

'What is it? Don't you want to…' I was too upset to finish the sentence.

'I'm going up to the turbines.'

'What? Why?'

He came over to the bed and there was enough light for me to see him running the tips of his fingers back and forth along the thread. He hesitated for a moment, then bent over and pressed his lips to my forehead chastely, as if I was a child.

'Get some sleep,' he said, and left.

19

Eileen

It wasn't how I'd imagined it. For a start, I hadn't expected any pain. I mean, my hymen had gone years ago, so it wasn't as if there was any obstruction. Nevertheless, it hurt, and he must have realised, because he said, 'Shall I stop?' or 'Do you want me to stop?', something like that. But I shook my head – if we didn't carry on, impregnation would not occur. After a minute or two, it stopped being painful and was just a bit uncomfortable. My research had suggested positioning myself so that my cervix was tilted upwards. He looked surprised when I reached for an old jumper that was lying on the ground. I folded it up and shoved it under my back to elevate my hips, then we started again.

We stopped once more, when my feet became tangled in his trousers, but after that it all became quite monotonous, and I have to say I did find myself wondering what all the fuss was about, particularly as it was far less pleasurable than when I was by myself, thinking about Jem. It occurred to me that perhaps that's what I was doing wrong. Perhaps I should be thinking about our Prophet.

I shut my eyes – his were closed anyway – and imagined that it was Jem's hands that were either side of me, her legs that were between mine, and rather than Leroy's huffing and puffing, I tried to imagine that I could hear Jem's funny whistling breaths, in and out, and in and out.

For a moment, I almost felt the start of something, but then it was all over. He stopped. The deed was done.

He part-rolled, part-shuffled off me, and lay on his back, pressed against the wall. At least he didn't want to engage in any contact unrelated to conception. I glanced at him out of the corner of my eye, but he'd thoughtfully covered his face with his arm, so we didn't have to look at each other.

I'd never been inside the hut before and when I'd followed him there earlier, I hadn't spent much time looking around. There was the table where I'd laid out my notebooks for Leroy to see – I'd have to remember to take them with me when I left. There were tools all over the floor, and ropes and cables looped over nails on the walls. There were buckets with more tools in them, and open containers of something that looked like grease. Against three of the walls were mattresses lying on planks of wood. One of them had clothes piled on it, which was the only indication that Willow and George had been there. There was no way that I would spend time somewhere so squalid when I was pregnant, I mean who knows what sort of diseases she was picking up. But then, that was Willow all over, too immature to understand the importance of personal hygiene.

There was a window above our mattress, which was wide open, probably to try and get rid of the horrible smell. I sniffed a few times, trying to work out what it was, but decided it was just a sort of general filth-smell.

I was hungry. My food-poisoning had completely gone, and of course I'd be eating for two now.

'Is there any food?'

Leroy shook his head without lifting his arm away from his face.

'What the fuck are you doing?'

Ed was standing just inside the doorway.

'Hi there,' I said, sitting up. Then I remembered that I should stay on my back for a while longer to give the sperm maximum opportunity to reach their destination, so I lay down again.

Leroy stood up but didn't say anything. Ed opened his mouth, then closed it, then opened it again, before he finally managed to think of something to say.

'Would one of you please tell me what the fuck is going on?'

Surely it was obvious? And frankly, if he couldn't think of anything useful to say, he might as well not bother.

'The Threads are Bound, Ed,' I said.

He looked down at me. 'Pull up your trousers, Eileen.'

His face was flushed. Now I came to think about it, he hadn't looked well for a while, maybe he was coming down with something. I hoisted my trousers up, making sure to keep my hips angled towards the ceiling.

Meanwhile, Leroy had sat down at the table and was tapping his fingers on one of my notebooks. He'd better not be thinking about trying to steal it.

'We talked about this,' he said to Ed.

They'd talked about it? Really?

'No, we didn't,' said Ed.

Well either they had, or they hadn't, which was it?

'We talked about you and Kat,' Leroy said.

'That's completely different.'

'Why?'

Ed looked at me.

'Don't mind me,' I said, 'I just need to stay on my back for a few minutes longer.'

Ed pointed at the door.

'Outside,' he said to Leroy, who hesitated for a moment, then followed, pulling the door shut behind him although thanks to the open window, I could hear everything they said.

'I told you about Kat and me in confidence.' Ed sounded

annoyed, and I realised he must be wishing that I'd asked him to do the sex, although given that we needed as many babies as possible, his chance would probably come.

'So?' Leroy was saying. 'You made it very clear that you weren't going to have sex with Kat again until she binds herself to the Threads.'

'I only told you because I feel awful about upsetting her. For the life of me, I can't see how you got from me telling you that, to you deciding to fuck Eileen.'

'You know what the Messages say as well as I do.'

Leroy must have moved away from the window for a minute, because I couldn't hear what he said next, but when he came back into earshot he was repeating word for word what Jem had said about how God had given fertility back to the Threads because we're the Parents of the Renewed World, and how it was a responsibility as well as a gift, and that you don't turn down a gift from God, or a responsibility. Of course, it's exactly what I'd been saying to him earlier, so I was pleased to hear that he'd remembered it all perfectly.

There was silence for a moment, then Ed said, 'But with Eileen? Really?'

He did sound quite upset that I hadn't asked him.

'Look, I know what you're thinking,' said Leroy. 'You don't have to spell it out. But she offered and besides, it all feels the same with your eyes shut.'

I wasn't sure I completely agreed with that. As far as I was concerned, it had started to feel better when I'd shut my eyes and thought about Jem. But maybe that's what Leroy had been doing from the start?

Their voices got fainter and I realised they were walking away from the hut. I waited another minute or two, then sat up. It was unlikely that I would feel pregnant right away, but something

243

definitely felt different and I couldn't wait to get over to Hinton and give Jem the news. She'd be so proud of me, and hopefully she might speak to God and tell It how tightly I was binding myself, so at Renewal I would be lifted higher than anyone else.

*

As it turned out, Jem wasn't as excited to hear my news as I'd expected. In fact, I would go so far as to say she was positively underwhelmed. Ever since Camman and Amber had killed their animals, it was almost as if there was a competition to do the best preps – preparations – for Cleansing and Renewal because no-one wanted to be left hanging. Being left hanging basically meant that you were still frayed and not tightly bound to God's rope, although what that actually meant in practice was unclear. Jem said we weren't yet ready to know the details about how it would all work. She needed to be sure that our preps were sufficient before God would let her tell us.

Of course, there was a lot of speculation about who might be left hanging and endless conversations about how awful it would be to be one of them, but I didn't get involved in talking about it. I didn't need to. I had the Book of Jem, and if I had a question, all I had to do was to read it and I'd find the answer. When I first started writing the Book, I hadn't realised how quickly it would become a handbook for how to be a good Thread, but of course, because I was writing everything down, it was an invaluable source of information about what to do, how to do it, and what everything meant.

So, by reading the Book, I was able to work out what it would mean to be left hanging, which was this: after Renewal everyone in Underhill was going to be saved regardless of whether they were Threads or not and because of that we would obviously be divided into two groups. Those of us who were most tightly bound to God's rope would be lifted up immediately, while everyone else would be left hanging. Those of us who were destined to be lifted straight away would become the leaders, receiving God's instructions about what to do after Renewal and being in charge of the others. And of course, it would be *our* babies that would be raised to be leaders after us.

Over time, everyone in Underhill would inevitably become a Thread, or at least anyone left hanging after a certain period would have to be cut off. A frayed thread is a weak thread, after all. But even after everyone had become Threads, some of us would still have to be in charge.

That much I'd worked out, which was more than anyone else had done. What I didn't yet know was *who* it was that was going to be lifted up by God immediately.

Besides me, I mean.

Anyway, the result of all the worrying about being left hanging was that there was a lot of effort going in to the preps. Lots of people had stopped working the Files, although personally I was a bit reluctant to stop because I enjoyed looking at all the pictures and the money certainly came in handy.

It was funny, really, but a lot of the effort being put into preps actually resulted in people doing less than they used to. Jem had told us that because God would provide everything after Renewal, if we spent time and energy now doing things that we would benefit from in the future, it meant we were doubting God's commitment to us or, as Jem said, picking at our binding with God. And picking at our binding to God was really bad, because it was one of the ways that we risked becoming unbound.

What this meant was that Threads who made things or repaired things had begun to stop making things and repairing things. One of the other most common preps was to do with the crops. Dust crops were coming into season, but the Threads who had always helped with the harvesting refused to do it any more, and a lot of things were being left to rot in the fields. Because Cleansing and Renewal would be happening at the next Whiteout and God would provide everything after that, it was understandable that people were wondering why they should break their backs picking bush beans. That's what they said anyway.

The unbound seemed determined to deliberately mis-understand our point of view, and there was a constant undercurrent of tension between us and them. There were pathetic attempts to annoy us, like when someone cut the Binding Area ropes. Also, during our meetings, people invariably turned up with the sole intention of shouting at Jem, trying and failing to drown her out. One time, someone hid all the stakes that we attached the rope to; and another time, a load of rotten food was dumped on Jem's speaking platform. I have to admit, that was disgusting and even when we had cleaned it all off, washing and scraping away for ages while Jem supervised us, the flies still hung around for days. But nothing the unbound did caused any actual harm until the fight.

The fight was exciting. I was upstairs working on my latest entry in the Book of Jem when I heard shouting outside. I could see people hurrying along the street, but no matter how far I leaned out of the window, I couldn't see what was going on, so in the end I had no option but to go outside and take a look.

By the time I got there, there was already a bit of a crowd, but I've always found that a strategic elbow to the ribs distracts most people enough to be able to push past them, so I managed to get a great view at the front. Fred already had blood smeared all over his face and I suspected that some of his nasal membranes had burst, presumably from contact with Scot's fist. It was the first time I'd seen fighting close-up, although it was quite difficult to concentrate because Lia was screeching away nearby, trying to get

Scot to stop punching Fred. Scot, who was one of those who lived out of the village, up on Back Hill, and who I had successfully ignored for years, always relied on Fred to help him pick his crops. At our last meeting, Fred had made a big deal about how he wasn't going to do it any more. *We must make big steps for the preps,* he'd said several times, looking ridiculously pleased with himself because he'd managed to find two words that rhymed.

Fred was on the ground and it must be said, he looked pretty awful. His right eye was swollen, there was a tear in the top of his left ear and he appeared to have lost a tooth.

Scot was standing over him, apparently trying to decide whether to hit him again, but instead he shouted, 'Fuck you, Fred. Fuck your Threads. Fuck your God. And fuck that stupid fucking troublemaker up on the hill.' Then he pushed through the crowd and walked away.

Afterwards, Jem told us that we should all be thankful to Fred, because people who were scared by the truth always wanted to silence it, and that by allowing himself to get hurt, Fred had shown them that the truth wouldn't be silenced. Fred tried to smile when she said that, but I think his face was still sore because all he did was lift his mouth up a bit at one side. Also, his missing tooth made him whistle whenever he said the letter s, and I was surprised that I was the only one who laughed when he said, *big steps for the preps.*

She was right though: the fight didn't put people off becoming Threads, because straight away afterwards there was a flurry of people who presented themselves at the bottom of Hinton's steps for Threading.

I have to say, I wasn't entirely convinced by all the newcomers and I did wonder if some of them had decided to hedge their bets. I mean they didn't have anything to lose by pretending to want to be Threads. That way, when Cleansing happened, they could claim they were one of us, bound to God, front of the queue for all the benefits God was going to bestow. If it had been up to me, I'd have been really strict about who could be threaded, but Jem was determined to welcome everyone.

Really though, how likely was it that someone like Lily genuinely felt the urge to be bound? It was her mother who had notified Jem, after all, and you can't tell me that Lily hadn't known what she was planning to do. Not to mention that she was Kat's best friend, the two of them always together, bitching away about everyone else. As I watched Lily kneeling at the foot of Hinton's steps, eyes shut, chin tilted, while Jem tied the thread around her scrawny neck, I resolved to keep a close eye on her.

After the fight, there was some concern about whether the resistance to the Threads might escalate or whether Scot or some of the other unbound might try and hurt Jem, but she didn't seem too worried. She said Hinton would keep her safe, and besides, there were always a few Threads hanging around if she needed any help. One thing that did bother Jem though was when Lorne left Underhill to go back to the Uplanders. She said she wanted to introduce Stone to his father, that she wouldn't be gone for long, she would come back, and although I couldn't care less where she was, I hated to see Jem annoyed. It was lucky for Lorne that she left before I had decided on an appropriate way to punish her.

However, all of this faded into the background on the day that Tish finally showed her true colours to everyone else and they saw what I'd always known. Namely what a bitch she was.

There had been a flurry of Messages, which of course I faithfully copied into the Book of Jem. Apparently, God was pleased with the way the preps were going. It particularly approved of some of the recent ones, like the animal killing and It had told Jem that because of our efforts there would continue to be an increase in fertility, or, as Jem said God said, *the cradle will soon groan under the weight of its load*, which was obviously a Message for me.

There were several other Messages about being strong for what was to come and constant reminders about not letting the unbound loosen our binding. These Messages are all in the Book of Jem, of course, along with helpful explanations for future readers so that they fully understand how to interpret Messages like these:

Cut the thread that refuses to be bound.
Keep your binding tight.
Be ready, for the rope may be lifted at any moment.
You are but one thread in the rope. Whatever you do to the
rope, you do to yourself.

On the day of the argument, we were in the Binding Area and Jem had just passed on a Message, I forget which one, when Tish shouted something. She was at the back and at first, I couldn't hear her over the shouts of other Threads telling her to be quiet. She pushed past everyone – she always was very rude – until she reached the platform and climbed onto it. It was only then that I could make out what she was saying.

'Why are we just hearing the same old Messages over and over again?' she shouted.

A few people called, 'shut up,' and, 'get off,' but Jem herself didn't say anything. She wasn't looking at any of us, she just unwound her scarf from her neck, then very slowly wound it back round again.

'Maybe God's Messages aren't always reaching us,' Tish yelled. 'Anyone else think that?'

What? How could she even think something like that? I mean we all knew what a nasty, spiteful person she was, but honestly, I had never imagined that she would have such un-Thread-like thoughts.

'We don't have much time left,' Tish said, throwing her arms out dramatically, almost hitting Jem in the face. 'The authority is watching us. At any time they may try and unpick our binding with God. Cleansing and Renewal are coming, we're making our preps, we are bound to God, and yet all we're hearing from the Prophet are the same old Messages over and over again. Why is that? Why?' She paused at that point, almost as if she expected someone to say something, but no-one did so she continued, 'Perhaps it's time someone else started talking to God. Perhaps we need a new Prophet.'

What little colour Jem had in her face had drained away and I wondered if she might be about to faint, so I started pushing my way towards the platform. I would catch her if she fell.

From somewhere behind me, a voice shouted, 'Jem is our Prophet.'

Tish bellowed back, 'Jem *was* our Prophet. But maybe it's time for a new Prophet.'

Then someone shouted again, 'Jem is our Prophet,' and I shouted it too and then more Threads started to shout the same thing, until everyone but Tish was shouting, 'Jem is our Prophet, Jem is our Prophet.'

Jem smiled and turned towards Tish as a deep flush started on her neck, spreading until Tish's whole face was red and blotchy. Jem put out her hands and patted the air in front of her until we all stopped chanting.

'Sometimes the rope gets knotted,' she said, and I was relieved to hear her sounding as strong as ever. 'Tish and I will talk, and together we will unpick her knots.'

*

I knew what Jem meant when she said she would unpick Tish's knots. I'd been present at several unpickings because there were only two or three of us Threads that she trusted to help her administer them. Even though I was thrilled to be one of the special ones, I hated to see how sad the unpickings made her. Why was it that people made Jem do things that were so difficult, that hurt her so badly, and made her feel so terrible? It always took days for her to properly recover after an unpicking. If only everyone could be a true and faithful Thread like me.

Jem asked Leroy and I to help Tish walk from the Binding Area up to Hinton while she went on ahead. The rest of the Threads didn't fully appreciate what an effort it was for Jem to prepare herself for an unpicking. She needed to speak to God, to make sure that her own binding was as tight as it could possibly be. Any frayed threads and there was a real risk that she herself might become knotted.

Tish struggled a bit when Leroy and I each took hold of one of her arms, but then she just went limp and I think she realised that she had no choice: if she didn't let Jem help her unpick her knots then she would never be raised up by God. Petra must have been totally embarrassed by Tish's outburst, but she forced herself to give Tish a quick hug, saying, 'You'll feel better when your knots are unpicked. I love you. The Threads are Bound.' Tish didn't reply.

It took a while to get up the path, mainly because Tish was being quite uncooperative, I think she was probably trying to put off the moment when she would have to face the pain she was going to cause Jem. In any case, Leroy and I had to drag her most of the way, which it seemed to take forever. I hadn't spoken to him since we'd done the sex, but he didn't try to talk to me, in fact, as far as I could tell, he was doing his best to avoid even looking at me, probably so we could prepare ourselves for what was about to happen.

When we finally reached the bottom of Hinton's steps, Jem was waiting on the platform, looking down at us. Leroy and I waited for her to give us the signal, and when she nodded we started to strip Tish of her clothes. Although we all knew Jem wouldn't be able to see the knots clearly unless Tish was naked, she put up a bit of resistance at first but after Leroy held her arms behind her back it was much easier for me to get her clothes off. I ripped her shirt, but that was a small price for Tish to pay to have her knots unpicked.

'Kneel.'

Jem's voice was gentle, floating down towards us from the top of Hinton's steps.

'Kneel,' she said again.

Tish was looking at her feet and did not move.

'Kneel,' Jem said, for a third time.

Leroy reached out and put a hand on Tish's shoulder, I did the same on the other side and together we forced Tish onto her knees. She reached out and held onto Hinton's bottom step, her breasts hanging so low that her nipples almost touched the ground. She closed her eyes and didn't move, even when Jem came down from the platform and stood next to her. I noticed that Jem had selected a particularly thin rope this time, which meant she had been able to tie more knots than usual along its length.

She lifted her arm above her head.

When the rope struck Tish's bare back she screamed, and I have to admit, I did think that Jem had made a mistake by not gagging her. She had to try several times before she found the best angle, but eventually she got into a rhythm and timed it so that with each lash, she shouted a word.

'You.'

The welts were deeper than in previous unpickings, probably because of the different rope that Jem was using.

'Are.'

Tish tried to get up, but Leroy put his boot on her shoulder and pushed her back down.

'A.'

One of the knots must have caught a vertebra or something because she really screamed after that one.

'Knot.'

Another scream.

'In.'

From where I was standing, I could see a line of blood tracing the curve of her ribs and dribbling onto the ground.

'Our.'

All the unnecessary screaming was really getting on my nerves.

'Rope.'

A final lash, a final ear-splitting scream, then thankfully Tish was silent.

Jem coiled the rope up and hooked it over her arm. She looked down at Tish who had fallen onto her side in the dirt, blood dripping from several wounds, forming a small puddle.

'We are but threads in God's rope,' Jem said, and because I knew her so well, it was clear to me just how upset she was. She was so selfless, ignoring her own feelings to help Tish unpick her knots. 'Whatever we do to the rope, we do to ourselves. Your knots are our knots. Your pain is our pain.'

I repeated after her, 'Your knots are our knots. Your pain is our pain,' and Leroy followed my lead. We chanted it together a few times although I noticed that Tish didn't join in. She didn't even bother to cover herself up – her breasts were still hanging out for anyone to see.

'The knot is unpicked, the rope is straight,' Jem said.

She stepped over Tish, walked up the steps, and disappeared inside Hinton.

Details of this and the other knot unpickings aren't in the Book of Jem. I can't see any reason why people in the future would want to read about such ignorant and un-Thread-like behaviour from people like Tish. Also, because it made me so angry to see how completely miserable Jem was when she had to help people unpick their knots, I just wanted to try and forget about it, so all I did was make a brief comment in the Book about Jem helping Tish straighten her rope and left it at that.

By sheer coincidence, it was the very next day after Tish's outburst that Jem received a significant new Message. Our preps were going so well that God had decided we were ready to hear the full details of what would happen at Cleansing. Not only that, but apparently God had said Jem needed to tell everyone in Underhill, not just the Threads. Everyone needed to be prepared for what was going to happen, whether they would be bound, frayed or left hanging, so Jem had decided she would tell us everything at the turbine festival.

I couldn't wait to hear what she was going to say.

20

Kat

Rumours were spreading that something was wrong with the turbines. When the mid-Dust winds arrived, they were so strong that the turbines had to be shut down to prevent damage to the blades. The flickers were immediate and prolonged, and it didn't take a genius to work out that there was far less electricity than usual stored in the batteries. Everyone was talking about it, and Ed was going to have to tell them all soon, whether he was ready to or not.

The levels in the purification tanks were critical as well, so the water was barely dribbling. Most days, we had to choose between cleaning ourselves or watering our plants, and almost every night we went to bed grubby. I spent a great deal of time scratching the flaky patches that were appearing all over my body and compulsively checking for Dust parasites.

The problems were compounded by the bickering that always emerged as the relentless heat wore on. Fuses seemed particularly short – several times I wondered if one ill-judged spark might send the whole of Underhill up in flames – and unsurprisingly, the focus of many arguments was Jem. Several families, like mine, were split down the middle, with some embracing the Threads, and the rest appalled by their stupidity. It wasn't at all unusual to walk along the street and hear arguments through the open windows, and once or twice actual fights had broken out. No-one had been seriously injured – although Fred had lost a tooth and broken his nose in a nasty brawl – but it did feel like it was only a matter of time before someone really got hurt.

I had my own issues to deal with of course, and since that awful night when Ed hadn't wanted to be with me, he'd started sleeping up at the turbines. When I did see him, we just ended up having the same arguments over and over again and no matter how hard I tried, I couldn't get through to him. Willow was going out of her way to avoid me, she'd missed several Wave appointments with the midwife, and I was becoming increasingly anxious about her and the baby. I was so thoroughly miserable that when I saw Lily walking up the steps with her gardening basket hooked over her arm, I followed her into the street without giving myself time to think about what I was doing.

'Lils,' I called. She hesitated, then stopped and turned towards me.

'Want some help?' I asked.

For a moment I thought she was going to refuse, but then she smiled.

'I'd love some. I'm going to pick berries for the festival.'

I fell into step beside her and at first, it felt like nothing had changed between us, but then I glanced over and saw the red thread tied around her throat and I felt horribly shy, as if she was a stranger that I needed to get to know all over again.

Obviously she didn't feel the same, because she was chattering away like nothing had changed.

'I can't believe it's that time of year already. It feels like no time at all since we were up at the turbines for the last festival.'

The turbines were the last thing I wanted to talk about, so I said, 'How's Ruby?' although the truth was, I didn't really care how she was.

Lily laughed. 'She's been trying very hard to force herself to be nice to me, but it'll be a long time before me or anyone else forgives her for bringing the authority here. She's barely leaving her room, although all the extra time she's got means she's knitting up a storm. She's already made me two new jumpers.'

We were passing the graveyard and she nodded towards it. 'Still visiting your elder tree?'

'Of course,' I said, surprised she would even ask.

She glanced at me, but didn't say anything, and we walked in silence for a while, climbing one of the tracks that led up Back Hill. It was lined with dense gorse, loaded with yellow flowers like tiny spots of sunlight. There wasn't enough room for us to walk side-by-side, so I let her go ahead. The heat was stifling, and I was relieved we wouldn't be going very far.

We'd picked berries together so many times, that we just settled ourselves on the ground a little way apart and started plucking them from the bushes. I wanted to say something, but the words stuck in my throat. It was ridiculous to feel so awkward. She might have a red thread tied around her neck, but she was still Lily, so I told myself to stop being so stupid, took a deep breath and forced out the words I wanted to say.

'I miss you, Lils,' I said, but so quietly that she didn't hear me, so I said it again, more loudly. 'I miss you.'

She turned and gave me the biggest smile, then reached over to give me a hug.

'I miss you too. I *hate* not talking to you,' she said.

'We must be able to find a way to deal with this. I mean, after everything we've been through.'

'I know. I feel the same.'

'Can we try and talk about it without getting annoyed? Do you think we can manage that?'

'You're the one with the temper,' she said, laughing. 'Do *you* think *you'll* be able to manage it?'

I grinned. 'I'll do my best.'

She turned back to the bush and plucked a berry, popping it into her mouth. She had a streak of dirt along her cheek – same old Lily – and I smiled, happy to be there with her.

'I'm so lonely, Lils,' I said. 'Everything is awful. Ed's sleeping up at the turbines, Ash is constantly miserable and I'm worried sick about Willow. My whole life has fallen apart, and I haven't the faintest idea how to fix it.'

Lily nodded and tiny drops of sweat glistened along the parting of her hair.

'You're always telling me that things are never as bad as they seem, give it some time, things will look different,' she said, and ate another berry.

'More time won't make this better,' I said. 'I'm running out of time, much more of it and Willow will be giving birth on the side of a hill, without me or any chance of medical help.' I couldn't bear it – every time I thought about all the things that could happen to her, I felt sick.

'I know you're worried,' said Lily, 'but...' then she hesitated, and I knew exactly what she was going to say next, 'Willow is where she needs to be.'

I swear, if anyone else said that to me, I'd start screaming and I might never stop. It was so frustrating. Why didn't they understand how dangerous it was for a pregnant fifteen-year-old to be living on the side of a hill?

'She needs to be at home, with me,' my voice cracked, and I swallowed hard. Tears would get me nowhere. Lily put her hand on my arm.

'She's fine.'

I pulled my arm away.

'She's not fine. I mean, even if she's okay right now, something could go wrong with the pregnancy at any time. I can't understand why I'm the only one worrying about her. She needs to come home, where she's safe.'

'She's safe where she is, Kat, we all know how special she is.'

'But that's the problem. Why can't you see that? *Of course* Willow is special. But she's special to me and to Ed and Ash. She's special to you, because you've known her for her whole life. But she isn't special to Jem. She's just being used by her. I mean, what teenager wouldn't want to get all this adulation? Who wouldn't enjoy being told that she's the *Mother of the Renewed World*?' I spat the words out. 'But come on, Lils, surely you realise that Willow is nothing more than a tool to Jem? A weapon to be used for her own ends. Willow is special because she's ours: mine and Ed's. And Ash's. And yours, too. But she's not Jem's. She just isn't.'

This time I let Lily take my hand and squeeze it.

'Look, Kat, if there's ever any reason, any reason at all, that you need to worry about Willow, I'll tell you. Okay?'

Of course it wasn't okay, but if that was all Lily was prepared to do then I'd take it.

'Do you promise?'

She nodded. 'I promise.'

It was better than nothing.

She turned her attention back to the berries, picking several in quick succession. 'You hate not being in control,' she said, putting the berries into the bowl. 'You always have. You know, you'd feel so much better if you'd just accept that you can't control everything. None of us can.'

She was right of course, but it wasn't that simple. Not with that woman living inside Hinton, kidnapping my daughter and convincing my partner not to sleep with me.

I decided to try a different approach.

'What do you see in her, Lils?'

Lily sat back and wiped her hand across her forehead, leaving another smear of dirt. I licked my lips, they were salty with sweat and I looked up, hoping to see some clouds, but other than a wisp above the top of the hill, the sky was empty.

Lily was watching me.

'I know you don't get it,' she said. 'But you will. You just need to give it some time.'

'No, I don't.' My voice was sharper than I intended.

'No getting annoyed, remember?'

I nodded, forcing myself to stay silent.

'I want to explain it to you, Kat. But it's really difficult.' She frowned, struggling to find the right words. 'It's like my life was fading away before she came, but now everything is bright and vivid.'

'Why don't I feel like that?' That's what I really wanted to know. Everything would be so much easier if I could see what they all saw in the girl.

'I've wondered about that too,' she said. 'I think the best way to explain it is that it's like Jem is many different people. Sometimes she says things to me that she might not say to the others. And then sometimes I hear her saying things to someone else, that she hasn't said to me. I wonder if maybe she just hasn't found the right way to talk to *you* yet.' She ran her finger along the thread around her throat. 'She hears me in a way that no-one has ever heard me before.'

'I hear you, Lils. So does Cooper. Most of the time, anyway.'

She grinned, her teeth purple with berry juice.

'I know, but it's different with Jem. She talks to my thoughts even when I can't find the words to say them out loud.'

'You know that's impossible, right?'

'I know, but it's honestly what it feels like.'

'In the past, they'd have called her a witch and said she was putting a spell on you.'

Lily shook her head. 'She's an incredible young woman, Kat.

260

Truly. It's like my life was on pause, while I was waiting for what she has given me.'

'And what is that? What has she given you?'

'The strength to make changes. By being a Thread, for the first time in a long time, perhaps for ever, I feel like I can achieve whatever I want.'

It was all so frustratingly familiar. They weren't the words Ed used, but it amounted to the same thing. It was all complete rubbish. I mean, what did Lily think she was going to make a difference to? And how? Apart from Cooper, I knew better than anyone how unhappy she'd been, but a lot of that was to do with her mother. Why couldn't she see that there was a difference between proactively trying to make things better for yourself, and wholeheartedly embracing an illegal religion?

'You do know that this is all in your head?'

She glanced at me but didn't say anything.

'You know that religion is just a false construct, right? A lie people tell themselves to… to… I don't know, feel better about themselves, I suppose, by pretending there's a God out there that'll make everything okay in the end.'

She shrugged and started stripping a branch loaded with fruit.

'You *do* still know that, don't you, Lily?'

She put the berries in the basket, then turned to face me.

'So what if it is, Kat? I mean really, what's your problem with it? I've never felt like this before. It's exciting, I feel alive. It's actually making me feel hopeful. *Hopeful*. Me. When have you ever heard me say that I feel hopeful about anything?'

'Right. So this isn't about God?'

'It's about everything. God, Jem, the Messages, the meetings. Each time someone new joins and another thread is added to our binding, I feel stronger.'

I stared at her. She didn't even sound like my Lils, she must be quoting Jem.

'I understand that you're using Jem to find the strength to stop working the Files and stand up to your mother.'

'Stop trying to unpick it, Kat. You always want to dissect everything. Can't you just accept that I'm happier than I've been in a long time?'

'Supposing I do accept it, Lils. Suppose I say I'm pleased for you. Well done. You've finally found a way to make some changes that you've been wanting to make for a long time, then perhaps you'll tell me how you can even begin to accept this crazy idea that everyone in the world is going to die? Except us lucky few in Underhill, of course.'

She looked a bit unsure for a moment, but then she sat up straighter, and said, 'I'll admit that did take some time to get my head around.'

'*Get your head around*? Seriously? You can't honestly think that this God of yours is about to kill everyone but us?'

'Jem says we must trust God enough to give up control of our lives to It, Kat. I know it sounds terrible, but it's all part of a plan to renew the world and our relationship with God.'

'*Sounds terrible* is a bit of an understatement, don't you think?'

'I trust Jem and I believe what she tells us,' she said, and obviously that was the end of that as far as she was concerned. She picked another berry and popped it in her mouth. I almost admired how thoroughly Jem had schooled them in what to say, how to shut down conversations, bat away the difficult questions. There was no doubting the girl's skills. It was just a shame she wasn't using her undoubted talents for something positive, because if she had she really might change the world.

'There's been talk in the village you know,' I said. 'Some people are saying there's another side to Jem, that she's not what she seems.' I hesitated – it was barely a whisper really, just a couple of people who were saying that Jem did some pretty awful things to punish Threads who stepped out of line.

'It's jealousy,' Lily said, shaking her head. 'There'll always be a few who can't accept that someone else knows better than them, is more patient than them, more kind than them. Jem is the most selfless person, she gives everything of herself for us, so it's hardly surprising that there are some people who make up lies about her.'

I wasn't so sure that was all it was, but as I watched her jabbing her finger into the ground, trying to work it through the outer crust, which was baked solid after weeks of endless sunshine, I realised that that was clearly the end of the matter as far as Lily was concerned. I could tell I was irritating her, but that wasn't my fault. *She* was the one who'd changed her views so completely that I couldn't begin to understand them, let alone share them. It was for *her* to convince *me*.

She clapped her hands together, as if she'd just thought of something. 'We're just going round in circles, Kat, why don't you remind me why you believe something you call the Elder Mother lives inside a tree?'

'That's completely different.'

'No, it's not. And I've never once made you feel that it's wrong to believe what you believe.'

She was right. The day I told Lily about what I did when I went to the graveyard, I'd already been talking to the Elder Mother for years. I'd been really nervous about telling her, but we were at the stage in our friendship where we'd covered all the important things, all the key milestones in our lives, all the things that had made us who we were, apart from this one thing. I wanted Lily to like me for who I was, not just who she thought I was and that meant that I had to tell her.

She'd listened in silence, and when I'd finished she said she was worried in case anyone else found out, because the authority might class it as a religion. But then she'd hugged me and said it didn't matter to her if I wanted to talk to a tree, she was still glad I'd come to Underhill. *Anything that makes our lives a little bit more bearable*, she'd said. Remembering that made me feel guilty – why couldn't I be as generous towards her new belief as she'd been to mine?

'Well?' she said, obviously not happy to let it go. 'Tell me again why you do it.'

'Talking to the Elder Mother makes me feel as if I'm not alone.' I laughed, bitterly. 'Freedom knows, I certainly need that at the moment.'

'But that's not really so very different from me, is it? I mean that's how I feel when I'm there with the Threads. Just the same as you with your tree.'

'You mean apart from the fact that the Elder Mother isn't saying that almost everyone in the world is about to die?'

She at least had the grace to laugh at that.

'Yes, apart from that. But until you're ready to surrender control to God, you won't be able to believe the truth of the Messages.'

I just shook my head and we let a silence settle between us for a few minutes and concentrated on picking the berries. A few of them had a whitish bloom on them, but neither of us knew if it was caused by some sort of disease, so we just picked them off the bushes and threw them away. My skin felt tight – I'd been outside for too long and I wished the sun would hurry up and dip behind the hills to give us some relief from the heat.

Eventually Lily broke the silence. 'What about the pregnancies, don't you think they're a sign from God?'

'What about the pregnancies?' I said, suddenly exhausted by the pointlessness of the whole conversation.

'Well as far as we know, they aren't happening anywhere else and it was supposed to be decades until we returned to this level of fertility.'

I'd been over and over this with Ed. 'It's just a coincidence, Lils. Yes, its unexpected, but the toxins were always going to clear, weren't they? It's just happening here sooner than predicted. It doesn't prove anything, certainly not the existence of a god.'

'Well I disagree,' she said. Of course she did. I had lost count of how many times Dandy had told me how people in thrall to the idea of God saw every single thing that happened through the lens of their religion. He called it the *fundamental illusion*. For example: good harvest, God is pleased; poor harvest, God is displeased. Anyone pointing out that the harvest was poor because the weather had been bad would get short shrift because, in the mind of a believer, it was a displeased God who had sent the bad weather.

'Can you understand why I find it so difficult to accept that you believe this stuff?' I asked, determined to try one last time to get through to her.

'Well, I certainly understand why it seems odd that I would voluntarily spend time with some of the Threads,' she said, shoving yet another large berry into her mouth – at this rate, there would be none left for the festival.

'Eileen, for example?' I said.

'Yes, well, Eileen has always been in a category of her own, hasn't she? I have to say though she does seem to have calmed down a bit. She's not quite so...'

'Strange?' I suggested, and Lily chuckled.

'She's definitely slightly less strange. She really does seem to have got herself more under control. And when she talks, she's barely stammering. Being around Jem is obviously really good for her. Which sort of proves my point, doesn't it?'

No, actually, it didn't. Not as far as I was concerned. But then a breeze stirred up some dust and I squeezed my eyes shut, trying to blink away the grit. Lily got to her feet and held out a hand. I let her pull me up and rubbed my eyes. She watched me, looking concerned, until I was sure all the dust was gone. I put my hand out but stopped short of touching the string tied around her neck.

'Why do you wear that?'

She reached up and ran a finger over it. Then she shrugged.

'Why not? Being a Thread means being part of something so much bigger than ourselves, Kat. I know that you won't ever be convinced that God is real, but there's no doubt that my feelings are real, and at the end of the day does it actually matter whether it's God that's making me feel so happy? Or the Threads? Or Jem? Or just some misfiring in my deluded, illogical synapses? Frankly, I don't care. Everything is changing and I feel great.'

Hearing the happiness in my friend's voice, I really did try to be pleased for her but, honestly, as hard as I tried all I felt was fear. Fear and exhaustion. I'd done my best to accept what she was saying, but as far as I was concerned, before we were born, everything had already changed. Half the world's population had died, and humanity had only just managed to survive. We weren't exactly thriving, not yet, but we were surviving, and there was reason to be hopeful that things would get better in the decades to come. So how could anyone genuinely be happy about the appalling idea that what remained of humanity was about to die? All those innocent people, struggling to make the best of what they had. All soon to die. Except us lucky few. It was ridiculous, but if they honestly, truly believed it was going to happen, how on earth could Lily, or any of the rest of them, seriously think that this God of theirs was something to feel happy about?

*

We walked back down the path and when we reached the road, I said I was going to go to the graveyard. Lily gave me a hug.

'It'll all be okay. You'll see.'

I didn't believe her, but at least we were talking again, so I just nodded and watched her walk away, then I turned and pushed my way through the undergrowth. My elder tree was heavy with berries, I'd have to come back with a basket and pick them. Unlike the fruit I'd just picked with Lily, we wouldn't eat elderberries, but I'd use them to make a syrup, which was invaluable when the Whiteout viruses started going around the village. Although if Lily and the others were to be believed, I probably didn't need to worry about having a Whiteout virus ever again. It was all so ridiculous.

I sat on the ground, leaned against the tree and closed my eyes, trying to calm my thoughts before I spoke to the Elder Mother. The problem was that there were so many things to worry about: Willow of course, always Willow, but also the turbines, and Ed, and all the anger bubbling away in the village. I'd seen flashes of the old Lily and I was sure she was still there somewhere, trapped beneath that stupid bit of string tied around her throat. I just had to hang on to the hope that all this Threads rubbish was just a temporary distraction. People were bored, sick of the same old life, this was just a bit of excitement which would pass like everything else did – hopefully before it could cause real damage to anyone, especially my daughter. Keeping my eyes closed, I rubbed my fingertips over the ground in small circles, trying to empty my mind, concentrating on what I could feel: the parched earth, brittle twigs, tiny stones, chips of granite. As my breathing slowed, I relaxed, just a little.

'Mum?'

I opened my eyes, squinting into the sunlight. Ash moved to the side, so his shadow fell on my face.

'What is it, love? What's wrong? Is it Willow?'

He shook his head.

'Have you seen her?'

He shook his head again. I reached for his hand, but he wouldn't let me take it.

'Is something wrong?'

He shrugged. Everything that was happening to me, was happening to him as well, but he was still a child, and he needed me. I took a deep breath and forced myself to smile.

'Why don't you sit down? We can have a talk. Or we'll just stay here for a bit. Whatever you want.'

He looked at the ground, then pushed some twigs out of the way with the tip of his shoe before sitting down awkwardly, as if he wasn't sure how to bend his legs properly.

'What have you been up to?'

I had to hide my irritation when he shrugged again. The last thing he needed was for me to be annoyed with him.

'Did you come here to find me?'

'I came to see the ash tree,' he said, much to my surprise because I had no idea that he'd even been paying attention when I'd told him about it.

'It's over there,' I said, pointing across the graveyard. 'Come on, I'll show you.'

'I've seen it before, Mum. I've been a few times. I bring water for it and sometimes I... I talk to it.' I smiled at him and he blushed. 'I wanted to bring water today, but there wasn't any.'

There wouldn't be, that morning we'd moved onto critical drought measures. There was only one level beyond critical, which was no water at all, and we just had to hope it would rain before it came to that.

Ash thumped his heel against the ground, over and over and I reached out to hold his leg still.

'How are you, Ash?' He shrugged again. 'Are you missing Willow?' Yet another shrug. It hadn't been all that long since Ed had taught him how to shave, and there was a rash along his jaw line. Where the rash ended, spots took over and he looked tired and miserable and I just wanted to give him a big hug.

'When's Dad going to start sleeping at home again?'

Didn't I wish I had the answer to that one?

'There's a lot to do at the turbines at the moment. You know what it's like, sometimes it's just easier for him to stay up there.'

He looked unconvinced.

'He'd love you to go and see him. Why don't you go? You know how much he likes it when you help him.'

'But *she's* up there.'

'Willow?'

'No,' he said, and the sudden anger made his voice sharp. 'That woman. That stupid, awful woman. She's taken Willow away from us with all her stupid talking, and now she's taken Dad as well.'

I had tried to keep the worst of my feelings about Jem from Ash, but here he was, as upset as me, and I couldn't think of a single thing to say to make him feel better. I put my arm around his shoulders, grateful that he didn't pull away, although I wasn't sure who was comforting who.

'It's the festival in a couple of days. We'll all be together up there. You know how much your dad loves it and we always have a brilliant time, don't we?'

'But she's even trying to take over that as well. Dad said that she's going to be making a speech to everyone.'

That was news to me, but I didn't react.

'There are always loads of speeches on festival day, Ash. You know that. Remember the year that your uncle Leroy had too much mead and was convinced that the turbines could talk to each other, and he could understand them? When he made you and Willow laugh so much you thought you were going to be sick?'

He nodded without smiling.

'Well, it'll be like that. We all love festival day.'

I tried to sound more confident than I felt. We had to maintain some normality in all the madness, and it was always wonderful when everyone came together up at the turbines. If that girl, or the Threads, any of the Threads, ruined our day, I wouldn't be responsible for my actions.

'I'm going to head back to the house, love. Do you want to come, or do you want to stay here for a bit?'

'I'll stay for a bit.'

'Okay. I'll see you at home?'

He nodded, and I bent to kiss the top of his head before he could pull away.

Back on the road, I could barely drag myself home. I was exhausted, I wanted to sleep for days but I knew that come bedtime, I'd just lie there imagining all the terrible things that might happen to Willow and everything would go round and round in my head and I'd have another sleepless night.

I was almost home when I saw Lorne half-jogging along the street towards me, although I hadn't realised she was back from the high lands. Stone was tied to her back with a piece of cloth and the top of his head bobbed up and down over her shoulder. When she reached me, she leaned forward and to my surprise, she kissed my cheek.

'You'll never guess what?'

Her smile was wide, but I really wasn't sure I could cope with anything else right then. I desperately wanted to get inside and have a cup of tea, but Lorne was determined to tell me her news.

'The most amazing thing's happened. I found Stone's father, but there's something even better. I still can't really believe it. Two of my people are pregnant. Isn't that wonderful?'

I nodded, but I had a horrible feeling that I knew what was

coming next.

'I told them about the Prophet and her Messages and they wanted to come back with me. They're with her at Hinton right now. She's going to Thread them immediately. She said that their pregnancies are a sign that God has bound them to Itself and by coming to Underhill they've already done major preps. I can't really believe it, Kat. It's so wonderful. Cleansing and Renewal are going to happen. It really is all going to happen.'

21

Eileen

Jem spoke from Lucy's top step at the turbine festival. She was dressed all in black, which set off her red scarf perfectly. In the Book, the speech needed a catchy title to mark its importance and after a lot of consideration I decided to call it The Speech at the Turbines. It comes at the end of the section called Messages.

Messages 9:1-20
The Prophet faced the assembled crowd and spoke the words that were known forever after as The Speech at the Turbines. This is what she said.

The Threads are Bound.

People of Underhill, I am here today to speak to you all. I'm here to speak to the Threads, and I'm here to speak to the curious. I'm here to speak to the old and to the young. I'm here to speak to those who have never left, and those, like me, who are newly arrived. To those of you who hate me, or who fear me, I'm here today to speak to you.

People of Underhill, I am no threat to you. I am not important. I am only the messenger. It is you, people of Underhill, who are important. It is you whom God has chosen for Its purpose. And by fulfilling God's purpose you will find a purpose for yourselves.

Your worries and your fears did not arrive in Underhill with me. I did not bring them. The drones that spy on you and count you and categorise you and tax you did not arrive in Underhill with me. I did not bring the Files that appal you and sicken you. The oppression you feel, your lack of purpose, your search for something more, these are not new feelings. I did not bring them with me.

People of Underhill, I brought only one thing with me, and that is a promise. A promise of a Cleansed world. A promise of a Renewed world, where you will be free from your worries and your fears and where all things are possible for you. I bring you the Message that the God that was, the God that is, and the God that will be, has chosen you, people of Underhill, to be saved when the stain of humanity is Cleansed from the earth. God has chosen you to bind a new rope with It, a strong and unbreakable rope, which shall connect you with God and with the Renewed world and with everything in it.

Many of you have asked me, 'What will happen at Cleansing?' and 'What will happen at Renewal?' but God would not permit me to answer you until the time was right for you to hear.

I can tell you now, people of Underhill, that God has pulled the Threads tighter, and today I shall give you the answers you seek.

When I was inside Hinton, a bright light shone. It was not sunlight, nor moonlight, nor any other light that I know of, since no light can penetrate Hinton's walls, but an old woman stepped through that light as if it were a doorway.

'I am the Elder Mother,' she said. 'The mother of daughters, defender of homesteads, healer of fevers.'

I asked her if God had sent her with a Message for me.

'I am not sent by God,' she said. 'I am part of God, I am one of the infinite threads of the God that was, the God that

273

is and the God that will be.'

And when I heard that, I knew that God was with me.

She stepped back through the light, which disappeared, but I was in darkness for only a moment because then I was outside, high above Hinton. One of his arms rose up towards me, the second stretched towards Underhill, while the third hung low to the ground.

I started moving through the air, faster and faster, over the highest hills and across vast plains and endless seas and I was alone but for the voice of the old woman.

'Consider the filth,' she said, and below me was a huge city and its foul blackness was visible, even through the great piles of snow that were banked along its walls.

'Consider the filth of those who blamed God for their actions,' said the old woman, and everywhere I looked people were rushing from place to place, heedless of the dirt and the poison and I knew that they did not remember the actions of those who had come before them.

'What was done in my name pierced my heart like a sliver of ice. And afterwards, their denial of me, their refusal to believe in my existence twisted the shard, forcing it deeper, freezing my love into hate, until now my fury is so cold that nothing shall survive it. I will destroy those who sought to destroy me. I will destroy them all. I shall not be assuaged until the world is Cleansed of everyone but those who I choose to Renew.'

And as I watched, an ocean of ice engulfed the city, freezing the people where they stood, breaking them into a million crystals, which fell upon the earth. Time stopped as the ice devoured the world.

Again, the old woman urged me to rise high into the sky, and we rushed through the air for the longest time until finally, I dropped towards the ground and stood among the lush greens of a meadow. And beyond the meadow was a lake of the brightest blue. And beyond that was fertile land and all about me there were plants and animals and birds. And there were people. And I saw how happy the people were and there was food to eat and water to drink and everywhere, everywhere, there were children.

And each person, young and old, had a gossamer-thin thread around their neck, visible only as a glint in the sunlight, a flash of red rising into the air, a tapestry of threads writhing towards a rope that hung from the sky. And the rope was made of the threads, woven together, dense and tightly bound. And although the people did not feel their threads or see them, or see the rope, they turned their faces towards the sky, calling out their gratitude to God for Renewing Its relationship with them and giving them a purpose, which was to live lightly on the world and be bound with everything on it and with God Itself.

People of Underhill, I say this to you today: I did not bring your fears and problems with me. I did not bring them.

Instead people of Underhill, the bound and the yet-to-be-bound, I bring you the resolution to your fears and the solution to your problems. God chooses you. It binds Itself to you, and when the first storm of Whiteout arrives, God will Cleanse the filth from the face of the earth with Its ocean of ice, but you, people of Underhill, you will not die because God has chosen you to be the saved ones. God has chosen you to Renew the promise. You, people of Underhill, are God's chosen ones.

The Threads are bound.

There were strategic pauses throughout the speech, so that the Threads could clap and cheer. Jem had also instructed us to repeat key phrases back to her so, for example, each time she said *I did not bring them* we all dutifully droned *you did not bring them*.

Even though I was writing everything down, all the stopping and starting meant that I had plenty of opportunity to observe everyone's reactions to The Speech at the Turbines. This was important because one of my duties is to decide what information is worthy of inclusion in the Book of Jem. There's no point cluttering it up with irrelevant anecdotes, and I find it useful to imagine a post-Renewal reader, turning the pages of my green notebook with white spots – or a copy of it, as the original will be so precious that it will be kept locked away somewhere – marvelling at my foresight in creating the prophet book, and I think what would *they* want to know?

It goes without saying that they won't be interested in how some of the unbound reacted to what Jem was saying. For example, I didn't mention that there was quite a bit of laughter when she said she'd flown over the world. I have to say, even I found that part of her speech quite challenging, but then she's the one who has the visions, she's the one that God speaks to, so who am I to say whether it's the truth or not?

Although the Book of Jem doesn't mention the inappropriate laughter, I did decide to include other, more interesting, reactions. For example, when Jem mentioned the old woman – the one she called Elder Mother – Kat looked really shocked, which is why I added a sentence saying: *among the unbound there was one, known by all for her unpleasant and wicked nature, who, when she heard the words of the Prophet, became as pale as a snowflake and swayed like grass in the wind before she sank to the ground, hiding her head in her hands*. I included this purely as an illustration of how people tried to divert attention away from Jem, but frankly, that was Kat all over. Always trying to be the centre of things, although she failed miserably, since no-one but me noticed what she was doing.

I must admit that I thought long and hard about whether to include any reference to the panic that followed Jem's announcement about a sea of ice killing everyone on earth apart from us. I mean, on the one hand, I'm not quite sure what people expected. After all, if we're the only ones left after Cleansing, then the rest of humanity are obviously going to die somehow, so they might as well freeze to death.

On the other hand, it did appear to come as shocking news to some people, particularly the unbound who hadn't really understood about Cleansing and Renewal until that point. There was a lot of shouting, and people were crying. A couple of the farmers who had been particularly annoyed when the Threads refused to help them because of preps, tried to rush up Lucy's steps and grab hold of Jem. It was okay though because after he'd been Threaded, Camman had appointed himself and his two sons as Jem's bodyguards, and together with some of the others, they formed a ring around Lucy and kept Jem safe. All in all, it was an unnecessary over-reaction to what was, when it comes down to it, good news. I mean, *we're* going to survive, so where's the sadness in that?

Because of the disturbance, Jem had to wait until people had calmed down enough for her to continue talking. I didn't want to stop and start The Speech at the Turbines in the Book, so I wrote it all down as if there hadn't been any interruptions and just made a passing comment about the fact that the speech had roused the crowd *to great emotion*.

When she finally finished, all the Threads started chanting 'The Threads are Bound', like usual. We made a lot of noise because Jem had made us practice over and over again so that when we did public chanting, we knew to speak loudly, enunciate clearly, keep our voices slow, and make sure we rose up a little on the word *Threads*, then do a tiny pause before saying *are Bound*. The result was that when other people were randomly shouting out stuff, for example, 'fuck off you freaks,' or 'there's no such thing as God,' our chanting drowned out what they were saying. It was quite hypnotic, and often people swayed from side-to-side while we were doing it, even some of the unbound.

Of course, some of the new Threads were Lorne's Uplander people. I hadn't yet had an opportunity to tell Jem what I thought about them being Threaded as soon as they arrived. Obviously she knew what she was doing, but I have to say, I didn't approve of this policy of being less picky about who was allowed to join. In the beginning, when there were just a handful of us, it felt special. I felt special. My connection with Jem was strong: she always made time for me and things happened when I was around her.

But with all these new Threads wanting to be with Jem, wanting to talk to her, to be seen to be doing their preps, the whole thing had become, well, a bit less special. Jem's priority seemed to be Threading as many new people as she could, handing out bits of red string to anyone that would take them. Sometimes, it felt like she had forgotten about those of us who had been there from the beginning. I suppose, in among all the visions of seas of ice and flying over the world and explanations about Cleansing and so on, God must have confirmed to Jem that she was doing the right thing by letting all these dubious individuals join, but that didn't mean that I had to like it. And I didn't. Not one bit.

The arrivals from the high lands had set up a sort of temporary camp not far from Hinton, constructing their shelters from grubby pieces of canvas and wooden poles. Jem had told us that we had to embrace them – not literally, thank goodness, as I wouldn't have been able to do that – because their pregnancies were an important sign, although after the burnings in Underhill earlier in the year, some of the Threads found the presence of Uplanders difficult to accept.

They invited me to go and drink tea with them, but I never went because it was obvious that they just wanted the reflected glory that they'd get from spending time with me: the original Thread. Worst of all though, was the way that they were always hanging around when I went to see Jem, and how they blathered on with the same ridiculous accent that Lorne had. It was so contrived, goodness knows why they didn't just speak properly. From the little I could make out they were always talking rubbish about respecting the planet, or maybe the plant, it all sounded the same to me.

I asked Jem, but she just gave me the usual line about how I should remember that although everyone's Thread is different, we are all part of the same rope. I knew that. I mean, she'd said it so many times, but as far as I was concerned, that didn't explain why these people had decided to become Threads. I even tried to talk about it to Leroy, after all, we had a duty to make sure that our baby would be safe, but he turned out to be disappointingly lacking in conversational skills. All he said was, 'We're Threads, Eileen. That's the only reason I did what I did with you. Just for preps. We're not partners.'

It took me a little while to realise what he was really saying. Ed must still be very upset because I had chosen Leroy and not him, which put Leroy in an impossible situation, with his loyalties split between his brother and the mother of his child, so I decided the kindest thing to do was to ignore Leroy altogether for a while, to avoid any more pain for them both.

Two of the Uplanders were pregnant, and so together with Willow, Lia and me, that made five of us in total. Five. There hadn't been so much fertility since before the Wars. I'd wanted to take my own turn to stand on Lucy's steps and tell everyone about being pregnant, but when I suggested it to Jem the day before the festival, she told me to wait.

'Why?' I'd asked.

'Until you're sure.'

'But I am sure. I stayed on my back with my pelvis tilted in an upward position and everything.'

'Nevertheless. We must only announce confirmed preps. God does not take false bindings lightly.'

'But it's not a false binding. It's true, and anyway, it's my turn to be pregnant.'

I was going to argue, but then Jem leaned close – we were both sitting on Hinton's bottom step – and for once there was no-one else nearby, except Camman and one of his huge, pale sons, but they were standing a little way away. I smelled Jem and squeezed my thighs tightly together.

'Eileen. Special one,' she said.

'Am I?' I asked, although obviously I knew that I was.

'You're the first of the Threads, you're tightly bound to me, and to God.'

I waited for her to say something else, but she didn't. She was looking across the hill at the Uplanders' camp. Since I'd last been to see Jem, they had got hold of some red cloth, which they had torn into strips and strung up between the tents. Their over-the-top efforts to be conscientious Threads really made me want to set light to their tents and burn their stupid camp to the ground. That would wipe the smiles off their smug Uplander faces.

They had somehow managed to dig a shallow pit in the rock-hard ground, and whenever I went up to the turbines now, they always had a fire burning. Ever since Jem had ordered all the Threads to only eat meals with other Threads – she said following her instructions on such matters would help tighten our binding

– the Uplanders had taken on the responsibility of making food for Jem and whoever happened to be at Hinton at the designated mealtimes. It was usually revolting but, by chance, I was often there at mealtimes so I forced myself to choke down whatever they produced. After all, I was eating for two.

Something was cooking now, and the smell of it wafting across the hill made me feel a bit sick, which reminded me why I had come to see Jem.

'So, about my baby?' I said.

Jem turned towards me. There were tiny beads of sweat along her hairline and I wondered whether they would taste salty.

'There'll be a lot going on at the festival,' Jem said. 'You know I'm going to be talking about Cleansing and Renewal, and Ed is going to be making an announcement.'

I didn't really pay much attention to what she said about Ed because I was trying to work out if it would be possible to collect all the drops of sweat off her face with just one lick, but then she reached over and took my hand and linked her fingers with mine, so I did hear what she said next, which was, 'It's not the right time to tell everyone, Eileen. I'll inform you when it is.'

Because I had only been half-listening when she said about Ed having some announcement to make, I really wasn't anticipating anything significant when he climbed up Lucy's steps after Jem had finished The Speech at the Turbines. Ed stood looking out at us all, waiting for things to calm down. Quite a lot of the punch had been drunk by then although obviously I hadn't had any, alcohol is bad for babies and in any case, I never drink too much. It was all very raucous because people were still trying to come to terms with the idea of the Big Freeze, as I had decided Jem's prophecy should be called.

Ed is not what you would call a natural public speaker. Not like Jem. He cleared his throat several times and said, 'Excuse me, excuse me,' but no-one paid him any attention. In the end, Leroy stamped up the steps and bellowed, 'Everyone, shut up and listen. Ed's got something important to say.'

Well. I was *not* expecting what followed.

The turbines are dying. Worn out turbines. Dying turbines. Soon-to-be-dead turbines. Whichever way he talked about it, it was shocking.

Not everyone understood what he was saying at first. Some of the people standing further away and the more inebriated didn't understand the importance of it, so there was a bit of a delay as the message got passed around. Lucy's blades were slowly turning above Ed's head – there was hardly any breeze – but they were still moving, which made what he was saying even more difficult to accept.

At the bottom of Lucy's steps, Jem looked up at Ed and nodded. He took a deep breath, then shouted, 'This is a sign that Cleansing and Renewal are close. God will provide for us, so we will have no more need of the turbines. They have turned for us for so long, and now they will be allowed to rest. No-one loves our turbines more than I do. But their work is nearly done. After Renewal, God will provide everything we need. The Threads are Bound.'

Ed turned his back on the crowd, stretched his arms out wide and wrapped them as far as he could around Lucy. He was crying. All around me people were crying. Jem started moving through the crowd, pausing every few steps to offer comfort to those who were distressed. None of them were Threads. She'd stand close, lean her head towards theirs, touch their hands or their shoulders and I knew what she would be saying almost word-for-word: *This isn't the end. It's the beginning. Underhill will be saved from Cleansing. God will save you. God has a purpose for you. Trust in God and you will be bound...* that sort of thing.

She offered a piece of red string to each person that she spoke to, and many of the people took them. Of course, that didn't mean that they were Threaded, but it was the first step – it was a sign that they were open to hearing more about being bound to God.

Meanwhile, most of the Threads themselves had drifted away from the main crowd and were gathering near Hinton. Although what Ed had said about the turbines was shocking – after all, they had been turning for my whole life, and for my parents' and probably my grandparents' lives before that – I wasn't that upset. What Ed had said was right, it was a sign and, in any case, after Cleansing God would be providing for us, so of course we wouldn't need the turbines.

I headed over to where Tish was apparently giving a speech of her own. Ever since her knot unpicking, there had been no more talk from her about another prophet, but I wanted to make sure she wasn't trying to cause any trouble.

'This is it,' she was saying. 'Our eyes are fully open. We see the signs. They've been there for months: the pregnancies, the coldest Whiteout, the worst Mudbound and the driest Dust that any of us can remember. And now the dying turbines. God is preparing us. Cleansing is almost here, and we must push on towards it. More preps, bigger preps.'

'What can we do?' said Lorne, holding Stone in front of her like a shield as she pushed her way to the front. The other Uplanders hovered around the edge of the group.

Then Fred called out, 'I've got a plan,' and everyone turned to look at him. His broken nose had healed with an unfortunate kink, swerving abruptly to the left half-way down his face and it still amused me when he whistled each time he said the letter s.

'I have a plan,' he said again, looking around, making sure that none of the unbound were within earshot, and waiting for us all to shuffle closer, before he said, 'There is something momentous we can do. Something that will prove to everyone that we are ready for Cleansing. Something that will show God beyond any doubt that we are worthy of being Renewed. It is time to make the greatest preparation of all.'

22

Kat

In the days after the festival, I did everything I could to avoid thinking about what had happened, but however hard I tried, memories of Jem at the top of Lucy's steps kept forcing their way into my thoughts. She had been so matter-of-fact when she was explaining that everyone on earth except us was going to die in an ocean of ice. How could so many of my friends and neighbours possibly believe it was true? The thing was, I knew how. I'd read all about it.

Group affirmation it was called in Dandy's books and even as I was reading about it, trying to learn as much as I could, I knew how fascinated my father would have been to watch it in action. Jem's ideas, as they left her lips, became waves that grew in strength as they washed back and forth between the Threads. Believers believed because other believers believed. Each person provided affirmation to each other person. Any doubts were diluted, then washed away, by the ever-growing tide of belief that rolled relentlessly around and around the group.

It wasn't so long now until Whiteout. Already the edge had gone from Dust and when the heat finally left us, and the first storm swept across the land, half the village had convinced themselves that the end of life as we knew it would arrive with it.

Then, of course, there had been the reaction to Ed's news about the turbines. Freedom knows I'd wanted him to tell everyone, but why hadn't I realised that something so devastating would push yet more people into Jem's arms? It was obvious with hindsight. Fill people with terror, tell them life as they know it will be coming to an end, really soon, and of course a proportion of them are going to want to believe someone who says that they only have to believe in God and everything will be okay.

I knew how much Ed would have hated standing at the top of those steps, telling everyone that Lucy and her brothers were dying. I wanted to go and stand there with him. And I was going to as well, until he started talking about how it was one of these stupid *signs*, like it was all a game or something. Except it wasn't a game, because Jem used what he said to prey on people's fear, manipulating it for her own ends, trotting out her glib rubbish, telling people that if only they would let themselves be bound to her God, then they'd have nothing to be scared about when the turbines stopped turning.

We would all survive. We were the chosen ones. That's what Jem kept saying to anyone who would listen. She went on and on, calmly, insistently, and as soon as she got someone to nod their head, or look interested, she held out one of those awful bits of string and told them to come and talk to her. And they did. There was practically a stampede up Front Hill the day after the festival, and by all accounts before they left, many of them bent to kiss Hinton's step and let the girl tie a bit of string around their necks.

It was a world gone mad.

Then there was Willow. Everything always came back to Willow. Before all the speeches, Ed had actually managed to persuade her to come and join us for a while during the festival and the four of us sat together on a blanket, pretending we were still a happy, united family. She looked really tired – the skin around her eyes was so dark it could have been bruised – but she insisted that she felt fine. I was nervous, not wanting to get into an argument but determined to try and talk about some of the things that needed to be discussed.

'Have you made any plans for the birth, Willow?' I said, ignoring the way she kept running her finger along the piece of string around her neck.

She shrugged and didn't reply.

'You must have had some thoughts?' I asked, doing my best not to sound like I was nagging her. 'Would you like me to ask the authority to arrange transport, so you can go somewhere where there's a midwife and doctors?'

'I'm not going away.'

'I'd come with you, love, you wouldn't be alone.'

'No, this is where I shall have my baby. Among the Threads.'

I had no doubt that if there were any problems, the authority would do whatever necessary to get Willow somewhere where there was proper medical help – there were too few babies being born for them not to do everything they could to assist – but if she wasn't at home, how would they possibly know if she needed help? How would I know? I frowned at Ed, hoping he would set aside his stupid beliefs long enough to help me persuade Willow that she needed to make a plan. He didn't take the hint though, and instead he changed the subject, saying, 'Have you thought about names for the baby?'

'I think the baby's uncle should name it,' said Ash. 'Fuchsia for a girl, or Teak for a boy. There's nothing like the name of a plant to give a baby a good start in life. I mean, look at us.' Beneath his forced laugh I could hear how hard he was trying to make everything seem normal, like it was any other turbine festival.

'You could start a new tradition,' I said, desperately trying to sound cheerful. 'You could give the baby a bird's name instead. How about Robin? That's a lovely name for a boy or for a girl. What do you think, sweetheart?' I looked at Willow.

'Me and George have already decided on a name,' she said.

'Whether it's a boy or a girl, we'll be calling our baby Jem.'

Well, that was it. I couldn't help myself. I told Willow exactly what I thought of that particular suggestion. I yelled at her, she yelled back, then flounced away. Ed shook his head, looking disappointed, then went after her. Beside me on the blanket, Ash was on the verge of tears.

'Don't get upset love, your sister's always been the same,' I said.

'No, Mum. It's you. *You're* always the same.'

'What does that mean?'

'You're always shouting, getting annoyed, telling her off. I'm not surprised her and Dad have left, why would anyone want to be with you?'

'Ash... I...'

'The world's about to end, Mum, and all you want to do is argue with Willow.'

He got to his feet and went to join his friends.

And just like that, I was alone again.

*

The memory of what Jem had said about the Elder Mother lurked at the edge of my thoughts, taunting me, and I pushed my chair back from the table abruptly and stood up. I couldn't let myself think about that – if I didn't hurry, I was going to be late for the delivery. Until recently, it used to take me days to collate, place, receive and distribute each week's orders, but there had been such a reduction that it only took a few hours now. Nevertheless, regardless of how much was coming, I still had to be at the touch-down site to meet the drone, swap the containers, and distribute the orders.

I set off along the street, but I was so weary, so worn down by fighting with everyone, that it was as much as I could do to put one foot in front of the other. Was it me? Maybe it was. It would be so much easier if I could just give in, believe what everyone else believed. No doubt Willow would find a new way to wind me up, but at least she'd come home, Ed would want to be with me and I could let Jem take over the job of worrying about what was going to happen to us all.

Other people seemed to have no problem accepting what she said. Of course, I wasn't the only one who was resisting the lure of Jem and her God, or who understood that it was all stupid, and wrong, and dangerous, but the voices of dissent seemed to be fading, while the monotonous chants of the Threads were getting stronger.

What would Dandy have done? I always asked myself that when I needed to find a solution to a problem. He approached everything logically and rationally, but nothing he had ever told me about and nothing in any of his books gave me any clue how to make the Threads see the error of their ways.

So. Okay then. Rather than trying to convince them to change their views, perhaps I should try working harder at changing my own. After all, I had no doubt what was driving people into Jem's arms: their helplessness, their vulnerability, their unresolvable problems. Freedom knows I had the same issues. All I had to do was turn my misery into belief. Could it really be that simple?

'I believe in God. The Threads are Bound,' I whispered to myself, testing the words, seeing how they tasted in my mouth. I said it again, forcing the words out through clenched teeth, 'I believe in God. The Threads are Bound. I believe in God. The Threads are Bound.'

The words were bitter. It was no good. No matter how helpless I felt and how much I might wish it were different, to me, they would only ever be lies. Yes, it would make things so much easier. Yes, I was desperate to have my daughter back home where she belonged, and yes, I wanted to stop fighting with Ed, but, whatever I did, I knew that there would never be any truth to be found in those words. I would never be able to make myself believe.

By the time I turned off the track and onto the sun-scorched stubble of the meadow the delivery drone was already above Front Hill. It followed the line of the ridge, skirting around the turbines, then dipping lower and I felt a sudden fondness for it – unlike so many other things nowadays, it was reliable, always arriving when it was meant to, always bringing what it was supposed to. There would be medicine for Molly, which I'd drop round as soon as I'd sorted the delivery, Laurel had ordered something to try and sooth Mila's on-going teething issues, and there would be lots of seeds, which would need to be planted as soon as possible. There were far fewer orders than usual, but no-one outside Underhill had questioned why and presumably no-one cared. Or maybe no-one had noticed. As far as I was aware, everything to do with ordering was done automatically, without the involvement of an actual person.

The drone flew lower, and I wondered whether it would still be making this journey in the future, when the turbines finally fell still, and the lights went out. Would anyone be here in Underhill? Would our community want to stay and find a new way of living, without the turbines? Was that even possible? Or perhaps we would never have to find out. Perhaps when Whiteout arrived, everyone on the planet would be killed by an impossibly cold sea of ice – apart from us in Underhill who would be Renewed and live a new life bound to God, whatever that meant. It was all just so ridiculous.

The drone was close enough now that I could feel the disturbance in the air as it swept across the fields, and came to a stop, hanging almost motionless above the touch-down site while it ran through its landing procedures. Because there were no clouds – although I was sure that the drought was preparing to break – the sunlight glinting off the panels was so bright that I had to look away which was why I glanced towards the barn at the edge of the meadow. Someone was standing in the doorway and I squinted, trying to make out who it was – everyone knew they weren't allowed in the field while the drone was here.

Above me, the drone engaged its landing pads, locking them into position below the curve of its belly, then dropped smoothly onto the patch of cleared ground. It rocked lightly and powered down, shuddering slightly as it switched itself off. I looked back at the barn, but there was no sign of whoever had been there. I reached my hand up to Wave the access pad. There was a brief pause, followed by the usual series of clicks, then the door slid open.

Inside, the containers rotated, moving into position. The drone had just begun to lower ours to the ground when the shouting started. I took a step back, so I could look past the drone's belly, towards the barn. People were running towards me – perhaps as many as twenty of them – and I didn't need to see the string around their necks to know that they were all Threads. Fred was at the front, closely followed by Camman and his two sons, carrying piles of ropes. Everyone else was trailing behind, bellowing at the top of their voices.

The drone's warning system must have detected something unexpected because it rocked slightly and powered itself up, then began to pull our container, which hadn't fully disengaged, back inside. It was only when Fred and the others started throwing the pile of ropes over the top of it that I realised it was a huge net. By the time the drone had finished retrieving our container, they'd managed to fling the net right over it and everyone had spread out in a circle holding it down, trapping the drone.

A high-pitched whine came from somewhere inside and it wobbled slightly on its landing pads. I went over to Fred, pushed him hard and yelled, 'What the fuck…' but that's as far as I got because he lifted a hand away from the netting and swung it in my direction, catching me painfully on the cheek.

'Stop this now,' I bellowed. 'You can't do this, they'll stop sending orders.'

I ran around the group, yelling, begging them to stop, telling them what a stupid idea it was. Lorne was there, but she shrugged me off when I screamed at her. No-one paid me any attention. Tish started chanting and they all joined in: *The Threads are Bound. The Threads are Bound. The Threads are Bound.*

They were all mad. Really, they were. I had to be witnessing a mass breakdown. How could anyone think that we could live without the orders? Why would anyone want to?

I tried again to make someone, anyone, listen to me, but the shouting just got louder, drowning out my voice and the awful noise of the drone.

Then Camman took something out of his pocket – it looked like one of the heavy metal hammers that Ed used up on the turbines. He crouched down, ducked under the netting and crawled towards the drone. His sons did the same, while everyone else shuffled around a bit, repositioning themselves, keeping the netting taut and the drone in place.

Camman and his boys started hitting the metal walls, timing it so that each swing connected with the curved outer shell at the same time as the others shouted the word *Bound*. At first, their efforts didn't seem to be having much effect and it looked as if the drone would withstand the attack. But then Camman reached down, aiming his efforts at what looked like part of the flight mechanism. He smashed the hammer in a frenzy and eventually the panel buckled. At that point, an alarm started blaring. It was high-pitched and painfully loud.

When Camman's eldest son, Lew, saw what his father was doing, he moved round so that he could attack a similar panel, slamming his hammer into it over and over, until it was twisted and buckled. Then for good measure, he forced the edge of the hammer underneath it, and managed to lever the whole thing off, exposing brackets and circuits and Freedom knows what else. He reached in and pulled out a fistful of wires. Meanwhile Camman's other son, Ali, was attacking the small control panel alongside the door – the one I used to check the inventory – battering it until it shattered.

The alarm blared, while the chanting went on and on until eventually, almost as if they were co-ordinated, the drone and the Threads both fell silent at the same time. Camman and his sons crawled out from under the net.

'What have you done?' I said.

They all looked at me, but it was Fred who replied, a huge, inane smile plastered across his face.

'It's the greatest preparation.'

I was appalled. I couldn't believe their stupidity. Most of our supplies of meat had been slaughtered and burned, and many of our crops had been left to rot in the fields, so how could we continue to live in Underhill if we couldn't order things? It just wasn't possible. I thought about Molly. She needed the drugs that were inside the damaged drone and there were several others who relied on the deliveries for medicine. Who knew if we would be able to get our container out? And even if we could, what would happen in a couple of weeks when they needed more?

This would be the end of Underhill. There was no way we could survive without the orders – we would have to request the relocation of the entire community. We would all end up being forced to work in a factory. How would the kids cope with that?

What sort of life would Willow's baby have? The stupid, blind, ignorant belief of these people had ruined everything for us all.

'We can't survive without orders.'

It was all I could think of to say and I didn't really expect a reply, but then Camman said, 'We don't need them. It's not long now until Whiteout. Cleansing will happen at the first storm.'

It was a nightmare. I was living in a nightmare. How had one young woman managed to bring our lives to this? I needed to get away, I couldn't bear to be near these people and their twisted thoughts. I couldn't bear to see the crippled drone. I needed to think, I had to talk to Molly, although Freedom knows whether she'd even be able to get out of bed without her drugs. I had to try and make a plan, work out what was best for me and Ed and the kids. I had to decide what to do about Willow and the baby.

I turned my back on them and walked away, reaching up to touch my cheek which was smarting from where Fred had hit me. My face was wet. At first, I thought it was blood, but I looked at my fingertips, then up at the sky. Above the hills, clouds had finally begun to arrive, bringing rain, and with it the beginning of the end of Dust.

I was nearly at the barn when I heard the drone shuddering back into life. Lights flashed, the landing pads disappeared inside its belly and there was a horrible grinding noise. I started running back towards it.

'Hold the net,' Camman was yelling. 'Hold the net.'

They all grabbed it and pulled down hard. Improbable though it seemed, the drone appeared to be trying to take off. The awful chanting started up again, and for a moment I wondered if I was condemned to be stuck in the field listening to them shout *The Threads are Bound* until I went completely mad.

'Pull down,' yelled Camman. 'Don't let it get away.'

They were all concentrating so hard on holding the ropes and chanting that no-one noticed Lew slip under the net. Camman was trying to get everyone to roll the drone over, to prevent it from taking off – they were heaving on the net, loosening it momentarily, then heaving again, and the drone was rocking wildly. On the far side, Lew had crawled even closer, smashing his hammer into the drone's base each time it tilted up towards him.

Too late, I realised what was going to happen. I yelled at him to move, to get away, to get out of there, but he couldn't hear me above the noise of the chanting and the last thing Lew would have heard before the entire weight of the drone rolled over him was *The Threads are Bound.*

23

Eileen

Not long after we had made the greatest preparation, Kat came storming up to the turbines. She charged around for a while bellowing Willow's name, yanking open the doors to the hut and the substation. When she didn't find her, she marched over to the Uplander's camp, still yelling Willow's name, but she wasn't there either. Eventually, she came over to Hinton where I'd been waiting to see Jem, who was inside talking to God and it was only thanks to me that Kat didn't barge her way straight up the steps.

'You can't go up there,' I said, standing in her way.

'I can go wherever I like,' she said, sounding slightly deranged.

'The Prophet is busy.' Words were lining themselves up so neatly and slipping so easily from my mouth now that I almost didn't have to think about it.

'The Prophet? *That's* what you're calling her?'

'That's what *you* should call her. It's about showing respect.'

'Grow up, Eileen, and get out of my way. *Get off me.*'

At that point, she pushed me. She actually pushed me. I mean, I'd barely touched her, just put my hands around her throat in a warning gesture, it's not like I'd started to squeeze or anything, but she completely over-reacted and pushed me so hard that I had to grab hold of the hand-rail so as not to fall over. I could have lost the baby.

'I could have lost the baby.'

Kat was already half-way up the steps, but she stopped and

turned to look at me.

'You're not pregnant, Eileen,' she said. 'Who'd have a baby with you?'

How dare she? Ed and Leroy had nearly come to blows over which one would be the father of my baby.

'There's a whole list of people who wanted to father my baby,' I called. 'And you know who was top, Kat? Can you guess?'

The bitch just ignored me.

'Ed.' I yelled, so I know she heard me, but she didn't say anything. She obviously couldn't bear to hear the truth. Well they do say it hurts.

She started banging on Hinton's door.

'Open the door, Jem. Open it, or so help me…'

The door swung open. Jem stood in the doorway, looking surprisingly unsurprised to find Kat on the platform.

'Jem,' Kat said.

'You must call her the Prophet,' I shouted.

'It's ok, Eileen,' said Jem, although she was the one that had made such a fuss, demanding that everyone call her the Prophet at all times.

'And she didn't kiss Hinton's bottom step. She shouldn't be up there without kissing his bottom step.'

They both ignored me.

'Are you hiding Willow in there?' Kat said, and pushed past her without waiting for a reply, only to reappear a moment later – I could have told her that her precious daughter wasn't inside Hinton. Kat put her hand out and grasped the railing hard, as if she might be about to fall over.

'This has to stop,' Kat said.

Jem put her hand on Kat's shoulder.

'I've been hoping you'd come and see me.'

What? Why? What possible reason could Jem have to want Kat

to come to see her? I didn't want to let myself think that Jem might be losing focus, but I couldn't help it. Threading all those unsuitables from who knows where and now, apparently, pleased to see Kat. It's not as if Jem didn't know exactly what I thought of the woman.

'What's troubling you?' asked Jem, arranging her face into her *tell-me-everything-and-I'll-make-it-all-better* expression. A hint of a smile, slightly raised eyebrows and tilted head – it was definitely one of her most successful looks.

'You've had your fun, Jem. You've let it go on much longer than it should have done, but someone's been killed. Enough is enough, it has to stop now.'

'You flatter me, Kat. People do what they want to do.'

'That's rubbish and you know it. These Threads of yours don't even dare breathe without your approval. You've spent months preying on the most vulnerable people in Underhill. You've picked them off one-by-one, told them what they want to hear, made promises that you can't keep. Now what?'

She paused briefly, but Jem obviously didn't think it was a question that deserved an answer, so after a moment Kat continued.

'Have you given any thought to how they're all going to feel when nothing happens? When they finally realise that you've been lying to them all along? Have you thought about that?'

I was trying to decide if it would be more satisfying to go up the steps and tell Kat exactly what I thought of her or give her a big shove to help her down them, but then Jem flicked her gaze towards me, just for a second, and I stayed where I was.

'I can't believe you've got nothing to say,' said Kat. 'Don't you care that Lew is dead?'

'Of course I care, I am bound together with all of the Threads...'

'Stop saying that. Lew wasn't just a Thread,' said Kat. I held my breath, waiting to see what Jem would do. Everyone knew how much she hated being interrupted – she'd told us often enough how interrupting God's Prophet was an indication that our own thread was becoming knotted, and of course no-one wanted to have to ask Jem to help them unpick their knots. Surprisingly though, on this occasion, it looked like she was prepared to make an exception to the *never interrupt the Prophet* rule, because she made no attempt to stop Kat talking.

'He was a young man with his whole life ahead of him. And because of you, because of your words, because of the lies you've spread, he's dead.'

Jem's expression changed to the no head-tilting, lips pressed together in a thin but firm line one, which meant *I-know-things-you-don't-but-I-also-know-that-it's-not-your-fault*, but she didn't get a chance to say anything because Kat was busy winding herself up into a full-blown tantrum.

'You have to make Willow come home. My daughter needs to be where she's loved. The baby's coming in a few weeks and she needs to be down in the village, where I can look after her.'

'Willow is at home. She is loved and looked after by us,' said Jem.

Seeing Kat's tears was wonderful. This was payback – she was finally getting what she deserved.

'I'll do anything,' she said. 'Anything you want. Just please tell my baby girl to come home before it's too late and she ends up like Lew.'

She really was working herself up into a very undignified state, what with the tears, snot and spit pouring out of her, together with a very convincing demonstration of some hyperventilating. She wiped all the stuff off her face with the back of her hand, then wiped her hand on her trousers. She really was a vile woman.

'Please, Jem. I'm begging you. All this stuff you say about

everyone being bound together – when really, it's just forcing us apart. My daughter won't speak to me, my husband is sleeping up here, and my son's blaming me for it all. And it's not just my family, you're tearing the whole of Underhill apart. And for what? For a made-up story?'

'Kat, Kat, Kat,' Jem said, in her most soothing voice. 'If only you would accept that you can't understand what it means to be a Thread of God by reading books. You can only understand what it means to be a Thread of God by *believing* in God. Let yourself believe, and you will have peace from your anger.'

At that point, I honestly wondered if Kat was going to have a heart attack – her face was scarlet and she seemed to be having a problem breathing. In the end though, she forced out a few pathetic words. 'It's *you* that's making me angry.'

'That's not true is it, Kat?' Jem said, all calm and serene. 'You were angry before I arrived. I did not bring your anger with me. Your anger is *your* problem, but if you bind yourself to God, you will find peace.'

At that point, Kat actually screamed, a completely unnecessary and overly dramatic scream that went on and on. When she finally stopped, she swallowed hard and managed to get herself under control long enough to say, 'Please just tell Willow to come home. Please,' she was actually moaning now, like a cow in pain. 'I'll do anything you want. I couldn't bear it if something happened to her, or to the baby. Please Jem, please, I beg you, tell Willow to come home.'

'I hear what you're saying, Kat,' said Jem, 'I understand you, and I will help you.' There was a brief flicker of hope on Kat's face, then Jem continued, 'Your words come from a place of fear, Kat. You're scared. Scared about giving up control, scared about your place in the new future. But I can help you find your way through this. Together we can confront your fear.'

She reached into her pocket and pulled out a length of red string which she dangled in front of Kat's face. Kat stared at it for a moment, then ripped it out of Jem's fingers and threw it over the side of the platform, where it drifted to the ground. Then she turned and marched down the steps, pushing past me. She was sobbing so hard I'm surprised she could see where she was going.

It was the funniest thing I'd seen for a very long time.

24

Kat

I got away from there as fast as I could. I couldn't see properly through my tears and at one point my ankle turned on the uneven ground, and the pain forced me to slow down. Pleading with Jem had been my final chance of persuading Willow to come home. I was desperate, I'd been reduced to begging, but she'd been unmoved, just looking at me with that pitying, arrogant look of hers.

I limped along the path. I was completely exhausted. I can't have been the only one who hadn't slept since the accident. Every time I shut my eyes, I'd see the pulpy mess of Lew's body, and hear Amber's terrible, harrowing screams. I'd see Camman lifting the remains of his son onto a blanket. I'd hear Tish, shrieking that Lew had made the ultimate preparation. And through it all, I'd hear the Threads chanting.

How had it come to this? How could it be that one of our own had actually died because of Jem's lies?

And yet. And yet. She knew about the Elder Mother. My Elder Mother. Mine. The mother of daughters, the defender of homesteads and the healer of fevers. That's what Jem had called her. I couldn't keep her words out of my thoughts any longer, and once I let them in, I couldn't stop thinking about how Jem had claimed that the Elder Mother had visited her, had talked to her when she hadn't said so much as a word to me in all these years. And it got worse. When I remembered how Jem had stood on the top of Lucy's steps, looking down at us all, saying how the Elder Mother had told her that she was *part of God*, I thought I was going to be sick.

For months, the question I'd been asking myself was why Jem was doing this, but alone on the path a different question forced itself into my mind and once it was there, it wouldn't go away.

What if the Elder Mother was part of God? What if, all these years, when I thought I'd been talking to her, I'd actually been talking to *God*? What if I'd been fooling myself, lying to myself, pretending to believe that everything about God and religion was evil? What if I'd convinced myself that the Elder Mother was just an innocent idea that I carried around with me for comfort, whereas the truth was that it was something far more sinister? That would make me as bad as Jem. For the rest of that lonely journey back to the village, my thoughts bellowed at me: you're just like Jem, you're as bad as Jem, you're just like her.

That's why I decided to find the axe. Ed's tools were always locked away, but I knew where he kept the key: in the kitchen drawer, behind the cutlery, tucked under a messy ball of string. My ankle was throbbing badly – I knew I should strap it and elevate it, but instead I took the key and limped to the barn, trying not to put too much weight on my foot. The axe was where I knew it would be, and I pulled it out of Ed's tool chest, feeling its heft, then I locked the chest and left the barn.

Out of the corner of my eye, I saw a glint from one of the Raptors. If anyone at the authority was bothering to check, there would be a record of the fact that I was walking through the village carrying an axe over my shoulder, but somehow the authority had become the least of my problems. No-one in Underhill asked me where I was going. No-one cared. These days, everyone was too wrapped up in their own concerns to bother about what anyone else was doing. The way things were going, our community would have disintegrated long before the turbines stopped turning.

It was one of the last hot days before the end of Dust, so after my hike up to the turbines, and all the running around up there, and hobbling back down the path to my house, the shade from the trees in the graveyard was very welcome. It was strangely quiet – there was no hint of a breeze and no birdsong – and standing in front of the elder tree the only sound I could hear was the deafening roar of my own thoughts.

'You betrayed me.' I spoke the words out loud, just like I always did, and she received my words in silence, just like she always had.

'You let me believe that this… you… were something other than God. For so many years I carried you inside me. But now… now… you let that girl tell everyone that you are *one of the infinite threads*.' I spat the words out, hoping they would pierce her bark and stab her tender, pulpy insides. 'How could you betray me?'

I lifted the axe up and over my shoulder, then heaved it down towards her. The blade glanced off her trunk. Until recently Ed had kept his tools in perfect condition, spending hours sharpening and polishing them, but they were one of many things that he'd stopped caring about recently, and the axe was blunter than usual. My arms were strong though, from the years of pushing the cart full of orders across the field, and I hoisted it back up and tried again. It sunk into her trunk with a dull thud. I pulled it out, and swung it again, slicing her bark open.

'Well hear me now, Elder Mother. I've given you no warning. I've made no offerings.'

I adjusted my grip and swung again. 'I hope you feel this.'

I tore into her flesh, slashing a deep gouge. I slammed the axe into her over and over, until finally, with sweat pouring off me, I had to stop to catch my breath. I listened, half-expecting to hear her screaming. But she was silent.

I hoisted the axe back up and urging all my anger and frustration into my arms, I swung in a frenzy, chopping and hacking, opening the wound in her trunk little by little.

'Mum?'

I spun round. There was a bowl of water cradled in Ash's arms. He must have come to see the sapling.

'Mum?' he said again, looking at the tree, then back at me, trying to understand what was happening. He knew I loved the elder tree. He may not have known why, or what she really meant to me, but he knew that after him and his sister, and Ed, I loved the elder tree more than anything else in the world.

'What're you doing?' he said, his voice cracking.

I shook my head, not trusting myself to answer. Instead, I turned back to the tree and put my hand just below the point where the lowest branches spread out. I pushed, hard. She was heavy with leaves, which trembled, and somewhere inside, there was a crack, but she stayed upright.

I swung again, and the blade of the axe sunk deep into her flesh.

Ash was crying, and when I heard his tears I started crying too. I knew he was scared, I was scared as well, but I needed to finish what I'd started.

I wiggled the handle of the axe, trying to pull it out of her trunk but the Elder Mother held onto it, refusing to give it up.

'Come on,' I yelled, fighting her, heaving on the handle until I forced her to let it go. I stumbled backwards and a twinge from my ankle shot up my leg, but still I wouldn't stop.

I lifted the axe one more time. Behind me, Ash was calling, 'Mum, please. Mum, stop it,' but I ignored him. My hands were cramping, but I ignored that too as I took aim and swung again. I thought of Willow, of my pregnant daughter and my unborn grandchild, and the danger they were in. I thought about Lew's terrible, unnecessary death and I thought of how much it hurt each time Ed turned away from me. I thought about Jem and everything she had done to my family and my friends. But most of all, at that moment, standing there in graveyard, I thought about the Elder Mother's betrayal.

I let my thoughts swell inside me, until there was no room for anything else. And then I forced my fear and grief and sadness down through my arms and into my hands and with a roar that could be heard on the hills, I swung the axe a final time.

The blade buried itself deep inside the tree's soft core, she rocked a little and then, with the axe still inside her, the last fibres of her trunk snapped, and she fell slowly backwards against the wall of the old church.

Tears streamed down my face and I gulped at the air in great heaving sobs as I lowered myself onto my hands and knees and crawled over to her. I wiped my eyes and waited for my breath to calm. It was only then that I leaned close, smelling her sap. I searched for a long time, but no matter how hard I looked, there was no sign of the Elder Mother. Or God.

THE FIRST STORM
OF WHITEOUT

25

Eileen

I had no intention of dying from exposure, so I put on multiple layers of clothes before I left for the Binding Area. A few of the Threads weren't wearing coats, still trying to outdo each other with their pathetic attempts to prove that *they* were ones most tightly bound to God. They kept saying things like *God will provide*, which was true of course, but they seemed to forget that God would be providing for us *after* Cleansing, which wouldn't help anyone who froze to death before it happened. I suppose it was one way of sorting out those of us who deserved Renewal from those who didn't.

On my way to the Binding Area, I walked behind some Uplanders who were jabbering away, and I accidentally kicked one of them. Honestly, it was only when she turned around that I realised it was the same one who had announced her pregnancy a few days before. I'd already added her to my List of Enemies, along with everyone else who was having one of the babies that *I* was supposed to be having.

His sub-standard and frankly amateur performance really should have alerted me to the fact that Leroy wasn't properly equipped for the purposes of fertilisation. He had the necessary anatomy, but clearly it wasn't functioning correctly. Since there was no doubt at all that God wanted me to have a child, I had concluded that I'd had a lucky escape. Once we were Renewed, and I received formal recognition as the first and most senior

Thread, then God Itself could choose the father of my baby.

The rope around the Binding Area was pink with a few darker patches. I'd queued up along with everyone else to let my blood splatter into a bucket. Jem said it was important that we all contributed, that by mixing our blood together, and then soaking the rope in it, we were creating a symbol of how closely we were bound. When she drew the knife across their palms several people collapsed, but I put a bowl underneath their hands, so at least their blood wasn't wasted. Presumably the darker patches came from the blood of those who were most tightly bound to God's rope. Like me.

Hopefully everything would be over before it got dark, but if we were still there when night fell, there were several large bonfires ready to be lit, and the Uplanders had constructed temporary shelters, although *shelter* is too grand a word for them really since all they'd done was stake bits of waterproof material into the ground on one side and attach them to poles on the other. They looked a bit like wide-open mouths and I supposed with us all huddled inside, we'd look like the teeth, smiling at God.

To begin with, we stood outside the shelters, facing down the valley because the first storm of Whiteout always comes from the east. There had been rumours going around about whether God would appear at some point in the proceedings. A few of the Threads were convinced that It would want to come and introduce Itself, perhaps give us a sort of presentation about how things would work from now on. However, others were equally certain that God would not come, that It would continue to relay Messages through Jem, just like It always had.

Jem herself was non-committal on the subject, although to be fair, she was exhausted from the enormous strain she had been under, making sure that everyone was ready for Cleansing and Renewal. Ever since she'd announced that God was keeping a record of how vigilantly we were reporting those who failed to do sufficient preps, there had been a huge increase in the number of reports, which had escalated even further after she confirmed what I'd known for ages anyway – that those of us who were best at identifying frayed Threads would be put in charge of the others after Renewal. It was inevitable that the increase in reports meant I was called on to assist with knot unpickings – one or two Threads even presented themselves for an impromptu unpicking – and, of course, each unpicking really took it out of Jem.

I knew God expected me to lead by example, so I made sure that I reported as many people as possible. For example, I reported Willow for not taking her turn keeping the Binding Area clean and tidy. As Jem had taught us: *The Prophet can only pass on Messages in a place of cleanliness*, but Willow seemed to think that just because she happened to be eight months pregnant, she shouldn't have to get down on her hands and knees and scrub Jem's speaking platform. I also reported Camman multiple times because since the incident with the drone, he had been really preoccupied and definitely wasn't fulfilling his guarding duties as well as he should be. All sorts of people had been turning up at Hinton to see Jem whenever they felt like it and considering that Camman still had one of his sons left, there really wasn't any excuse for such inattention on his part. Sadly, despite my diligent reporting, Jem didn't think that either Willow or Camman needed help unpicking their knots and of course, it wasn't for me to question the decisions of the Prophet.

Almost all the Threads were assembled inside the Binding Area by the time the leading edge of the storm swept through the valley. Only Ed and George were missing. They'd been around at the beginning, but Jem took Ed to one side and spoke to him for a while, then Ed left, taking George with him. Frustratingly, I hadn't been able to get close enough to hear what Jem had been saying to Ed, so I don't know where they went. But the rest of us were there and we lifted our faces towards the sky as the first storm of Whiteout arrived above us.

Snow always reminds me of my Dad. He called it *nature's marvel* and every year, right up until he died, when the snow came we would go outside and he would take my hand, laying the back of it flat against his palm, and together we would catch a single snowflake. We'd look at its intricate design and Dad would remind me how every snowflake was unique, and we'd gaze up at the vast slab of grey sky and wonder how something so complex and beautiful could come from it. Every time the first snow arrived, I wanted more than anything to be with my Dad, catching snowflakes. But this year was different. This year I was with Jem and I was excited.

As the temperature dropped, and Dad's grey slab loomed overhead, the anticipation grew. We'd been waiting so long for this day, it was difficult to believe it was finally here. I was so happy that I almost joined in one of the conversations going on around me. I must admit however, I hadn't anticipated that the whole Cleansing thing would take quite so long and after a while it began to feel like I'd been standing in the Binding Area forever. The wind was driving freezing rain straight into my face, my nose and cheeks were painfully cold, and I was struggling to catch my breath. I congratulated myself on having had the foresight to wear both pairs of trousers, four pairs of socks and all my jumpers. The inappropriately clothed Threads were shivering violently, and I distracted myself from how cold I was by trying to work out which one of them was likely to be the first to die from exposure. I thought Tish might be about to go, but then someone decided to light the bonfires.

Once everyone had warmed up a bit, we did some chanting, but after a while the periods of silence grew longer. Jem went between us, talking quietly, putting an arm around a person here, a person there, until at some point she climbed onto the platform, and everyone fell silent and dutifully shuffled round to face her. She was wearing the same clothes she had worn the day she'd walked into Underhill: black trousers and jacket with her red scarf tied tightly around her neck. How life had changed since that day.

I got out my notebook, but my fingers were freezing so I didn't bother to write all the usual stock phrases out in full and consequently I ended up with a lot of notes like:

Thds are Bound.

First storm of Whtout = C and R.

God knows the preps done.

God abt to Renew Its relationship with ppl of U.

Every now and then, I did make the effort to write out what she was saying in full, mainly to try and stop my fingers from going numb.

The Threads must keep the binding tight. Those left in Underhill who have yet to believe will need your help to understand why everyone but God's chosen ones had to die. They will need your strength to embrace Renewal when all that remains of humanity is bound to God's rope and to each other and to everything on earth.

By the time she reached that point in her speech, the valley floor had turned white and Jem was shouting to make herself heard above the wind. The weather was too bad to carry on making notes, but it didn't matter, because she'd almost finished.

'The first storm of Whiteout is here,' she bellowed. 'The world will be Cleansed. Rejoice my Threads. Rejoice for you are bound to God and you will survive.'

I caught a snowflake. This is it, Dad, I thought. I am a Thread. I am bound to God. I will be Renewed.

All around me people were shouting things like, 'I am ready,' and 'I am bound,' and 'Cleansing, Cleansing, Cleansing.' We took hold of each other's hands and I was next to Jem which was as it should be and although I also had to hold Lily's hand, somehow it was more bearable than usual. *The Threads are Bound, The Threads are Bound, The Threads are Bound.*

Cleansing had begun.

This was it.

'God is among us,' yelled Jem.

I have to say, even taking into account the limited visibility, I'd seen no sign of God and I was pretty certain no-one else had either.

'God does not want Its Threads to suffer. God will keep you warm. Do you feel God's warmth?' she shouted.

Some people called out things like: *I feel it* and *I am warm*, but that was hardly surprising since they were the ones closest to the fires.

'God shall give Its Threads the gift of sleep while It Cleanses the world. When you wake, you shall be Renewed. But for now, accept God's gift and sleep.' She stopped shouting then, and her voice got slower as she repeated the word *sleep*.

Just like we'd practised, we started chanting *sleep, sleep, sleep* and all around me, people lay down in the shelters, huddling together as close as possible to the fires. Even as they closed their eyes, they continued to murmur *sleep, sleep, sleep*. I was too tired to stay standing, so I found a space inside a shelter and lay on the ground, pulling the hood of my coat around my face.

The chanting had stopped, and I was nearly asleep when someone behind me started wriggling around, which was incredibly annoying, and it was a relief when they got up, stepped over me and left the shelter. I pushed my hood back a little and watched whoever it was walk slowly away from the fires. They stopped, bent over for a moment, then straightened up again and carried on towards the ropes. It was only when she briefly turned and looked back that I realised it was Willow. I knew it. I *knew* that all these months she'd only been pretending to be as tightly bound as the rest of us. She was so frayed.

Jem appeared from the other side of the fire, walked over and put her hand on Willow's arm. At that point, I tugged my hood back around my face and over my eyes, and my very last thought before I slept was that Willow was so lucky to have Jem to help her unpick her knots.

26

Kat

It was finally here. The storm that would change everything, according to the people gathered halfway up Front Hill, in anticipation of, well, what? No-one I'd asked had actually been able to give me a proper explanation of what they expected to happen. I knew what Jem had said of course, her so-called vision, or prophecy, call it what you will, of a sea of ice covering the world, killing everyone but us lucky few in Underhill. But despite all the talk, all the anticipation, no-one seemed to have the first idea about the practicalities.

I'd ask, was it the whole of the earth that was going to be buried beneath the ice, or just places where people were living? What about all the plants and animals, surely this God of Jem's didn't want those things to die? And, although it might be Whiteout here, elsewhere in the world it was Dust – or whatever name they had for the season that used to be called summer before it became so arid – so perhaps they could tell me how exactly the ice would form in all the places where it was currently really hot? Also, was everything going to happen instantaneously, or would it take a while for this ice ocean to spread? How big an area around Underhill would remain ice-free? When would the ice melt? And when it had, what would happen to all the dead bodies littering the world?

The list of questions for which no-one had any answers went on and on, but whenever they were asked, the Threads would narrow their eyes and stare into the middle distance, as if they were actually expecting to see God looking back at them. They would purse their lips for a moment, before saying, 'Only the Threads can fully understand Cleansing and Renewal.' I had to give it to Jem, she had drilled them well, they trotted out their responses perfectly time after time, pretending that they had some sort of special knowledge about how it was all going to work, but of course there was no special knowledge, because it wasn't going to happen.

Needless to say, I wasn't the only one who couldn't bear the endless repetition of such mindless, meaningless rubbish, but the problem was that almost all of the Threads, aside from the handful of Uplanders, were our family and friends. They were our people. We loved them. I mean, obviously we wanted them to realise how ridiculous they were being, but at the end of the day what were we supposed to do?

If we notified them, they'd almost certainly be forced to leave Underhill. If we tried to physically stop them spending time with Jem, we'd be hurting our own. Those of us who had family among the Threads talked and talked about it, but in the end, we decided that we really had no option but to let the whole thing play out. After all, at least the girl had provided an end date for the whole stupid fantasy. The first storm of Whiteout would arrive, and once it had passed, once they saw that nothing had changed, surely then they would face up to how foolish they'd been and how thoroughly they'd allowed themselves to be swept along by empty promises of a better life.

I hadn't yet had official confirmation about whether the authority had accepted my explanation about the attack on the drone – I'd said it was a skirmishing group of Uplanders – but they had at least agreed to send transportation for those villagers who wanted to leave before we were cut off by Whiteout. Of course, the Threads didn't expect the vehicles would ever arrive, due to the rest of humankind being murdered – sorry, *Cleansed* – during the storm.

Those residents who had asked to go, who had agreed to give up their homes and make a new life in a city were generally older people who had no family in the village, although a couple of them had told me they were going because they no longer recognised the Underhill that they'd lived in for their whole lives. *She* was to blame for that. I was devastated by the break-up of our community, but too few of us were taking our situation seriously enough to make the decisions that needed to be made. I kept on telling myself that all this nonsense would be over soon. After the first storm of Whiteout, when the Threads saw that absolutely nothing at all had happened, we could talk properly about our future.

So for the first time ever, I was happy that Whiteout had arrived, although that didn't stop me standing at the kitchen window, watching the storm sweep down from the hills, while I compulsively raked my nails along the scarred flesh of my arm. All I could think about was Willow. *Hang on in there my love*, I thought. *Get through this, see for yourself that all Jem's talk means nothing, and then come home.* I wished more than anything that I was with her, but Ed had made it clear that I wouldn't be allowed to be anywhere near their stupid meeting place. He said that if I insisted on going up there I'd be forced to leave, that if it came to it, some of the others would be prepared to hurt me to keep me away. In any case, he was convinced that no matter what, our daughter was going to be completely fine because of God. I wanted to take God's rope, the one that Jem went on and on about and choke her with it, until she was incapable of saying the words God, Thread, rope, or bound, ever again.

'God only wants the Threads to gather in the Binding Area,' Ed kept saying.

'Really?' I'd reply. 'And how exactly do you know that? I mean, did God actually tell you in person? Did It Wave you? Please do enlighten me as to how you know where God wants you to be.'

'You can try and make me feel stupid, Kat. Freedom knows, I'm used to it. But it won't work. God has said the Threads must be alone in the Binding Area during Cleansing, so that's what will happen.'

A couple of times, I had caught myself walking towards the graveyard to talk to the Elder Mother about everything, before I remembered, with a feeling that was like a kick to my stomach, that she wasn't there any more.

The closer we got to Whiteout, the nastier the arguments with Ed had become, partly because out of sheer frustration I had resorted to saying things like, 'You don't want me there because you want to spend time with Eileen.' Every time I said it, he'd clench his teeth tightly together, then spit out, 'For Freedom's sake, Kat. How many times do I have to tell you? Nothing happened between me and Eileen.'

For what it was worth, I believed him. I knew better than anyone what a vindictive lying cow she was, but it was easy to keep flinging the accusation at him and I wanted to hurt him, just like he was hurting me.

Inevitably though, it wasn't long before our arguments returned to Willow and we went round and round in circles until eventually I was forced to accept that my friends and neighbours, people I'd known for years, really would be prepared to do whatever it took to stop me being up on the hill with my daughter during the storm. My only comfort was knowing that at least Ed would be with her.

Outside, the snow was falling more heavily, the wind had picked up and the kitchen windows were rattling. Ed had been promising to sort them out for months, it was yet another thing that he hadn't done. The street was deserted: with the arrival of the storm everyone who wasn't on Front Hill was tucked up at home. At least I knew that one of my children was safe – I could hear Ash pacing around his room. He was miserable but safe. I hoped Willow was warm. I hoped they all were really, apart from Jem, who I would cheerfully let freeze to death.

The bang on the front door made me jump. There was another, and an another, someone was thumping it insistently and I rushed into the hallway hoping against hope that Ed had finally come to his senses, that he'd come home and brought our daughter with him. Ash ran down the stairs. He got there first and as he opened the door, a gust of wind caught it, slamming it against the wall. Lily stood on the doorstep. She pushed back her snow-covered hood and fumbled with the scarf wrapped around her face. I was already reaching for my coat and boots by the time she got the words out.

'It's Willow. Something's wrong.'

Beside me, Ash was pulling on his own boots.

'Ash, stay here,' I said.

'I'm coming, Mum. She's *my* twin.'

We couldn't waste time arguing. I grabbed a blanket. Was there anything else I should take? I couldn't think straight. I had to get to Willow.

It wasn't until the three of us were stumbling up the path, leaning into the wind, snow blowing into our mouths and eyes that I thought to ask Lily how long Willow had been in labour. The wind took my words away and I had to bellow the question several times before she heard me.

'I don't think she is,' Lily shouted over her shoulder.

My relief was only momentary. 'So what is it? What's wrong?'

The wind whipped Lily's reply from her mouth, so I reached

out and pulled her arm, forcing her to stop. The three of us huddled together, our heads touching, and I asked again, 'What's wrong with Willow?'

'I think Jem might be going to hurt her.'

'Hurt her?' She wasn't making any sense.

'Those rumours you heard about Jem hurting people?' Lily said. 'I think they might be true.'

The wind hurled snow against our backs and we leaned closer.

'Dad wouldn't let anyone hurt Willow.' Despite everything, Ash's confidence in his father was touching.

'Your dad's not there,' Lily said.

'Why not? Where is he?' I was appalled. Surely he hadn't left Willow.

'I don't know, he was there at first. But he and George left before the storm started.'

My poor baby was all alone. I broke free of our huddled group, the wind catching my wail, carrying it up the hill.

'He promised. He promised he would look after Willow.'

I pushed past Lily, almost knocking her over in my panic. I stamped up the path, calling to Willow over and over again. Willow. Willow. Willow. The shape of my daughter's name filled my mouth, pushing me through the snow, parting the wind, driving me towards her. Nothing was going to stop me reaching my baby girl.

All the months of Threads walking back and forth to their Binding Area meant the path on the lower part of Front Hill was relatively clear but even so, my lungs burned even as tears froze on my cheeks. Ash matched me footstep for footstep, so when I turned off the path and stamped through the snow to their meeting area, my boy was right there beside me.

Flames from several fires lit up a row of little shelters and inside, people were lying huddled together on the ground. Were they asleep? In the middle of a storm? Were they all actually insane? I scanned the rows of bodies frantically, but Willow wasn't among them. Nor was Jem. Then Lily caught my hand and led Ash and I away from the shelters and around to the other side of the fires.

At first, I couldn't see anything, but then my gaze dropped and I saw my baby girl. She was on her knees, arms outstretched, hands gripping the step in front of the platform, snow piled on her back. The rounded bulk of her stomach rested on the frozen ground.

I rushed over and crouched beside her, saying, 'Willow, sweetheart. I'm here.'

She was shivering so violently that her body was jolting as though she was having a fit. I brushed the snow off her as best I could and put the blanket over her, tugging it around her bump.

'Are you hurt?'

There was no indication that she even knew I was there. Ash knelt on her other side and rubbed her back. I touched my head to hers, she was chanting, so low I could barely hear the words, but I didn't need to. I knew what she was saying. *The Threads are Bound. The Threads are Bound.*

I put my lips against Willow's ear. Her skin was so cold. 'Has she hurt you?'

Willow shook her head, just fractionally, then, without removing her arms from the step, she turned her head to look at me. Behind her blue lips, her teeth were chattering.

'I need help to unpick my knots so that I can be certain that I'll be a Mother of the Renewed World.' She tried to smile, but her mouth wouldn't co-operate and her face twisted grotesquely.

Ash scrabbled at her hands, trying to pull her away from the step, to make her sit up.

'Willow. Come home.'

She did sit up then, resting on her haunches, letting Ash and I hold a hand each. Her right glove was missing, so I took mine off and slid it over her poor, frozen fingers, then leaned close to her, kissing her cheek, desperate to remind her of how much love I had for her.

She looked at me. 'I was scared. I wanted to come home. But then the Prophet explained how it was just knots in my thread making me feel that way. She said she'd help me unpick them.'

'It's okay to be scared, Willow.'

She turned her head away like she was trying to stop my words reaching her ears.

'I won't be scared when all my knots are unpicked.'

'Think of your baby, Willow. What if it came now? Imagine how cold it would be for a tiny baby up here in the snow.' I hesitated, steeling myself for what I was about to say. 'If your baby is born here Willow, it might die. Is that what you want?'

A moan tore itself free from somewhere deep inside her. 'I don't want my baby to die.'

'Then you have to come with us.'

She leaned against Ash and he put an arm around her.

'Don't let your baby die, Willsy,' he said, and I almost broke down when I heard his childhood name for her.

'I want to go home.'

That was all I needed to hear.

Ash supported her on one side, and Lily held her from behind and I pulled her up, as gently as I could. I don't know how long she'd been kneeling on the snow-covered ground, but at first she couldn't stand on her own and we held her steady, waiting for the feeling in her legs to return. How twisted and evil would someone have to be to let a heavily pregnant girl kneel on the ground in the snow? And then to just leave her there. Where was Jem? Where was the monstrous person who had made my daughter believe that all would be well if only she had her *knots unpicked*? I wanted to kill her.

Making sure that Ash and Lily had hold of Willow, I climbed the step that my poor deluded daughter had been hanging onto and stood on the platform. The wind flung snow at me, stinging my face as I stared into the night, trying to see Jem. Shadows flickered, but they were just phantoms created by the flames and each time I turned to look at them, they slipped away. Beyond the fires, inside the shelters, no-one was moving. How could they possibly be sleeping?

As I climbed off the platform, Willow reached for my hand. She needed me.

Jem could wait.

27

Eileen

When I woke up, I didn't feel very Renewed. The storm had passed, but the first day of our Renewed lives was dull and overcast, which I must admit, wasn't what I'd been anticipating. Also, since there would now be hardly anyone left alive, I had expected the world to feel bigger, more spacious, but as I lay on the ground, trying to get some feeling back into my arms and legs, everything felt much the same as it had the day before.

All around me Threads were standing, stamping their feet and clapping their hands to get the blood flowing, before lining up to take their turn to squat behind the wooden platform. Obviously being Renewed wouldn't stop us having to perform basic bodily functions. I looked around to check everyone was there. Ed and George hadn't returned, and there was also no sign of either Willow or Lily. I wasn't surprised – God had obviously severed the frayed Threads.

It looked like Jem hadn't taken advantage of God's gift of sleep because her face was drawn and her eyes were bloodshot. We gathered in front of her and despite the inauspicious weather, there was a lot of hugging and kissing and general excitement that we'd been Renewed. There was the inevitable chanting which of course I joined in with, although I wished Jem would just get on with telling us what was going to happen next. No doubt she would start by confirming my elevation to senior Thread, and then I could help her tell everyone else what to do.

The Threads are Bound. We are Renewed. The Threads are Bound. Renewed. Renewed. Bound. Renewed.

Jem watched us, unsmiling. Somehow, I had expected her to be happier. She took a deep breath and we immediately fell silent, but before she could say anything, we heard the unmistakeable sound of a vehicle coming over the hill. We all turned and squinted into the distance. It was difficult to tell but as far as I could make out there wasn't just one vehicle, there were three or four.

'God is coming,' Tish screamed.

I suppose it was possible, but it seemed unlikely that God would have appropriated a fleet of old vehicles for the purpose of visiting us. I mean, this was the God that had flown Jem over the world, so would It really rumble slowly towards us down a hill? In any case, surely the vehicles should have been buried in the ocean of ice, along with the people that used to travel in them.

I watched Jem watching them. She looked as grey and cold as the sky.

Tish and a few of the others were still calling out things about God being on Its way towards us, but everyone else stood in silence, watching as the vehicles bounced past the turbines, occasionally disappearing behind the rise of the hill.

Then they were with us. Four vehicles stopped beside the Binding Area, a door slid open and a man stepped out.

'God is here!' Tish yelled, despite the man looking just about as un-Godlike as it was possible to look. The man, or God, looked startled when about a dozen Threads fell to their knees, while a few others shuffled backwards, away from him.

'Good morning,' said the man, or God. 'I've come to collect the people who've asked to leave.' He looked at us all dubiously. 'I wasn't expecting so many of you though.' He took out a tab and Waved his hand over it. 'I've only got space for twelve.'

For a moment, nobody said a word, then Petra stepped forward.

'You need to go down into the village. We're not the ones who're leaving.'

'You're not?' The man, who was clearly *not* God, sounded surprised. 'Then why on earth are you all standing around in the snow?'

Without waiting for a reply, he shook his head, climbed back inside his vehicle and carried on down the hill towards the village, the others following closely behind.

Jem had climbed onto the platform. She was crying.

'Threads,' she said, wiping away her tears. 'While you were sleeping, God tried the rope and found it frayed. It looked inside your hearts and saw that you were not yet ready for Cleansing and Renewal. You did not prove yourselves worthy. Your preparations weren't sufficient. You must work harder to strengthen the rope. You must bind the loose ends, so that none remain. Only then will you be ready. God told me that if you fail again, It will look elsewhere for people to be Renewed.'

I knew it. I just *knew* that some Threads didn't deserve to be bound with God. For a moment, there was silence in the Binding Area, then there was a collective groan and all around me people fell onto their knees, sobbing.

'We have failed you, God.'

'We will do more.'

'Do not leave us God.'

'Do not let us die in the ocean of ice.'

'We will do more.'

'We will do better.'

More. Better. We will. We will. Better. Better. More. More.

On and on they whined, louder and louder as they tried to outdo each other in their efforts to prove that they were worthy. Pathetic.

Jem was staring at me from the platform with an expression that I hadn't seen before. I studied it carefully. Suddenly, I understood. She was asking *me* for help. She needed me to tell *her* what we had to do. This was the moment that I had been waiting for. I was the first, the best, the most tightly bound Thread. Only I would be able to bind us all to God forever. And I was the one that could do this because I had something that no-one else had. I had The Book of Jem. I alone knew what God really wanted because I alone understood the truth-behind-the-truth. I was the only one who didn't have to rely on Jem's words. The Book of Jem would tell me what I had to do to bind us to God forever.

I nodded once at Jem, then turned and walked away from the Binding Area.

I was ready to do what had to be done.

28

Kat

If I'm lucky, if I live long enough, then perhaps one day the memories might fade of leading Willow away from that place and making the terrible, endless journey back to Underhill.

Lily went first, stumbling along, doing her best to keep us all on the path. Ash and I each held onto her coat with one hand and one of Willow's hands with the other. I hadn't been able to stop Ash from giving his sister his coat, making her stand with her arms out while he'd tugged it over her own. In return, he'd taken the blanket and tied it around his shoulders. The ground was slippery with snow and with every step our feet threatened to slide out from under us. The wind taunted us, moaning constantly as it threw snow into our mouths, our noses and our eyes.

Willow frequently needed to stop to catch her breath, and while she did we all huddled close, freezing, desperate to get home. Every now and again she'd start crying, and at one point she actually tried to turn back, mumbling about unpicking her knots. Ash wrapped his arms around her then, whispering into her ear. I don't know what he said, but after a minute, she nodded, and he unwrapped his arms, took hold of Lily's coat and our little procession continued its painfully slow progress. My poor, wonderful boy. He didn't deserve this. But which of us did, really, when it came down to it?

We must have been more than half-way down the path when the snow suddenly stopped falling and at the same moment, the wind died. One minute it was howling, and the next, we could hear each other breath. It was only then that I began to believe that we would actually get Willow to safety and I let myself begin to think about what needed to be done. The four of us stumbled on, putting one exhausted foot in front of the other over and over, but by the time we eventually reached home, I had the outline of a plan.

Lily followed us into the house, trying to talk to me, wanting to explain, but she had to wait because I couldn't think about anything until I'd sorted Willow out. I jammed wood into the log burner, wrapped the kids and myself in as many blankets as I could find, and waited for daylight.

*

It was several hours before they came, but that gave me the time I needed. I had to try several people because at first, I couldn't find anyone who would give up their seat. I understood, I really did, but I had to get Willow away from Underhill. In the end Clare, who lived three doors down from us and who had known Willow since she was a baby, agreed to give up her place. There would only be one spare seat. I had to make a decision: send Willow alone to get the help she needed, or keep her in Underhill with me, with no help at all.

There was no choice, really, and in the end I think Willow must have understood that too, because for once, thank Freedom, she hardly argued.

'Look after her,' I begged the others in the vehicle, after shouting down the man from the authority when he tried to say he couldn't take anyone whose name wasn't on his list. I helped Willow inside and wrapped a blanket around her. I leaned in and kissed her cheek, 'I love you.'

'I love you too, Mum,' she said, and she sounded so young.

I cried as I watched my daughter being carried away from me, and Lily held my hand and led me along the street, down the steps, through her front door and into her kitchen. She made me a cup of tea and then another. When my tears eventually stopped falling I listened as she told me how Jem had commanded everyone to go to sleep and they all did, except she, Lily, was cold and unhappy and already wondering what she was doing on the hill in the middle of a storm. She'd still been awake, which is why she'd seen Willow try and leave the Binding Area, and then seen Jem stop her and lead her behind the fires.

'I wasn't certain she was going to hurt her, but I couldn't take the risk...'

She got up and went over to window sill where she started to push her little pots of herbs around, fidgeting with them until they were arranged to her satisfaction. I knew she had more to say, so I just watched as she filled a cup with water and poured a little of it into each pot, waiting for her to continue.

Eventually, she stopped fussing, took a deep breath, and turned to face me.

'I've been so stupid, Kat. So fucking stupid.'

I got to my feet and hugged her. We held on to each other and after a minute when she tried to pull away, I wouldn't let go. I held her close and said, 'Tell me it's over, Lils. Please tell me it's all over.'

I let her go then, but she kept hold of my hands and said, 'It's over. You kept telling me, but I wouldn't listen. How could I honestly have believed that being on the side of a hill in a snowstorm was going to reveal some sort of deeper truth about life? All that happened was that I nearly froze to death watching other people sleep. Can you believe it? Nothing happened, Kat. Absolutely nothing happened. Until Willow tried to leave, all Jem did was wander around.' She laughed, bitterly. 'She's just like the rest of us, she's nothing special. She's no mouthpiece for a God. How could I be so stupid? I'm so, so sorry, Kat.'

'It's not you who should be sorry, Lils. You promised you'd tell me if Willow was in danger. And you did. You came to get me, and Willow is okay. She will be okay.' If I said it enough, surely it would be true? I thought about my daughter who at that moment was travelling far away from me and swallowed hard.

'It's not *you* who owes me an apology, Lils,' I said, 'It's Ed.'

I had no words to explain how furious I was. How could he leave Willow like that? She was his daughter. She should have been his priority, above all else. And where was he now? How could he have left me to deal with this by myself? How dare he? I had to find him. I didn't care what he was doing up there on Front Hill. I didn't care if God Itself really had appeared and was walking among them, Ed needed to come home. He needed to be with me, and with Ash. He needed to help me decide what to do next. We had to work out how to arrange transport for Willow and our grandchild, once the baby was born – please, please, let everything be okay – back to Underhill, or whether it would even be possible during Whiteout. There was a very real chance that Willow and her baby would have to stay wherever they ended up until snowmelt, and if Ed thought he could just let Ash and I spend the whole of Whiteout worrying about her while he bound himself to a non-existent God, then he had another thing coming.

And then there was Jem. I had unfinished business with Jem. The hatred was like a wild animal pacing around my body, growling, straining to be released, so it could pounce on her and rip her to pieces. I had never hated anyone as much as I hated that girl. She was responsible for everything. She was to blame, and I was going to make her pay for what she had done to my village, to my family, to me.

29

Eileen

I sat in my bedroom with the Book on my lap, trying to ignore the commotion going on outside. The leavers were abandoning Underhill, just as God Itself so nearly had. They had been allowed to take nothing with them, everything would be provided for them where they were going, but that didn't stop some of them dragging their belongings along the street and surreptitiously trying to load them into the vehicles.

Then Kat appeared. I should have known that she'd get involved. She had Willow with her, a blanket wrapped around her shoulders. So, she'd run home to mummy, had she? Pathetic, frayed Willow. I always knew her binding was loose.

There was a lot of shouting, mainly by Kat, although the man that we'd seen up on the hill did some shouting as well, but eventually Willow got into one of the vehicles. Once all the leavers were inside, the doors slid shut, and when the vehicles started making their way down the street towards Front Hill, I was finally able to turn my full attention to the Book of Jem.

I opened it at the first page and spent a while admiring my handwriting. My grandmother would be so proud of me. My parents would be proud too, I was sure of it.

I turned the pages. The answer would be there, there was no doubt about that. I just had to find it.

To begin with, I couldn't see it. Then, when I did, I couldn't believe it. Not at first. But the more I read and the closer I looked, the clearer it became. The clues were hidden in plain sight and once I knew what I was looking for, they were everywhere. Flipping through the Book, reminding myself of the Messages, re-reading her speeches, I realised just how many times Jem had said things such as: *you, people of Underhill, are the chosen ones, not me* and *I am nobody and I am just the Messenger* and *I am not important and God's rope will remain strong without me.*

How could I have missed it? How hadn't I seen it before? How had it taken me so long to see what had to be done? I don't want to suggest that I didn't have doubts at first. I mean, I loved Jem. But when I read these words – *What sacrifices must we make to ready ourselves for the Cleansing of the earth and the Renewal that will follow? Each of you must ask of yourself, what must I do? What is God asking from me?* – I was certain that my interpretation was correct.

I gathered together what I needed. There wasn't much. From my Treasure Cupboard, I took the syringes, and the little bottles of drugs that my parents had been working with before they died. It took a while to find a suitable piece of rope but eventually I found one under the stairs and I put everything into a bag. I left the house and had almost finished securing all the locks when I realised that I had forgotten the Book. Obviously I couldn't leave it behind, so I had to unlock everything and go back inside. I took off one of my jumpers, wrapped the Book in it and tied a piece of red string around it, then I put it into the bag, taking care not to stab myself on the syringes. Finally, I locked everything up again and with my house secured, I went to find Jem.

30

Kat

And there I was, back on the path. A few hours earlier, fear had driven me up the hill, this time it was fury.

I stamped along, rehearsing what I was going to say to Ed. There was a long list: his selfishness, his stupidity, his neglect of Willow, the danger he'd put her and the baby in. That was just for starters. I didn't need to rehearse what I was going to do when I found Jem though – that would take care of itself. I was so wrapped up in my anger that I didn't see the line of Threads heading down the path until they had almost reached me.

I have to say, awful as it might sound, when I saw some of them crying, I was relieved. Finally, they had seen the girl for what she really was. Yes, I was sorry for them. Yes, I knew how much they had wanted to believe that they'd found something that would solve their problems, make them feel better, change their lives – all of the reasons that had driven these people to spend the night on Front Hill in the middle of a storm – but all I could think was: thank Freedom it was over.

I was determined to find Ed, so I didn't really want to speak to anyone, but then Camman, Amber and Ali reached me, and when I saw how upset Amber was, I stopped and put my hand on her arm.

'I'm so sorry,' I said. What else could I say? I mean, I couldn't imagine how they must be feeling. They'd killed their animals, and then lost their son, all in the name of a lie. How could they possibly begin to recover from that?

'We thought we'd done enough preps, hadn't we love?' Camman said and Amber nodded. 'But we haven't,' he continued, 'Not yet. There is more we must do.'

I had expected anger, I mean they certainly deserved to be angry, or if not anger then possibly embarrassment or even shame at having been taken in by the girl and her lies, but what I hadn't expected, what I really did not expect, was that they would say that they had *more to do*. More *what* to do, exactly? I mean, how could they really think they needed to do more? Surely they could see that they had done too much, given too much already. I was about to carry on walking when Amber reached over. Her hand was freezing and she crushed my fingers painfully in hers.

'It's our fault Cleansing didn't happen. All of us Threads. It is *our* fault.'

Her voice was flat and toneless, like she was reciting something she had learned by rote. She stared at me, she wouldn't let go of my hand and was shaking it up and down for emphasis.

'Our preps weren't good enough. We haven't done enough. We let the Prophet down, we let God down. God needs us to do better preps before we will be ready for Renewal.'

Her intensity was chilling, and she was swallowing convulsively, obviously trying not to cry. I tried to think of something to say, but there was nothing, and in the end I just pulled my fingers away and walked on.

More people trailed past, looking upset, stunned, broken, but I didn't stop again until I reached their meeting place. There were only a handful of people inside and it would have been difficult to identify it as the place that we'd rescued Willow from only a few hours before. The rope that had fenced it off was on the ground, half buried in snow and there were patches of burnt ground where the fires had been, but there wasn't much else to indicate that it was a place that had contained so much hope, and disappointment.

There was no sign of Ed, or Jem. Tish was kneeling beside the makeshift platform, face in her hands, Petra squatting by her side, stroking her head, but I ignored them and went over to Leroy, who was pulling the rope out of the snow and coiling it into a heap at his feet.

'Where's Ed?'

He looked up briefly, then carried on tugging the rope towards him.

I yanked it away from him and threw it on the ground. 'Don't ignore me. Tell me where Ed is.'

He looked down at his hands, flexing his fingers inside his gloves as if he was still holding the rope.

'For Freedom's sake, Leroy. Tell me where your brother is.' Each word left my mouth with a puff of hot, angry breath that hung in the air between us. 'Answer me.'

'Ed went to the turbines.'

'See?' I said. 'That wasn't so difficult was it?'

I'd already turned away, when he said, 'Jem asked him to make the final preparation.'

I shook my head, I couldn't care less what the girl had said, I just wanted to find him.

'He went to destroy them.'

I spun back round. Leroy's face was wet with tears.

'Destroy what?'

He didn't reply, but this was too important for silence.

'Do you mean the turbines? Ed went to destroy the turbines?'

He nodded, then bent to pick up the rope and started methodically tugging it towards himself again.

For moment, I thought I might be sick, and I took a couple of deep breaths, swallowing hard. I had to find Ed, had to make him realise how insane this was. A part of me still hoped that he had made up the issues with the turbines, or at least exaggerated them, so that he could claim they were one of Jem's so-called signs, because despite everything – the flickers, the rationing, all of that – Lucy was still turning and, most of the time, so was Faraday, although I had no idea if Hinton was working. As far as I was aware, since Jem had started living there Ed hadn't even tried to get Hinton moving. I had absolutely no doubt however, that if he really wanted to, Ed knew exactly what to do to make sure that Lucy and her brothers would never turn again. And if he did that, if he destroyed the turbines, that was it. Our lives in Underhill would be over.

I hurried back to the main path. Above their meeting area the snow was deeper and with each step it tugged at my boots, reluctant to release them. The air seared my throat and my lungs ached horribly from the cold. Then snow started falling again and within minutes I couldn't see anything, not the path, not the top of the hill, nothing. The only way I could tell I was still walking uphill was by the stretch of the muscles at the back of my thighs.

I was almost at the top when I slipped and fell, and for a moment I lay on the ground, my hip throbbing with pain, half-buried in the snow, flakes the size of my hand falling onto my face. But then the thought of Ed smashing his way through the turbines, destroying them for good, pushed me to my feet and, trying my best to ignore the pain in my hip, I stumbled on and up the final rise to the plateau. As I came over the top the wind slammed into me, almost knocking me off my feet. The turbines rose out of the snow, tall and proud, but the blades on all three of them were still. There was no sign of Ed.

The snow was getting heavier – a second storm must be following close on the heels of the first. I limped over to the hut, hoping against hope that I'd find him there, that I wasn't too late.

337

There was no-one inside, but Ed had obviously been there because his coat was slung over the back of a chair, his gloves were on the table and there were tools all over the floor. I crossed the field to the nearest turbine, which was Faraday. At first, I tried to jog, but the snow made it almost impossible and, in any case, my hip was really sore. At the bottom of Faraday's steps, I looked up and the door was closed, but I climbed up to the platform anyway and tried the handle. It was locked.

I stood on the platform for a moment and looked around, trying to see Ed. There was a brief break in the weather and just for a moment the snow stopped. In the distance I could see the Uplanders dismantling their camp, as swiftly and efficiently as they had put it up. With any luck, their love-affair with Jem was over and they were moving on, melting back into the hills as quietly as they had arrived. Out of the corner of my eye, I saw Lucy's door move. I stumbled back down Faraday's steps, clinging onto the handrail so as not to slip and headed over to Lucy as fast as I could, limping and stumbling several times as my boots disappeared into drifts of snow.

When I finally reached her, the door was ajar, and I climbed up, terrified by what I might find. I took a deep breath and pulled the door wide open, letting the flat Whiteout light inside.

Ed was there, sitting on the floor.

'Am I too late?'

He lifted his head. He looked terrible. His face was streaked with oil, but that was the least of it. His eyes were puffy and bloodshot, his skin was cracked and raw in places and he looked so, so tired, as if he hadn't slept in months.

I crouched next to him, ignoring the pain in my hip and the soaked trousers clinging to my skin.

'Are the turbines ok? Are they still working?'

Without his coat, he was only wearing a thin jumper and he

was shuddering with cold.

'The turbines? Tell me, Ed. Please. Are they okay?'

He ran his fingers around the edge of Lucy's doorframe, and I held my breath, both desperate to know and terrified to find out. Finally, he spoke.

'I couldn't do it. I couldn't do what she wants me to do. I couldn't make the final preparation.'

He sounded so broken that despite everything, I held out my hand. He stood up and pulled me towards him; we hugged, stiffly at first, almost like strangers, but after a moment we relaxed and held each other like our lives depended on it. I turned my head, letting my breath warm his skin. Then I put my lips to his ear.

'Willow's gone with the leavers. I need you, Ed. Will you come home with me?'

He nodded, his cheek brushing against mine, and for the moment that was enough. There would be time later to say what had to be said.

He turned his head and pressed his lips to mine.

*

I suppose it was inevitable that I would go over to Hinton while I was waiting for Ed to get his things. I didn't have a plan, but if she was there, if she was that stupid not to have fled while she had her chance, then…well…she would have to take what was coming to her.

Hinton's door was ajar, but it wasn't until I was half-way up to the platform that I heard a thump and a muffled cry. So, she hadn't gone. I climbed the rest of the steps and pulled the door fully open.

It took my eyes a few moments to adjust to the gloom inside, and I didn't immediately understand.

Jem was lying on the floor with Eileen kneeling beside her, syringes and glass bottles scattered around them. Jem's neck was bent at an unnatural angle, head thrust back, saliva bubbling from her mouth, heels thumping the platform. At first, I thought she was having some sort of fit and it was only when I stepped inside Hinton that I saw the rope around her neck. Eileen held the ends, twisting them round, the rope tightening with each turn. Jem's eyes were bulging, her hands scrabbling uselessly at her neck.

I stayed where I was.

Eileen tightened the rope.

I didn't move.

I didn't move.

But then Eileen glanced up at me and smiled. She gave the rope another twist and she actually smiled and, finally, I moved. I jumped, literally jumped, across Jem and tried to shove Eileen away from her, but she braced herself against the floor and stayed exactly where she was. I tried to prise her hands off the rope, but her grip was too strong. Below us, Jem's feet had stopped thumping the floor. She was motionless. I looked behind me, grabbed a glass bottle and smashed it into the floor so it shattered. Taking the biggest piece, I stabbed the jagged edge into the back of Eileen's hand. She howled and let go of the rope. Before I could do anything else, Eileen shot out of Hinton, clattered down the steps and was gone.

My hands were covered in blood and I was shaking badly as I unwound the rope. There was a livid red line around Jem's throat.

I had no idea if she knew I was there, but I took her hand in mine and said, 'It's okay, I'm here.'

I couldn't even tell if she was breathing but then she moved her head towards me, just slightly and I leaned close, ready to hear whatever she might say, but the only sound was the pop of a bubble of blood on her lips.

'I'm here. You're not alone,' I said.

What else was I supposed to do?

Her eyelids flickered and with a huge effort, she forced them open. Broken blood vessels stained her eyes a vivid scarlet. They briefly widened, as if she could see something and her lips moved, soundlessly. I followed the direction of her gaze, but all I saw was the dark column of Hinton's walls stretching far above us. After a moment, her hand slipped from mine.

When I was certain it was over, I picked up a blanket from the corner of the turbine, laid it over her body and went to find Ed.

31

Eileen

This is my final entry in the Book of Jem. Her story is complete.
There is nothing more to tell.

Eileen 1:1-3
*It was only the one who had listened most carefully to the
Prophet who knew what must be done.*

*It was only the one who heard the truth behind her words
who could understand, even when the Prophet herself did not
understand.*

*It was only the one who loved Jem the most who could
unpick the final knot.*

Jem's story may be complete, but mine has just begun.

I am alone on the hill when I speak to God and say, 'I have made
the final preparation. I am ready. I am bound to you and I am part
of you. I cannot be unpicked from your rope.'

And even as I speak the words, the sky splits apart and I know
God is coming.

Acknowledgments

This novel would not exist without an unbroken chain of people who encouraged and supported me.

I am a firm believer that you can be taught elements of creative writing. You may not be able to learn how to find the ideas, but you can develop a toolset to shape the ideas when they arrive. I have been incredibly fortunate to be taught by some of the best, and to each of these people I acknowledge a deep and abiding debt of gratitude. Bernardine Evaristo – Booker Prize winner – is not only an immensely talented writer but is a truly inspirational teacher. Being taught by Bernardine on a six-month Guardian/UEA creative writing course in 2011 was a life-changing experience. She imbued me with such an unshakeable passion for writing that three years later I abandoned my career as a solicitor in order to write fiction.

After leaving the law, I undertook an MA in Creative Writing at Goldsmiths, University of London, where I not only met an inspiring and talented group of writers, but had the immense good fortune to be taught by both Francis Spufford, who has the gift of making his students truly believe in their own writing, and Erica Wagner, who is one of the most supportive and generous people in the industry. I now count myself lucky to call her a friend.

I wrote this book while undertaking a PhD at Swansea University. It is a rare talent to inspire creativity and dedication in others month after month, year after year, and yet this is just what my supervisor, Alan Bilton, manages to do. I am delighted that his most recent novel *The End of the Yellow House* is a stablemate to my own at Watermark Press.

This book is dedicated to my family. My parents, Gill and Terry, gave me one of the most precious things a parent can give their child – the self-confidence to pursue my dreams. Mum nurtured my love of reading, and (thankfully) disregarded the local library's rules about which books were deemed suitable for a voracious young reader to borrow. And in 2014, while in New Zealand visiting my brother and sister-in-law, Andrew and Fi, they gave me a pep talk at precisely the right time. They refused to indulge my doubts about leaving my law firm. They were right, I left shortly afterwards, and the firm continued just fine without me.

While writing this novel, my family expanded to include two dear friends. Gaynor and Dave believed in this novel from the beginning, cheered me on relentlessly and plied me with restorative gin on countless occasions. Dave did not live to see this book published but his love and support is bound together with the pages.

My husband encouraged me to apply for the Guardian/UEA course. He also gave me an ultimatum. Either I took up the place I was offered, or I never mentioned my desire to write novels again. It was a wonderful, life-changing ultimatum. If it wasn't for him and his unwavering support, writing would still be a dream and so to Pete, I owe everything.